WISH
UPON THE
STARS

MALCOLM TENT

WISH UPON THE STARS

A Superhero Cultivation LitRPG

Book 6

MALCOLM TENT

Timeless
Wind

First published by Timeless Wind Publishing LLC 2024

First edition

Line editing by Lorne Ryburn. Proofreading by Daniel E. Olesen.

Cover art by Denis Belinski.

Recap of Book 5

After the battle over the Cavalcade, Shane and his team gain control of the **Starburst Pavilion,** and their focus shifts to the upcoming **Moonsong Glade Tournament. Abel** and **Mel,** the Pavilion's leaders, commence rigorous training to enhance Shane and Callie's teamwork and combat instincts. This culminates in the duo unlocking the Minor Paired Dueling Mastery Skill.

Seeking a break from training, the team returns to Valen. Shane, Callie, Jessie, and Benny all reconnect with family, friends, and allies. Shane meets Amelia, Callie's mother, and grants a Wish that makes her an Ascendant.

When it's time to leave, Shane and Callie reflect on how far they've come, and the team returns to the Starburst Pavilion reinvigorated. Shane and Callie jump into preparing for an expedition to **Doomtown,** a dangerous, lawless dark district—and Abel's old stomping ground as the masked Apollyon. It's an unofficial gathering place for Moonsong Glade Tournament hopefuls and a prime place for information gathering.

The tournament only accepts teams of four, so Jessie and Benny won't be participating, and they stay behind to train.

Shane, Callie, Abel, and Mel kick things off with enchiladas at the Raving Baby, where they exchange information. Before long, they encounter other Moonsong Glade hopefuls who have traveled from off-world. Notably, they befriend **Lament** and **Wren** of the **Spear Legion** and **Sydney** and

Megan of the **Wave Warren.** They also meet **Mordaunt** of the **Darkling Institute,** who invites them to the **Walking Silence Auction.**

After a few days of training with the Spear Legion and Wave Warren, the day of the Walking Silence Auction arrives. Tensions are high as powerful Ascendants from across the Gloryfire System converge. The Starburst Pavilion successfully bids for a blank **Skill Crystal.** Notably, the Darkling Institute makes no bids at all. Shane knows that something is amiss.

The auction is violently interrupted by **Pietro Verralan** of the **Black Sorrow Cult,** who seeks revenge for Aiden's death (which happened during the scavenger hunt). A chaotic battle erupts as Pietro and his hired cronies, including Mordaunt, fight off other Ascendants.

Shane faces off against Pietro and his E-rank guard. Unexpectedly, Shane's mask devours the E-ranker. With the powerful guardian dead, Shane has a choice—to spare Pietro, or end him. Shane weighs the decision, and ultimately decides to kill Pietro.

Shane's team leaves the auction early, deeply unsettled. They return to G-district to regroup and prepare for the Moonsong Glade Tournament.

Chapter One

AFTER LEAVING THE AUCTION, we went back to the Pavilion. Before it had been a quick stop where we waited for the four F-ranked guards that Callie's uncle, the Nothing, had sent to protect the two of us. Now, though —now we were home. Our home. Our place, that we actually owned. Not like the house Zeke bought. And speaking of my uncle, he was waiting for us when we got into the Pavilion.

"Hey, you're back," he said casually from his spot on the bench. To my shock, every other Pavilion member was clear on the other side of the tent, not training, but trying to press themselves into the wall in the tightest possible configuration. When he saw where my eyes went he chuckled wryly. "Ah, sorry. I felt the trouble at the auction and figured I'd wait here for you to get out just in case. When that E-ranker picked his fight and I warned him off, I might have been a little annoyed. My aura leaked a bit."

That certainly explained the looks of existential terror plastered across the faces of some of the most hardened battle maniacs I'd ever seen. I grimaced at him. "Yeah, about that." I held up the mask. "What the actual fuck? I've been wearing this thing on my face and it eats people? That's pretty messed up." I was still uncomfortable putting the mask back on and had used my old scarf to cover my face on the way back up here.

Zeke cracked up. "I can't believe he actually triggered it. What a dumbass. I did warn him. I guess I was a bit too gentle with the aura. I didn't want to go full blast and fry a bunch of randoms." He shrugged. "As for the mask… it did its job. It was supposed to protect you. I can make you a new one if you want. A weaker one. But I have to warn you that including the defenses lets me skirt the edges of what I'd normally be able to put into something like that. If I make a new one it won't be a thousandth as good."

I climbed up on the stands to drop down next to him bonelessly, letting the mask clatter to the ground. I wasn't worried it would break. He looked amused but didn't mention it. Callie followed me in, sitting next to me and not saying anything. She'd been hovering since I killed Pietro, the arrogant young master of the Black Sorrow Cult. I'd been worried she would be horrified, but all I felt through our bond was a sense of worry. The others all headed in, giving us space as they went to check on the traumatized Pavilion members.

"You know… I always figured this mask was too weird to be low level. How can I even use it? I assumed it was impossible to use gear too many ranks above you. This thing has to be at least E-rank to have killed Pietro's guardian so easily. How come it didn't crush my soul?" Trying to leverage an item with that much Impact would probably do something dramatic like that. Either way, I knew it should be impossible.

He shrugged. "Because I cheated. There's an Impact seal on it. My Voltomancy can manipulate masks I make in ways that wouldn't normally be possible. It slowly releases portions of that power as you rank up. Still, that material has the toughness of B-ranked wood. The emergency defenses I put on it are well within the tolerance level of something that durable."

Now that he mentioned it, the mask *had* jumped right off my face before it ate the guy. Presumably so it could channel that Impact without crushing me. That was… "Zeke, what exactly can your ability *do?* That sounds more like an AI than an enchantment. Is this mask *aware?* Because I don't care how strong it is, I'm not wearing a living being trapped in a hunk of wood on my face."

He chuckled. "Don't freak out. It's not aware. That was a preprogrammed response, to use your computer jargon. A conditional enchantment. There are countless tiny runes on that thing you can't see, and they form some pretty complex instructions, but they aren't anything close to an actual entity. It's like a personal alarm. Someone too strong tried to hurt you so it went off."

I wasn't sure why that made me feel so much better, but it absolutely did. "Alright," I said slowly. "What about Pietro, did you see when I…" I didn't know what his senses could do, but he'd been able to see the E-ranked guardian well enough to scare him off. I cleared my throat. "Is that going to be a problem? Will the Cult start trouble because Pietro died here?" I'd been pretty confident that wouldn't happen, but "pretty confident" isn't "sure."

My uncle actually sneered at me for the question. "Honestly. No. The Cult isn't going to attack a pseudo D-ranked planet. Nothing here is worth starting even a minor skirmish over." He paused. "Maybe you, at least to some of them. But the kid didn't know who you were. He was just some typical spoiled little elite who was far too confident in Daddy. They're a credit a dozen back at the clan, and pretty much everywhere else. So, no. They won't declare a war."

Callie cleared her throat. "What about the others?" I looked at her in confusion. "The rest of the Cult's team. They're a four person group, right? Were they all down at the auction and disqualified, or are we going to be meeting a team from the Cult with an alternate thrown in? That seems like something it would be good to know."

Shit, I hadn't even bothered to check that. I should have asked to make sure the rest of their team was around. Zeke didn't seem bothered, but then, I doubted the sun exploding and swallowing the planet would bother Zeke overly much. Being at B-rank couldn't possibly be good for your scale measuring problems in relation to normal people. Speaking of ranks, I'd gotten my wishes in on the way back and been paid in stats, putting me that much closer to F-rank.

Yesterday's wishes were all used up on escape prep, though shockingly none of my teammates had actually triggered them. The spells had been keyed to potential lethal danger, which they'd all thankfully avoided. Benny hadn't really engaged so much as stuck to the edges smashing things with a hammer, Jessie had let Randall do the fighting, and Callie had been working with me and our teamwork, keeping her from being exposed too much.

Sadly, to afford a full-on teleport all the way to the Pavilion, they'd had to keep things specific, which meant limiting the time covered by the escape.

3

Regardless, I didn't consider the wishes a waste even if they never triggered. Better to have them and not need them than need them and not have them. Still, that last available wish and the other five I had on hand added eighteen points to my total, putting me that much closer to rank up. My stats were looking pretty good, actually. I'd added the eighteen points to my Creation, bringing it up to an even 160. I'd also gotten topped up with some owed attacks from my teammates.

Wishmaster Candidate Status: G-rank.

Ability: Beginner Wish—Five times a day, grant a Beginner wish in return for proper compensation. Wish must be feasibly achievable by the candidate's own efforts within a three-day period with current statistics.

Might: 160
Impact: 12
Fantasy: 180
Vitality: 130
Focus: 148
Perception: 150
Creation: 160
Progress to next rank: 940/1000

Stored: 10 shadow attacks (two in reserve waiting to be granted), 9 fire attacks, 10 triple-strength tranq blows, 8 triple-strength density-shifted attacks, 8 spider leg attacks, 10 heal bursts (26 in reserve waiting to be granted), 10 gravity attacks, 10 shadow clones, 27 scan heals (I-rank)

Pet: Wolf named Jin

Skills: Beginner Doom Sovereign Mastery, Beginner Enchanting Mastery (four charges per point of Impact), Lesser Cooking Mastery, Lesser Inventing Mastery, Lesser Stealth, Lesser Paired Dueling, Minor Piano Mastery, Minor Gymnastics Mastery, Minor Swimming Mastery, Minor Guitar Mastery, Minor Singing Mastery, Minor Poker Mastery, Minor Archery Mastery, Minor

Boxing Mastery, Lesser Balam Mastery, Minor First Aid Mastery, Minor Herbalism Mastery

I'd gotten sick of not being able to tell how close I was to the next rank without doing math, so I'd tinkered around with trying to change the way I envisioned the stats themselves. As I checked my sheet though, I noticed something much more interesting. I'd been so caught up in Pietro dying and the fallout that I hadn't even noticed the change in my bond with Callie. My eyes snapped to hers. "Holy shit, Cal—did your Paired Dueling Skill rank up to Lesser too?"

As I listed off my stats to her, I also explained how I did the progress bar tweak. It was mainly an exercise in Fantasy. The representation of our stats was itself part of the same system that gave us abilities, so it could be affected by stats. Not much, and not to any real use, but little alterations were more than possible. Once I finished, she checked her own stats and shared them, confirming her Skill up.

Calliope Reynolds: G-rank

Ability: Beginner Shadow Embodiment—The ability to control and shape shadows, either molding them into constructs or imbuing them into specially prepared objects to enable enhancement and control.

Might: 198
Impact: 12
Vitality: 142
Fantasy: 120
Focus: 58
Perception: 175
Creation: 135
Progress to next rank: 840/1000

Pet: Wolf named Rellia

Skills: Minor Tracking, Beginner Stealth, Beginner Trap Mastery, Beginner Disguise, Lesser Balam Mastery, Lesser Paired Dueling, Beginner Shadow Manipulation Mastery

Aside from the rank up, I was even more shocked to discover something else. "Wait... I'm closer to F-rank than you?" I stared at her in dumbfounded astonishment. Callie had always been stronger than me. I mean, granted, she still was. My stats were far too spread out, while hers were concentrated in her main specialties. Not to the extent of someone like Jessie of course, but she had nearly forty more Might than me, just to name one stat. Still, my total was higher now.

She sighed, giving me a fond smile. "Yes, idiot. For a while now. It's not a surprise. You've been training hard and doing more than a bit of extra work with the Beast Lord Garden. I admit though, I didn't expect you to be a full hundred points more advanced. I guess I wasn't keeping track of your overall stats." It wasn't hard to notice (with the bond and my own knowledge of her) that her smile was a bit strained.

"Hey," I said, reaching out to take her hand. "I get that it's weird, but don't forget we have the same end point. We're both stopping right before F-rank for the tourney, and we have a whole week to get you there. That'll be a hundred and five points." I paused. "Shit, that means we're going to be short. I have some of my elixir total left I can use to make up the difference for me, but we'll have to rush yours during the tournament itself."

She laughed sweetly and leaned up to kiss my cheek. "I know. I don't begrudge you the advancement. It's just weird. We met only a few months ago and you're already stronger than me. But I know we're a team and I'll catch up. The tournament should last a week or two, so getting us both to the peak of G-rank in time shouldn't be a problem—don't worry so much."

Zeke rolled his eyes. "Well, this is getting uncomfortable for everyone who isn't you two. I'm going to go check on the minions I traumatized. Anything is better than watching you stare soulfully into each other's eyes. Seriously, you two even make *me* sick, and with my Vitality that shouldn't be possible."

I laughed along with Callie as Zeke walked away.

Chapter Two

By the time we rejoined the others, Mel and Abel had mostly managed to talk down the terrified members of the Pavilion, though most of them were still shooting fearful looks at my uncle. Zeke ignored them, of course, and was sitting with Alden, who had offered him a beer. Alden was having a grand old time talking to the younger man. Although… I wasn't sure how true that was. Alden looked older, but Zeke was a B-ranker. For all I knew my uncle and parents could be thousands of years old.

Once everyone was calm, Abel and Mel distracted them with the Skill Crystal and talked about using it to teach them all martial arts. I'd assumed Callie would be the one to imprint on it, but someone suggested Abel, and no one could really argue the validity of the suggestion despite all of us having been so focused on Callie.

Callie herself joined in the discussion, and as she did I walked over to slump down next to Alden and Zeke. "You two look thick as thieves," I said wryly. "I should have expected the two drunkest people I know would have some things in common." I pointed at Zeke. "Him I get, but Alden, aren't you worried about the tournament? Your disciples are going to be in it. Even if you aren't concerned for the two of us, there are other Master Candidates coming. Hell, might be more than a few, who knows how strong the other forces in the Gloryfire System are."

Zeke rolled his eyes. "Please. I'm surprised even a pair of Master Candidates popped up near here. Maybe if it was in the Unity Hub I could see a reason to worry, but the Gloryfire System is a wasteland. You might see more impressive people in the Glade Itself. This particular tournament is for the System as a whole, and all hundred Systems in the Axiom Cluster will be sending their best."

That brought up something important I'd been putting off asking. "Ok, so what the hell is up with all that? Clusters, Systems, planets—how is all that related?" I'd heard plenty of that kind of talk in passing. All I knew at the moment was that we were in the Gloryfire System on a D-rank planet. "Actually," I cut in before he could answer, "why is it happening here anyway? Wouldn't a higher ranked planet be better?"

That got a chuckle from my uncle. "No. Weaker planets work better, means the locals are less likely to try to assassinate the visitors. As for why it's happening here... Well, let's just say that the WCP doesn't want anything going wrong and arranged for it to be in the territory of someone inclined to ensure that. The Gloryfire System is right on the edge of Cult space, as you may have noticed from their bullshit theatrics."

Huh... so they had set this up because Zeke was around? I assumed that was what he meant. I didn't bring that up in front of Alden though. He might know Zeke was powerful, but that didn't mean he knew everything. Zeke nodded approvingly at my silence when the bearded man wasn't looking, then continued. "You're right though. You should know the layout of the local area at least. The planets thing isn't necessarily important— every System has multiple planets, depending on their size."

He looked genuinely interested in the topic, and I listened with rapt attention as he informed me about how the universe worked. "The Gloryfire System is a three-star System, and every star has multiple terraformed planets surrounding it. There are several D and even C-ranked planets among that number. As I mentioned earlier, Gloryfire is one of a hundred or so Systems in the Axiom Star Cluster, and among those Systems there are other three-star, four-star, and even five or six-star Systems. The stars can, of course, be spread out and have multiple planets in their orbits that never intersect, though they all orbit a central star in the System, even if that star isn't easily visible from each planet."

Ok, that made some sense. So we were orbiting one of the outer stars, which was orbiting the interior star of the System. "So the Axiom Star

Cluster is the territory controlled by the Unity? Star Clusters are the same thing as Galaxies right?" I'd looked that up when I heard the term System. While information about the actual political formations of Systems was obviously not available, the structure of the physical phenomena was common enough.

Zeke shook his head. "No. Not even close. A Cluster is an agglomeration of Systems, and a Galaxy is an agglomeration of Clusters. The Unity's territory is the smallest of the five factions, with only a single Galaxy to their name. This is because the Unity himself is the youngest god. Older and more powerful factions have several, in the case of the Empire and the Faerieland. Technically speaking the entire five faction alliance occupies a single Galactic Cluster, but we mostly just use the Universe as shorthand because there are no known civilizations outside the Cluster."

"So the Gloryfire System is one of hundreds of Systems in the Axiom Cluster, which is in the single Unity Galaxy?" My head was hurting at the concept of how fucking big the world was, and how many planets that would have to be. He mentioned multiple planets around each star, which could mean into the double digits, and the scale as that went up was mind-boggling. I knew farming renown was important, but still, to expand to that scale…

Seeing my shock, Zeke smiled. "Yeah. The Chiron Galaxy. Most people just call it the Unity Hub. The Conglomerate is the managing government of the Axiom Cluster, to put things in perspective. Anyway, like I said, the 'geniuses' in this System won't be worth much. It's the ass end of nowhere and there are less than a dozen planets. Being able to spawn a pair of Master Candidates is already decent. You might see a few freaks with rare abilities or weird racial traits, but probably not many people on the level of Abel or the spear wielder. Maybe one or two more tops, since there are a few C-rank planets in the System." He said that like it was irrelevant.

"You said that the Black Sorrow Cult's Galaxy is near here?" I focused on another relevant issue. The Cult were enemies of mine and especially of my mom, who was a Saintess of the Red Revenant Church. From what I knew, Black Sorrow and the Red Revenant were old enemies from before they ascended, and this had carried over to their factions. Being able to kill the son of a Saintess would be a huge coup for the Cult.

"One of them." Zeke said with a shrug. "They have a couple. As I mentioned, the Unity is the youngest of the gods by a large margin. Black

Sorrow and the Red Revenant each control two Galaxies, including their central and original territories—the Night Demon Abyss and the Holy Dominion, respectively. Those are nicknames, like the Unity Hub. Most Galaxy names are pretty nondescript.

"Anyway, the closest Cult Galaxy to us is the Extreme Void. The Gloryfire System is right at the edge of it. Probably how the Darkling Institute made contact with the Cult in the first place."

Yet another reason to get off Callus. Zeke wouldn't be protecting me forever. Once I hit D-rank, I'd be a Master ranked Ascendant and officially recognized as being able to take care of myself. Ignoring the fact that I couldn't even reach D-rank on Callus, even if I could, I wouldn't dare to do it so close to the Cult's territory.

Once we finished our adventure in the Moonsong Glade we'd go out on our own. Maybe visit the central Cluster of the Unity Hub, or even take a look around the Empire or Faerieland. The latter was pretty insular, but they still maintained decent relations with the Wish Curse Palace.

Not having our own territory made it possible to be uniquely entwined with the entire five faction alliance. Though now that I knew how big the Universe (or Galactic Cluster I guess) was, I doubted that was exactly literal. The WCP probably had a home planet or even a System. Just no Galaxies to our name.

Alden looked mildly fascinated by hearing about things at this level, but not as much as I'd expected. Sure enough, he probably came from a larger force originally. Maybe not at the Galactic level like the factions, but still. Though that brought up an interesting question.

"I've heard there are a lot of powerful clans. Are they all part of the factions? What about the WCP? We have a lot of branches don't we?" I knew anyone who reached S-rank like my grandfather was eligible to start a branch. Theoretically they could even start a new clan, though I was told that didn't really happen.

"They're all part of the factions. Or they live among their territory anyway," said Zeke. "Most of the Galaxies outside the main Galaxy of a faction are controlled by an S-rank clan. They're top officers of the faction. The Kings of the Empire are all S-rankers who serve the Emperor directly, for instance. Not every S-rank clan runs a Galaxy of course, but they mostly have their own territory.

"Our branches usually operate at a Galactic level, working alongside S-rankers in that specific Galaxy. Sort of like how the Deacon of the Rajak WCP operates alongside the local Unity leader. Being spread out like that keeps us from being too big a threat and lets us get along with the other factions, though of course the Wish power certainly doesn't hurt our PR at all."

I decided that was enough learning for the day. My brain was already exploding with new information and if I kept going, I wouldn't be able to focus on anything. I knew Zeke tried to ration the amount of this stuff that I learned to keep me from being overwhelmed and discouraged by the size of the Universe. I had a feeling you could take a century long class on global politics and force distribution and not even scratch the surface of the full picture.

Seeming to sense my train of thought, Zeke laughed and clapped a hand on my shoulder. "It's not good to get too caught up in that stuff. You only really need to worry about the here and now, kid. This planet, this System. Soon the Cluster maybe, but nothing past that. Galactic matters need Galactic power, and you aren't even close." He said this kindly, not meaning it as an insult, and I took it that way too. I didn't want to go swimming in deep water until I was a shark.

With a solemn nod I exhaled. "You're right. I just need to win the tournament and get that Moonglow Dew. Having the extra Impact will make me that much stronger compared to others my rank. Even if I run into some crazy monster with Master rank Skills at F-rank, it's useless if they can't hurt me."

Not that I was confident the Moonglow Dew could even *do* that. That was a big gap to close. But it would definitely help. In the end, this all seemed complicated and scary, but it came down to the same thing Ascendant stuff always did. Want to be left alone? Get stronger.

If I wanted to adventure and see the Universe with my friends, I needed to have the muscle to back it up. I'd better get to work.

Chapter Three

IN THE END, Abel was the one to use the Skill Crystal. Despite Callie's interest in trying it and passing on her Balam techniques to others more easily, Abel was a Master Candidate in Ragam. The martial art was extremely powerful and dangerous based on what we'd seen from him, and if we wanted the best possible results from the crystal our best bet was to let him do it.

Sadly, since it had been prepared for Callie, the crystal was only G-rank, and couldn't contain an Intermediate Skill. Abel was able to imprint only the Beginner rank insights from his martial arts easily enough though. The more important factor was that Abel would be around to *teach* them Ragam. With his high standards he was able to help them advance much faster than Callie could.

"Actually, I always wondered about that," I couldn't help but interject. "Where did you learn Ragam? It's not the same style that Mel and Alden use. I'd have figured if you used a martial art it would be the one your teacher uses. Alden mostly uses a grappling style that complements his gravity ability, but Ragam seems to be a striking art based on how you use it. Did you create it yourself?" I didn't think he had. I remembered Cicero's lackey telling me Abel used a powerful art and he'd alluded to it being old.

Abel just laughed. We were all lounging on the steps drinking soda from Alden's cooler (except Zeke and Alden, who were still drinking beer). "Not even a little," he said in amusement. "I found it in an old book. It was mostly just exercises and some insights. Only enough to get me to Beginner, but past that point you really need to make your own way in any case. Not that some guidance wouldn't have helped but… what are you gonna do, right?"

He sighed wistfully. "I picked the book up for a few chits as a kid and became obsessed with learning it. Alden actually tried to talk me out of it more than once, but I was a stubborn little bastard."

"Was?" muttered the red bearded man. "I admit I underestimated you, boy. Even so, you got lucky. That book was a treasure. Still not sure how it ended up there. Probably some Fate sense malarkey. That doesn't mean you'll hold up against other geniuses though. That Spear Legion girl sounds like a legitimate threat to you, don't go assuming you're unbeatable because you're the biggest bully in a small playground."

Abel's grin was so feral even the wolves looked disturbed. "Oh don't you worry old man. Complacency is the last thing on my mind. I'm so excited for this fight I can't even sleep. There are so many things I need to test and confirm that no one close to my level can help me verify. Too strong, too weak, all the same problem. The chance to pit my Ragam against a true warrior on an equal footing…" He looked over to Callie. "How early can I face her? I know the layout of this thing will be team fights first, then single elimination, but do we know anything about the lineup?"

Callie snickered at his childlike enthusiasm. "I've been asking around. As far as I can tell there will be eight rounds in the team battles, with ten thousand contestants spanning twenty-five hundred teams. Of those, only forty teams will make it to single elimination. Five rounds of that to pick the top ten. That'll be the main tournament that will have all the spectators. The thirteen rounds prior will be split up all over the city and happening all at once mostly, otherwise there would be no way to get it all done in any reasonable timeframe."

"Thirteen rounds, and then a top ten elimination tournament," I said excitedly. "We're working as a team for the first eight at least, so that should help our chances. Personally I can't wait for the five solo rounds. What are the chances we'll fight each other early into that?" I sucked at math, so it was more convenient to just ask one of the others. Focus made your brain work better, but mostly at stuff you already used it for.

Benny surprised me by answering. "Gets higher the longer it goes on, but in the first round, not that high. Single digit percentages. If you add in all the other people we know and assume that they'll make it far enough to be an issue, we start seeing much higher chances of running into someone that could pose a problem. How far you get is a matter of luck as much as anything. If you run into a Master Candidate first round you'll be pretty much fucked."

I nodded grimly, but that reminded me. "Speaking of Master Candidates, can't we start looking into the other teams more? The ones not in Doom-town will be around in Rajak to feel out right? Cal, do you have a way we could bump into them? I'm not really a social person but they have like… galas and stuff to celebrate big events, right? No way they miss the chance to wine and dine the bigwigs from the more powerful planets in the System, *right?*"

Callie's face lit up. "Oh! That's a great point! I got so used to thinking about things from a martial point of view I completely overlooked that we can go to parties!" Everyone looked at her and she blushed. "I… I like parties. Big fancy galas were kind of a family thing for my mom and me when I was younger. They're good memories."

"I'm glad to hear it," I said with a smile. "I know jack and shit about formal galas. I'll need plenty of help from you, Benny, and anyone else who we can rope in to be presentable." I looked at my best friend. "Speaking of being comfortable with formality, is your girlfriend available for etiquette lessons?"

If there was one person we knew who would definitely be able to help with political maneuvering, it was Celine. Callie had learned some of that stuff by necessity growing up, but Celine was raised for it. From what Benny had told us, her mother was a high ranking elven official, and even though Celine wasn't her only child, or even one of the more important ones, she'd been brought up to be a chess piece in that kind of environment.

It actually bothered Benny a lot. As someone who essentially blew off every attempt his mother made to force him to play the good little rich boy, knowing Celine did everything her mother said frustrated him. He'd confided in me that he wished he could just help her see that it was all bull-shit because she deserved to be happy, but in the end it wasn't his choice to make. She did what she did, and he cared about her so he was along for the ride.

As such, my suggestion that we embroil her in a bunch of political intrigue was met with annoyance, but not outright rejection. He knew Celine would most likely want to take part, he just didn't particularly like that I was getting her involved in the first place.

Eventually he sighed. "Fine," he spat. "I'll bring it up and let you know what she says. But you need to try not get her sucked into an assassination plot or something."

"Hey," I protested, "I'm not a magnet for assassins…" I paused. "Actually, now that I think about it that's fair. I'll make sure we keep an eye out. Damn, I am a magnet for assassins, when did that happen? Other Ascendants get into cool fights and punch monsters and I have to worry about getting backstabbed by crazy cultists. That's unfair as hell."

Callie snickered, patting my shoulder. "Just the price you pay for being awesome. Who told you to be so good looking and talented." Her tone was solemn and sympathetic, but there was a sparkle of amusement in her eye. "You've attracted the envy of the universe."

I glared at her for a second before her twitching smirk broke down into peals of laughter. My expression made it worse and she almost fell off her seat cackling.

"I never mock *you* for *your* pain," I grumbled. But I was smiling too. I was glad to have friends who would make light of this kind of shit. Otherwise I'd turn into some angsty edgelord who spent all his time whining. I had fun being an Ascendant for the most part, and I wanted to keep that going. It was why I had a team in the first place. Everything was more fun when you did it with a bunch of friends.

Jessie rolled her eyes at our antics. "I can help too. My brother took me to a few galas during our visit here, and when we were younger I got plenty of lessons on etiquette from Harvest. She's surprisingly socially conscious for a hermit that lives in the woods and plays with dirt all day."

I laughed at that harder than I probably should have. Turning to Callie, I waited for her verdict. As team leader she would be making these calls, even more so since I knew nothing at all about politics. She was in a better position to decide who would be allowed to help out. Even my question about Celine was just a suggestion, though the two of us were in sync enough that I doubted she would shut it down.

She mulled it over for a bit before nodding. "Jessie and Celine helping should be fine. We're going to be in Rajak proper, not some dark district. Rajak has laws and rules. Even if villains sometimes break them, none of them will be stupid enough to attack a high-ranking Ascendant gala with most of the Unity leadership there." She grimaced at that last part, and I knew why, but she forced herself to move on. "Anyway, the WCP should be sending a delegation too. They're one of the major organizations on this planet, so they won't miss the fun."

Which meant Alexander would be there to act as support when she had to deal with her dad. I hadn't met Midknight yet and honestly wasn't looking forward to the experience. My own issues with his behavior aside, Callie wasn't going to have an easy time seeing him after so long. I reached out to grab her hand. "You can always skip this you know. You don't have to deal with him."

She shook her head. "No. I'm sick of letting him control me. By avoiding him I'm just giving him more power. I may not be up to his level in terms of rank but I'm already strong enough to stand on my own. I'm part of a team and I'm not afraid of him anymore." She squeezed back, and I felt her fear and resolve through our bond.

"Alright," I said. "But if things get too heavy let me know and we can bail. There's no reason to torture yourself if it's too much—you can always face him again later. Whatever you need to do."

Midknight shouldn't be willing to throw away his rep by trying anything overt, and even if he did Alexander could stop him. If he attacked me it would go even worse. Callie deserved the chance to say her piece in a safe environment and I knew if she didn't get it, she would be bothered by it for a long time.

Knowing this had gotten too serious, we changed the subject, speculating about all the potential events and which to go to once we found out when and where everything would be. We still had a week of relaxing to do, and plenty of wishing, but nothing said we couldn't be productive *and* relax. Who knew what this next week would bring?

And after that... the tournament would finally begin.

Chapter Four

THE NEXT WEEK flew by in a blur. We did end up talking to Celine, and upon consulting her we decided to wait to attend a gala. According to her, none of the really impressive forces would bother going to the pre-party because they hadn't shown off their strength yet. Without proving what they could do it would be harder to operate from a position of social superiority. Celine estimated that ninety percent of the important guests would wait until the end of the first round to make an appearance, so they could pressure the others with their performance.

The biggest change that happened was obviously that I managed to max out my G-rank cultivation, reaching exactly one thousand points. I needed sixty points to do this, and at three points per wish that ended up being twenty wishes from the Beast Lord Initiates. It brought me up to a nice round one hundred and ninety in Vitality. Since I had thirty five wishes to burn over the week, that left me with fifteen, which I of course used to bring Callie up another forty-five points before the tournament.

Callie decided that her Perception had been slipping, and since she was going to be synergizing a new ability on rank up, she wanted to stack her highest stat as high as possible to see if she could stumble into some amazing ability like Jessie. The forty-five points brought her Perception up to a full two hundred and twenty, with plans to take it even higher as she went. Perception was one of the main components of her build, even with the addition of her Shadow Manipulation Skill. You had to be able to keep track of fine details to manipulate and adjust them.

Paying the wishes off was an issue, of course, but we managed to come up with a pretty solid compensation. Callie often used her powerful Stealth Skill to hide us, but since it was more powerful than mine and I found it useful, she was able to use stored Stealth charges to pay off her debt, giving me ten and promising another five. In fact, I was over the moon about the discovery, because having used two of those charges (leaving me with three left on top of the base ten I could hold), I realized something amazing.

Experiencing a higher level of a Skill I already had a decent grasp on let me increase my understanding of it. Not to the level of ranking up immediately, but I was pretty sure if I kept using Stealth charges, I could get my Stealth Skill to Beginner and even match Callie's expertise extremely quickly.

It opened up an entirely new way of training. Granted, the circumstances were pretty specific, since I was positive it wouldn't work with Skills I'd granted myself, but I was sure I could find some Skills my friends had that I did too and experience them so we could learn faster. Hell, we could probably do it with Paired Dueling if I granted some wishes to Abel and Mel, at least if I hadn't used up all my wishes for the day already. I was going to focus on Stealth for now though, at least until Callie hit her cap. We needed her there by the end of the tournament after all.

Regardless, we were in our best condition, and that was why we were all extra excited to find ourselves standing in the Varia Coliseum in Rajak, waiting for the announcement of the beginning of the tournament, as well as the selection for everyone's first round battle. It wasn't just us and our team either. Benny, Jessie, Alexander, Sloane, Cark, Melinda, Baric, Croll, Lament, Wren, Sydney, and several other friends from Doomtown were all crowded together in the stands of the massive white marble structure, staring down at the circular stage in the center.

"So," Benny asked curiously, "what is the point of this huge extravagant ceremony? Because I feel like they could have just picked the lineups out of a hat and sent us all a text."

Celine snorted out a laugh at that, getting shocked looks from everyone who actually knew her. She gracefully ignored them before clearing her throat. "It's a sign of status. A show of the resources and manpower that the Unity can bring to bear as hosts. It's—"

"It's dick measuring," cut in Callie, the only one of us who didn't seem happy to be here. I knew she was expecting to see her dad, so I didn't blame her. "They want to show everyone how impressive and grandiose they are. It's a petty attempt to save face preemptively because they know their teams are going to get crushed." Our Doomtown acquaintances who didn't know Callie's story seemed surprised by her venom.

Alexander nodded under his darkened cloth wraps. "Midknight has always been very concerned with appearances. In some ways it makes him a better Ascendant, and in some ways it limits him. While reputation is certainly important, you can only make so much of an impression with a carefully curated image. To truly inspire awe or even terror, one must step outside the conventional and do things the masses wouldn't ever expect."

That drew a snort from where my uncle sat behind us. "Shock and Awe versus PR is an age-old debate among Ascendants. I personally hold to the former school of thought. A real legend grows in the telling—trying to prune every branch of your story to perfection just slows it down. Only cowards who are afraid of recursion bother with that much image management. It's a sign of subpar willpower."

Cark's sister Cass, who was here with the group, turned to glare at him. "Hush Uncle Zeke, it's starting!" Despite yelling at a literal force of nature, Cass seemed completely unworried and turned back to watch the stage as a dark figure climbed it. Zeke shot Cass a fond smile, but Callie tensed up. I stared down at the black armored form that had to be Midknight as he strolled to the center of the stage.

The Rajak branch's Unity Guild Master had presence, I'd give him that. Granted, so did every E-ranker I'd ever met. You needed to be something special to make it to the peak of cultivation for a planet, even when that peak was as low as it was here. Midknight strode across the white marble stage, swept along on a carpet of rolling shadows that spilled from his pauldrons, tumbling to his feet like a cape only to buoy him aloft like some sort of ghostly warrior general.

I took Callie's hand, letting her grip my fingers so tightly I lost feeling in them as she glared down at the man attracting all of the attention from the now silent crowd. Midknight stopped in the center of the stage, glancing around slowly as if choosing his targets, both in terms of words and who he would address.

19

Finally, he spoke. "Conflict," he intoned. "War, by another name." His voice was deep and resonant, almost hypnotic. I'd expected him to sound weaselly. Guess I had been making assumptions.

"Some would say this sentiment belies our purpose here today. To gather in celebration and pit ourselves against allies. They would speak of peace. Of togetherness. Of… Unity."

That got a bit of a chuckle, though it was diffuse. People were too wrapped up in what he was saying to laugh. It wasn't really going in an obvious direction.

"Fools!" He barked, making everyone jump. "War does not make a mockery of alliance. It lends it strength. It does not contradict peace, for even in the tamest peace must we do battle with our inner selves. War is our nature. Our purpose. Our core."

"Is he serious right now?" I whispered to Callie, making sure to use Stealth to prevent my voice from being overheard. Apparently my Stealth Skill wasn't good enough to hide my words from someone at Midknight's level, because the blue eyes in the helmet, the ones that looked so much like Callie's, snapped to my face.

Far from being agitated, my girlfriend… Well, smiled would be a generous description, but she bared her teeth in something approximating the gesture. She didn't bother to use Stealth when she responded. Or keep her voice down. "Unfortunately. The old man has always loved to hear himself talk. Shame he's too self-involved to notice no one else likes hearing his voice as much as he does."

You could have heard a fucking pin drop. Every single eye in the whole arena swiveled to fix on Callie, who was still baring her teeth at Midknight in that same not-smile. The man sighed. "So many years Calliope. Yet you remain so disrespectful. Your mother's influence I assume. Amelia never did know how to keep her mouth shut. Silence yourself girl, I'll deal with you when this is over."

"The *fuck* you will." I snarled. I'd like to claim that I was trying to lure him into attacking so Zeke could smash him like a bug, but honestly I hadn't even known I was speaking until I said that. I also hadn't noticed myself standing up. "You come near her and I'll fucking kill you. I might not be able to fight you in a head on conflict, but I bet you'd have some real trouble surviving an E-ranked spike of metal through the eye while you sleep."

I admit. That wasn't the most… diplomatic thing to say. But I could feel Callie's rage and hate through our connection, not to mention my own because I *liked* Amelia, and fuck this guy for blaming her when he'd been the one who humiliated and left her.

I expected him to get angry, to try to lash out at me, but fortunately for my anonymity, someone else had something to say, too.

"Enough, Paul," said a quiet murmur from our side. "This is enough. Have you really become so pathetic and pompous that you need to poke at your own daughter's wounds for all to see?" I noticed he used Midknight's real name this time, and realized it was because Midknight had done the same to Callie. Alexander was letting his brother know that anything he did to her, The Nothing would pay back in kind. He was offering her protection.

Not to be outdone, Melinda snorted from the other side. "Please, like there's anyone on the planet who doesn't know Midknight is a brown-nosing rat bastard who sucks up to the public and treats everyone around him like shit when no one is looking. If there's a Hypocrisy Skill his is probably at Master rank." Her mocking sneer was so unlike her I had trouble even processing it for a second.

On second thought, though, the Unity and the WCP were public enemies. Not to mention Melinda was allied with our Pavilion and I was a guest elder of the Beast Lord Garden. She was making her stance clear, probably because if Midknight chose to make an issue of this he would be effectively challenging three E-rankers—Melinda, her weasel companion Travis, and Alexander himself.

The man's blue eyes bored into our group, icy with rage, but to my surprise, he just chuckled. "Criminals and trash will always show their true nature. By all means, put on your show, clowns. I'll accommodate you. I imagine our guests would love to see such a comedic performance."

Melinda looked livid. Alexander shook his head, and with a begrudging nod she sat back down. The E-rankers all stared at each other for a moment before returning to the matter at hand.

I winced. Midknight was good. Any further provocation would vindicate him and make the other two look like children. It was the same thing the triplets had done back in Valen. He'd diffused that way too easily.

21

Still, I wasn't stupid enough to think this was over. His cold blue eyes had locked on me and Callie as he resumed his speech. We'd challenged his authority, and he wasn't going to let it pass.

That was fine. I might not be able to fight him, but I had ways of making his life harder. He could bring it the fuck on.

Chapter Five

I VAGUELY CONSIDERED THROWING fruit or something at Midknight, but that was clearly beneath my dignity—and also I didn't have any fruit. Instead I just held Callie's hand as the armored bastard returned to his obnoxious soliloquy.

"Now," he rumbled, "as I'm sure you know, today we will be selecting your primary opponents. In the spirit of fairness there will be a random selection rather than a structured match schedule."

Callie's snort told me she agreed with my assessment that Midknight wasn't the type to care about fairness. My guess would be that he didn't want to get assassinated by some overzealous E-ranker from a higher rank planet because he fucked up their chances by putting them against a ringer.

"If you will all look under your seats!" Midknight boomed. "There should be an envelope. If you have more than one per team, simply leave them be and they will randomly switch places until all contestants receive their assignments."

Huh. Considering we picked our own seats, that actually did seem random. However, we were on a marble stadium style bench seat. There was no underside to check.

Looking down though, I could clearly see a stone tablet set snug against the bench. Levering my fingers into the seat I lifted it up and let Callie grab our envelope. The other groups nearby grabbed their own and began to open them.

Callie checked the stiff white card inside ours. "Halls of the Nether," she announced. She flipped over the card. "Team captain: Selariam. Team members: Sennec, Vile, and Runk." She stared at me blankly. "I... have no idea what any of these words mean."

I was about to respond when Megan's voice cut in. "Wait, you guys are up against the Nether? From the sound of it you got the Screaming Specters too." The Wave Warren Ascendant paused. "Huh, could have sworn those guys were dead."

"They are," Sydney said in puzzlement, her rabbit ears swiveling. "They're ghosts."

Megan just glared at her sister. "That's not what I meant you smartass. Anyway, the Nether isn't from our planet, but it is from one of the others orbiting our star. We've had dealings with nearby worlds a time or two. Selariam and his brothers all managed to find a spectral catalyst and synergize a ghostly racial trait. Energy attacks work better than physical damage for that group."

"Noted," Callie said, smiling. "Who did you guys end up drawing? It's not anyone we know, is it? It would really suck for you all to end up fighting Lament's team in the first round or something."

That got a snort from Megan. "Please, we're luck manipulators. Granted, with all the Impact behind this tournament, it's unlikely we'll do much for the overall situation later, but with this many people involved things are pretty damn in flux. Tweaking our odds with all this colliding fate to work with is just child's play."

It was interesting to hear more about their ability. Sadly, I didn't get to hear too much, because a booming voice cut us off. "Since you all have received your battle assignments, we can discuss the rules of the tournament," Midknight said. Everyone settled down, even us, because as much fun as it would be to fuck with him at the moment, we needed to know the rules so we didn't get disqualified over something stupid.

"First, the rank limit. If, under any circumstances, anyone breaks through to F-rank during the tournament, their entire team will be immediately ousted. Most of you are at the edge of F-rank due to the requirements for entry into the Moonsong Glade. However, to make sure the contestants don't vary too wildly in strength, you've been required to put your break-throughs on hold."

We'd known that already, but it was nice to know what the consequences were if someone tried to break through. Not that I'd refuse to do it if needed (I'd keep my friends safe no matter what) but still, forewarned is forearmed. "Second," continued Midknight. "The use of offensive F-rank artifacts is considered forbidden during the tournament. As the matches aren't designed to be fatal, defensive gear is permitted."

That was a relief actually. Our F-rank armor would be a huge boon during all this. "And finally—intentional killing will be cause for dismissal from the tournament."

Where the other rules had been a net benefit to us, this one wasn't. Not because we were murder hungry lunatics, but because he'd said *intentional*. Which meant it would be possible for someone to kill us and then claim after the fact that it was an accident.

While Midknight couldn't do anything to me because of Zeke, that didn't mean none of the Unity could. Based on his petty personality as mentioned by Callie, I wouldn't be surprised if the Unity teams closest to him had orders to try and kill me.

That might be a bit paranoid, but he'd looked right fucking at me when he'd said it. Callie looked just as upset by the implications as I did, possibly more so. Where I was just cautious and annoyed, my girlfriend was so livid I was worried she'd literally burst into flames from anger.

Pulling my hand out of hers and flexing my sore fingers, I put an arm around her and pulled her close. "Hey, don't let him get to you. He can't do shit to us directly, and I refuse to believe he has a team of G-rankers that'll be a threat." After all, we had Abel on our side, and I didn't think any of Midknight's assholes were Master Candidates. Our team would crush any of his people.

"That's only helpful in the first eight rounds," she insisted. "The five single elimination rounds will give him plenty of chances to try some-thing. I know you're plenty strong Solomon, but the Unity is a big organi-zation. Some of the fighters on this planet *are* dangerous, despite how low ranked it is. I bet you at least a decent chunk of the Titan Twenty make it to the single elimination rounds, and some of them are from the Unity."

I pulled her into a hug. "Hey, I'll be fine. I'm a scary bastard. Plus don't we have a few more days before that? Maybe a week or two. That's plenty of time to get even stronger. Although I admit I'm a bit surprised. Like, this is a three-star System right? Even if every star has a bunch of planets around it, lets say ten, that's still only thirty planets. How the hell are there twenty-five hundred teams competing?"

"Oh, that," Megan interjected. "C-rank planets are much bigger than D-rank planets. Gralter is the weakest C-ranked planet orbiting our star, and like I said, we barely got an invite. We're really only pseudo C-rank, like this planet is pseudo D-rank. The real C-rank planets have much scarier forces, and plenty more of them. The strongest person on a pseudo C-rank planet is still D-rank, even if there are a lot of them. Real C-rank planets have *actual* C-rankers. Every force from places like that can send multiple teams to an event like this."

That made sense in a way. I was guessing the true C-rank planets were the top of the food chain in a small Star System like this one. Once we got into the wider Cluster I imagined they would be much more common, with pseudo B-rank planets maybe even showing up. Regardless, Megan and Sydney's reveal about the Wave Warren and Slime Hall being the only contestants from their planet and Zeke's explanation of the Star System had massively thrown off my estimate for how many people we'd be fighting.

Granted, a large number of the contestants were probably from local forces. I imagine the bar was much lower for locals, especially since we hadn't had to take any tests or anything to qualify. Most of them were clearly just there to fill out numbers and make the main matches more exciting. Higher end teams like the ones from the Unity and the WCP factions would be the real competition from Callus, and even then, the System forces probably didn't care too much about them.

Abel cleared his throat. "Stop getting in your own heads, idiots. We aren't here to play patty cake, though to be fair I would absolutely crush a patty cake tournament." I saw him pause, hands twitching, and I scooted away from him as I imagined massive hand images descending from the sky to crush his enemies in rapid succession. He shut it off quick with an elbow from Mel though. "Oh, sorry. Point is we don't need to worry so much about this kind of thing. Our options have only ever been to win or lose. The strength of the enemy doesn't change that. Win or lose, just fight as hard for the former as you can."

A bark of laughter sounded from behind us, and I turned to see Zeke grinning down at Abel. "I like this kid. He gets it. So many Ascendants get too caught up in nonsense. Move forward, don't hesitate. If something stops you then you were never going to make it all the way to begin with, but you gave it your all."

It had been a long time since I saw Zeke so enthusiastic about anything. I think Abel reminded him quite a bit of himself, which looking back I could kind of see.

Alexander nodded his agreement with my uncle's sentiments. "Exactly." The Nothing turned to his own team. We'd met them all when he showed up, but they weren't really friendly or talkative, so they'd mostly been standing in the background. "Abigail, are you prepared for this fight? To put it all on the line even if your opponents are stronger than you are?"

The tiny, tanned girl with blue-streaked black hair and aqua eyes nodded gravely. "I am, my lord." Her tone was overly polite and formal. "For the moment however, I suggest we retreat from this place to strategize and talk amongst ourselves. So long as none of our number are pitted against each other, such a confluence should be quite advantageous, and as you can clearly see, the water darkness slowly swallows the skies."

At all of our confused looks, Alexander just sighed. "She means it's going to rain." He paused, looking up. "Which actually is a good point. No roof on this place. Good call Abigail." He stood up, gesturing for us to follow. "If you'd all accompany me, I can pay for a meal while we talk. I assume we all have things to share about our enemies, or at least some of us do, and if any of us did get matched up we can simply decline to discuss such topics."

Callie shrugged happily. "Works for me. I'm hungry. Plus if you're treating, uncle Alex, I bet the place will be great. Can we bring the wolves?"

Alex just chuckled. "I'm an E-ranker. You could bring a whole damn forest if I decided you should. The wolves will be fine. Though I don't think the bear will fit. Where is it by the way?" He gestured to Jessie. "I thought the two of them were bonded."

Our blonde teammate looked sullen. "I had to leave him home. They wouldn't let him into the meeting." Her scowl quickly morphed into a sunny smile. "It's fine though, I can just bring him some food to go. I'm sure you wouldn't mind me getting some carryout."

Alexander agreed easily, but it was my turn to chuckle. Poor bastard had never seen how much an F-ranked bear could eat, clearly. Oh well—better him than me.

Chapter Six

THE PLACE ALEXANDER took us was *huge*. I was expecting something like one of the pubs we had been to before. Something with a bar and wooden tables and a seedy backroom feel. This new place though... it was really upscale. It reminded me a bit of Rantano's back in Valen, but not as obviously geared at mortals.

The new place, Deva, was a much larger building for one. Where Rantano's was the size of a normal restaurant, Deva was, at least on the inside, almost as big as a sports field. I expected given the size they would need columns, but there were none. It was all a single uninterrupted space except the tables, which were only about a foot tall and surrounded by plush pillows with intricate designs of a dozen types.

The ceiling was arched, but despite it being so high up, it was easy to see the pictures painted on the surface of the domed structure. Gods and monsters battled among the clouds, hiding behind still images as they threw bolts of lightning and fire literally out of the painted surface and across the gap to the other side of the dome. The deities and demons would sometimes die, only to fade into a normal still image upon their demise—only for one of the still images to awaken, some seeming to heal from fatal damage to begin anew their tiny war.

Though the place was far from empty, the sheer size made it feel much more private than it was. Which was good because we had a large party, and everyone needing to crowd around one huge table was already taxing to the space without trying to work around strangers. The wolves flopped down on the cushions nearest the door when we got to the table and the rest of us set up wherever we could get a spot with someone we wanted to sit with.

"So," I said as I sat down, "that was bracing." I looked at Callie. "Sorry to say, babe, but your dad is every bit as big an asshole as I was expecting. Sucks you had to put up with him all those years."

Alexander sighed. "Yes. Paul has gotten much worse. I truly wonder how much of that was early recursion before he built his reputation as a hero. Powers like ours are perceived a certain way. It's more than likely he was unduly influenced before he built his current image." He held up his hands quickly as if to forestall comment. "Not that it excuses him. Just... be careful about growing too fast. Recursion can become overwhelming if you get too much of it at once. Faster growth can make it harder to withstand."

I hadn't known that actually, but it made plenty of sense. I suspected we wouldn't have that problem, however. Most of our points came from wishes which should dilute the effect quite a bit. We would still have plenty of recursion, but it should be easier to resist for us at least.

Callie held up a hand. "I appreciate the support, guys, but let's just eat. I don't want to spend any more time thinking about that bastard than I have to." She grabbed for a menu on the table I hadn't even seen there. "What does this place have, anything good?"

I smiled as I grabbed another menu, realizing they were stashed in small compartments just under the table. Scanning over it I noted dozens of dishes. "It would be more useful to ask what they don't have. And the answer is not much. I'm in the mood for gumbo today I think. How about you guys?" The gumbo looked fantastic, and I was sure based on the pricing it would be made with high-ranking ingredients.

Our whole party went about ordering. Benny, Jessie, Abel, Zeke, Alexander, Abigail and her team, Lament and her team, Sydney, Megan, Cark, Melina, and even MacGregor. I was wincing internally for Alexander by the time we got to the wolves because this was going to cost him a fortune. The puppies got steaks, and Jessie ordered a massive to-go box of meat for Randall to be prepared right before we left. Alexander didn't even make a sound about the expenditure though.

Once the food was coming, we turned to Sydney and Megan. "So, you mentioned knowing something about our opponents in the first round? I admit I've never fought ghosts before. If it's a racial trait, did they give up their abilities when they made the shift?" I'd never been clear on that one. Some of the nonhumans I'd met were able to use jobs or abilities fine, and some seemed to have switched over to an ability based on their new species.

"They have both racial traits and abilities," Megan said flatly. "There are obviously some common powers between them, like intangibility. Other than that they have different tricks. Cold, sound—each one of them developed as a ghost uniquely, at least from what I heard. I don't know too much about them. As a D-rank force we never had much interaction with the Hall of Nether. I just know about them because all of them synergizing the same trait is considered odd."

Callie cursed. "Damn. We'll need to do some research on them before the fight. But it's fine, that's more than we knew before." She scanned the table. "I don't believe that with a group this big we won't find answers to help everyone out. This is a huge pool of potential information. So, who does everybody have to go up against?"

I knew that Callie had two reasons for doing this. One was definitely to help our friends, but she could also gather valuable information on people we might have to fight in the future. Statistically not all of the teams here would win. Some of them were shoo-ins like the Spear Legion team, but some like Silent Dagger's team were local and not particularly strong. I was sure Alexander had taught them well, but with so many D-rank forces sending out fighters who wouldn't be well trained?

Lament held up her card. "I got the Cave Spider Cult." She paused. "Actually saying that out loud, it's kind of a weird coincidence given our fight in Doomtown, but there are so many forces in the Gloryfire System it's not that surprising. Anyway, they're a D-rank force who mainly use variations on spider transformation. Not a racial trait, but more like your Beast Lord Garden."

MacGregor, who was with us for this little powwow (we'd been friendlier with him after he helped out in the auction fight) nodded. "Truth. The cultists are swift and dangerous, but should you avoid their projectiles they are no threat to one such as you. Do not allow them to bleed on you, however. Their blood is highly toxic and corrosive."

Lament look unmoved by the information, but Wren nodded in appreciation. "Thanks." He turned to glare at his captain. *"Some* of us worry about things like that. We appreciate the heads up." Lestri and Vector both nodded in appreciation, while Falken, who was sleeping on the table from all appearances, held out a lazy thumbs up without actually sitting up at all.

That got a snicker from Megan. "We got matched up with the Dead Iron Brotherhood. No one I've heard of before, so they probably aren't from any of the planets near our star. Or they are and they're just super weak. I'm hoping for the latter, given the work we put in to tweak the drawing in our favor."

Wren nodded at that. "Bit of column A bit of column B. The Dead Iron Brotherhood is only a D-rank force, and they're mainly defensive. They use a body transformation art to shift their bodies into metal. The type of metal varies depending on the person, synergizing different abilities can change that kind of thing. They're a pain in the ass to wear down, but you two are fast enough that they shouldn't be a threat. Just a long annoying battle."

I noticed that Megan didn't seem pleased with the news, and I had to hold back a snicker. Looked like her luck had come through in the most irritating way.

Sloane spoke up next. "Sky Wolf Temple. Never heard of them before either, not that I was expecting anything different. Anyone know what they can do?"

Sadly it seemed no one did, but then, with twenty-five hundred teams we were bound to see some unknowns, and our little alliance mainly spanned three or four planets. A few of the others spoke up, and some of them likewise had opponents we didn't know about. Despite the size of our current group, twenty-five hundred teams were far too many, especially given how many planets were probably involved.

Of course, some of them we were able to dig up more information on. The Burning Heaven Abyss was a well-known D-rank force that both Lament and MacGregor had heard of. Cark was up against them, and upon finding out they used some kind of cold fire, he immediately started making countermeasures. After that we all kind of broke off into our individual groups to converse and try to come up with ideas.

32

Our team discussed all the possible details. As we tried to figure out a countermeasure to the ghosts, Jessie perked up. "Oh hey, what about that dagger?" We all looked at her blankly. "You know? The ghost stabbing one we got in the Necropolis. That thing was G-rank wasn't it? What ever happened to it?" I blinked as I remembered it, then turned to look at Callie, who had handled the loot.

"We still have it." She said with a shrug. "Zeke made it sound impressive, so I kept it when I sold off most of the other stuff. That's a great idea, though, Agria. They won't be expecting that I bet. I'll dig it up and bring it along." She cocked her head in thought. "Maybe we should give it to Apollyon." She glanced at Abel. "Think it would be helpful?"

To my complete lack of surprise my teacher just shook his head. "Ragam isn't a weapon-based art. I can use a dagger, but it won't be as effective as my fists. Besides, I don't think my manifestations even count as physical attacks. I should be able to slap ghosts around just fine."

Callie nodded. "Fair enough. We can do some training tonight. The first round is tomorrow, so we obviously need to warm up. The next one will probably be a few days later. They need time to hold all the matches. Twelve hundred and fifty fights isn't going to be quick."

I groaned aloud at the idea of more training, but it was good natured. After some downtime I was up for some combat. Plus I really did want to be in peak form for this fight. Once we won we would be going to one of the local parties, and as much as I didn't look forward to formal attire, I figured we'd have more chances to try some good food.

Before long, my gumbo arrived. I dug into the delicious stew as I reached down to pet Jin and enjoyed the sights and sounds of Deva with my friends while we talked over our next moves. Tomorrow would be the first fight of the tournament, and I was betting those ghosts had some interesting tricks up their sleeves. I was confident we'd be ready no matter what they threw at us.

Chapter Seven

THE NEXT DAY found us reporting to one of the way too many arenas in Rajak. "Seriously," I complained, "why are there like three hundred of these places in town? Do people not *do* anything else?" I knew they did, actually, because tons of Ascendants spent most of their day hunting monsters for various bounties or Academy points. There was zero reason for them to be so bored as to run off to a random arena to mess around.

Callie giggled at my annoyed tone. "Arenas are a time-honored tradition among Ascendants. They give us an excuse to show off in front of a bunch of people, and they make money at the same time. Granted, places like this are way more regulated than arenas down in the WCP, but the Unity is still an organization for cultivators, and they'd be stupid not to take advantage. You need to make a name for yourself to get stronger, and for people outside of the major organizations this is the easiest way."

"She's right," chimed in Abel. "This is pretty much universal. Arenas are a valued commodity on almost every planet. They give poor and underexposed Ascendants a method of showing off and getting attention. More than one of the current E-rankers were arena-born. Hell, most of them scout their best talent from places like this. By that logic, do you honestly think in a city this size that three hundred arenas are a lot?"

Now that he said it like that... "Huh. Now I'm wondering why there aren't more of them." Before either of them could speak I held up my hands.

"It's just a figure of speech, I understand the concept of diminishing returns. Anyway, with twelve hundred and fifty fights spread over three hundred arenas the first round should only be four fights. If that's the case, why the gap between the fight days?"

Callie gestured around. "Buzz. This whole thing might be for selecting slots, but every one of these contestants is a possible recipient of a ton of renown. Most of the factions here are live streaming this back to their own planets and territories. Burning out the viewers with constant repetitive fights would be a waste. By having only one fight a day or so, they can keep people excited and milk the most out of the attention."

That actually made a lot of sense—I could understand why they would agree to it to. Under the assumption the others would do the same, they could reap a ton of benefits. Sadly I couldn't learn more about how this would work because the announcer for the arena called our names. "Alright," Callie said. "Everyone remember your roles. We practiced this last night." She drew the dagger we'd looted from the necropolis.

We had practiced, and as we made our way down the tunnel leading to the arena proper, I went over the various strategies in my head, trying to make sure I could react with a moment's notice. As we walked, I triggered Touch of Tears and Consecration of Flames as usual. If nothing else they would theoretically allow my cane to make contact with the ghosts.

Once we stepped out onto the sand, the previously roaring crowd cut off completely. Looking up, I could see them still yelling in the stands, but their mouths weren't producing any sounds. Some kind of barrier maybe? It seemed to only cover the actual arena pit. Interesting.

My eyes, which had been scanning the arena, finally fell onto the group of four beings standing across from us, clearly waiting for us to arrive. The one in the lead, who I assumed was Selariam, didn't look like much. Just a super pale guy with silver hair and delicate features. He was short, maybe five foot six, and his icy blue eyes were calm and analytical.

"Hello," he said as we approached. "You must be our opponents. We represent the Halls of the Nether, a D-ranked force located on the planet Vakram. My name is Selariam, and these are my brothers, Sennec, Vile, and Runk. Might I have the honor of knowing what your faction is called?"

I opened my mouth to answer, and quickly had to break off the response as my senses screamed at me that I was about to be attacked. It took me almost too long to realize I wasn't the one being targeted. I spun on my heel, lashing out at the air behind Callie with a Flurry of Blows enhanced smash of my cane. There was a crash as the head of my weapon met the blades of a huge double headed axe, and another figure faded into view.

As he did, the largest of the four enemy combatants dissolved into silvery mist. I bared my teeth at him and triggered one of my fire attacks through my cane, releasing a giant burst of slightly corrosive flame. Granted, it wasn't as effective as actually using the skills synergized with the attack, but it was faster and much less of a strain. The massive bearded ghost warrior's eyes widened and he flickered backwards unnaturally as the wave of teal fire swallowed the space he'd been occupying.

While I was distracted, the other three had attacked, but Selariam himself and the one I was pretty sure was Vile had both been intercepted by Abel, while Mel had snagged Sennec in a flame cage. That left Callie and I to do what we did best. I dashed forward, annoyed that our plans had been spoiled, but we'd made contingencies for a surprise attack (what kind of moron doesn't expect to be jump scared by a ghost?). I brought my cane down overhand at Runk's head, imbuing it with a triple-stacked density-shifted attack.

As he backpedaled, a wall of darkness about a foot high sprouted behind his feet, and he tripped for a second before seeming to remember he didn't need to obey the laws of gravity and just... stopping, midair.

A massive stockade of shadow jumped off the ground, clamping down around his hands and neck. Apparently shadow constructs counted as energy because he had to plant his feet to get the leverage to tear free.

The second he did I triggered Sucking Mud, along with a shadow attack. Runk managed to tear free of the stockades within seconds, but by that time my tendrils had already caught his legs. The shadow imbued earth held him where I knew regular earth wouldn't, and Callie took advantage to split off into half a dozen clones and surround him, her armor making her own form just as deceptive to the eye as the shadow simulacra.

Planting a foot, I spun out off the ball of my foot, letting my cane ride the axis of the spin to build up momentum as I synergized Balam and triggered another triple stack density-shifted blow. Sadly, the brief period of confusion from our barrage had worn off and Runk was ready for me, catching the blow on his double-headed axe with a grunt and using the force to catapult him out of the shadow mud.

I saw his grip tighten as the blade of the axe cracked slightly under the force. He lunged forward to swing his axe at me, and I pulled up my cane to block, only to get bodied by one of Callie's clones before a swing from behind could take off my head. The ghostly form I'd been looking at faded into smoke as Runk appeared behind where I'd been standing, grinning nastily.

Damn. This one was tougher than expected. I looked over to check on the others and saw Selarium manifesting some kind of huge ghastly face that screamed at Abel, only for the thing to get belted in the mouth with a fist manifestation. I was pretty sure Selarium's was an ability, not a high Intermediate Skill. I climbed to my feet, groaning slightly as I glared at Runk.

"Ok." I said testily. "That was uncalled for." I mean sure, that wouldn't have killed me with my armor, but still. I considered using my magma leg to finish things, but I knew it would mess me up. My head was twinging a bit already from the shadow swamp. Besides, I needed to stop relying so much on big finishing moves. I wouldn't be able to hold my own against stronger opponents if I let things turn into a competition of trump cards.

I noted, interestingly, that Runk had avoided getting too close to Callie. I wondered if he could feel the spectral severer, because she'd put the thing away temporarily to avoid letting him see it, presumably waiting for a shot. Since that was our best bet against him, I rushed forward to play distraction again, hurling myself up into a forward flip to smash an axe kick down on the bastard, imbuing it with yet another triple stacked density shift.

As my foot slammed down on the axe, I had a second to think while I was in the air. Despite the number of exchanges, due to our speed and Perception, we had only been fighting for a short while. I considered trying to stall him and letting Abel take care of this, but dismissed the thought almost immediately. I'd be fighting solo soon enough, which meant it was imperative to sharpen my one-on-one combat. My team wouldn't be there to bail me out later.

Which is why, as he raised his axe to block the kick, I lashed out and triggered Cloud Step. Through a tricky bit of maneuvering I managed to bounce off a pair of Cloud Step spots in the air, and combined with Flurry of Blows and a triple stack density shift, along with Mercy Kill, Consecration of Flame, and Touch of Tears (otherwise it wouldn't have even landed) I hammered a kick directly into the side of his head, completely bypassing his defense before he could even process what was happening. Though not before he could snap out a backhand to my ribs, bouncing me away from him.

As he staggered, a storm of razor-sharp shadow snowflakes burst out into a cloud of destruction, coming right up from his shadow to swallow him nearly whole, with only his legs being visible. There was a scream, and I got the vague impression of someone waving an axe frantically, but he was too obscured from view for me to keep track for long.

Callie appeared next to me. "You okay?" she asked unhappily, glaring at the ghostly fighter. "Because that looked like a nasty hit." My ribs ached, mostly because that had been blunt force (and how much bullshit was it that they could use physical attacks fine but ours wouldn't work), but I wasn't too bad off. I triggered a scan heal heal-burst combo, and since it was just bruising it wouldn't take too long to patch me up.

I went to move forward, but she held up a hand to stop me. "Wait. I have an idea. We need a big finisher, and neither of our abilities does that well from range. My constructs can be large, but it makes them less solid, and your attacks are for close range mostly. Will you let me try something?"

I could hear in her voice that what she was really asking was if I trusted her. I did, so I nodded.

Callie closed her eyes and held out a hand. Then I felt a pull. Not like when I channeled skills into her—that was always directly physical, like with Abel's punch. This time she used the bond to literally synergize with my skills, and what's more, use my stored attacks. From the ground in front of her crawled a huge dragon construct, not unlike the wyvern we fought in the necropolis, though obviously smaller.

She poured skills and attacks into it. Stone Limb, giving the whole thing solidity, Touch of Tears and Consecration of Flame imbuing it with poisoned flame, bolstering it with a fire attack, even adding Mercy Kill to give it a boost. By the time she was done, the massive black flaming magma dragon looked so terrifying that Runk froze as the cloud of snowflakes melted away.

Callie swayed, clearly having taken most of the soul weight on herself for this, but was still aware enough to make it pounce. As it crashed down, I had to grin to myself. Our bond was getting stronger and this was bound to make a hell of an impression.

Chapter Eight

"WHAT THE ACTUAL FUCK WAS THAT?" Abel said as he strolled over. The two ghosts he'd been fighting appeared to be sprawled on the sand leaking some sort of mercurial substance I suspected was ghost blood. He didn't even notice though as he stared at the spot where the dark magma dragon that Callie and I had made with our Paired Dueling Skill faded into a cloud of darkness and green sparks.

I smiled smugly, pulling Callie against me as she laughed at his expression. I held up a hand to high five her as she proudly proclaimed, "That was our first Skill used through the bond." I was pretty sure he knew that and just wanted us to have a chance to say it, but still, she sounded so proud I didn't want to interrupt.

The dragon had been cool as shit. I was pretty sure I couldn't have managed it on my own either. While I could use shadow attacks, sustainable constructs weren't viable for me. But using my skills through the dragon meant Callie could still reinforce and control it, her Shadow Manipulation turning it from a big hunk of burning darkness into a dangerous weapon. The Stone Limb skill had also made it much more solid, even with only sand to work with.

"Damn," Abel said. "I knew you made it to Lesser, but I didn't realize you were already at that level. Not bad. Be careful with that bond, though. It's a big strain using it for Skills—as you may have noticed." He gestured to where Callie was practically hanging on my arm.

I grimaced. Without waiting for her response I scooped her up with an arm under her legs. She squeaked in surprise and glared a bit, but I could see a little smirk on her face.

This would normally be a bit over the top for public interaction, but after I'd felt how little strength she had in her legs, I realized walking out of here was a pipe dream. Better the audience see me being a bit affectionate than see her showing weakness. Luckily the barrier prevented sound from escaping so no one had heard what he said. Callie waved theatrically to anyone as I carried her out, and when we got back to the waiting room I set her down on a bench.

She seemed a bit out of it. I snapped my fingers in front of her a few times. "Hey, stay with me. You alright?" She was alive and conscious, so she wasn't in any real danger, but being this loopy wasn't exactly a good thing. I didn't realize she'd overdone it so much. I wished Benny was here with his spiritual calming belt.

"M'fine," she mumbled, waving me off. "Jus' tired."

I sighed, picking her up again. We had wanted to stick around and soak up some attention after the fight, but she was completely out of it—and I wouldn't leave her alone. We could see people at the after party. The audience should be pretty distracted, anyway—they held a few non-tournament exhibition fights to entertain people since official matches didn't last that long. One fight a day wasn't a reason for people to show up at this kind of place en masse.

Getting her home was easy enough. We were back up in the orange house that Zeke had bought since the Pavilion was a bit too far for a daily commute. Once we got back, I borrowed the effect of Benny's belt (I was definitely going to trade for a few charges of that after we got Callie up to the peak of G-rank) and helped her get back on her feet. Once her head cleared, the loopiness became pain, and she ended up curled on the couch groaning, which was what I'd been expecting.

"Ow," she whimpered. "Is that what you feel like every time you overuse your soul strength? Because if it is, I'm so sorry—and also you're an idiot." I laughed at that, plopping down next to her as I took off my mask. She winced again. "Ow. No, bad noise. Don't be so loud."

I chuckled more softly, lowering my voice as I responded. "Sorry, but it's just funny to hear you yell at me about this when you bit my head off about testing the magma leg in person. But hey, at least you took my 'do something stupid' philosophy to heart." She glared at me venomously, but I just winked back. "It's fine, just don't do so much next time. Honestly I'm surprised you could stack so much on the construct as a rookie. I think it had something to do with using your ability as a base for the effects instead of a half-assed Enchanting Skill."

Sadly I couldn't grant wishes unless people made them, so mobilizing the wish power to act as a base for my DS Mastery wasn't feasible. That meant my soul had to be a lot stronger than most to get the same effects, hence the unusual amount of pain I had to go through.

She nodded, wincing at the action. "That sounds right. Still, you're not wrong about me overreaching." She gave me an embarrassed look. "I guess it's easier to get lost in the thrill of combat than I expected. I'm sorry I got so mad at you last time."

"Don't be," I said gently. "You were right. Which means you actually did do something dumb this time. And not healthy dumb, like picking a fight with your childhood nemesis. Legit dumb. So it's my turn to tell you to be more careful. Messing with soul weight is dangerous. Soul damage could kill you or worse if you screw up using it. We can work out some training now that you can use my skills, and I'll work on learning to use yours."

I was pretty sure I could use her ability with practice, though I was positive she couldn't use mine—if it were that easy to gain access to the wish power, plenty of people would have it. I was also looking forward to learning that dark dragon construct thing. I could even most likely use her Shadow Manipulation Skill.

"So," I said tiredly, "I think we made a good enough showing to hit one of the galas. Assuming we're still going. Your dad might be there and he could cause trouble for us."

She snorted. "Don't be ridiculous. He wouldn't start a fight with his daughter at a formal event. I'm not bored enough to start one with him either. I vented plenty at the arena and seriously messed with his plans anyway. As for the rest of what I owe him…" She looked at me worriedly. "I can just wait it out. We'll be E-rank before too long, and then we can kick his ass. Speaking of, given how high some of my stats are getting, I should get a really impressive upgrade when I synergize this time. Maybe not something like Jessie has, but still something great."

I was looking forward to that too. Callie's stats were pretty damn concentrated at this point. She was right that she probably wouldn't get something as broken as Jessie's ability. I'd looked into it and breaking through with the percentage of Vitality she had was almost unheard of. Still, Callie would definitely get something good.

Though she acted like waiting was fine, I could tell that it frustrated her. I took her hand. "If you don't want to wait we can find a way to mess with him now. I was already planning to pressure him politically with my ability."

She smiled at me sweetly. "Feel free. But leave any real revenge to me—I want to handle him myself. Once I break through to E-rank, especially if I manage to get more Impact before that, I'll be happy to show him how unhappy he's made me and Mom over the years." Her sweet smile turned sharp and feral, and I grinned back and kissed her softly.

I noticed, though, that she mentioned *hurting* him specifically—not killing him. I was glad. I hadn't thought she would take it that far, but given how much she hated him anything was on the table. I didn't think Callie, at least *my* Callie, would survive killing her dad, no matter how much he deserved it. Hell, wanting to handle him herself was almost a way of protecting him. She wanted to kick his ass for everything he'd done, but she knew she personally would be willing to hold back and not take it too far.

As much as I disliked him, what I wanted most was for her to be happy with how things ended. If she wanted to break both his legs and smack him around that was her prerogative.

"So, we're going to one of the galas. I assume you have a specific one in mind?"

Her mood, which had been souring talking about her father, brightened. "I talked to Celine about that quite a bit actually. We decided to go to the Mindbender's Ball. Solana the Mindbender is an E-ranked illusionist and is known for throwing some of the best parties. The gala she's putting on for the visiting dignitaries should be absolutely amazing!"

"Sounds good," I laughed. "You know I'm hopeless at parties. Just get me the clothes you want me to wear ahead of time and I'll be there. Well, and my mask of course." I looked at the wooden face covering with a compli-cated expression. It was powerful and useful and naturally protected me from attacks... but it was also creepy. "Man, I cannot get used to that whole defensive measures thing. I try not to think about it most of the time but..." I shuddered in revulsion remembering the sight of that E-ranker getting *eaten*.

Callie grimaced. "Yeah, it wasn't pleasant to watch. But if it keeps you safe I can deal with a bit of creep factor. As for clothes... I'm sure we can find you something nice that won't clash with it. You won't need your armor at least—the gala will have intense security. Plus if anyone too strong shows up, Zeke will be there too." She grinned conspiratorially. "I may or may not have already arranged for him to bring a date."

Knowing she must have arranged to fly Stella over from Valen, I couldn't help but grin. It was always fun seeing my uncle off balance, and I suspected this would accomplish that.

"What about Benny and Jessie?" I asked. "They can still come even though they aren't in the tournament right?" Also Randall, because seeing a bunch of famous people try not to react to a giant bear, possibly in clothes, sounded hilarious.

Of course, since she knew me pretty well, Callie just rolled her eyes. "Yes to them, no to the bear. Don't think I didn't notice what you wanted to do. As much fun as that would be we're trying to make inroads with visiting factions, not make everyone below E-rank piss themselves. I'm already talking to Jessie about what we're all wearing to the ball, so don't worry about your clothes. Celine is obviously picking Benny's. We'll also be helping Cass decide what she's wearing, though Cark is picking his own stuff."

I smirked at that. While it might seem presumptuous, they just knew us well enough to anticipate that none of us cared about formal wear or any of that other stuff. Letting them pick our outfits just meant we didn't need to do it. Well, Benny and I specifically. I knew Cark liked to make an impression, so him picking his own outfit made sense.

"Alright," I said. "When is this ball anyway?" I wanted to make sure I was mentally prepared for this before we went, after all. I really hated parties.

"In an hour."

I just stared at her.

She gave me a sly grin. "Kidding. It's the day after tomorrow."

I sighed. Not far enough away.

Chapter Nine

THE MINDBENDER'S Ball was apparently being held at the ballroom of a local hotel in the city. The Ventralia was an upscale hotel catering to visiting dignitaries and high-ranking Unity and WCP personnel from other cities. Since most of the E-rankers were concentrated in Rajak, they mostly saw F-rank visitors, but considering these people were all influential local powerhouses, the place was still pretty swanky.

Climbing out of the carriage, I looked back at it in awe. "Ok, how the hell did you guys even find a carriage in this day and age? Especially such a nice one. Who the hell uses G-rank horses to pull a carriage?" I looked apologetically at the driver. "No offense, it's a beautiful carriage, just the concept seems kind of old fashioned to me for some reason."

He just shrugged. "You paid for a ride didn't ya?" I opened my mouth to retort but came up short because… I had no response to that.

"Well played," I said with narrowed eyes, and he tipped his hat to me and gently spurred the horses to move along.

As we stood outside the venue, I took in everyone's clothes, and I had to admit that our various politicos had a pretty good eye for fashion. Even Cark looked upscale in a nicely tailored suit and waistcoat. Cass was wearing a ball gown that she looked thrilled to be in, while Jessie had on a floor length dress that looked like it was made from leaves. Given her power that might actually be true.

Callie had decided to go with a black evening gown that looked like solid darkness, but she had a shawl of roiling shadow over her shoulders and back. Her dark dress matched my own suit, which paired well with my dark wooden mask.

Celine was dressed in an emerald green velvet dress, with Benny wearing a similarly colored suit that went shockingly well with his eyes. Zeke was in a rumpled but upscale looking suit of dark grey that went well with Stella's shimmering starlight silver dress. Melinda was there with Travis, looking regal in dark green silk, with Sloane trailing behind in black. We had more than a few nature-inclined people in our group and it showed.

Alexander hadn't come. I suspect he didn't want to be here without Amelia, and I didn't expect she had any interest in being at a party where her ex-husband and presumably his new wife would be in attendance. I knew Callie would prefer to avoid Annie as well, and I didn't expect her to approach us. She'd been keeping her distance like Callie clearly wanted ever since we'd moved out of the Unity building.

"Alright," I said, "how do we go about making our entrance here?" I shot Callie a sulky look, my voice whiny as I said, "We *could* have been escorted in by a giant bear in clothes. I still say it's not fair Melinda got to bring her companion and Jessie couldn't bring hers."

Callie looked at me incredulously. "Travis is a weasel! He's the size of my forearm. Randall is a bear the size of a small bus." With my mask on she couldn't see my smirk, but she could hear my tone and knew I was just teasing. She played along because it amused her.

"Yes, dear," I said dramatically. Then I put an arm around her and pulled her close. "You look amazing by the way." I put on a faux haughty tone. "Not as amazing as me, but then, we all have our burdens to bear in life, and being drop dead gorgeous is clearly the heaviest of my responsibilities."

She giggled and poked me in the ribs. "Talk to me about your magnificence when you can dress yourself, stud. I'm pretty sure you might have shown up wearing pants on your head if I hadn't picked out your suit." She gestured at Cark. "Why can't you and Clockwork be like Tony. He can pick his own clothes."

I gasped in mortal offense. "How dare you. I am a very stylish individual. I have style... ish." That got another giggle. "Anyway, we should head in.

Don't want to keep everyone waiting." I removed my arm from her shoulders and held out my elbow formally. "Shall we, milady?"

She actually curtsied in response (albeit pretty sarcastically) before taking my arm and leading me inside. The others trailed behind us. Benny and Celine caught up, and my friend nudged me. "So, Cel says this place is going to be crawling with local power players. Anyone we might know?"

Callie nodded as we walked toward the entrance to the hotel. "Oh yeah. Several people we've met, a few we've heard mentioned. The Moravian is going to be here, which is huge—he rarely comes out of seclusion. The old man likes to spend his time alone from what I'm told. Duncan the Liar will be here, though he tends to mess with people at functions like this. Unless you want to break your teeth biting into a diamond or something steer clear. He's the obnoxious blonde guy in the bright yellow doublet."

She had her Stealth Skill active as she filled us in to keep us from being overheard. As we got close to entering, she stopped talking and dropped the skill, smiling at the man guarding the door. "Nightstrike, here by invitation from The Nothing." I hadn't known we needed an invite, but it made sense. Alexander being able to get us in wasn't a surprise either, even without him being here. The Nothing had a pretty sizable reputation, even up here.

Realistically, Melinda was with us and could have just walked us through the front door herself, but since we were trying to make connections, Callie decided to use Alexander's name.

The door guard, a hulking beefy man with thinning hair and a neck as thick as my thigh, nodded and waved us through without a second thought. Walking into the building, we followed a trail of floating candles in elegant crystal sconces that bobbed in the air over a red carpet. Soon, we arrived at a pair of open double doors where the party was being held, and when we reached the threshold, we all stopped and gaped.

A cosmos of rioting phenomena blazed dizzyingly over the room. More than just stars. Waves of fire, storms of lightning, swirling cascades of luminous water, mist, clouds—shimmering blobs of light and gel and a million other things wove an inexplicable tapestry through the darkness of space, transforming and combining and breaking apart into components again and again.

The array of lights and colors that played across the dark marble of the floor seemed to be just on the edge of overwhelming without actually becoming too much to deal with. I noticed the cascade of colors was passing through a cloud of nearly invisible white light that kept it from overpowering the crowd with the sheer spectacle without disturbing our ability to withstand it.

Even with the filter, it was easy to see how it could be used as a mental attack if the caster was so inclined. Mindbender indeed.

"Holy shit," Benny said quietly. "You guys weren't kidding about this being a crazy party." Focusing past the light show (which was only possible because of the filter I suspected), we glanced down at the party itself. Among the guests floated cloaks full of nebulas, with dark hoods covered only by masks. They each had a pair of floating white gloves holding up trays of food and drinks as they circulated.

The decorations and the help were only part of what made the place so amazing though. The guests were almost as impressive. Suits of living flame, dandelion dresses, doublets made of storm clouds with real lightning striking out. I'd thought we'd gone all out getting ready, but we'd dressed conservatively compared to some of the wild fashion statements.

Far from being upset, Callie clicked her tongue in amazement. "See," she said to Jessie, Celine, and Cark. "I told you it would have been a mistake to go big. No way we could have kept up. Better to let our reputation do the talking."

As we stepped in, one of the cloaked nebulas floated over, extending a pair of trays in a way that told me those gloves were not attached to any arms. Mine had some mini quiches, and I snagged a few before tapping into Callie's ability via our bond for a second and condensing a plate from shadows.

Damn, that was convenient. It wasn't very sturdy, and it wouldn't last, but since it was so flimsy I barely had to strain my soul at all to make it, plus I could just disperse the thing when I finished eating. I made a second one for Callie because I knew my girl well enough to know she'd want some food, too, and slid a few bacon and scallop mini quiches onto it.

When I passed the appetizers over she smirked at me. "They do have plates, you know? But this works better for me anyway. Thanks babe." She hopped up gracefully to give me a peck on the mask, just before my wooden face covering receded so I could eat, allowing me to return her grin.

I popped a quiche into my mouth with a groan. Smoked gouda and pepperoni. Odd combo but very delicious. "This is great," I said as we headed out to mingle. "Wonder who did their catering." Popping another in my mouth, I saw Callie had already eaten all of hers and dispersed the plate. I chuckled. "Clearly you liked them too."

The others had mostly broken off when we came in, with Jessie following Cark and Cass, Benny and Celine disappearing into the throng, and Sloane trailing Melinda, leaving just the two of us as Zeke and Stella got lost in the dance floor crowd.

"So, who do we talk to first?" I asked Callie. "This is your show—I don't know what's what here."

She looked around uncertainly. "I'm not sure. Usually I had a reason to talk to people at parties when I was younger." She bit her lip as she paused for thought. "Let's try someone our age we actually know. Maybe Cold Snap is around. His mom is E-rank, and he could make an introduction."

I wasn't sure he would actually want to do that—the guy had been an arrogant tool back when we'd worked together to defeat the Heartrippers during the scavenger hunt. Still, he hadn't seemed too hostile in the end, so it couldn't hurt to ask, especially with security here.

As I turned to follow her into the crowd, I felt a twinge from my bond, meaning Callie had picked up something coming at my back. I sidestepped easily and was shocked to see a pulled pork sandwich fly through the air where my head had been.

"Hah!" bellowed a voice from nearby. "As expected of my nemesis."

I knew that voice. I closed my eyes silently and breathed out an exhalation of annoyance. I turned to see the crowd retreating as a familiar form strolled out, a blazer over his usually shirtless torso. I should have figured this was coming. His dad *was* an E-ranker now.

He shot me a challenging grin. "Bet you didn't expect to see me again so soon, did you, Solomon?"

Callie stepped up next to me, and I felt her own annoyance through the bond as Punchin' Carl cornered me right next to the dance floor. Well, this should be fun.

50

Chapter Ten

I SIGHED DRAMATICALLY at the sight of the other man. Hard to forget someone who threw a rope of sausage at your face during your first patrol. "Carl," I said, not even bothering to feign enthusiasm. "So good to see you... No, wait that isn't true. I see you, you're here. Where's your buddy Stephen?"

Carl sneered. "They wouldn't let him in because he wasn't wearing shoes." I hadn't considered that. He glared back at the door. "They even tried to say I couldn't come in because I'm not wearing a shirt! Stupid. I obviously have this jacket on. That totally counts."

Callie actually snickered a bit at that, and I rolled my eyes because she really shouldn't encourage him.

"I take it your old man is around here somewhere?" I ran my eyes over the room, because even in this crazy bedlam there was no possible way I could miss someone like Mr. Jack-tastic with a brightly colored spiked mohawk.

"Nah, pops doesn't have time for parties like this. All these boring people doing boring stuff. He sent me to chat up some of these randoms before the tournament. Get the low-down on what they can do." I assumed he was also supposed to be making connections for if he managed to get off world, though having seen how strong some of the forces in the tournament were, I judged the likelihood of that to infinitely approach zero.

Everyone around us was looking at Carl with an unhappy expression, presumably because he'd said that last thing pretty loud and people don't like being referred to as boring randoms. A long sigh came from off to the side as a girl stepped out of the crowd. She had brown hair and peaceful golden eyes, flanked by a pair of twins in suits each wearing a half mask.

Joy. Serenity and her cronies from Sanctuary Hall.

"Carl—I could swear that I told you not to openly insult anyone here." To my surprise, rather than sneering and gloating, she mostly just seemed exhausted. I almost felt bad for her—I wouldn't want to deal with Carl all day. She gave the two of us a soft smile. "My apologies for the crude manner of my companion's speech. It's wonderful to see you both again. You've certainly gotten much stronger."

I expected some kind of animosity or anger (we'd killed a bunch of the Peace Lord's people in the battle for the Pavilion, after all) but she seemed genuinely affable.

Even Callie, who was used to hero and villain bullshit from her time growing up in the Unity, looked off balance. "You don't... hate us? We kicked your asses and then ransomed you back to your faction." That wasn't a particularly political way to phrase that, but it was weird enough to see her being so friendly that it didn't seem too out of line.

Serenity just shrugged. "That's life. Play stupid games, win stupid prizes. We knew the risks of attacking the Cavalcade. We took a shot and failed. We're members of the Wish Curse Palace. Not to say we don't hold grudges, but you could have killed us or been quite a bit rougher than you were. We no longer have any need to be hostile, so why waste the energy?"

That... staggered me. We'd killed their people, beaten them mercilessly (although, in retrospect, there'd been a *bit* of mercy), and sold them back to their bosses like used books, and they just... didn't care?

Beat (at least I think it was Beat given his gloves) snickered at us. "You have a lot to learn about how things work downtown. Today's enemies are tomorrow's allies. We don't have defined sides like the Unity does. Not to say I won't enjoy kicking your asses in the tournament if we run into you. You're not the only ones who have been getting stronger."

Carl groaned. "This is so boring! Can we go? I wanna go punch some stuff." He looked at Serenity. "Also I didn't insult anybody. These people are all randoms to me, and someone has to be boring or how can anybody be awesome? Also, Solomon, I'm totally gonna punch you in the tournament. I'm way stronger than last time. You won't even know what hit you." He brought his fists together near his stomach in a flexing motion, and the jacket he wore ripped loudly across the shoulders.

Serenity closed her eyes, from all appearances counting to ten, and exhaled slowly. "Carl... Fine. We can go." She fixed her gaze on us, her previously serene smile turning sharp. "Just wanted to let you know there's no hard feelings, so when our team crushes you in the tournament, you'll know it's nothing personal."

She gestured for Beat and Sever to follow and grabbed Carl's arm, dragging him away into the crowd.

I blinked. "Wait, *Carl* is their fourth team member? That's... How is he even strong enough?" I knew that my cousin Natalie had been working with the Jerks and Sanctuary Hall for a while, but helping Carl grind up that high since I'd last seen him was still impressive. I guessed that they'd probably maxed his elixir cap at each rank, too. Still, I'd crushed him the first time we fought.

Clearly able to sense my disbelief, Callie chuckled. "You were H-rank the first time you fought Carl. Abilities at that rank are so low level they barely work. Almost no stats to fuel them. A high G-ranker isn't anything like they were at early H- or I-rank. He might actually be pretty tough. Plus who knows what Skills he picked up on top of whatever his ability is."

I knew M-jack's ability was some kind of animated animal tattoo conjuration. I wasn't sure if Carl inherited the same one, made his own ability similar through synergy, or just had some of those tattoos placed on him by his dad, but I'd heard that M-jack made sure his son was protected. If he was at our level maybe he could be a real threat, especially with backup like Beat, Sever, and Serenity.

Callie sighed. "Their group will be tough for us. Serenity isn't quite a hard counter to Abel, but she's the closest I've seen. He can dominate one or two of the others in a fight against most groups, but against them... Well we've already seen that she can keep him busy."

I hadn't considered that. Abel was a monster (we'd seen him crush everyone he came up against like bugs) but Serenity had managed to keep him busy solo. That hadn't seemed too scary at the time, but having experienced his strength firsthand, that made her fucking terrifying.

Seeing how troubled I was, Callie just smiled and reached down to squeeze my hand. "Hey, no worries. She's a bad match-up for Abel, but that doesn't make her invincible. We'll come up with some countermeasures for her ability. No power is impossible to beat. For now, let's hit the dance floor for a bit before we try to meet up with other attendees. Won't do us any good to try making connections all keyed up like this."

I stepped back, sweeping into a bow and holding out a hand for her. "Fair enough. Then may I have this dance, milady?"

"Of course, kind sir," she said with an exaggerated curtsy, then took my hand, only to squeak when I spun her around and caught her.

We stepped onto the dance floor, and for the first time I started paying attention to the music. There was a graceful serenity to the tune that I hadn't even noticed. In fact, it wasn't just an emotional reaction—I felt a familiar sensation as I immersed myself in the sound of the instruments.

"Is this—" I said, stopping. It took me a second to put my finger on it, but I finally realized what I was picking up. "Does this music replenish soul strength?"

Callie paused too, her eyes widening. "It is. This is the same kind of sensation as Benny's spiritual calming belt. You can do that with music? That's amazing." It had to be an ability, but an ability like that must be insanely hard to come by. It might even be necessary to be born with it directly, but even if it wasn't, the stat requirements and the skills needed to synergize it must be crazy.

We danced for a while, and because I could, I decided to take advantage of the time to train a bit. The replenishment was a good opportunity, it would be a shame to miss it. I triggered Cloud Step, but I used my soul strength to alter the skill, creating a single huge platform for Callie and me to step onto. Then, with a serious effort, I moved the platform, lifting us both up into the air so we were dancing above the crowd.

This was an Ascendant party, so flying wasn't anything huge—it mostly just got a few laughs. One or two of the other couples used their own abilities to join us in the air, though. I saw a few fire users flying above the crowd, and one or two people using wind and even a gravity ability or two. One pair of ladies were dancing above the crowd on what looked like a cloud of purple starlight, and I even saw Abel and Mel join the party, with my mentor using his spatial ability to eliminate the distance between his feet and the ground while still standing midair.

Dancing up here, we could see the riot of forces and stars right above us, and it was staggering to be up among the illusion the Mindbender had set up for this party.

"Flashy entrance, kid," my uncle's voice called from behind us. I turned to see him and Stella standing on a miniature galaxy courtesy of her cosmic witchcraft. I knew that high ranking Ascendents (D-rankers and above) could fly regardless of ability and was pretty sure Zeke could just forcibly defy gravity with raw stats, but he was keeping a low profile and seemed content to let Stella fly them.

I shrugged. "Anything worth doing is worth doing big." I doubted this counted as a great deed or anything, but I was sure it would at least generate a bit of buzz for me in terms of making connections. Callie could definitely use it as an icebreaker.

Zeke cracked up at that. "Well said kid, couldn't have phrased it better myself. Anyway, don't spend the whole night up here. With this Soul Soothing Song, you probably could, but you'd miss the food and the company." It was Zeke's way of telling me to start mingling soon. I desperately wanted to stay up here, since the "Soul Soothing Song" was good training for me, but I knew that as a Wishmaster Candidate, making connections was integral and it was something I needed to learn.

With a sigh I waved to the others and lowered the Cloud Step platform to the ground. As we touched down, Callie went up on her toes and planted a kiss on my mask, smiling up at me happily. "Thanks for the dance, handsome."

Then she dragged me over to one of the floating cloaks to get some food. We filled a few more shadow plates with hors d'oeuvres before looking around for the next target we needed to schmooze. We settled on Burning Fist, or Edgar as he preferred to be called informally. The E-ranker was off in the distance talking to Cark and Sage, with Saffron nearby. I already knew Sage was Edgar's daughter, but seeing them all together, it was clear Saffron was his daughter, too. I should have guessed the relation from their names honestly, but I figured they might be cape monikers.

With an internal shrug, I followed Callie over to talk to them. I had to admit, this really was turning out to be a hell of a party.

Chapter Eleven

WAKING UP THE NEXT MORNING, I was incredibly exhausted. Between helping Callie schmooze "randoms," as Carl called them, and training (I absolutely wasn't going to waste a chance to train my soul strength nigh-limitlessly), my brain was fried.

I was still tired when I woke up. Not physically tired, since my Vitality was pretty high, but mentally tired. Constantly expending and refilling soul strength was a unique kind of exhausting I'd never experienced before. Still, I'd made considerable progress last night. I was pretty sure I could handle using Magma Leg without instantly exhausting my soul strength now, which was a huge boost to my abilities.

When we woke up, we found an envelope pinned to the door of the house with our next opponents listed inside. We would have been totally in the dark about who they were, except we'd been chatting up everyone last night and had managed to dig up quite a treasure trove of information on the other teams. The team from the Divine Stainless Temple had been precisely one of the teams we'd heard about.

It wasn't actually a shock that they'd come up, because the main combatant of the Divine Stainless Temple used an extremely weird primary weapon. His first-round opponent from the Turtle Breath Monastery had complained endlessly about how stupid and ridiculous it was that he lost to a guy using a mop.

"Ah shit," Benny said as he read it. "You guys are fighting mop guy? He's pretty strong right? Honestly, how does a person train mopping to a Beginner or even Intermediate Skill? And where the hell do you get a G-ranked mop from? I still say those turtle guys were just chumps."

Abel, who had crashed with us at the house rather than head back to G-district, shook his head. "Nope. Their team leader was actually decent. You get a feel for martial arts aura. I'd say... Intermediate rank, probably somewhere in the middle. Not a standout favorite, but still, decent. Plus I haven't seen him fight but 'Turtle Breath' makes me think defensive art. Those guys are always a bitch to deal with."

Jessie snickered from her spot at the counter. "So you're saying they got... cleaned up?"

We all groaned at the bad joke, though I secretly sidled over to give her a fist bump for the hilarious pun.

Abel rolled his eyes. "I'm just saying not to underestimate him because his weapon is weird. Don't we have a guy on our team who can beat people stronger than him with video game Skills? Stupid to assume other people can't do interesting things with underwhelming Skills. Mopping is a new one to me, but I could see how it could be useful in a fight. I mean, it's basically a net on a stick."

"No," Callie said. "That's a butterfly net, and it's already a thing, but I see your point. Also I really hope we don't ever have to fight someone who uses a butterfly net as a main weapon. I think mops are about the most ridiculous form of weaponry I can stomach."

That set Jessie off on another round of giggles. "You guys clearly didn't hear about the team with the guy who fights with a mug." We all just looked at her, and she put both hands up. "Hey, I swear that's not a joke. Mug guy crushed his first-round opponent. They were whining about it all night."

Ignoring the ridiculousness of that, I turned to look at Callie. "I wasn't listening to any of the other stuff they said about the Stainless Temple." I grimaced. "Sorry, I was bored at that point, so I started training with Seek Hidden to pass the time. It doesn't have any outward signs so figured it would be okay." Naturally I needed to take best advantage of the music, and while dancing had helped, using my other skills was useful as long as I actively altered the skill during execution.

She just smirked at me and patted my arm. "I know sweetie. I could tell. But don't worry, no one else could. You did a good job of pretending to be interested. If it wasn't for the bond I might not have noticed. But it's fine. I noted everything down. I know you aren't a fan of those kind of events and that you put plenty of effort into meeting people for most of the night."

I just shrugged. I'd pick up people skills eventually. Unless… were there people *Skills?* Celine probably had some, but for now it didn't matter. I had enough Skills to deal with trying to upgrade all the subskills for DS Mastery.

"The other members of the Divine Stainless Temple are okay, but nothing overwhelming," Callie continued. "One of them can grow, which is interesting, and one of them can create swords. The last one just uses lightning blasts, but he teams up with sword guy mostly and they're pretty effective."

"Wait," I said in surprise. "He can *grow?* Like… make himself bigger? How does that even work? Does he gain more Impact with size? Less? Is there a limit?" I'd heard of a few impressive powers, but that one was kind of over the top even by Ascendant standards.

She sighed. "Sadly, no one could say. I can pretty firmly say no to the first. Even your ability isn't that broken. I don't know if he has relative Impact or if, like you said, it diminishes as he grows. There's obviously a limit, of course, since he has limited stats. I'm not sure if he has a stat multiplier when he gets bigger, but if not, the power isn't that impressive. Just gives him better reach. Smart play would be to use it in small measures, making himself slightly larger. I'll look into it before we decide how to handle him."

"That's a good idea," I said. "We have a few days until the next round anyway."

I called Callie to the training room, waving off the others, though they didn't try too hard to follow. When she got down there I grinned at her. "Not sure if I mentioned, but yesterday I officially hit a thousand points. I'm capped for G-rank. Which means my wishes going forward are all yours. Since I was getting all my points from the Beast Lord Garden, I'm even prepaid on my contract with them for quite a while."

She squealed with joy. "Awesome! I was a little worried about that. Today and four more days, that'll put me at seventy-five points. What do you have left of the attacks I traded you before?"

I could see how excited she was, but I was pretty curious. "What are you going to focus on endgame? I know you wanted to try to qualify for a stronger ability when you synergize by making sure one stat was much higher than the others. Still going for Perception?" That was her highest and her original specialty, as well as extremely important for anyone who fought with Stealth. It would even have benefits for her constructs, allowing her to make them more detailed and make better use of her Shadow Manipulation.

She nodded. "I have a general idea what I'm doing, but yeah. As much as I love the extra Might, Perception is my bread and butter. I've been able to focus so hard on other stats because it was so high, but my fighting style is heavily influenced by my ability to move unseen and deceive the senses, not to mention find blind spots for my shadow attacks."

"Speaking of which," I said, frowning, "I can channel your ability through the bond as far as I know, so stored attacks don't seem as useful. Any ideas for what you can use to pay?"

She nodded. "I was thinking about that. The bond makes it tricky. My best idea was just to go out solo and make some money. I took a few missions while you were doing your thing with the Beast Lord Garden leading up to the first round. Nothing crazy, but enough to save up some chits." She passed me a small bag. Fifteen G-ranked chits. "I worked for them myself and not as part of the team, so they should still serve as payment, right?"

I wasn't positive, but I suspected they would. Team goods and stuff from the Pavilion were partially mine so it wouldn't work as payment, but money she went out and made on her own should be fine. I nodded to her, and she grinned. "Awesome, I wish for fifteen points of Perception. Paid for with fifteen chits of our same rank."

Wish detected. Grant wish?

I confirmed. The usual stat requirements rolled across my vision, and I was pleasantly surprised to see that I could actually queue up wishes like that. It made things much easier than listing them out one by one, especially if I got the payment all at the same time. Realistically though, it was just a minor timesaver. I still had to let the five wishes build and grant them individually.

The chits worked fine, each of them containing more than enough Creation to be a viable payment, and they also weren't so valuable as to tip the scales the other way. Callie got all fifteen points dropped right into Perception, bringing it to two hundred thirty-five points and her full total to nine hundred out of a thousand. Callie gave a happy sigh once all the wishes were finished. "Man, it feels nice for my Perception to spike like that. I'm pretty excited for my breakthrough when the tournament ends."

"You going to tell me about it?" I asked with a laugh. "Or do I have to guess?" With Beginner rank Shadow Manipulation and a high concentration of Perception, I couldn't think of what she might unlock. Something related to infiltration probably, but she seemed to have a specific direction in mind. Given Jessie's Lifeweaver ability and how well it conformed to her future goals, Callie's long-term aspirations might affect it. We'd have to wait and see.

"Nope." She grinned at me mischievously. "Not that I know for sure how it'll turn out. I know what I'm aiming for at least. You'll just have to wait and be surprised like the rest of them."

I rolled my eyes at that but didn't really mind. I was excited to see what she would end up with.

I kind of wished I could synergize my ability sometimes, but doing it at this point would be pure stupidity. The main benefit of the Wish power was fast growth, which in the end was the most impressive power you could have in a world like this. Stats decided everything, and getting more of them made all my other abilities much stronger. Once I reached a high enough level I could think about finally synergizing my ability to get something new.

I suspected that given the massive jump in needed stats, once you reached A or B-rank being able to get even ten or twenty from stats wouldn't be a huge advantage, otherwise my old man would have held off on his own change until he became a god. I wasn't anywhere near strong enough for that to be an issue for me though.

For now I was destined to keep my ability unaltered. With my stockpile of attacks and modifiers from DS Mastery, though, I refused to believe I wasn't one of the best at up front combat among Candidates my level.

I guessed I'd find out if I fought my cousin Natalie in the tournament. I was really looking forward to facing her.

Chapter Twelve

"THIS SUCKS," my girlfriend groaned as she slumped down on the couch. "I'm an Ascendant. A powerful G-ranker who is probably going to hit F-rank before I turn nineteen, and I have to *work* to make money to pay my own boyfriend. I became a superhero to avoid this kind of nonsense. I hate hunting monsters. I can't even bring you along to help because if we earn the money together it doesn't *count.*"

I just snickered at her. "You're lucky I already confirmed that I could take cash for wishes. Not that it's surprising. I think that's where most of the WCP's startup funds came from. And honestly, you're ranking up much faster than anyone else our age could even dream of. Four days and you're already only five points from hitting three hundred perception, and forty points from the cap. Can you really complain?"

She turned her head to glare at me, but there was no heat, it was just sulking. "I can complain about *anything.* I'm being petty—didn't you tell me to do more dumb things for myself? You're supposed to listen to me vent and say how bad you feel for me."

I would have, but at seventy-five G-ranked chits I was quickly saving up enough of a nest egg to replace my weapon. The cane was getting a bit old. Not that I'd do it during the tournament since they banned F-ranked offensive gear, but that just meant I could save more and get something really nice.

"I do feel bad," I said with mock sincerity. "I have to listen to you whine every day, it's a terrible feeling." Callie pouted and hurled a pillow at me, which I easily dodged, sticking my tongue out at her. "But honestly, it's fine. You're almost capped, and then you can just focus on training. Speaking of which, the big fight is tomorrow. Did you manage to dig up any more background on the others?"

She scoffed. "With my copious free time? Do you know how much work I've been doing? Without a team I have to take smaller missions and making enough to pay off my stats is breaking my back." Her face lit up. "So of course I did. In fact, I found out something absolutely huge."

I rolled my eyes at the misdirect but urged her to continue. She looked around dramatically, as if someone would be listening in while we sat in the living room of the house we shared with a B-ranker. "Apparently... mop guy is a Master Candidate."

"Bullshit," I spat. "There's no possible way. Didn't Megan say they're stupid rare around here? I mean, I knew there would be some maybe showing up in the tournament, but there's no way the guy is at peak Intermediate in *mopping.*" There were limits to how ridiculous Skills could get, and that stretched the limits for me. Like, how would you even train that? And what the fuck was his original ability?

Callie just shrugged. "It's what my sources say. Which is to say Celine. Which is to say the information hall at the Academy." She saw my horrified expression and giggled. "Oh calm down. We have our own Master Candidate to counter him." Her expression turned serious. "I admit though, I am a bit worried, so I already talked to Abel, and he's giving us special training today."

I blanched. "*Special* training? Abel's training is already about as special as I can take without dying. If it gets any more special they might not find all the pieces of me."

"Yeah," she said with a wince. "I'm not looking forward to it either. But if it needs to be done it needs to be done. It's not like the other team will go any easier on us. And while Abel can keep him busy, going up against someone like that, there's no telling if he might manage to get a stray shot in on us." She stood up, holding out a hand.

"Wait, now?" I grimaced. "I'm not mentally prepared. You mind if I go hide under my bed for a few hours?"

Raising an eyebrow at me imperiously, she just left her hand out.

"Alright fine, I'm coming." I grabbed her hand and made her physically pull my body off the couch as an expression of my discontent. She just rolled her eyes but didn't complain. If she could whine about nonsense I could too.

In reality I wasn't... *that* worried. I knew he wouldn't really kill us. This would likely suck a lot. But if he thought it would make us safer I was all for it.

We met Abel down in the training room and found Mel sitting off to the side nursing a hot cup of tea... without her mask. We just stared at her blankly.

"I... what?" I said. I'd only seen her take it off once, so it was a bit jarring.

She grinned at us. "Welcome to the team kids. For real. We were impressed with the last fight, and we figured since we're in this together we'd show a little sincerity." She jerked a thumb at Abel. "Drama king over there only takes his mask off when he's going to kick some serious ass, but mine I just leave on out of habit. So... hello again." She waved casually. "I wouldn't let it distract you too much though. This is going to be rough enough as it is."

Abel cracked his neck, starting to stretch and loosen his muscles in a way that utterly terrified me. Abel didn't stretch. Abel didn't need to prepare to fight anyone. This warmup implied he was taking us seriously. Deep down, I felt a thrill of excitement. My teacher had always been a mysterious existence. We'd seen him get pissed and ruin someone's day, but we'd never seen him get serious. He'd never needed to.

"This next fight," he said calmly, "is going to be different than the last. I can't tell you that the opponent will be as strong as I am. But I can't tell you that he won't. I am not going to allow you two to participate in this fight until I'm satisfied that you can survive a battle with someone like me. This training is going to force you to adapt to combat on the Master Candidate level, at least enough to live through it. Are you willing?"

He obviously had no plans whatsoever to let us continue if we said no— he'd just made that clear. I personally didn't want to, though. I had plenty of heals in reserve to use, and I wanted to see what would happen. Still, I felt the need to at least ask. "Are you sure we can? We don't have any Inter- mediate Skills between the two of us."

The solemn demeanor slipped as he rolled his eyes, looking to Mel in exasperation. "It's like they haven't ever heard a word we've said? Do I just have an ignorable voice? The first thing you should have learned at the Pavilion is that combat is more than Skills and stats. Sure, you two aren't at Intermediate, and that's going to hold you back. But battle isn't just numbers. I trained my Ragam to peak Intermediate because I love the art, but I was still a member of the Titan Twenty before I was a Master Candidate. I won't say I can train you to beat someone like me in a few days, but surviving should be doable."

That thrill of excitement sparked and became an inferno. *This.* This was what I wanted. The reason I craved combat. There was still fear, I wasn't a moron, but the idea of being able to fight above my weight class, to be more than my stats, was intoxicating. If I wanted to walk much further in the Wishmaster Candidate race, I had to evolve. To adapt. To learn.

I nodded slowly at him, readying myself. I felt the fierce determination in my gut echoed in the bond as Callie took up her own stance.

Abel grinned. "Now *that's* what I like to see. You kids will bring a tear to this old man's eye. But don't think being proud means you won't get beaten. Spare the rod spoil the child and all that."

Without an ounce of hesitation he unleashed a fist at us, the manifestation easily the size of a fucking bus. He'd chambered the punch from his hip, so while it wasn't overwhelmingly strong it was *fast*.

I panicked for a split second as it approached, freezing under the pressure, before forcefully dragging my attention to the attack. I grabbed Callie's hand, and she pulled up a shield in front of us. Rather than using my skills alone, we shared the burden, just like we'd been shown in that invocation, only much faster and easier. Stone Limb, modified, Consecration of Flames, modified.

The dome of darkness hardened into black magma, and it stayed stable just long enough for me to trigger Cloud Step and Leaf on the Wind to drag Callie out of the way. We barely avoided the shattering earthen darkness. The pressure knocked us flying, and I hit the ground, already dragging her up to move again as another massive fist bore down on us.

We erected another shield, dodging again, and Abel clicked his tongue as he watched us madly scramble. "Your foundations are too unstable. I said earlier that Skills and stats are only part of the equation. Using soul strength to constantly toss out powerful moves to counter my casual punches is a good way to get exhausted to death. You might be able to survive an intentional attack, but if you need to mobilize that much power you'll get crushed by the first sneak attack."

I panted as I pulled Callie to her feet. "You're a Master Candidate using your fist manifestation. How the hell are we supposed to survive it without Skills?"

He just shrugged. "Your business. I'm just saying this isn't sustainable. Skill use is fine, but you need to take your long-term survivability into account. I'm not going to let up anytime soon. You've got dozens more of those to survive if you want to make it through this."

With a grimace I adjusted my stance and shot Callie a meaningful look. I flicked my eyes at a spot. She seemed confused for a second before finally nodding. He'd mentioned that Skills were fine but had specifically told us that using soul strength would wear us down. He was probably right—I'd built up more soul strength with my training, but even sharing the burden with Callie I couldn't keep going indefinitely.

When he confirmed we were ready, he chambered another punch and a massive fist image hurtled out of the void at us. Without a second thought, I hauled on Callie's arm and used Balam to flip her over my head, creating a foothold for her with Cloud Step. She used her own Balam Skill the same way, using the step-off point to pivot me, and the two of us floated out of the way on the still active Leaf on the Wind.

Another fist fired out, and another Cloud Step allowed us to dodge it by a hair, but the third hit me in the shoulder and cracked my arm bones and several of my ribs. I triggered a heal burst and a scan heal together. Callie looked terrified and barely dragged me out of the way of the fourth blow, but I was already healing.

Luckily Abel wasn't punching rapid-fire or we'd both be dead. I was surprised Callie's safety wish hadn't triggered, so he must still be holding back, even if I couldn't tell.

Finally he let up, letting us catch our breath for a minute. He didn't say anything, just waiting for us to be okay to go again. Once we reset our stances the training resumed. Gods this was going to be a long day.

Chapter Thirteen

ABEL STOPPED BEATING us early enough that we were able to get a few hours of sleep. Our match was at eleven in the morning, so we had a bit of time to rest, but Abel wouldn't let me and Callie heal ourselves until after we woke up. Aside from the natural healing of Vitality, he also knew the blast of energy from the heal burst would stop us from sleeping and wanted us to maximize the amount of rest we got.

I healed us up with one heal burst each while we scarfed down breakfast, and then the four of us headed for the arena again, the same one we fought at last time. When we arrived, it was just as packed as before. There would still be exhibition matches from those who couldn't enter the tournament after our fight (we'd kind of gotten in the back door because Natalie pulled strings), but we were the main event.

Just like before, we waited to be called out and entered the arena, but unlike last time, Abel wasn't carefree and bored. He looked focused, keyed up to a razor's edge, and he had a gleam in his eye that I'd only seen a few times. No, not the same gleam. I'd seen him enraged, interested, but this was something else. He was honing himself for battle, truly baring his fangs for the first time. Even against Serenity he hadn't been pressured. Her artifact had been enough to hold him back for a bit, but nothing more than that.

As we stepped out onto the sand and saw the other team, I felt like his enthusiasm was infecting all of us. Like there was an invisible war drum beating in time to all four of our hearts, and I knew that the training yesterday was only the beginning. These people were strong, and this battle was for real stakes.

There were four of them, of course. The one in the center was a tall skinny man with shaggy brown hair and a goatee. He had a long face and he was pale, almost sickly looking, so thin that I could see the bones in his face. He leaned against a mop handle, with the head over his shoulder, and looked like a strong wind might blow him over. The other three members of the Divine Stainless Temple stood a bit back from him, as if giving him space to attack, but I could see that the three of them were experienced in teamwork.

They stared at us for a moment after the battle was called to start, and then the one on the far end, an olive-skinned man with long red hair, barreled forward, expanding as he did. He went from normal size (about five ten) to almost twenty feet tall.

As he charged, a massive sword erupted from the sand to one side of him, called by the blue haired man with the single earring I knew was the sword summoner. It came up hilt first, and he grabbed it and swept it horizontally at us, even as the final member of their team, a very small man with a yellow ponytail, hurled a massive bolt of lightning at the shimmering blade.

Whatever the sword was made of, it conducted the electricity flawlessly, and the sight of the massive electrified blade might have frozen me in place... yesterday. Now I just grabbed ahold of Callie's hand and put my other hand on Mel's shoulder, activating Leaf on the Wind in conjunction with a Cloud Step for each of us to get out of the way.

Abel stayed behind, staring at the only unmoving member of the group, the mop wielding man, as he casually slapped out a hand to each side, one creating a fist image, and the other manifesting a palm that allowed the crackling sword swing to arch over where he was standing with a simple window wiping motion. The spatial lubrication channeled through the image forced the sword up and over, cleanly sliding by our teacher.

Abel's fist, though, never made contact. The blow aimed at the supersized team member was slapped aside by the image of a huge wooden pole as mop guy finally made his move. The pole wasn't the last of it either, as the other side of the mop spun up and a massive manifestation of the mop head appeared in front of us.

I'd wondered how the hell someone could possibly get mopping to peak Intermediate, but that terrifying attack told me absolutely everything I needed to know about the Skill. A fucking *canopy* of tightly woven wool strands appeared around us, each one winding itself like a striking snake to try to entrap and bind us from a different angle. Net on a stick indeed, this was absolutely horrifying, and I desperately tried to compensate for the attack with another Cloud Step, but I had nowhere to go.

Another hand image appeared around us, spatial lubrication smoothing the way along our path and allowing us to glide through the world around the grasping chords. Rather than a single palm, this one traced a myriad of paths in the air with expertly twisting fingers, creating not just a spatial waterslide for us to ride, but a series of intercepting spatial streams that forcefully turned aside each mop strand.

My eyes were wide as saucers as I saw what Abel was really capable of for the first time. The fine control, the speed and dexterity. It was like watching art. Knowing we had zero chance of interfering with those two, I Cloud Stepped again, bringing us down on the far side of the arena. Triggering a shadow clone, I sent it sprinting across the sand, then used it as a focal point to cast Sucking Mud.

The clone slapped its hand down on the sand, and the experience of working with Callie through the bond enabled me to trigger the skill through the clone, but the thing burst because I put too much soul strength into it. Still, the skill worked, and the massive sword wielder's eyes widened as he began to sink into the already unstable sand. A wave of swords burst up from the ground through the quicksand and another several arcs of lightning lit them up, but the other two team members couldn't take the time to follow up.

From what I could tell the sword conjurer could manipulate his blades, and was currently doing so to help the gigantified guy lift the enormously heavy blade. The lightning caller had to keep a steady stream of electricity going into the weapon to keep it electrified.

With Abel's help, we finally landed. Callie and I split from Mel, who moved to attack the lightning caller because we didn't have much of a counter for lightning.

We both attacked the sword conjurer, and as we closed in he (unsurprisingly) conjured a pair of swords to meet us. Mop guy tried to intervene, but in a blink Abel was there in front of him. His fists blurred out, weaving and snaking through the air in bizarre arcs that wouldn't have been possible without his ability, and the sickly-looking Master Candidate's expression became fierce as he whirled his mop.

Wooden staff knocking the punches askew and writhing mop head tangling up the strikes, I saw the spatial distortions melt under the threads of the mop, causing Abel to snarl. This would be mop guy's ability I guessed. Some kind of cleansing, amusingly enough. The images of fists and mop crashed together in the void above us, but Abel wasn't able to overpower the other warrior because he was still engaging the huge guy with his off hand.

Turning to Callie, I indicated for her to protect me while I tried something, and she seamlessly stepped in without me needing to speak aloud. I stepped back and triggered another shadow clone. Utilizing all my necessary skills, I stacked poison fire, Afterburner, Mercy Kill, a Triple Stack tranq blow, and Kidney Blow on the clone, then, using the connection to Callie, I hauled on Beginner Shadow Manipulation.

The soul weight of changing the composition of the clone from "clone" to "giant knife" was nothing to sneeze at, but once I did, I snatched it up (barely able to carry the damn thing because of the size) and triggered Double Trouble. Appearing behind the giant, I slammed the oversized shadow blade infused with super augmented poison and tranquilizer into the massive form, which as I had hoped was *much* more vulnerable.

Impact couldn't be amplified like his other stats, which meant all of his was spread out over his body. It was why mop guy had protected him from Abel. He probably assumed we wouldn't be able to cause harm to him on a large enough scale to matter without Abel's Skill.

He was wrong. The giant staggered as the G-ranked super-boosted poison tore through his body. He was forced to shrink back down so his Impact would return to a more condensed state to resist it. That, or he passed out from the tranq. Either way, he slumped over onto the sand, letting the giant sword fall to the ground and massively relieving the pressure on Abel while letting me drop my Sucking Mud.

Unfortunately that freed up sword guy completely, and the massive sword thumped to the ground unmoving as he gestured to the wave of blades from earlier and hurled them right at me. Fortunately, I still had nine charges of Afterburner after that dagger. With the single greatest pull of soul strength I could manage, I triggered Stone Limb and pulled the strength of the earth over my entire body, simultaneously using a triple stacked density shift on my whole form.

Sand or not, the dirt beneath me was still earth, and G-ranked earth at that. Afterburner's tripling effect was stacked on top of it. With the triple-strength density shift combined with the triple-strength stone limb, my entire body became a living statue too dense for any of the swords to penetrate, which combined with my F-ranked armor meant I took zero injury from the attack.

My mind was on fire—I was barely coherent at this point. The soul strength needed for this was at the very edges of what I was capable of. Forcing stone limb to cover my whole body would have broken me before the night of the gala, but all that training had massively increased my tolerance, so I could just barely hold on.

Feet digging into the sand from the weight, I would have probably been swallowed up even having dismissed Sucking Mud, except I still had Leaf on the Wind active and was able to offset some of it. I felt the sword barrage rain down on me, pinging off my skin like sleet. These were conjured weapons, not high-ranking crafted blades, and they were only as strong as the Creation and Might of the sword conjurer himself.

He was so distracted by the attempt to avenge his buddy that he even ignored Callie to attack me, which was not at all wise. She pummeled him the second he dropped his guard, creating a heavy mace from shadows and beating him violently about the head and body, presumably in anger at seeing me get swallowed by a cloud of dangerous cutlery.

Finally, there was a loud snap and the image of the mop above us vanished as Abel landed a strong hit on the mop handle and snapped it in two, breaking mop guy's momentum. Without his weapon the Master Candidate was helpless in front of my teacher. The whole fight had been so interconnected that once the first domino fell the pressure overwhelmed them and things ended within a minute or two. I let the Stone Skin (as I was calling it) skill fade as I slumped to the ground, barely conscious.

I was grinning like a loon as I heard the announcer call the battle in our favor. We'd gotten our second win.

Chapter Fourteen

As SOON AS Mel finished taking down the lightning caller, Callie was at my side in a flash. "Solomon," she said worriedly, "are you okay? Where are you hurt?"

I was confused for a second, before I realized the bond was probably dumping an assload of agony from my brain into hers. She saw me get stabbed a few hundred times and then experienced horrifying pain and assumed my defenses didn't hold up.

I groaned as sat up slowly. My armor being F-rank would have protected me from the actual stabbing, but without the Stone Skin defenses the impact trauma of the blades would had beaten me to mush. That guy had way more Might than I did based on the speed those had been going. It made sense since swords are a physical object and need to be durable to be useful, but still, I was glad I'd made that call. I wouldn't have died, but it would have sucked.

"My head feels like a scrambled egg, but I'm fine," I mumbled. "I overdrew my soul strength again." Afterburner was still going too, with another six attacks left, and once I used them I was pretty sure I would drop like a rock. I considered using a heal burst to try to ease the pain, but I was ninety percent sure it wouldn't work and might even make things worse.

She frowned at me but nodded with a sigh. "I get it. Sometimes risk is unavoidable. You weren't being reckless or anything, just desperate." She shot the sword conjurer a dirty look, though I don't think he noticed from where he was bleeding profusely and twitching on the sand.

Standing up, she held out a hand to me, and I let her pull me to my feet. "I can't believe we won that," I said in shock. "Like... holy shit. They were way stronger than the last team." I'd been expecting another series of sectioned off individual battles, not that madness.

Abel chuckled as he strolled over. "Damn right they were. That really got my blood pumping. Danny boy over there is the best fight I've had in quite some time, though I suspect Lament will be a bigger challenge." Despite the seriousness of his earlier demeanor, Abel looked just as carefree and lackadaisical as usual. This had been fun for him but I could tell he hadn't been genuinely pushed. Not like we had.

Mel rolled her eyes as she approached. "What he means to say is good job. That dagger move was a smart play Solomon. Your poison was much more effective on the big guy than I expected. Apollyon never would have been able to snap that mop fighting them two on one." Abel looked annoyed at that assessment, but didn't disagree.

We turned to the other team, who were still gathering themselves. Callie smiled at them respectfully. "You guys fought a good fight. Almost got us." Her gaze flicked to the sword guy, chilling for a second, before warming back up to match her sunny expression.

Danny the mop guy (and when the hell had Abel had a chance to learn his name?) nodded. "I didn't expect another Master Candidate, especially a local. I know the Spear Legion has one, and I heard the Primal Hatred Domain is supposed to have a guy who uses a gun of all things, but no one mentioned you."

The incredulity about the gun user seemed a bit absurd from a guy who fought with a mop, but to be fair guns were not common Ascendant weapons, so I could kind of see it. I filed the information away anyway, and we spent the next minute or two making small talk before heading back to our own entrances.

I was still holding back my Afterburner charges, but I knew that wasn't sustainable long term. I'd have to use them eventually, and it was straining my soul even more holding them in, but I'd have to deal with that when the bill came due. Once we were out of the pits, we headed up to meet with our friends, and everyone seemed incredibly enthused about the match.

"That was fucking *awesome!*" crowed Benny. "That statue defense was amazing—when did you come up with that?"

It had been inspired by him learning to use his abilities across his whole body, and by my own growth in soul strength actually, so I was glad he liked it. "About half a second before those swords hit me," I admitted. I wasn't going to sugar coat how close that had been. "Still, won't be doing it too often. Combined with your density boost I was able to withstand a ton of damage, but it's a huge strain. More of a last resort, since being super durable is pointless if you can't move or black out from pain."

He grimaced and put a hand on my shoulder, and I felt a cooling sensation roll over me, taking the edge off the blazing star of agony kindling in the back of my skull. I sighed with relief and did my best to soak up as much of the feeling as I could. "Anyway, glad you guys had fun watching. Pain aside I'm pretty proud of how we did, you think the other fighters noticed us?"

Zeke, who was leaning back against the empty bench seat behind him, chuckled. "Oh yeah. They noticed. That was middling to decent in terms of this part of the universe. Of course, most of the credit goes to the punchy kid, but still, that'll turn some heads." His expression flattened into a serious frown. "But you should be careful, not all attention is good, and not all tournaments are fought in the pits."

I wanted to tell him he was being paranoid, but Zeke knew Ascendant culture much better than I did. If he thought people might pull something, then they probably would. Callie nodded gratefully to him as she leaned against me, and I smiled softly at the realization that she was propping me up in case I fell over when the skill ended, while making it look like PDA.

"Speaking of the tournament," I said uncertainly, "do we know who our next opponent is going to be? I'm hoping we don't end up against one of the top teams like we did this time."

Zeke snorted at that. "Top teams? Divine Stainless Temple is middle of the pack at best. They have a Master Candidate sure, but the other three were all absurdly weak. Plus, who told you that Master Candidates are the only ones who can be strong? Skills are important, but as you well know, some abilities are just stronger than others from the start."

He didn't have to specify that he meant mine. But come to think of it he wasn't wrong. Serenity had been able to keep up with Abel. Maybe he could have overpowered her if he went all out, but I'd seen him crush F-rankers without much trouble. For her to be able to hold him back naturally meant she was much stronger than I'd given her credit for.

"D-rank factions," Zeke said seriously, "are all led by Masters. Most of them have complete inheritances of complementary Skills to help their descendants get as strong as possible. Not to the level of some of the inheritances from bigger factions, but synergizing powerful abilities wouldn't be hard." He nodded to Jessie. "With the right knowledge about the stat and Skill requirements of certain abilities, making powers like hers is more than feasible."

Which really put things into perspective because Jessie was a powerhouse for our rank. Honestly she was the strongest of the four of us within her area of specialization. I sighed. "Ok, point taken. Still, can we ask about our opponent? Forewarned is forearmed. We waited for the note last time, but I never asked if we actually had to."

Callie looked over to Abel and our mentor shrugged. "I can go ask about it at least. Might be a good idea to have the info. We only have two days until the next fight right?" Three hundred arenas and twelve hundred teams meant two fights a day for two days. That would bring Callie to the cap counting today's wishes, which would make me feel a lot better about going into whatever fight we had coming up.

As he headed off, I turned to Callie. "When he gets back we should get out of here. Though I did forget to ask, how did the others do in their fights?" I was planning to go see them fight at some point, but I'd mostly been busy with wishes and training. Maybe we could see who had a fight tomorrow and drop in to take a look.

She grimaced. "Silent Dagger and Beast Lord Garden lost their fights. Cark's team and the Twilight Order won and advanced to the next round. Sloane was pretty upset about it, and my uncle wasn't thrilled either."

I winced at that. Realistically, some of our people wouldn't make it past the second round. In fact, it was probably impressive they all made it through the first. I hadn't actually checked in on their next opponents at the ball, and I felt like kind of a dick for not thinking of it.

"Excuse me." It was kind of a surprise when our conversation was interrupted by a frail looking guy with baby blonde hair and blue eyes. "I was extremely impressed with your battle just then. I thought I'd come introduce myself." He held out a hand. "My name is Alec Brightwind. I'm a member of the Heavensong Tower. I was amazed by your performance just now. I actually wanted to invite you to a little gathering my Tower is holding for all the most promising teams."

I deferred to Callie on this of course, since she was the leader and the one who dealt with political stuff. However, she didn't look convinced. Zeke had just told us to be careful about who we trusted, and this guy was so meek and inoffensive looking it made my teeth itch. He reminded me of Aiden. Not in terms of being a cultist or anything, he didn't have that vibe. It was more that he was definitely a wolf in sheep's clothing.

My instincts were decent enough to pick up on Mordaunt, though I'd ignored them like a moron, but this guy didn't strike me as that kind of threat. He was a threat though, and Callie could see it too. Noticing her expression he held up both hands placatingly. "We don't have any nefarious intentions here. This is Rajak, there are dozens of powerful E-rankers keeping watch. It's better to make friends than enemies. Tournaments end, but friendships can last a lifetime."

Callie seemed to weigh things for a bit before finally nodding. "Alright. When is it? If we have the time we'll make an appearance. You don't mind if we bring some friends right?" Going alone would be stupid. While Rajak (the normal city anyway) forbade things like higher ranked Ascendents killing lower, if we got mobbed by other G-rankers they might not bother to step in.

He beamed. "Of course! It's in two days, right before the start of the third round." He pulled out a card and passed it over. The piece of cardstock had only an address printed on it. "Anyway, it's been nice talking to you, I have a few other teams to invite so I'll be going. I hope to see you there!" Cheerfully turning around, he strolled off into the crowd, stopping to talk to several other teams as he went.

I watched him go uncertainly. That had been odd. I got a sense of extreme danger from that guy, but not malice. I had a feeling he was going to make it to the later rounds, and that we might be up against him in the future. The sense of oppression I felt from him was no less than what I felt from Lament, though it was... different.

He'd be a tough opponent. I couldn't wait.

Chapter Fifteen

THE NEXT DAY, we decided to come in and watch Lament and Wren's match. Zeke actually came along too for some reason, and I was curious as to why. As we settled in to wait for the match to start, I decided to just ask. "What made this fight interesting enough to check out with us?"

Zeke turned to look at me. "Lament. Not many people manage to train their soul strength to that level out here in the boonies. There's three or four kids here who made it to the same point, and that's solid talent without any sort of heritage or guidance, though it isn't something you can do further up. At least not nearly as easily. There's a reason that even at G-rank they call them Master Candidates."

The way he was talking made it sound like they'd hit some kind of standard. "Is there a method of gauging soul force comparatively? Like some kind of metric people can use?"

That got me a grin. "See, that's the kind of question you should be asking." He was clearly pleased I'd brought this up. I was guessing it was basic cultivation info he was allowed to share, but only if I asked. "Yes. There is. Soul strength is gauged through color. I-rankers have an ivory soul. H-rankers are pink, G-rankers have a red soul, F-rankers have orange, so on and so forth. To clarify, you're maybe ten percent into red. It's much easier to train your soul at low levels, and the hammering method you and the others here use only really works well at red."

"So Abel and the others are at the peak of orange?" I guessed. It made sense that since they were almost Experts they would be at the top of the orange soul strength bracket.

Zeke just laughed. "What? No. They're barely orange. Listen, kid. Soul strength is incredibly important, for reasons that won't become apparent until you get much more powerful. Most people however, never cultivate soul strength. Despite that, even basic ass cultivators are able to rank their skills up to a single rank ahead. Intermediate at G-rank isn't impressive, not like peak Intermediate. Orange can take you to the peak of Intermediate, but it's impossible to break through to Expert without breaking through to F-rank—unless your soul reaches yellow grade."

"So they're at orange, barely, which means despite being right up against the barrier, they can't push through that last little bit without way more effort?" I asked uncertainly. Abel had made it sound like his soul was just a drop away from strong enough, but it seemed like that drop was the difference of an ocean.

He nodded. "Sure. And when they rank up that process happens naturally. The process of ranking up is a sublimation. The weight of your stats condenses and you become heavier, your Impact rising. In the process your soul becomes tempered and categorically rises one rank."

I frowned at that. "So there are ten ranks of soul strength, just like cultivation ranks?" Well, eleven but I wasn't counting gods because who knew how the hell you became one of those.

"Not exactly," he said wryly. "But don't worry about that for now. As far as you're concerned there are ten for the moment. Tempering at red can be done through your current method, it's called hammering. Being able to hammer your soul to orange is no mean feat. All those kids are geniuses. Maybe not monster level existences, but they have a natural strength of heart that most people can't match. The soul gets harder to temper through hammering as it condenses. You're at maybe ten percent, like I said, but it's going to take you years to get to orange even with all your advantages."

My displeasure at that must have been obvious, because he just laughed. Undeterred, I pressed on. "Ok, if hammering isn't the way to temper your soul, what is? Is it really something that only large clans can do?" I refused being relegated to space hick for the rest of my life. All the powerful combat techniques in the world were useless without the soul strength to mobilize them.

That seemed to be the right thing to ask. "No. Other people can—" The symbol on his forehead flared, and he gritted his teeth, forcing his breathing to even out. "Shit. That's too much. Fine. There…" He stopped to think over his words. "There is a *place*, where anyone can temper the soul. I can't tell you much more, but I can tell you this—after your soul reaches Master rank it becomes too sublimated to change. Blue is when tempering stops."

Something about that was important. He couldn't say what, but it was clear from the geas flaring that he'd been about to tell me something related to cultivation secrets that were outside the scope of the competition. I tried to puzzle it out, but Callie got it first.

"It's important that we go to this place early. Probably during F-rank. You mentioned people able to support Skills two above their rank before. If we can only go up two ranks, then if we wait until we're E-ranked, we can't go up two full ranks—we'd stop at green."

Zeke beamed. "I knew there was a reason I liked you." Then he winked. "Not that I can, of course, confirm the statement you just made. That would be beyond the scope of my role. But I feel a completely unrelated need to comment on your cleverness at this seemingly random time." His eyes flicked to the pit. "Anyway, enough talking about soul strength, your friends are coming out. I want to see what the spear girl can do. She and your little buddy are the most interesting two here."

Lament, Falken, Wren, and Lestri came out onto the sand as a unit. Lament was in the lead, with Falken dragging behind. I didn't know what Falken could do, but I was pretty sure he was strong. Apart from Lament he seemed to be the strongest team member based on how the others acted. Not a Master Candidate most likely, but still powerful as hell. "Who the hell are they fighting by the way?" I asked Callie.

"Blood Fiend Society," my girlfriend said with a grimace. "Nasty bastards. Sacrificial abilities that can induce temporary berserk modes. Finding information about them was easy since they aren't exactly subtle. Of course, that's just their core heritage. How much each person uses their faction's unique Skills and methods and how much they rely on inborn abilities is up in the air, as we saw in our last fight."

The other party did kind of look... Blood Fiend-ish. They all wore deep crimson robes and stylized demonic masks. Couldn't tell anything about their appearances except their eyes were red like fresh blood. As they stepped out, they glided over the sand, not literally, but with dramatic swooping strides that trailed their long robes across the ground. Sadly, the isolation barrier stopped us from hearing what was said, but judging by Lament's bored expression, it wasn't anything too interesting anyway.

The society members spread out around the Spear Legion, taking up a four corners position before two of them dashed in, transforming mid stride into slavering red-furred beasts. Lestri and Wren stepped in to deflect them, the larger brother whirling out his massive spear to keep them at range. Lestri used a rapid-fire stabbing technique that relied on the spear sliding through his hand like a pool cue, driven by the grip he had on the base with his other palm.

The other two members of the society raised their hands and called forth a storm of sanguine energy. Crimson fire and blood-red lightning pooled together above their heads in a vortex. As that happened, the sand in the arena began to glow an ominous red, and energy started to flow out of it, siphoning up into the vortex. The more energy that fed into it the more terrifying it became, growing in size and ferocity even as the red sand dimmed.

"What the fuck is that?" I asked in horror. That attack was much stronger than it should be coming from two G-rankers. At this point the vortex had firmly pushed into the realm of F-ranked attacks.

Zeke whistled. "Crafty. They used the vortex invocation as a focus for a blood sacrifice art. That arena has seen a lot of bloodshed over the years. It's baked into the ground at this point. Shouldn't be able to take all of it, though. Even both their souls together couldn't handle that kind of pressure. I expect they're just about done with the buildup."

True to his words, the siphon of sanguine energy cut off. Rather than charge it more, the two casters raised their hands and pushed, slowly forcing the cloud of roiling energy to shrink. They condensed the power slowly and steadily, and as it shrunk it started to shape itself. By the time they finished there was a giant head that resembled the creatures the first two had turned into.

It became obvious that the two creatures were playing distraction for the casters, and I expected Lament and Falken to take the time to attack, but neither did. Lament just watched the huge head of bloody fire and lightning form in the air, and Falken appeared to be napping, held up only by his spear.

Lament cracked her neck, smiling confidently, and started to spin her spear. One rotation, two, hand over hand as she whirled it in a slowly accelerating circle. The shaft of the weapon began to spark. The hooded figures threw their hands forward, and the head began to descend, its giant mouth opening in a soundless roar. Or soundless to us—based on the way the sand moved it wasn't soundless to the rest of them.

Each pass made the electricity gather more densely, and soon the spear was a blue glowing blur in front of her. She'd closed her eyes as she did it, ignoring the descending head, but as that terrifying blood monster approached her eyes snapped open. Her grip *changed*, the spin turning into a brutal upward thrust with every ounce of her body behind it.

She grabbed low and dipped, and the rising spear skimmed just over the ground up to full extension in a flash, ascending like a pillar of heaven. Above her head, the image of a colossal spear formed, driving upwards with all the momentum of a blue volcanic eruption. The spear manifestation smashed into the howling beast head, impaling it straight through. The spear rose past it and smashed headlong into the dome over the area.

And the dome fucking *cracked*.

Thankfully it didn't break and release the attack into the audience, but the head exploded into a massive conflagration of bloody flame and blue and red lightning. The two casters clutched their heads and fell to their knees, and Falken's eyes snapped open, his spear snaking out as his form blurred. He smashed into the monster Wren was fighting and sent it hurtling into the wall of the arena. Wren seamlessly turned to attack the one besieging his brother.

Everyone just stared in wonder as the match came to an end within only a few minutes of starting. I'd certainly learned a lot. First that Lament had a lightning ability, second that the blood people had been strong, even without a master candidate. They'd forced Lament to, if not go all out, at least put in effort. Third was that Lament was way more terrifying than I had expected.

I swallowed hard as I turned to look at Callie. "We... should probably train some more."

Chapter Sixteen

AFTER WE WATCHED THE MATCH, we invited Lament's team to the party we'd heard about from Heavensong Tower. We agreed to meet up tomorrow to head over together.

Callie made her wishes for the day and again the next morning, paying me another thirty G-ranked chits and getting another thirty points of Perception, bringing me up to a full E-ranked chit worth of personal funds.

We met up with the Spear Legion around sunset. Since it was a younger generation party, Zeke, Stella, and Melinda stayed home. It was just me, Callie, Benny, Celine, Jessie, Abel, Mel, and Lament's cohort. The party was apparently formal dress, so I got another use out of that suit from the Gala.

We all drove to the address on the card together, and by the time we got there it was dark.

"I'm starving," I announced as we headed into the nondescript building. "You guys think they'll have any decent food?" The surrounding area was eerie. We'd come to a back street where the lights were dim and there weren't many people. I'd have thought it was a trap except I could see a few other formally dressed people our age filtering into the building, so I guessed the people here just prized secrecy.

Callie chuckled. "Probably. Formal parties usually have decent stuff. Canapes and the like. I hope they have crab puffs. The gala didn't and I really love those. They were basically the only good part of some the parties I went to as a kid."

Benny rolled his eyes, faux muttering to Celine. "These two, I swear. We're lucky Nightstrike is so obsessed with loot or I'd worry they would eat us out of house and home." When he caught us looking, he stuck out his tongue at us, and I flipped him off.

Deliberately raising my voice, I stage whispered to Callie, "Did you know that when Clockwork was a kid, he used to have a phobia? Specifically, he used to be terrified of owls."

"They're creepy!" he rebutted with fervor. "What kind of animal can turn its neck all the way around? You're the weird one for not being bothered. They swoop up mice and small mammals and shit out whole skeletons. It's horrifying. They're like living nightmares."

I cracked up at his defensiveness, but we didn't keep sniping. The bouncers at the door were well hidden, but when we got close enough, they resolved from the shadows to block our way. Probably some kind of Stealth Skill.

"Invitations?" the one on the left said blandly. I fished out the card and handed it to him. He inspected it and then gave it back with a nod, ushering us in.

The inside of the building was much more lavish than the plain exterior suggested. It was probably a hotel based on the decor, and a fairly upscale one, but most likely catering to more... discreet clientele. It made sense some of the shadier forces wouldn't want to stay in a noticeable spot.

"Well," said Jessie as she took it all in, "this is much less dramatic than the last party, but I feel more comfortable here, I think."

"I get what you mean," I said contemplatively. "It's stuffier but less otherworldly. The lack of crazy illusions helps, but the lack of E-rankers also makes it feel less restrictive. We're among peers so I don't feel so stiff."

"I'm happy to hear it," an amused voice interjected. I jumped slightly and we all spun to see Alec. He looked just as harmless and pleasant as before, with a bland smile in place as he virtually appeared out of nowhere. What a creepy guy. "I'm glad to see you could make it." He smiled at Lament and co. "And you brought friends—the Spear Legion if I'm not mistaken. I heard about your showing in the second round, very impressive. Please, make yourselves at home, mingle and get something to eat. I'll be around if you need me."

I expected him to stick to us and be a pain in the ass, but he just waved and melted into the crowd heading into a large ballroom. Not everyone was in the ballroom, though—there were sporadic groups in the halls, people who felt more comfortable talking then dancing or shuffling around the edges of the more formal setting.

Surprisingly, we ran into some old friends. Megan, Riley, Sydney, and their fourth team member, Sam, had noticed us walking around and come over to greet us. Megan, being the more gregarious, was the one to flag us down. "Hey guys. Good to see you. You got invited to this too, huh? That Heavensong Tower sure has some pull to gather this many guests across so many arenas."

I hadn't considered that actually, but she was right. "I wonder how they booked this place. It doesn't seem like its existence would be common knowledge. Interesting group of people. Anyway, what's their purpose for all this do you think? Like sure, getting information on other teams and making connections, but there were parties already happening where they could do that. Why throw their own?"

Callie shrugged. "If I had to guess, these are all the teams they consider a threat. Speaking of which." She turned to Megan and Sydney. "Congrats on passing your second round you two. Kind of wish we'd seen your fight, but maybe next time. Who did you end up against?"

Megan grimaced. "Treepoem Grove. I don't want to talk about it. Suffice to say they were annoying to beat. Riley did most of the heavy lifting on this one, though we should be playing a bigger role as we move on. Heard from Sloane you all took on Divine Stainless Temple and even beat a Master Candidate. Damn impressive."

Another voice cut in. "Divine Stainless Temple?" We turned to see a few teenagers around our own age in incredibly upscale looking clothes. The one at the front, a girl with short black hair and a bright smile, held out a hand as we noticed her. "Oh, sorry to interrupt. I'm Laura, from the Solemn Vow Guild. If you guys just took on Divine Stainless Temple then you must be the team from the Starchaser Pavilion."

Callie took her hand, looking slightly uncertain. With our Master Candidate going against another, it made sense they would have heard of us, but the timing on that introduction had been a little too coincidental. Like they'd been waiting for us. I hadn't heard of her organization, but Callie either had or was pretending to make them feel better. She took Laura's hand with a smile of realization. "Oh, Solemn Vow. I've heard of you all."

Laura looked pleased. "I'm glad, because we're going to be facing each other sooner rather than later. I have it on good authority that you're going to be our next opponents. I couldn't believe my luck when I heard you mention Divine Stainless Temple."

I couldn't believe her luck either. Literally. I didn't believe for a second that her "bumping into us" was a coincidence. Callie didn't tense externally, but I felt a burst of suspicion over the bond. "Well isn't that funny. I guess we're in luck too, getting to meet our future opponents so early. We couldn't even find out who our fight would be against yet, and we checked."

Abel had come up basically empty handed looking around. He'd been given a date and time but not told the enemy. Presumably they were waiting until the last minute because so many teams had been so prepared last round. Which gave rise to the obvious question—how had these people known who they were fighting when no one else did?

Laura just smiled disarmingly. "Ah, well you know, we've always been good at making friends. We'd love to be friends with you all too. You seem like impressive people. It can be so uncomfortable navigating situations like this. Don't want there to be any hard feelings between the teams after the matches. I feel like if we form a good rapport now, even if you were to end up losing, we could still be friendly. We could even try to cheer you up. I'm always generous with my friends."

That... was an attempt to get us to throw the match. I wasn't the most politically savvy person around, but even I had enough sense to see that they wanted us to fold. Callie's demeanor cooled, her smile becoming forced. I personally didn't begrudge them the attempt, but it seemed like the unfairness of trying to bribe us had upset my girlfriend. Not that I thought we should take the deal, but you don't know if you don't ask.

"That's kind of you," Callie said frigidly, "but I think we have our hands full at the moment. We already have quite a few friends. Maybe we can make some time to get to know you after the tournament. Don't worry about hard feelings on our end though—we don't plan to lose, so it shouldn't be an issue."

Laura seemed more amused than offended, putting both hands up in surrender. "No problem, just something to think about. I know that you probably have high hopes for this tournament, but I wouldn't count your chickens before they hatch. Certain parties have a vested interest in making sure the proceedings happen in a specific way. Teams like you and I are just boats on the current. Best to know when to dock and get off the water."

Her words sounded threatening, but her tone was almost... apologetic. Like we weren't the only ones in a bind here. Someone was pushing certain teams to give up in order to get their personal picks through the rounds. My immediate thought was that it was the Cult, but not everything could be because of them, right? Then again, Pietro's presence showed they weren't even trying to be subtle about their involvement in the tournament, so maybe it was them.

With a cheerful nod, Laura turned and strolled away, her lackeys going with her. I turned to Callie. "What the hell was that?" I was sure she'd caught more about what had just happened than I had.

I felt a tug as she resonated her Stealth Skill to prevent anyone from hearing us. "That," she said grimly, "was a complication. Solemn Vow is a Guild, which is a type of organization most common in the Empire. With Pietro showing up, it means that at least two factions have teams in the tournament. How they managed to get them entered I have no clue, but it seems like the factions involved are starting to apply pressure."

"Wouldn't that be against the rules?" I knew they were open about interference in the WCP, but the Unity usually put on a more upright face.

She just shrugged. "Maybe. They tried to bribe us first—the threat was potentially just a warning. It's possible it wasn't even coming from them. They might have been trying to clue us in to the Cult's policy of doing the same. This System borders Cult territory, so there's no way they don't have other teams in the lineup. The Empire probably does too. We need to talk to Zeke and my uncle. This just got a lot more complicated."

I knew getting Impact in advance was huge, but this tournament was attracting more attention than I'd expected for something so low stakes. I could see how Natalie had been drawn here. In fact—"Let me get in touch with my cousin. I haven't talked to her since things started, and I think we're due for a sit down."

I wanted to know what the fuck was going on. Because I was pretty sure this was more dangerous than I'd been told.

Chapter Seventeen

WE DIDN'T STAY TOO long at the party. We chatted up a few random people and made some connections, but we were both still worried about what we'd learned. Benny and Jessie had fun, and Abel and Mel gathered a decent amount of attention just by being themselves. Still, the whole night was mostly a blur to me.

I texted Natalie about a meeting after the party, but I was more concerned about Callie. Through our whole relationship and even before, she seemed so... unflappable. She was right there with me ready to jump into danger, and I was right there with her. But finding out that the Empire and the Cult might both be involved had scared her. I could feel it through the bond, the creeping taint of fear.

She was quiet the rest of the night, and finally when we got home she broke. "I think we should quit the tournament."

I'd been expecting a talk about her worries, some kind of request for us to be careful, but to actually quit... I just stared at her uncomprehendingly. "Cal, I know this is getting a little dicey, but we always knew things would get dangerous. We still have Zeke watching our backs—"

She cut me off. "Until we break through. Then E-rankers are fair game to come after us, and we'll be helpless." We were in her room, and she stood up and started to pace. "The Cult stuff isn't your fault, Shane. I get that. I'd never blame you for your parents' baggage, and I'm here for it all. Just like you're here for mine. But the Empire... We're fucking G-rankers, Shane. We aren't supposed to be messing with things like this."

Her voice was high and panicked and my stomach clenched as I felt her fear. I stood up and stopped her, putting my hands on her shoulders. "Whoa. Hey, calm down. We can talk this over. If you really think it's best to quit, I'm down. You're the boss, and more than that, we're partners. But this is a chance we might never get again, and it can help us move forward in our goals. Are you really willing to just bow out?"

"What goals?" she shouted, throwing her hands up. "Why are you even doing this, Shane? Any of this? Is it just for the fun? For the adventure? I want to surpass my dad, Jessie wants to bring back her brother, and Benny is looking after you, even if he'd never admit it. Why do you even want to be the Wishmaster?" She was shaking, her eyes burning as she stared at me. "Is this just a game? Is that it? It has to be more than that."

"How long have you been worried about this?" I asked her quietly. She flushed and looked away, and I groaned. "Damn it Callie, what did I say about trying to be perfect? If you wanted to know what's going on in my head why not just ask?"

Not that I knew really. Was this just a game? Was I doing this purely for the adventure? I wasn't sure honestly, but I'd have thought about it if she asked. I wouldn't have brushed her off. How long had she been worrying herself sick over this?

She looked away. "You're always there for me. Helping when I need it. It didn't feel right questioning you like that, implying you didn't care. But with the Empire... it's getting out of hand." She paused for a moment. "Shane... I won't say we need to drop out, if you can tell me why you're really doing this."

The first answer I came up with (doing what I wanted and having fun) sounded stupid, silly, and immature. But thinking about it, that wasn't right anyway. If it had just been that I'd have been fine dropping out. But I wanted to keep going. I wanted to win. Wanted to go to the Moonsong Glade and continue to grow, not because it would be fun, or exciting, but because...

"It's what I want." I said with certainty. She looked at me, confused. "Moving here. My dad wanted that. Becoming a Candidate, my dad wanted that. Maybe. I think. The point is, all my choices up to now *haven't* been. It's my 'destiny' or my 'bloodline' or whatever the fuck. The Cult hates me because of my mom, the WCP supports me because of my dad. But they're not here. It's just me. It's my choice. I want to get stronger. I want to do it my way. Because I want to and for no other reason. Because it's my life."

I ran my hands over my face. "But it's your lives, too. All of yours," I said quietly. "I won't push this if you think it's getting too dangerous. We can still grow and get stronger without winning. I have a contract with Natalie, but it's for an alliance, not a commitment to do all of the tournament." I'd pushed Callie to make decisions more geared to her own interests. I'd be a massive hypocrite if I ignored her request to pull back for our own safety.

Callie didn't say anything for a minute. She just stared at me, then blew out a breath. "I can't exactly fault you for wanting to be your own person. Not given my own motivations. How long have you felt like this? Why didn't *you* tell *me?*"

I shrugged. "I'm not introspective. I didn't really realize it until it came time to quit. But this is important to me." I looked her in the eye. "It's just not as important to me as you. This is your call. That's not fair in some ways, but I can't be objective here."

"No," she said firmly. "You have a reason for wanting to go ahead. It might not be one most people would get, but I do. We continue." She held up a finger. "But. If the Empire or the Cult start putting overt pressure on us directly, we bail. I'm willing to see this through as long as we aren't getting in the way of their plans too much. I'm not sure how willing they are to interfere in things under the noses of the other forces. Having the WCP and the Unity around might be enough to keep them in check, but if it's not—"

I grinned at her, wrapping my arms around her and kissing her soundly. "Of course. If things get to that point we're out. We can talk to Natalie too. She might have some kind of insurance set up to keep them off her back. She knew about this way before I did and I suspect she has a better handle on the situation." Natalie wasn't any more in touch with the family than I was as far as I knew, but she was older and had been doing this longer. She most likely had way more connections than I did, and I doubted she'd have jumped into the middle of a fight between factions if she knew it would kill her.

I stepped away from Callie, happy to see she seemed to be more relaxed after I mentioned Natalie. She had a point though. When it was just the Cult, we were dealing with a specific force with reason to harm me, but we had countermeasures for that and other options to pressure them. If there were multiple factions fighting over the winner of this tournament, we had to be careful or we'd get crushed by accident without even knowing how we died.

It meant a lot to me that she was willing to take the risk now that she knew what it meant to me, and I swore to myself that if it looked like things were getting out of hand, we would take a step back. My team's lives were most important.

"We should tell the others," I said after we both sat down. "I'm glad you have my back here, but it doesn't seem right to go into this kind of danger without letting them know. When we were just in the tournament, they weren't really involved, but if we piss off a faction and they come after us, they'll target Benny and Jessie too." I paused. "Well, and maybe Abel and Mel, but those two can take care of themselves. We'll tell them too of course, but I doubt they'll care. Abel will probably think it's cool."

Callie chuckled at that. "You aren't wrong. But yeah, I think telling them is the right choice. Knowing the two of them I doubt it'll change much. Jessie needs your help to have any real shot at bringing back her brother, and Benny won't let you go into something like this alone." She held up a hand to forestall my comment. "Yes, I know you have me, but you know what I mean. He's got your back."

He did. Always had really. As for Jessie... I felt bad that she might get sucked into this out of some kind of obligation. Callie was right though. Most people in the System would probably never make it past E-rank. The further out from the larger factions you went the harder it was to rank up. Jessie had an amazing power, but that wouldn't be enough to get as high as she needed.

I would do everything I could to help her, even if she decided to back out, but she was also fiercely loyal. She wouldn't take my help and abandon me. I was just glad she had Randall to watch her back. Her combat capabilities weren't nearly as impressive as Benny's, despite all her power. Having the big bear as backup made her much safer, especially if he kept growing and reached E-rank.

Despite everything though, I felt... different. Knowing more about my reasons for doing this was cathartic. It sounded stupid for someone to do something without knowing why, but people lied to themselves all the time. I guess it took real pressure for me to finally understand what was making me tick. Granted, I wasn't sure going on a universe spanning adventure because I wanted to make my own decisions was exactly reasonable, but it was probably better than aimless drifting.

As for what I wanted to do in the long-term with that freedom... who knew? I didn't have a plan for now, but being able to not have one was a luxury on its own. I'd help my friends as best I could.

I did have a few goals in mind, though. I wanted to find my mom once we left the planet. I'd never met her, and I'd really like to see what she was like. Finding my dad at some point would be nice, though whether it was to give him a hug or punch him in the throat I couldn't say. Maybe both.

There was a buzz on my finger and I confirmed that Natalie had gotten my message and was responding to me. She couldn't meet up tonight, and tomorrow was the next round of matches, but we made plans to meet after our fights to talk over our next moves.

In the meantime, I didn't have much time to think things over. We were busy figuring out countermeasures to the Solemn Vow Guild. After all, tomorrow was the next fight, and this whole thing was kind of moot if we lost.

Chapter Eighteen

CALLIE DIDN'T USE her wishes the next morning. We decided to hold them in reserve. Not that we could use them during the tournament with everyone watching, but better to have them and not need them than need them and not have them.

We got to the arena early so we could prepare and ask around for more details on the Solemn Vow Guild, because what we had on them so far wasn't much. As far as we could tell Laura was the captain—no surprise since she'd done most of the talking. As for abilities... nothing. One of them had some kind of transportation ability, but apparently the visual aspects of the power were so confusing that no one in the audience had any clue what was actually happening. Something about broken glass and teleportation. The others hadn't used any obvious powers. There had just been a lot of movement and blood and then their fights had been over.

Whatever they could do, they didn't fuck around.

We'd come in early to try to get some more leads, but their first two opponents had been so thoroughly outmatched they hadn't needed to show anything. So as we stepped out onto the sand, we were all grim-faced at the battle ahead. Well... Callie and I were. Mel was wearing a full-face mask and Abel mostly just looked intrigued.

Laura greeted us with a friendly smile when we stepped out, her teammates all lined up behind her in single file: A short dark-skinned girl with green eyes and a stoic expression, a tall, pale redheaded guy with freckles and a bushy beard, and an olive skinned guy with a bright smile and wavy dark hair. "Hey there," the team leader said warmly. "Good to see you again. I take it you decided to stick with your original plan? I respect the guts honestly. We aren't going to hold back on you though, I hope you know that?"

Callie seemed relieved by that. We'd expected Laura to be condescending or rude about us deciding to fight. Not that we cared, but her not being too pushy meant at this point in the tournament things hadn't gotten too serious. That, or they were super cocky and thought we would definitely lose. Either way we'd take it.

Before she could respond, Abel apparently got bored of the banter and threw a punch at the enemy team.

The fist was the size of a bus, but to my shock, it didn't land. Not because they dodged or anything, but because as it hit the air in front of them, the space *shattered*, exploding outward in a cascade of silvery shards.

Mel and Abel both dodged as I grabbed Callie, Leaf on the Wind and Cloud Step getting us clear of the shards as they tore the air apart. They eventually stopped, floating in a giant web of fragments that looked like nothing so much as a suspended explosion that had stopped mid blast— except without the blast force and with mirror shards instead of shrapnel.

"Huh," Abel said. "That's... new." Even he sounded impressed.

Laura, whose eyes were now reflective silver all the way through the sclera, grinned at us. "You haven't seen anything yet. Charlie, Olivia?" The green-eyed girl and the guy with wavy hair each reached out to touch a shard. The ones in the air flashed twice before Laura said, "Blaine." Her tone sounded like a judge declaring the final verdict of a death row inmate.

Blaine, the red-haired guy, spun on a heel and threw a punch containing a mass of condensed black energy at the closest shard. The thing flashed, as did the rest of them, and then a fucking torrent of black energy blasts exploded from every one of the shards.

I cursed and Callie and I danced back, using our synergy and my Cloud Steps to dodge most of the blasts as I activated the overlay for both of us. I still took one in the shoulder and one in the thigh, while she got hit in the ribs, but despite feeling like we'd been shot we pressed on and dodged the rest.

The actual energy broke on our armor, thankfully. Based on what it was doing to the sand, I didn't think I'd have enjoyed taking a blast like that to unprotected flesh. One of these matches we would meet someone like me with armor piercing powers and I wasn't looking forward to it.

For the moment we dashed behind Abel, who had been using spatial lubrication to divert the attacks and protect himself and Mel.

Laura clicked her tongue. "I wasn't sure from the reports on the last match, but that confirms it. Spatial manipulation *and* a Master Candidate? Nasty combo." She nodded at Callie and I genially. "Impressive moves by the way—him I expected to get away, but the two of you managing is a surprise. You should be proud to avoid our invocation. Few teams have the coordination we do."

Callie grunted. "Thanks so much, that means a lot to my cracked ribs." I frowned and put a hand on her lower back subtly, triggering a heal burst for each of us. My thigh and shoulder, which had been killing me, felt much better. She gestured at the shards. "Invocation huh? I'm guessing the spatial breakage is your ability, then probably some kind of teleportation layered with a bilocation ability, so every attack comes out of all shards at once?"

Laura clapped slowly, an impressed look on her face. "*Very* nice. Yeah, pretty much. You're in the ballpark at least. It's stupid to confirm or deny the exact mechanics, but knowing the basics of how it works won't make dodging any easier." She shot Abel a pitying look. "Pretty sure you won't be able to throw punches when you're on the defensive. Looks like this isn't going so well for you."

She didn't sound mocking, just matter of fact, which actually made it feel *more* like she was mocking us. I considered how I could take her out and break the effect, but my only real shot at that would be to use Double Trouble to get behind her, and then I'd be standing right in front of all her friends. That would just be asking to get crushed.

I triggered one of my Stealth charges, covering up my voice as I addressed Abel. "This seems like a space thing—any chance you know how to stop it?"

He shook his head as he watched them carefully. "No—it's a mishmash of abilities. I could probably move the shards, but I'd have to basically do it one at a time, and there's no way they'd give me breathing room for that.

The whole superposition thing is probably a two-way street though. Since anything that happens to one of them happens to all of them, if we can damage one it should break them all."

Which meant our best bet here was probably Mel. I turned to our red masked teammate. "With Abel out of commission on defense, do you think if I juice up your orb with a few stacks of powerups you could smash one of those shards?" I was already going over which abilities would give her the best edge.

She nodded. "Sure, single target attack drills are part of my training. Flexibility is key, but being able to condense all my flames into the smallest area and land a single blow is an important part of controlling my powers. It'll likely backlash through the shards though." She glanced at Abel. "I'm sure they have defensive measures for that kind of thing, but can you stop the resulting explosion from seriously injuring us?"

He waved her off with a snort. Question answered, I reached out to put my hand on the focus crystal we'd gotten her. Touch of Tears, Mercy Kill, one of Cark's flame attacks, Consecration of Flames. I stopped there because I was pretty sure using Afterburner or some of my other abilities would be overkill. Even so, imbuing that kind of power into the orb was easier than imbuing it into a person since my ability recognized objects. It didn't take much soul strength.

Mel raised her orb-wielding hand toward the nearest shard and growled with effort. I could practically see the space around the orb warp for a second, and then a pinprick of light, like a firefly, lit the air. The light got brighter, and brighter, growing slightly but maintaining its basic size. It was green, and so bright it hurt to look at. Mel groaned from the strain. "Could use a highway."

Abel flicked a finger casually, and a massive manifestation of the digit appeared in the air, swiping the space between Mel's condensed star of fire and the nearest shard. She pushed it forward with a snarl of effort into the lubricated space. It flashed across the space almost too fast to see.

The whole combination had taken us a split second to pull off, and with Mel being behind Abel, the star hadn't been visible from a distance until it was too late.

Laura's eyes widened in horror and she punched out with her own fist, shattering more space and whirling her hands to bring the shards together into a mosaic dome of warped reality. The others reacted pretty quickly, I'd give them that. When their boss started moving they all dived under the defensive barrier. Just as they covered up, the star hit one of the shards.

I saw a blaze of energy in every single one of them, like a supernova being unleashed in a thousand mirrors, and they all blew apart at the same time. Green flame ripped the intervening space inside the field apart as Abel cursed, folding his hands over us and interlacing his fingers to create a defensive manifestation. We'd massively underestimated the amount of generated force.

Callie raised a barrier inside the construct and pulled on the bond, using Stone Limb on the small dome where it came in contact with the sand. Abel snarled in pain and I saw his hands actually catch fire, which I didn't know could happen, and I put a hand on his shoulder, triggering a heal burst.

We dropped the defenses, looking around at the devastation in the arena. Solemn Vow were all alive, thankfully. With the force I'd been worried, but the blast had torn apart their shield and seriously messed them up. They were burned and battered from the backlash, as well as poisoned. I was just glad that hadn't killed them by accident.

"Wow," I said, looking around at all the melted sand. "That was... flashy. Note to self—maybe avoid mixing random power interactions outside of controlled circumstances." Mel had predicted backlash but that had been... impressive.

We walked over to Solemn Vow carefully, taking our time to crunch across the sand, making sure not to get sucker punched or anything. They didn't bother. They were all heavily poisoned, the toxic fire having seeped into their bodies at multiple points.

We turned to the crowd and Callie raised a fist, and the announcer called it once they didn't move for a bit. Luckily we could still hear that even through the isolation. Once they called our victory, I reached out and switched off my Skill, eliminating the poison.

Laura's team slumped onto the sand from where they'd been writhing in pain, Vitality already getting to work on the damage. Laura grinned up at us. "Ok. Ow. Good fight."

Callie laughed and offered her a hand to help her up.

Chapter Nineteen

OUR MEETING with Natalie was later that night, after their own match, so we said our goodbyes to Laura and her team. She seemed to be excited to find a powerful opponent (or potential ally) and insisted on getting Callie's scan ring number. Despite the rough first meeting, she was so enthusiastic about it that Callie couldn't bring herself to turn down the contact details. She also invited us to another party tonight, but we took a pass given the meeting and all the parties we'd been to lately.

After she got Callie's details, her smile slipped a bit. "You should be careful. We aren't the only group hoping to guide how the tournament progresses. If you run into some of the others next round… Let's just say they won't be as personable as us. We got our fighting assignment early through back channels, and we aren't the only ones. There are people inside the Unity who are less concerned with victory than a payday."

That was unsettling, but not unexpected. We hadn't known for sure where they got their information, but a traitor had been one of the more likely options. Unfortunately our ability to address that was limited, given who was in charge over there. I doubted Midknight would listen to us even if he cared, which was pretty up in the air.

We thanked the others and left. I triggered Stealth so I could ask Callie a question. "What are the chances you could get us a meeting with someone high up in the Unity who isn't friendly with your dad? You said he's always fighting with some of the other E-rankers to maintain control right? Could we get in touch with one of those?"

Midknight was a dick, and if he had it out for us there was no rule saying we couldn't back his enemies. I had a contract with Melinda and the Beast Lord Garden, but they didn't use all my wishes or anything. I'd have to recheck the terms but I was pretty sure the exclusivity clause in there was specific to the WCP.

Callie looked contemplative. "That… might work. It depends on what we offer them and how much they dislike Midknight. I never really checked into his enemies—that would have meant getting involved in all his political nonsense and I was outspoken about wanting no part of his life. Still, I bet Uncle Alex would know."

I nodded. At least we had a secondary plan at the moment.

We headed home right away to get ready for our meeting with Natalie, with Callie planning to do some research before we left. She did get a chance to make her last day's wishes, finally bringing herself to the cap at three hundred thirty-five perception and me to a hundred fifteen G-ranked chits. It also marked a breakthrough for my own Wish granting as I was finally able to give four points on her final wish.

That meant I probably could have done it earlier, but hey, live and learn.

With two three-point wishes and one four-point wish, that left two more for the day, which I used on Benny, topping up two of my triple-strength density-shifted attacks. He put those eight points in Focus, which balanced it with Might. Benny had decided to do a combination of Focus for Inventing and Might for usage as his model for stat distribution. It might not be as over the top as Jessie's full Vitality allotment, but splitting most of his points between the two should still open up interesting possibilities.

Callie, in the meantime, planned to start Skill training hard, making sure her Shadow Manipulation broke through to Intermediate before she ranked up and had to synergize it. She was at the upper edge of Beginner, but the jump to Intermediate wasn't so easy to manage, so she had quite a bit of work to do. Given our plans for the night, she'd elected to wait until the next day to begin since we had a few days before our next match.

After a few hours we finally headed out to the meeting, with Natalie insisting we meet in G-district at the Pavilion. Our ability to move undetected was much greater in the WCP, especially in lower-end districts where we were less likely to run into over-the-top abilities or people with absurd Perception. When we arrived, my cousin was sitting in Mel's office, feet up on the desk as her two henchpeople loomed on either side of the door. I'd never heard either of them speak, they just kind of... imposed. But they were pretty decent at being imposing.

Natalie was looking extra relaxed, sipping from a tall, thin glass with a wild looking straw and an umbrella. We didn't have those here, so I wasn't sure where she'd gotten it. Her eyes lit up when she saw me, and she took an extra large slurp before putting it down on the desk. "Baby cousin!" She said with a beaming grin. "Look at you. Fourth round already. I'm so proud. I knew teaming up with you was a good idea. Congrats on the victory against the Empire's B-team. Even that much is impressive."

My stomach sank as she said that. Solemn Vow had been strong. If they were the B-team... Well, it explained why the Empire hadn't tried to put the squeeze on us harder. Speaking of. "So you knew the Empire was involved? Because we didn't. That would have been good information to have."

She shrugged. "Not really our business. Faction bullshit is for the big dogs. They can't pressure us with anyone too strong so we might as well not worry about it. Besides, the Empire won't go overboard. You have more to worry about from the Cult. Heard you whacked one of their little dictators. Good on you by the way. No one really likes them. They aren't unique to the Cult of course, but their structure makes useless arrogant fops more likely to spring up."

"Not the Empire?" I'd have figured nobility would be a sure way to make sure nepotism ran rampant. Granted, I wasn't in a position to throw stones, but still, it was a surprise.

She snorted out a laugh. "Gods no. Nobility is rank based. That's their whole cultivation system. Not that there aren't absolute bastards there, it comes with the territory, but useless up-and-coming nobles get killed off for resources long before they can become strong enough to be a problem. I won't go into details—it involves the way the Empire farms renown—but suffice to say people are very motivated over there."

"Fine," I said, waving that off for another time. "But what about their F-rankers? They can send them after us and our guardians can't do anything about it. Isn't that a huge loophole?" I'd been wondering why they did the two-rank buffer up to this point, but I couldn't exactly ask Zeke. Natalie might have some workaround though.

To my surprise she laughed again. "It isn't a loophole. They leave us vulnerable to people one rank higher because it tests our resourcefulness. Guardians are WCP resources to keep us from getting swatted like flies by high rankers, but they don't want us to get complacent. While WCP resources we don't pay for can't be used to protect us from F-rankers, our personal forces *can*. Allies too."

Callie made a sound of understanding. "That makes sense. It's all part of the test. With the wish ability, being able to recruit F-rankers and even E-rankers should be a snap. That's why the guardian's duties end at D-rank right? Because by that point the Candidate should be established enough to protect themselves."

"I like this one," Natalie said approvingly. "She's much smarter than you— hold onto her." I flipped her off and she just cackled at me before responding to Callie. "Pretty much. It can be hard to build up momentum at the lower ranks since newbies have no rep. From what I could find, there was a big problem with Candidates getting murdered early into the process to prevent more Wishmasters from being added to the WCP. The guardian system was an answer to that."

"Where's yours by the way?" I'd never met Natalie's guardian and I was a bit curious.

She shrugged. "Who knows. She's a C-ranker so she has enough Perception to listen into anything that happens on this planet. Not like she needs to babysit me directly. I'm sure your own guardian is entertaining himself too. Probably has a few contingencies to keep you from getting randomly butchered though."

I shuddered at the thought of my mask eating that guy. She had no idea. "Should we be making contacts with some of the stronger locals in case we need them to deal with faction pressure?" That was pretty much what we'd been looking at doing anyway. We already had three E-rankers on our side who could step in if any F-rank pressure came our way. I hadn't really considered what a deterrent that was, but it would be hugely useful to us since Zeke could handle the E-ranked threats.

In my head I'd made the mistake of matching E-rankers against E-rankers, falling into the same trap most of the people on Callus did by noticing how much more powerful higher ranked and more centralized warriors would be. But even the faction geniuses who could fight up a rank would be mostly able to contend with very early E-rankers, and all of our allies were in the late E-rank coming up on D.

But the WCP wouldn't be enough. I looked at Callie and found her looking back at me. She nodded, and I could feel through the bond that she agreed with me—we needed more than ever to make sure that we got one of the higher-ranking Unity members on our side. With the WCP being an outside faction, involving them would give Midknight a chance to move against us. While our E-rankers could handle themselves against our enemies, if the Unity E-rankers ganged up on our people, Zeke wouldn't be free to intervene when we weren't in direct danger.

Natalie seemed to sense the tension and gave me a reassuring smile. "Hey, chill. It's not a big deal yet. We're early enough out that no one is going to be exerting their full pressure. Just watch out for potential assassins and you should be good. The Cult is vindictive and not to be screwed with. Especially if you get matched with one of their teams. An Impact advantage is priceless at lower levels. It makes people your own rank substantially less dangerous to you, and that advantage sticks around for the rest of your life."

It would definitely do a lot to alleviate the danger of the early phases of a rank, where your stats couldn't keep up with all the more powerful Ascendants who had been there for a while.

This had been more reassuring than I'd expected, and I was able to put some longstanding fears to rest. My biggest need here was to do what I had been doing from the start. Making alliances and using my ability to gain favors. I was still pretty annoyed to be stuck at G-rank for the next few weeks, since I'd be losing lots of potential points, but I'd make do. It would be tight getting my friends to F-rank in time for the Moonsong Glade, though on the upside they would be able to rank up as soon as they hit the cap because they weren't in the tournament themselves.

We thanked Natalie and headed home, already making plans for where to go from here. I was worried about those assassins, and I wanted to make sure we were prepared.

We decided to try to get a meeting with one of the Unity higher ups tomorrow. Now we just had to pick who we would approach.

Chapter Twenty

GETTING a meeting with an E-ranked member of the Unity was surprisingly easy. I'd expected to have to go through channels and maybe bribe some people, but we managed to get something on the books without any trouble once they realized who Callie was. Apparently her well-known hatred for her dad as well as the whole scene at the opening ceremony was more than enough to get us in the door.

We still had to work around their schedules, so we had a few hours to kill. We decided to get Benny's wishes in. We had to space them out because of how much they took out of him, but we got them all done. One triple-strength tranq blow, two triple-strength density-shifted blows, and two spider leg attacks, bringing me to a flat ten in each, for twenty points (my new daily max). He had all the points added to Focus, bringing him up to a hundred thirty-three points in that stat, his highest until he evened up Might.

"I still think I should go with you," my friend said belligerently. "I've been getting left out of everything lately, it's total bullshit. Jessie and I can still be useful, even if we aren't in the tournament."

I sighed. "Yeah, I know man. But this isn't tournament business really. I mean, it kind of is, but it's mostly Callie's family stuff. I'm only going for moral support and because my ability might be an asset we can leverage. Nobody is downplaying what you and Jessie can do—hell without you I'm

103

pretty sure Mordaunt's attendant would have killed me—but this isn't a place you can help. I know it sucks, but that's what all the stat gains are for right? Just work on your soul strength. Now that we actually know what the hell we're aiming for with that, it'll be much easier to keep track of."

He grimaced. "Don't remind me. Eight percent into red after all the training I've done. Honestly it's soul crushing. I thought I'd already overtaken you. Not to mention neither of us is even close to breaking orange like Abel has. Is Zeke sure about those measurements?"

"Not really." I said with a shrug. "He was ballparking it. Not like he has a skill for soul reading; he says he can just kind of tell from experience. There's a special piece of gear you can get that measures the soul, but they're expensive and hard to get. For the moment we just have to deal with the estimates. As for catching up…" I shrugged. "I've been training hard for months on this, it's obvious that you would be a bit behind. Coming that close to catching up after just a week or two shows how much of a bullshit advantage you have with that belt."

That at least got a smirk. Before he could say something annoying though, Callie's voice cut through the house. "Shane! What's the hold up? We've got to go. We have a meeting with Frostbite. She was more than willing to talk once I got ahold of her and she found out who I was, but I still had to actually reach her. I got in touch with Cold Snap and he agreed to put us through… for a fee. So we can't miss the appointment—we might not be able to get another one."

That didn't shock me. Cold Snap was a mercenary asshole. If he hadn't been, he wouldn't have worked with Aiden in the first place. But since he wasn't the one doing the actual brainwashing, and because we couldn't afford to have two E-rank Unity executives as enemies (not to mention that he actually fought with us against Aiden), we'd mostly let things lie. Given how we met, it was actually surprising he was even willing to go that far.

I sighed and nodded to Benny. "Alright man, looks like we're out. Don't worry too much about all the politics, just focus on your training. I have a feeling we're going to need all the soul strength we can get."

Jessie drove us to the meeting. As we headed there we sat in silence for a while. Eventually Callie shot me a concerned look. "He's worried about you. I mean, we all are, but you two are close right? It must be hard for him to see you in so much danger and not be able to help."

104

"Honestly I'm almost glad for it," I admitted. "Seeing you in so much danger already terrifies me. Having one less person to worry about is kind of a relief." She snickered at that, and I shot her an apologetic smile. "Makes me wanting to do this even stupider doesn't it?"

She just shrugged. "It's fine, I knew you weren't too bright when we got together. At least you're pretty to look at." Jessie, who was pretending not to listen from the front seat, tried unsuccessfully to muffle her giggles at that, but I just rolled my eyes.

"No respect," I grumbled. "But seriously, it just feels different. You've had your whole life to train for this—it's easier to put my faith in your abilities. But Benny... he's Benny. My best friend. It's not that I don't have faith in him, it's just... different."

She smiled at me as she reached out to squeeze my hand. "I get it. You grow up with someone, it's hard not to remember their flaws. Doesn't mean you don't love them, just means you don't have them up on a pedestal. I don't begrudge you some worry, Shane. You don't need to explain yourself to me."

It was hard not to feel guilty anyway, like I should be just as reluctant to let her be part of this. Which made me feel like an asshole for pulling her into it. But that wasn't a productive line of thought so I decided to focus on what would be useful right now.

"So..." I said, changing the subject. "Tell me about Frostbite. I assume you did some research into her. This is going to be your show for the most part."

She smiled fondly at me. "I know it is. And yes, I did plenty of research. There's a lot out there on her. Like I mentioned, Frostbite is famous for being a pretty biased person. She takes care of her own first and everyone else second. In some ways that isn't ideal, but it makes her an excellent person to be in an alliance with. If she decides to take your side, she follows through. Not sure if that's recursion or just her way of maintaining her reputation, but either way it's good for us."

"Assuming we can actually get her to commit to working with us," I pointed out. "No guarantees she'll be willing. She's one of your dad's rivals?"

Callie snorted at that. "There are more than a few of them. But yes, she's definitely up there on the list. His tendency to try to promote his own people to positions of power out of paranoia is inconvenient for someone like her. Part of taking care of her own subordinates is helping them accrue power, and the old man doesn't share well. Add in the fact that she's considered pretty powerful among the top brass, and she's too much of a threat for him to ignore."

"How does that even work in the Unity?" I asked. "In the WCP people like that try to undermine and kill each other by proxy, but the Unity has an image to maintain. How do they act against each other?"

"Politics," she said tiredly. "There are a lot of ways to compromise someone's power base. I won't get into it now—we don't have the time. But she'll still step in personally if needed, which is what we're looking for. We need insurance against enemy F-rankers without dragging the WCP into a regional war."

I nodded in acknowledgement. I knew that already, but if she needed to talk things out to remain calm I was happy to listen. I could feel her anxiety through the bond—a bit of repetition was the least she deserved.

"So where is this meeting anyway? I forgot to ask." I hadn't really cared to be honest. Callie would have mentioned if we were walking into something dangerous, and I preferred the surprise if I could get it.

"It's called the Crystal Palace," Callie said, her tone shifting to something a bit more excited. "Frostbite built it herself out of specialized ice. Never melts, not too slippery. It's supposed to be absolutely gorgeous. It's a huge tourist attraction. Unlike the WCP, the Unity E-rankers are spread throughout the city, each one with their own territory to manage and control. Keeps them out of each other's hair."

That was probably a better system in some ways, but I could see why the WCP wouldn't use it. Because of the existence of the deeds, no one actually owned territory in the WCP. You could lease it, but in the end the WCP was the true ruler. Without the restrictions placed by the Unity and their own reputations, letting the E-rankers establish their own territory was more likely to cause frequent bloody battles among civilians. While the WCP wouldn't care as much about what people thought about their methods, that would be a waste and prevent the rise of lower rankers.

I knew that renown among Ascendants was more powerful than renown from mortals, so raising plenty of low rankers to feed the machine was important. It was natural for the WCP to make sure they had a place to grow. Hell, that was the whole point of planets like this wasn't it? Lots of mortals to feed the low-rankers, and once you outgrew that you headed up to a higher-ranked spot.

Shaking my head, I tried to focus. I got existential when I was nervous, and I really was nervous about this. Despite this being Callie's meeting to succeed or fail in, I wanted this first one to work out. The longer we waited, the more danger we were in. Not to mention Callie would feel so much better knowing she secured us aid on her own merits. Her having a way to fight back against her dad and the other dangers in our lives would mean a lot to her, I could sense that easily.

As the car finally came to a stop, I checked my mask and hopped out. Turning to Jessie as I did, I said, "We'll be done in probably an hour—you have any places nearby to hang while you wait?"

She waved me off. "There's a plant nursery I wanted to check out about ten minutes from here. I looked it up when Nightstrike gave me the address. Go to your meeting. I trust you guys to do your best for us." As I turned to leave, she spoke up again. "Hey."

I froze, focusing back on her.

"Benny does too. And you should trust him more. None of us are the same people we were when this started. That's kind of the point."

Her voice wasn't reproving or condescending, just matter of fact, but I slumped a bit all the same. "Yeah, you're right. I'll... I'll keep it in mind. See you in a while." I shut the door and the car lifted off the ground, speeding away and leaving us alone in front of the crystal palace.

"Alright," I said nervously, "Let's go meet the ice queen."

Chapter Twenty-One

THE CRYSTAL PALACE WAS... palatial. The whole place looked like a massive crystalline castle. Some of the ice was frosted, and some was clear as glass, and the combination created an effect like windows and walls in what was essentially one big ass piece of carved unmelting ice. It wasn't just ice, either—looking close I could see millions of tiny runes around the edges. This thing was enchanted, and judging by the scale, it must be absurdly high-level material.

"Does she have a stockpile of high-ranked materials or something?" I asked. "Because this is E-ranked ice. You said she created this right? She didn't make *all* of it did she?" I wasn't surprised that she'd made something her own rank, but this place was absolutely massive. Being able to create an ice castle on this scale and then enchant it... Frostbite must have a ludicrously high Creation stat, even for an E-ranker.

Callie just shrugged. "Hard to say. Obviously, 'she built the giant ice castle herself with her bare hands' is a much better story. You have to question everything you hear about Ascendants, especially high rankers. They're masters of media manipulation. Nine out of ten things you hear about them could be bullshit. Of course, that tenth thing is the one that'll kill you if you assume it isn't true, so you can't dismiss anything outright."

I raised an eyebrow at her dryly. "Wow. That's so helpful. Don't believe anything you hear. But don't not believe it either. Because it could be true. Or false. Any other wisdom to drop on me?"

She smiled at me sweetly. "Yeah—don't make fun of your girlfriend if you don't want to sleep on the couch for the next two weeks." She winked to let me know she was teasing and then the smile melted off her face. "But seriously, just... be careful. All the E-rankers we've met have been either allies or constrained by circumstances. Frostbite is too when it comes to dealing with you, but if she decides to take out Midknight's daughter..."

"I'd throw myself in the way and let my mask swallow her whole," I said icily. "Not to mention that small scale faction war or not, Alexander would fucking murder her if she hurt you. Frostbite is an E-ranker at the top of one of the biggest organizations on this planet. I refuse to believe she'd be stupid and reckless enough not to know the consequences of killing either of us. Plus if she was going to off us it would be stupid to invite us here to do it. Make more sense to assassinate us somewhere unrelated to her. Blame it on one of the visiting factions."

Callie's jaw dropped as she looked at me.

I shrugged. "I've been putting lots of thought into possible assassination strategies. I don't want to get backstabbed by some cultist because I wasn't paying attention, and you have too much on your mind for it to be fair to expect you to do it alone. Politics might be beyond me, but figuring out ways someone could kill us I can totally do."

She smiled and stood up on her toes to kiss my mask, then pulled back slightly with a grimace and kissed the side of my jaw.

I snickered at the reaction. "Yeah, I would prefer you avoid kissing the mask too."

Chuckling lightly, Callie looped her arm in mine and we headed to the massive double doors of the palace. She reached up and rapped three times on the opaque ice. The boom that shook the area was much deeper and more resonant than expected, like she'd been knocking on a sheet of metal. After a minute or two the door slid open to reveal a small pale woman with bright blue hair and icy eyes. Her blue lips quirked up in a smile as she saw us.

"Can I help you?" the F-ranker said in a melodic voice. Her frozen blue eyes seemed to crack and shift around the irises, like there was a pair of crashing glaciers being projected through a pair of wheel-shaped viewing screens. She was so pale it literally almost hurt to look at her and it took me a second to notice that her ears (behind which she'd swept her long hair) were pointed like Celine's. Some kind of ice elf maybe?

Callie smiled, holding out a hand. "Yes, I'm Nightstrike; this is Solomon. We're here to see Frostbite. She should be expecting us?"

Her lips curved up in a paradoxically warm smile. "Of course," she said, her voice like the wind through a forest of icicles. "My name is Rime. I'm Frostbite's personal valet." She stepped back, swinging open the door with a gentle tap of her fingers. As she did, we could see that she was much taller than she'd looked before, having been leaning out the door. I'd have put her at six feet, though the silver heels under her shining silver dress might have been throwing me off.

Her blue hair was held back by an icy crown and was lost in a bloom of white fur draped over her shoulders, spilling down her back to very nearly sweep the floor. Some kind of thick pelted animal, and not a small one. She gestured us past her and we both nodded our thanks as we entered.

"This is a lovely building," Callie said politely, clearly not sure what to say to the woman when we'd spent so much time focusing on how to address Frostbite.

"Yes," Rime said happily, "it is."

We... had no response to that, and both decided it might be better to just shut up.

We mounted a set of spiral stairs along the perimeter of the building and began to ascend. The external steps led us along the outside edge of an absolutely massive space inside the castle. Along the edge of the space were balconies that acted as floors, leading out into the external parts of the castle away from the towering hall. Crystalline walkways threaded between the balconies and across the vast open expanse, reminding me of nothing so much as that crystal spider web back in the cave in Doomtown.

The sun reflected through the icy canopy above us was diffuse in most places because of the opaque ice, but there were a few clear spots like skylights that shone beams of startling light down into the atrium, each beam hitting the walkways and scattering into prismatic rainbow cascades that crisscrossed the open space.

"This... is amazing," Callie said breathlessly. "Now I see why they call it the Crystal Palace. You live here? It must be wonderful getting to see this every day."

Rime shrugged. "You get used to it. It's still pretty, but it starts to lose some of its impact after the five thousandth viewing. Though I imagine it loses its appeal much slower than an office building, so I suppose I'm still lucky in that regard."

She stopped talking again, but we weren't in the mood to gape silently now that we had the ball rolling. "Do you know Cold Snap?" I asked politely.

That drew a snort from the F-ranker. "I changed his diapers as a baby, so yes. That explains how you got this meeting. Frostbite isn't usually so accessible to the younger generation." She shot a sideways glance at Callie. "You might have managed it just from the sheer amusement of your little display at the opening ceremonies. Though admittedly it probably wouldn't have been so quick."

So she knew who we were. She could have saved us the intro at the beginning, but then again, I suppose that was just basic politeness.

Finally, after minutes of walking, we approached the top of the massive atrium. As we climbed, the balconies began to take up more of the space as the castle narrowed, the catwalks and rainbow-filled nothingness condensing until finally we stepped off the stairs onto a large floor with only a relatively large hole in the center you could look down from.

Rime led us across the floor, which alternated opaque and crystalline squares in a *deeply* unsettling and yet incredibly majestic way. She stopped before a huge pair of double doors carved from what I was pretty sure was black permafrost.

I looked around. "Is there like... nobody else here? Because this place is a total ghost town from what I've seen. Seems weird to have a castle this big with no people."

The blue haired woman rolled her eyes. "Of course there is. They're in other parts of the palace, on the floors and in their offices. The steps and catwalks are transport—people don't spend time lingering there. The prismatics can be disorienting with long term exposure, even for Ascendants." She raised a hand and rapped three times on the black door. "Wait here until the doors open, then go inside. She'll arrange for someone to pick you up on the way out…" She paused. "Or throw you out the window. Probably not though. She hasn't done that in months."

With that last very unsettling statement, she turned and strolled away, seemingly unbothered by the idea that we might be thrown from the top of a castle… or possibly just fucking with us. I took hold of Callie's hand just in case, readying Leaf on the Wind. Better safe than sorry, I always said.

Callie smiled at me wryly, and I felt through the bond that she was just as sure that had been a joke, and just as disturbed by the possibility that it wasn't. We stood there like that, waiting, for a few minutes, before the doors creaked slowly open, allowing us inside.

We stepped in, and my breath was taken away by the sheer majesty of the room we entered. The scale wasn't as grand as the main hall or its prismatic walkways, but the *detail* of the icy carving here was staggering. It was a large room with a vaulted ceiling, and every single inch of it was absolutely perfectly carved.

The furniture was shaded various colors of blue and purple and black that somehow seemed like a full spectrum with only dark winter hues. A fireplace sat to one side of the room with a crystalline carving of flames so realistic, it looked like they were leaping. As light danced through the facets, it glowed with a rainbow radiance.

In the back, behind a large black desk of shiny ice, sat Frostbite.

With all the grandiose pageantry I'd expected her to be flashy and dramatic, but she just looked… normal. A pretty girl who seemed only a bit older than us with a cornsilk blonde ponytail and bright blue eyes, wearing a T-shirt and jeans. Her one nod to her Ascendant identity was a long snow-white trench coat she wore draped over her shoulders, her arms not even in the sleeves. To cap off the image, as she watched us calmly as she popped a huge pink bubble, slurping the gum back up to continue chewing it.

She looked interested, if not terribly enthused by our presence, and I saw her flip a folder closed on the desk as she stared at us. She seemed to mull over what to say for a minute before she finally opened her mouth. "So," began the E-rank executive of one of the most dominant factions on the entire planet, "you guys want some ice cream or something? It's homemade."

Chapter Twenty-Two

"MAN THAT IS GOOD," Callie said as she practically slurped the spoon clean after finishing her dish of butter pecan. "You weren't kidding about the homemade thing huh? I have to say though, this isn't what I imagined you being like, I figured you'd be more…"

Frostbite grinned. "You thought I'd be a megalomaniacal ice queen who sits up in her tower planning how to screw everyone else over to get the biggest advantage possible?" At Callie's blush, the woman laughed. "Hey, no judgement, if I had a dad like yours I'd have figured the same thing. Honestly, in some ways you aren't off the mark. I'm more than capable of being a bit coldblooded to get my way. I figure I owe you two though, so no harm in being approachable."

That got my attention. "Owe us?" I asked curiously. "How so? I mean, we're here to ask for a favor and…" I looked over to see Callie glaring and cleared my throat. "I'm going to stop talking now."

That had been a fuckup. Callie was supposed to do the talking. I'd gotten wrapped up in her pace and started being casual. I hoped I hadn't given away anything important. Still, it seemed weird to me that she would consider herself owing *us* a favor.

"My son," the blonde woman said with a smile, "is a fucking idiot. He's useless and arrogant and often stupid. He makes bad decisions on impulse and hardly does anything right… and I love him more than anything in this world. You could have killed him for what he pulled. I got it out of him later, and I honestly wouldn't have blamed you. But you didn't and I owe you for that. So yes. I took this meeting and I'm treating you like potential allies because you deserve it. And because watching Midknight try not to lose his damn mind in front of all those people was the highlight of my year."

That got a genuine smile from Callie. "I enjoyed it too. Probably too much. Which is kind of why we're here, we wanted to talk to you about—"

"Protection," said Frostbite matter-of-factly. "Wasn't exactly brain surgery figuring out that much sweetie. Your pals from the WCP are limited in what they can do without potentially kicking off quite a bit of trouble. Your boy toy here is basically bulletproof when it comes to the big wigs, but mid-ranking execs are still a threat based on our observations, and I assume you want some insurance in case those threats apply pressure."

To my surprise, Callie sighed in relief. I guessed that she figured since Frostbite knew why we were here and accepted the meeting anyway she might be amenable to our terms.

Sadly, it wasn't going to be that easy. "My question," the blonde said as she ate a bite of rocky road, "is what's in it for me? I like you kids, but that's personal. This is business. I don't give out alliances for being swell folks. What benefits are you gonna bring me?"

"That's fair," my girlfriend acknowledged. "There are the obvious benefits, of course. Destabilizing my dad's regime for one. You're competitors, and not only would recruiting me to your side make him look weak, it would give you an excuse to rub that weakness in his face and gloat over his help-lessness as you did it."

Frostbite took another bite of ice cream, smirking at Callie as she did. "You know, I knew I was going to like you. That sounds hilarious." Her smile dropped. "But I don't make business decisions based on amusement. Get to the point or get lost. You're becoming less impressive by the second." The tonal shift from warm interest to icy indifference was jarring, to say the least. I could see what she'd meant earlier about being willing to make harsh calls.

Callie wasn't bothered though, her own smile curled up wickedly, and I got the impression through the bond that she'd been waiting for that exact response. "Oh by all means. We're willing to offer similar terms to the ones we set with the Beast Lord Garden. Similar, though not nearly as generous. After all, you weren't the first person on board."

She reached into her jacket and pulled out a rolled-up piece of paper—specifically, the contract we'd signed with Melinda. I hadn't realized she was bringing that, but I didn't much mind. She handed the paper to an amused-looking Frostbite, who unrolled it casually, then glanced over it. Her condescending smile froze, and her eyes widened, flicking back up to Callie, then to me.

"Well… that makes *way* too much sense." She slapped the papers down on the desk with a scowl. "I knew you got in good with the puppy huggers, but I didn't know the details. The WCP doesn't share with us much, especially not about things like this. They more than anyone know about the necessity of keeping this kind of thing quiet. You realize that the Unity is going to be *much* less airtight? If you sign on with me people will find out about this." That comment was aimed at me, not Callie.

I nodded. "It was going to happen eventually. I'm confident that my guardian can handle anyone who causes a problem, at least as far as people on your level or higher. Below that I'd need to rely on you and our other allies. As long as we have you as an excuse though, Callie says that even if Melinda or The Nothing have to make a move, it'll be considered inter-faction jockeying, since they'll technically be under your aegis."

"This is true," she admitted. "But you mentioned being less generous with me than with the puppy huggers. How much less? Getting a favor from a Candidate is useful, but not as useful as wishes, and I'm assuming you aren't willing to sign up for any long-term deals in that regard given your participation in the tournament and presumably, you hope, in the trip to the Moonsong Glade?"

That was true. I was working on getting up the cash for a buyout on the contract with the Beast Lord Garden. I'd prepaid plenty for wishes, but we didn't have the option of staying here forever. Luckily, since I wasn't an idiot, I'd made sure to leave an out in the contract, though if I did it the right way we could maintain our current relationship for a certain number of wishes per year, which was what I was aiming for. I didn't foresee much problem with it—no one sane would give up access to wishes for no reason.

Callie took back over negotiations. We'd talked over what was plausible for us here and had come to a hard line that would let us accomplish our goals and still give them something to work with. "We're willing to offer a flat rate. The biggest benefit to wishes is increased cultivation, though of course you aren't obligated to wish for anything specific. We're willing to offer you exclusive access for twenty-five wishes, provided you pay for the wishes in G-ranked elixirs."

Given the time crunch, we were going to be absurdly tight on getting Jessie and Benny to F-rank before we left for the Moonsong Glade, provided we made it. In the worst case we could approach Natalie to double their growth rate, but her payment would be steep. Since neither of them had used any of their elixir allotment for G-rank, they had a hundred stats worth of bottled growth available, and if we could get that as payment for something we had to put up anyway, it was a win-win.

Clearly Frostbite knew how wishes worked too, since she didn't try to negotiate an out for the payment. The actual contract would be wishes for protection, but that wouldn't do anything to mitigate prices, since we were leveraging scarcity rather than the actual wishes to be granted.

I'd coached Callie on some of the finer points of the contract, and she requisitioned a piece of paper and a pen and got to work outlining terms, letting Frostbite weigh in on what to nix and what was appropriate. Despite going through the motions, I was pretty sure Frostbite was hooked already. Callie was just giving her a good deal to make sure she thought of us as actual allies.

The E-ranker knew it too, and she seemed warmer as the two of them worked, even pointing out a few loopholes I'd missed in the wording. Despite my experience and training, my Focus was presumably much lower than hers, so I wasn't shocked she picked up a few threads I missed.

Finally, the two of them finished writing up the contract. Frostbite gave it a final once over, had us do the same, and once we agreed the terms were fair we all signed it. "So," I said once that was done. "I have to ask. Are you planning to use your wishes on Cold Snap? Having him boosted to F-rank so early would be a coup for your force, since you would be on track to have another E-ranker in your... what is your force called? I don't know how the Unity works in terms of subfactions."

She smirked at that. "Fimbulwinter. And yes, we can have our own subforces. But no, my son will not be receiving a boost. I wouldn't trust him with that much power so quickly. He has more than enough time to grow into his rank the natural way. Rime would be a more likely target for my usage of wishes. You can grant wishes to higher level Ascendants right?"

I blinked at that. "I… think so?" I paused. "I know I can, but they might not be as effective." I wasn't sure I'd ever granted a wish to a higher-ranked cultivator before. I was positive it would work, but considering how much easier I'd found it to grant them to lower-ranked people, there was a good chance the efficiency would be reduced. I could do four points of stats to someone my rank, but odds were it would be much less at F-rank. It had just never really come up.

She nodded, clearly unsurprised. "That's fine. Worst case I'll focus on grinding up some more of my G-rankers. Having more F-ranked hall members would be a big boost to my capabilities too, and I know some of mine are pretty close. Anyway, we can look into it later. For now, I suspect you have more to say. You don't seem to have relaxed after signing the contract."

Callie nodded. "That's true. Now that we've entered an alliance officially, we had something we wanted to bring to your attention." It was a risk mentioning the leak to Frostbite before we had any insurance. If it had been her, she might have tried to silence us. Now that we were in the same boat though, even if it was her we could just promise to keep our mouths shut about it.

My girlfriend explained, mentioning the Solemn Vow Guild and noting how easily they'd gotten our information. Frostbite looked more annoyed than worried. "Sadly problems like that aren't uncommon for Ascendant organizations, even big ones like the factions. Most of the people working the tournament signed confidentiality contracts, but those always have loopholes, and there are people with Oathbreaking abilities you can hire to get around even the ones that don't. I'll look into it, but I wouldn't expect miracles. Your best bet would be approaching it from the other side."

At our confused looks, she gave us a wolfish smile. "The Unity isn't a brokerage organization. Even if someone has the info, they wouldn't have the channels to actually sell it, and unless they were idiots they wouldn't just wander up to random factions and offer them insider information for cash. I'd look into middlemen in the WCP if I were you."

I grinned under my mask. I'd been hoping she could just give us the name of the leak, but that… that I could definitely work with.

Chapter Twenty-Three

WITH THE NEW lead from Frostbite, we officially had options looking for the leak. If we'd had to search in Rajak proper among the Unity directly, things might have been dicey, protection or not. Since this was WCP business we had more options for people to watch our back. On top of that, as per the protection clause of our contract, Frostbite had an F-ranker follow along with us in case we needed backup. Specifically, she sent Rime along.

I was pretty touched she dispatched her most powerful F-ranker to keep an eye on us, though I knew at least some of that was because she wanted Rime to make some of the wishes. The F-ranker had brought along a large amount of valuable elixirs as per our deal, and I would be able to grant her wishes without compromising our efforts to boost my friends to F-rank before we left. Though Benny and Jessie had both informed me that they'd finally been seeing some reputation gain from the fight in the auction, with Benny getting another twenty-five points of Might (presumably from swinging around that giant ass hammer) and Jessie getting twenty points of Vitality.

I was glad to see they were benefiting. I'd thought it was odd we hadn't seen any renown from that mess, but from what I could tell people had kept it under wraps for a while and it took time for rumors to disseminate. I knew sometimes great deeds were only counted after the incident was considered over in the minds of those involved too, like the scavenger hunt, so maybe that had something to do with it. It just kind of sucked Callie and I didn't benefit, having already capped our stats at the peak of G-rank.

We brought Rime back to the house, introduced her to everyone, and then consulted the resident WCP expert, Zeke. "So," I asked my uncle as we all settled in, "who should I talk to around here to find a middleman for brokering information? I know wishes aren't great for finding secrets, but we act as go-betweens on enough stuff that I'm sure we have specific protocols for where to find those kinds of people. Or can you not tell me that?"

He shook his head. "No, that I'm free to share. You'll need to pay for the actual information as per the rules, but directing you to where you can purchase those services isn't an issue. Let's see…" He stroked his five o' clock shadow. "I would say you should talk to Duncan the Liar. From what I've heard, he's in everyone's business."

"The compulsive liar is a reliable source of information?" I asked in confusion. "Isn't that a bit… counterintuitive?"

He shrugged. "If you can get him to talk. Believable lies come from a place of truth. You need to understand something in order to obscure it. If anyone would know it would be him—even if he isn't the broker, he should have an idea of who is. Provided you can motivate him."

"I'm surprised you know that, honestly. Rajak isn't your city, and you've just been kind of hanging around since we got here. I know you don't want to take over this branch, so why the research?" Not that I was complaining of course—this was pretty useful to me. Still, it made me wonder if his senses were just so monstrous that he passively picked up secrets from all over the planet or something.

My uncle just shrugged. "I got a dossier from the branch head, Facade, when I arrived. He included a brief introduction to all the E-rankers within the WCP, and most of the power players in the Unity. I suspect he was trying to make sure I wouldn't have a reason to go poking around for information if a question came up. He's good at managing problems before they arise. It's how he's managed to remain in power so long."

I remembered Callie having mentioned Facade. He was supposedly a party animal without much real skill who relied on his lieutenants to do most of the actual work, but we'd both guessed that was as much of a cover story as his name suggested. Seemed like Zeke actually had a bit of respect for him,

119

based on his grudgingly appreciative tone, and that said more in his favor than any number of rumors.

"Alright," I said with a sigh. "How do we meet Duncan the Liar? I didn't hear anything about him having a faction. Is he in the E-district? Can you *be* in E-district if you don't have a faction? Those buildings are huge—are there people who just hang out alone in there?" I hadn't spent much time in E-district, and I was honestly curious about how the most upscale part of the Rajak WCP functioned.

Sadly, based on his sigh, the knowledge I sought was not to be. "Nah," Zeke said with a wave. "He spends most of his time in the dark districts, the higher end ones, but there are ways to get in touch and arrange meetings. Has to be since according to the dossier, he moves around *way* more than necessary."

He pulled out a piece of paper from... somewhere, maybe a spatial artifact? Regardless, he started scribbling out instructions from memory before he passed them to me. "The locker in question is in the terminal, so you won't even need to go down into the WCP. Just write out a note and then slip it into the front slot."

I briefly considered asking why he hadn't just written the note, but the reason was obvious. He couldn't interfere in my business. He was able to tell me how to arrange the meeting, but getting a note from a B-ranker would have basically obligated Duncan to show up, which would be direct action on Zeke's part.

Callie had been showing Rime around while Zeke and I talked, but after he confirmed the contact method for Duncan, I went to find her. Then the two of us plus Rime headed for the station with the entrance to the WCP. We let Rime drive, which went fine, and I added another reliable driver to my mental checklist. Benny hadn't ever learned to drive a shuttle, much like I hadn't, and Callie would kill us all, so it was nice to have a new option for transport when Jessie was busy.

Arriving at the place, I saw Rime look around in interest. Callie noticed it too because her immediate response was to ask our F-ranked protector, "Have you never been here before?"

It seemed crazy to me that someone could live in Rajak and never visit the WCP, but thinking about it, there was at least some logic there. The WCP and the Unity were competitors, and the Palace was almost another city compared to Rajak proper. We hadn't done much exploration of the world above, given my connections to the forces beneath us, but someone like Rime wouldn't have that. This would be enemy territory.

The F-ranker's blue hair cascaded as she shook her head. "Never had a reason. It's... interesting. Some of the lower ranks from the academy and such spend time below, but I've been part of Fimbulwinter since I was a child, and the boss lady doesn't send us down here. Too dangerous she says."

"You'll be fine with us," I assured her. "We're sticking to the mixed rank areas anyway, and between our identity and our connections, the E-rankers down here won't mess with us. Assuming no one gangs up on you, most F-rankers shouldn't be a problem right?" She was high up in her rank from what I understood, and being Frostbite's second meant she was probably pretty scary on top of that.

Rime seemed taken in by the food kiosks, venders, and various other interesting attractions inside the massive stone building that was the entrance to the WCP. As per our instructions, we ignored the tourist attractions and followed the tile floor back into the depths of the building, away from the people. We turned off into a side hallway that shrunk down from the huge open area to a claustrophobic mashup of two walls so close together I had to turn sideways to walk down it. We emerged in a dark and somewhat cramped low-ceilinged room.

The dim room was, as we'd been told it would be, full to the brim with squat, dark metal lockers. "Alright," I said, checking the paper. "We're looking for... Z34962." Closing my eyes with a sigh, I said, "Can one of you guys please tell me that the plates on the closest lockers don't start with the letter A?"

Callie leaned over to peer at one of the plates on the lockers. "A00032. Sorry sweetie."

I sighed in defeat. That was just great. Thus began our journey through the locker hall, constantly checking the plates as we went. Duncan the Liar was either a huge dick or extremely paranoid, possibly both.

When we finally got to the locker in question, I pulled out a sheet of paper with the prepared directions, folded it around one and a half F-ranked chits (bringing my personal coffers down to exactly one E-ranked chit, or one hundred G-ranked chits) and then proceeded to spin the wheel on the locker's door in a series of very exacting and complicated patterns. A rune lit up on the metal after the third spin, and I slipped the paper through the slot on the front, jumping as a loud bang shook the door.

"Did it… work?" Callie asked cautiously. I consulted the paper, going over several of the addenda on the note. There were a few details on confirmation, and… got it, the bang on the door was a good sign. Probably.

"It did." I confirmed. "Or a giant energy chicken is about to burst out of the locker and try to eat us. But the note says that would have happened about thirty seconds after the bang, and since it hasn't, it seems like we're all good. Now… we wait." Duncan would get our message and show up to talk to us, though how he would manage that I had no idea—the note just said to wait here.

Rime looked annoyed. "Of *course* the first time I come to the WCP I have to spend the whole visit in a cramped locker depository. Does it say how long it will take for him to arrive?"

"Oh," said an amused voice from behind us. "Not long, I would imagine."

We all froze, having completely missed anyone appearing until the voice spoke up. We turned slowly to find a foppish, brown-haired man with a scraggly goatee and predatory amber eyes leaning against the inside of one of the opened lockers as he stared at us.

The yellow doublet and tights were the same as I'd been told about at the gala, and his hands toyed with a brass flute as he watched us. I felt like a bug under a microscope. Even knowing that he was E-rank and I was protected didn't blunt the edge of danger I felt from him. Like he was insane and capable of anything.

Of course, given his title, it was hard to say how much of that was a real impression and how much he'd purposefully cultivated the feeling to put people off their game. As "the Liar," I expected Perception was his bread and butter, and aside from stealth, I supposed Perception would be excellent for giving false impressions. Either way, he was here now.

He held up a familiar folded piece of paper, sans money. "I heard you were looking for some information."

Well, that was a good start. Probably.

Chapter Twenty-Four

"I was under the impression that we'd paid for your services with that little… deposit earlier," I said as the E-ranker casually plopped down on a bench. "So what do you mean you're *charging* us for the information we want?" I'd expected once he accepted payment that he'd just show up and tell us what we wanted, but the yellow-clad sneak seemed completely unmotivated to reveal anything. In fact I thought he was basking in our frustrations.

The grin that crept onto his face was even more annoying than the idea of paying twice. "Oh, no no. You paid for me to come and *listen* to you. One and a half F-rank chits isn't enough to pay for my *services*. It just got you this audience to impress me." He put a hand to one side of his mouth, stage-whispering. "It isn't going well." He closed his eyes and put the brass flute to his mouth, fingers flying as he played a particularly catchy sting, seemingly ignoring us completely.

That was a problem. Because while I personally was safe from Duncan, and I doubted he'd be stupid enough to attack the others (as a person who specialized in Perception and gathering intel, there was no way he didn't know who I was), we couldn't do shit to him, either. Maybe down the line, but I doubted, "I'll beat you up someday" was a decent motivator. So I only had one real option.

"You want a wish," I said flatly. He probably wanted more than one, but if I kept making long-term contracts I'd never get off this fucking planet. Plus I couldn't afford the delay in stat gains for my friends. So I'd offer one, and if he pushed I'd deal with it.

To my surprise, Duncan the Liar just came out and admitted it. "Wouldn't say no. But it wouldn't be for now. I know enough about the Wish power to figure that your ability to affect an E-ranker would be laughable. I'll wait until after the tournament, but I want it in writing before we move forward."

I cocked my head at him. "I'm pretty shocked you just came out and said that. Shouldn't you have slowly maneuvered me into your web with deception?" I was half joking, but still it seemed off to me.

He just shook his head. "People make that assumption quite a bit. But no, not really. See, I'm not a compulsive liar. I lie often and with ease, but lying loses its effectiveness if you never say anything true. If every word out of my mouth was false, everyone would just know I meant the opposite of what I said. I do tell the truth, and sometimes I lie, and sometimes I do both at once, because the truth from a liar can be even less believable than fiction."

That... had been a really long, convoluted way of telling me absolutely fucking nothing about him. Which I suspected was his entire point. I really disliked cryptic bullshit. I got enough of that from Zeke courtesy of my dad's bullshit geas. "You understand," I said archly, "that I can't just give you a blanket promise to grant a wish after I rank up without knowing what it is?"

My issue was less with the wish and more with the open-ended nature of "after you rank up." It would be easy enough for him to wait and cash that in later. And I had no interest in being dragged back here when I was higher-ranked because of some old marker.

I could have and would have covered all that in the contract, but since he was being so up front I figured I'd do the same. He grinned at me. "Oh no, that's fine. I can include provisions for when exactly I'll make the wish." He didn't mention limitations on content, but he didn't need to. His limitations would be the same as everyone else's—what my stats were capable of accomplishing.

Slipping out a blank piece of paper I started writing. With over a hundred Focus and Perception my handwriting was excellent, and I could write pretty damn fast, so it didn't take long to dot my I's and cross my T's. Duncan looked it over and nodded, filling in the last bit of info, an exact date for the wish.

I let Callie look over it before I signed. We were partners and while she wasn't quite as well trained in contracts, she was smart and careful. I valued her opinion. She smiled softly at me as she took the paper, scanning through it for a minute or two in a way that told me she was taking her time and doing multiple read throughs before handing it back.

"Alright," I said as I signed. "Now, we were told you're the guy to see about information. We need you to help us locate someone who has been selling it. We suspect they used a middleman from the WCP but the person them-selves is Unity. If you don't know them, I'm sure you can find out."

I'd been careful not to mention specifics in the information request, lest it be intercepted or Duncan decided to warn whoever it was before coming to see us. Still, he didn't seem too surprised by the request. Granted, it was possible he was just hiding signs of that surprise with his excellent lying skills, but who could say?

He nodded thoughtfully. "I can help with that information. Honestly you're lucky we did it this way. I'd probably have turned you down if we hadn't already signed the contract. I don't owe them anything, but burning primary sources isn't beneficial to a broker. Do you just want the source or do you need the middle man too? Because one of those will be much more annoying for me."

He was hinting that he might need to dissolve the contract (we had provi-sions for that on both sides in case of extenuating circumstances) if I went after the middleman. Luckily I didn't need to. "Just the source is fine," I said firmly.

Depending on who it was, we might not even be able to do anything to them in the short term. Rime and Frostbite both seemed unhappy (if resigned) about the leak, so if it wasn't someone related to Fimbulwinter we might be able to use them to take care of it, but they hadn't been able to make any promises.

Duncan nodded approvingly. I expected him to just give us a name, but the unusual E-ranker turned his amber gaze away from use, and, staring off into the distance, started speaking. "I've always been enamored with information you know. Not just its acquisition, but its application. Whether by virtue of its absence or presence, truth changes many things about the world. Learning the truth of others lets me know my own, and you can't lie to other people properly if you're lying to yourself."

Despite the apparent non sequitur, I didn't interrupt and Callie followed my lead. Duncan kept talking. "I started learning other people's truths and met other people on the same grand quest. I've met many people like that over the years. Some of them hungry for knowledge, some of them desperate to learn more about the reality of this storybook world, to see past the lies that even the universe tells us."

"The person you are looking for," he said firmly, "is not one of those people. He doesn't want to learn more truths or see past the facade. He wants power. This insults me. Lies are art—they are a delicate and subtle manipulation of the minds of others for the purpose of shaping your world. They are not commodities."

I had to admit, this was not what I had expected of the guy everyone hated, who someone had recently turned into a fish. "I didn't expect you to be so… philosophical," I said carefully.

Duncan's stoic and distant expression cracked, becoming a manic grin. "Maybe I'm not? Maybe I just like playing with baby cultivators. I can smell confusion on you like cheap cologne." He waved his hand dismissively. "No matter. Believe or don't. No business of mine. I've decided that I dislike this person, and so I will hand them over to you. Take that as you will. You're looking for an F-ranker who works at the Unity building. He goes by the name Kalway."

Callie and I both looked at Rime, who shrugged. "No clue—name doesn't ring a bell. If he works at the main building he's probably not entirely unconnected though. I'll look into him and get back to you."

Nodding, I turned back to Duncan and… blinked. Nothing. There was no one on the bench. The locker he'd come out of was still open, but there was nothing in there that might explain his disappearance. When I looked back down, I noticed a note where he'd been sitting and picked it up. I unfolded it, to find a picture of me unfolding a picture of me unfolding a picture. Which then exploded. Into confetti. Sharp confetti.

Luckily my armor and mask took all the cutting edges, though the locker next to us wasn't so lucky. Callie and Rime were behind me and therefore untouched.

I sighed. "Now I get why people don't like him."

Callie leaned over next to the locker, giving a deep sniff. "Especially since I'm pretty sure these are poisoned. Nothing super dangerous, I think just a mild paralytic. Though I wonder why he would bother to—" There was a puff and about two hundred pounds of glitter dropped from above. "Ah. Keep us in place. Well... that worked I guess."

I didn't see any particular reason for that little prank, other than amusement. I could see why others were tempted to turn Duncan into a fish—I might need to use a wish to get all the glitter out of my armor.

I turned to Rime. "So, you said you can look into Kalway? If Frostbite can plug the leak before we get too much further in, we can possibly avoid a lot of trouble."

Callie nodded. "Especially if she makes a production of it. If other locals see her crack down hard on someone leaking tournament info they'll be much less likely to try it."

The F-ranker sighed. "Which I'm sure would be her intent, but it depends on who the guy is. There are certain factions in the Unity that make dealing with things like this... tricky. Some of the executives claim priority on their own subordinates and will give them a slap on the wrist instead of actually punishing them. They consider it a blow to their own reputation for their subordinates to be held accountable."

"Isn't Frostbite like... *infamous* for that?" I asked carefully. I'd heard Frostbite was incredibly biased toward her own people, which, granted, was nice since that was *us* now.

Rime grinned at me. "Yeah, like that. So we might not be able to pin it on him in an obvious way. Of course, some of the executives are more objective. Really depends who he works under. Or if he's just rank and file, his ass is grass. I'll get into it."

"Sounds good," Callie said dryly. "Now let's get out of here. I want to go home and wash all this damn glitter off. We can use Stealth to leave."

I nodded, and we each put a hand on Rime's shoulder, getting ready to boost her stealth as we left, before stopping.

I closed my eyes and sighed. "Ah. That would be why he used glitter. All that excess light shifting around makes Stealth *much* harder. Okay." I triggered one of my stored up Stealth charges, synergizing it with my own Stealth skill, and Callie added hers in. We were barely able to make it to the parking lot without being noticed.

Yeah. Definitely understood the impulse to turn him into a fish.

Chapter Twenty-Five

THE NEXT DAY WE HAD... nothing to do. Not absolutely nothing, granted (we had training pretty much daily), but there were no big important tasks other than getting ready for the following day's match. We slept in late, got up and had a big breakfast, and then had a big meeting with the others to catch them up on what they might have missed, as well as making sure they all knew Rime (Cark hadn't met her yet).

Once that was done, I granted Rime all five of her wishes, confirming that I could in fact grant full stats to an F-ranker, and possibly an E-ranker. Which was good information to have, if nothing else.

In repayment for her wishes she put up elixirs as requested. Each wish of four points was paid off with a G-ranked elixir worth five, and she was easily able to supply the Focus elixirs Benny needed for the day, bringing his focus up from one hundred thirty-three to one hundred fifty-eight, his total coming up to four hundred and twenty-eight points. At this rate it might be possible to get him and Jessie up to F-rank before it was time to leave.

Me and Callie sat on the couch with the others, strategizing for possible enemy fights based on the opponents we were sure had passed the third round already. "I have to say, I kind of wish the elixir limit wasn't a thing. Like, I understand it, but this is *way* more convenient than bartering individual points. It would have made ranking up a snap." I looked at Zeke. "Any chance it's possible to integrate elixir points perfectly with wishes?"

He seesawed a hand back and forth. "Anything is possible, but it's not cost effective. It's an Impact thing, so it only really works on people lower ranked than you are, which limits your options. That's a much bigger change than you might think, so even in those circumstances the cost is prohibitive. The only ones who really bother are incredibly rich cultivators who can pay *much* stronger wish-granters to get their kids back on track."

Rime nodded at that. "I could see how that would be a rare and valuable commodity. It can be enticing to constantly get stronger like that. There are plenty of people who don't believe they can ever rank up and just decide to ignore their elixir limit entirely and artificially pump themselves up to their next rank limit."

I froze and went back over what I knew about elixirs in my head. That would actually work. The elixir limit wasn't an inherent thing, it was the formula for what part of your core self could be artificially inflated before your soul would be too weak for a rank up. Which meant it *would* be possible for people to pump themselves up to the edge of a rank. "Ok, I hadn't realized you could do that but that makes sense. Why don't all the E-rankers do it then? Shouldn't they all be at the peak of E?"

Rime shook her head. "They can't. We don't have nearly enough E-ranked Alchemists or materials to supply all of them. Hell, we have almost none. Any time E-ranked elixirs show up they get snatched up almost immediately, and usually not by the same person."

"It's much more common elsewhere," Zeke chimed in. "With D-rank being a watershed, E-rank is as high as a lot of people manage to get, so you see a lot of people who completely abandon the hope of advancement to artificially pump themselves up to the peak of E. Happens all the time on real D-rank planets where materials like that are much easier to get."

Rime sighed. "Even F-rank pills and elixirs can be hard to find here. I hit my cap, but I'm in the minority. Frostbite had to put in quite a bit of effort to boost me up so much. Luckily, G-rank is low enough that there are plenty to go around. We had a stockpile for some of our lower-level members, and I didn't even clean the whole thing out."

Well that was good for us. Honestly, even once the twenty-five wishes were past I would probably work with her for a while if possible, since at that speed Jessie would still have seventy five points left on her cap.

I also cursed myself for never trying to give more points when they were lower ranked, since I'd had no idea it worked like that. I probably could have gotten them to G-rank much faster. Assuming they could pay for it of course. I hoped that Callie had mentioned her whole part time job thing, since they would need cash to pay off the points blitz, especially in the last month. At the very least, once I broke through to F-rank, getting Jessie ready in time would be much easier.

Focusing back on the matter at hand, I had to point out the obvious. "As nice as getting everyone to G-rank on time is, it's not exactly going to matter if we can't win this. We really need to know who we're fighting."

Benny snorted. "Anyone else amused at the irony of us doing our level best to get the leak busted when we could really use his services?" He looked at Rime. "Any chance he's still active and they're like… gathering evidence or something?"

She just smirked. "We're the Unity. We don't need to do stings on flunkies." Her smirk dropped off into an annoyed scowl. "He was picked up right after I called in and is currently having… words, with some of our interrogation specialists. Probably won't lead anywhere sadly. Either he's a greedy opportunist or whoever was pulling his strings did it carefully, but either way he's apparently not going to give up anything of value. Not the best outcome I admit."

That was unfortunate, but it could have gone worse. Still. "Does that mean there's not a high chance of him going down for this?"

"Oh that's already happening," she said casually. "He's screwed, it's just that he's the *only* one who's screwed. The threat is a lot weaker if she just wrecks the one guy. Since we couldn't get his bosses, anyone else who wants to leak info through a cat's paw will be emboldened to try it for themselves. Though Frostbite is having people put in place to keep an eye on all the bigger names who have access to things like fight info, so at the very least they won't be quite so overt about it next time."

I slumped at that. "Does that benefit us at all though? Getting our hands on some random minion isn't likely to scare off the people behind him."

She shook her head. "Nope, but you're not thinking of this the right way. Whoever was backing him won't dare act a second time. While some of the middle management might risk it, whoever he got that information from has to be careful now that everyone is being watched. One data point means nothing, plenty of people could have given him that little tidbit, but the more times it happens the more vulnerable they are. They won't dare try it again while being watched. Which means whichever faction bought that information lost their main connection in management."

Callie cut in, bringing us back to the point—strategizing for our next fight. "We need some kind of plan on what we'll do, and since we don't know what we're facing, more than one plan would be best. Something general, maybe some formations we can use or something." She looked at Abel, who was leaning back on the couch nearby with his eyes closed, though the angle of his head and his breathing showed us he wasn't sleeping, just relaxing as we talked. "Any ideas there, Apollyon?"

His eyes opened, focusing on me. "Maybe," he said with deliberation. "I'm not sure exactly. Honestly I think we have enough figured out in terms of roles that we don't need too much more work there. Our best bet is to continue the training we were working on before, forcing you all to react to my attacks and try to survive them. That's training that will give you instincts you can't get from studying a team's win record."

I grimaced. I'd been afraid he'd say something like that. I'd hated that training. Callie didn't seem thrilled either, but she nodded. "That might be best. Realistically, not knowing the opponent isn't too much of an imposition as long as we're in top form, and your... special training is nothing if not effective." She shot Benny and Jessie a jealous look. I completely sympathized. Those lucky bastards.

Abel popped to his feet, moving almost too quickly to track. "Well then, guess we have a plan." He grinned at us wickedly. "You two might want to get warmed up. Wouldn't want you to move too slow and get hurt."

I was pretty positive given the massive strength difference Abel wouldn't accidentally kill us, but he might purposefully maim us, given Jessie's presence here as insurance.

Speaking of which, I looked over at her. "Hey Agria, can you do me a favor and stick around for this? Even if he doesn't break our knees or something we don't want to fight exhausted tomorrow. If you patch us up, we can train hard and still be in good condition."

She shrugged. "Sure. I was planning to go visit Randall and the wolves, but I can do it later." With Randall coming up here we realized the house wasn't going to cut it for keeping the animals, so we'd cleared out a shed behind the house that Zeke hadn't bothered telling us about. The wolves had claimed it as a den pretty much, and Randall mostly just slept in the back and let them do their thing unless they woke him up.

With a sigh, we headed for the training room to prepare for the fight. Realistically, I knew this was a smart move. Abel was a monster in battle, and learning to react to him (even in training) took our ability to avoid attacks to a whole new level, but I was getting cold shakes remembering the last time we did this. The feeling of his fist whistling by me so fast I could barely track it was something I would never get used to.

When we got down there, I saw that Rime had come along with us, deciding to sit off to one side and watch. To my surprise Mel walked over to sit with her. The two of them had started chatting and apparently hit it off. I found the dichotomy amusing, since they literally couldn't be more different. The red-haired fire user and the blue-haired ice user were a study in contrasts, but it couldn't be a bad thing for Rime to get better acquainted with everyone.

As we took up position and started warming up, Abel strolled into the ring and stripped off his coat. He left the mask on, which we were thankful for, since Mel had told us that Abel was only ever *really* serious in battle when he took off his mask. But still, knowing he was going harder this time was terrifying.

Focusing on our bond, I triggered the overlay for both me and Callie, making sure we'd have the best chance to avoid the attacks and to learn from this. Once he saw that we were ready, Abel gave us that same blood-thirsty smile that had been seared into my brain last time.

"Fight."

And then all I could see was fists. This was going to be a long day.

Chapter Twenty-Six

It was time. Round four.

Rime got her wishes in before we left and Benny started taking his elixirs (all for Might this time, set to bring him up to one hundred and sixty-four). Meanwhile, we all made our way to the arena, with Rime coming along just in case since she was our bodyguard. Surprisingly, the Silent Dagger quadruplets made another appearance and followed behind us too. I supposed it made sense, since Alexander was bound to want to keep Callie safe.

I could feel from the Impact difference between them and Rime (I wasn't as good at gauging the differences in F-rankers, but I could get a general feel for it) that they weren't on her level, but they would be solid backup. With Rime intervening they would have an excuse to jump in and protect us from any F-ranked threats without starting a war, which was the more important part.

Everyone got set up in the stands and the four of us headed down to the prep room under the stadium. When we got down there, we found the guy waiting to send us in and finally had a chance to ask him about our opponents.

He smirked at us when he heard the question. "Well at least some of you little bastards are in the dark. Last round only one of my teams asked who they were facing. I think it's more exciting this way though, don't you? No chances to prepare for your opponent. The first rounds were a bit too predictable, so they wanted to shake things up."

He looked at us suspiciously for a bit, as if it had only just occurred to him that we hadn't asked him last time, but eventually rolled his eyes. "Oh well. Too late for any last-minute planning anyway. Fine. Let me see." He walked over to a desk and pulled out a clipboard, flipping through it. "Ah. You're up against the Seven Seas Armada. C-rank faction. Pretty good results so far."

There was no further elaboration, which was annoying, but at least we had some kind of idea now. Probably some kind of water based force? He walked back over and sat down in an old wooden chair, ignoring us and closing his eyes as he waited for it to be time to dispatch us to the sand pit. After a few minutes of looking around the cramped, moist stone space, his eyes snapped open and he looked over at us. "Alright. Go on out. Good luck."

We nodded to him and the four of us walked out into the arena. The sun was beating down, and as usual it was silent despite the cheering crowd because of the sound barrier around the combat area. When we came out and saw the other team... we all stopped.

Pirates. We were fighting fucking pirates. Long leather coats, tricorn hats, pistols, swords, the works. I wasn't sure what was up with the pistols since aside from that Master Candidate I heard not many people used them, but the rest of their gear gave the impression of brutal efficiency and *lots* of practice.

My heart started pounding in excitement as I grinned at them. I got the distinct impression this would be a fun fight.

"Well now!" the leader sneered. "If it isn't our opponents. You certainly don't look like much, but then again, I suppose looks aren't everything."

I snickered at the comment. "It's okay, I'm sure plenty of people will like you for your personality." Callie rolled her eyes and Abel chuckled while Mel just shook her head. The enemy... er, captain smiled wolfishly, seemingly unbothered by the comment.

He opened his mouth to speak, but before he could I got a... feeling. Whether it was my fate sense, my diviner instincts, or just luck, I got a strong impression I needed to *move*, so I did. The sand rippled like lapping waves and one of the pirates (the shortest, who had his whole face wrapped in bandages under his hat) broke apart into shards of glass as an exact copy of him emerged from the ground, wickedly sharp blade aimed right at my fucking eye.

Callie reached out and grabbed my coat, casually pulling me the rest of the way clear. She'd started moving when I had, since our bond made it easier for her to see something coming if I did.

The form of the pirate dropped back toward the sand, but as he fell Abel's fist lashed out like a speeding car, about to smash into him.

The captain crossed the distance within a blink, his sword coming free at the same time as his pistol and chopping down roughly at Abel's hand while his gun came up at Mel and fired. Rather than a musket ball or something, which I'd have expected to come out of the barrel, a cannon-ball of green smoke erupted from the gun, and Mel's eyes widened as she called a wall of flames to stop it from reaching her.

Abel, who was about to follow up, jerked his head toward her and bellowed "No!" before vanishing in a swirling line of shifting space as he tackled his girlfriend out of the way. He barely got them clear before the gas made contact with her flame defense, erupting in a huge gas explosion.

The captain had already spun on us to attack, but I wasn't giving him a shot. I got a dangerous feeling from him. I unleashed a blast of flame I had stored up from Cark, releasing it through my cane which I'd already coated in poison fire.

The scruffy blonde man snarled but stepped back into the watery sand, falling beneath the "waves" and vanishing to reappear next to the others alongside the bandaged one. The closest to them, a tall red-haired woman with piercing green eyes, stepped over to put a hand on them and... fuck, healed them. We hadn't fought a team with a healer yet, and as I watched the soothing water wash away their wounds, I realized this would be even tougher than expected.

Abel stormed back over, slightly singed and looking as genuinely annoyed as I had seen him in one of these fights. He stripped off his jacket and shoved it into my hands. "Stay here," he snarled as he stalked toward the other team.

I looked at Mel uncertainly and she just snorted and shook her head. "Stay on alert. We'll jump in if we're needed, but I doubt we will be. That other team isn't bad, but they aren't on the same level as some of the ones we've fought so far. Let him work it out."

Shrugging I sat and watched, waiting for my mentor to do his thing. I was kind of curious to see how this would go for the pirates. I hadn't met anyone who could really push Abel. The closest was the Master Candidate with the Mop Skill, but even he'd mostly given the man a light workout.

As Abel advanced, the captain flicked a hand. He and the bandage guy both vanished into a ripple of waves on the sand. At the same time, the redheaded woman stepped back and the last man, an absolutely massive guy with bulging biceps showing through a sleeveless leather vest, hurled himself forward.

He shot forward like a cannonball, curling his legs and arms as he turned to steel midair. Abel hauled back and smashed his fist headlong into the flying man, and I saw a slight ripple in the air of a fist image between them just long enough to crush the big man into the sand before Abel's elbow caught a previously unseen slipstream of warped space. His body contorted like a fucking spinning top, his elbow smashing into the face of the now emerging bandage guy.

As that happened the captain emerged from the sand, cutlass stabbing up at Abel's throat. My mentor's spare hand waved in the air, creating another spatial slipstream and guiding the sword harmlessly away. Before he could press the attack, the pistol came up and a roaring wolf head made of blue flames erupted from the barrel.

Abel shifted his whole body back and to the side, his physical form jerking in several rapid directional changes I don't think I'd be capable of with years of practice. When the wolf head caught up, it smashed into Abel headlong, only to hit sand as Abel's form blurred, revealing it to have been a fucking *afterimage* as Abel appeared behind the now-open captain.

The blonde man hissed and yanked his hand free from a pocket, hurling out a cloud of black dust that Abel guided away from his face with spatial lubrication. The redhead had been sneaking over to heal bandage guy as the steel guy dug himself out, and they now swarmed Abel, converging to attack from all sides.

I moved to go help but Mel stuck out a hand and put it on my shoulder, shaking her head. I supposed it was fine—Abel had already showed off everything he could do, he'd just done it *very* casually. He wasn't giving away any new abilities here, just proving he was way fucking stronger than most of the people here. If anything, this would hide some of our own possible trump cards.

I had to give them credit. The four pirates together were scary. Not the same level of cohesion that me and Callie or Abel and Mel had, but a different kind of teamwork. Where our cooperation was a perfect melding of our styles, theirs was almost the opposite. They were so perfectly out of sync that it made reacting to them at the same time nearly impossible. It was so discordant it was almost beautiful, and if it had been me I'd have been screwed.

The captain drew and fired, a massive cloud of red smoke in the shape of a bear trap snapping towards Abel while the big guy hurled himself at my mentor's legs and the redhead fired some kind of blowdart at him, covering the bandage guy who leapt toward Abel's back. They knew exactly what the others would do, and instead of fitting their attacks together, they made them so wildly different that there was no way to counter them all.

Except if you were Abel. With barely a thought, he dropped to a knee, swinging a hand up behind him to create a slide of spatial energy over his back. The metal guy hit the slipstream and changed direction, arcing up over Abel's back to take his place. The red energy trap closed around the metallic pirate and he screamed in agony, the metal fading from his skin. Bandage guy landed on him as the red trap was closing, and the smaller pirate stiffened but made no sound as blood welled from the injury.

Abel slid forward through space, leaving them to drop onto the sand, the dart from the healer having hit the big guy head-on as my teacher engaged the captain alone. A series of short, sharp punches launched from outside the captain's range that hit despite being too far away disabled the pirate leader before Abel knocked him out with a brutal smashing blow to his chin.

Abel turned to the redhead slowly, glaring without emotion. The pirate girl dropped to her knees, hands behind her head to show the people outside the dome she surrendered. Abel snorted and pivoted, walking away in disgust, and she breathed a sigh of relief before scrambling over to treat her friends.

Fingers crossed she had an antidote to whatever was in that dart, because metal guy was turning purple.

As I watched Abel walk back toward us, I swallowed audibly. Note to self—never mess with Apollyon. After this display, I doubted I was the only person thinking that, either.

Chapter Twenty-Seven

"WELL," I said in shock. "That was… terrifying." I looked over at Callie. "Why do we even fight? Like, we could just have Apollyon carry the team through the whole first half of the tournament. Not like it would be hard for him." My tone was joking and light, but honestly I kind of wished she would agree. As much fun as some of these fights were for me, I could always get my fill of that in the single elimination rounds.

Abel just snorted. "No."

We both looked at him and our mentor chuckled. "You're thinking too short term. We have four more rounds of practice to get you ready for the single elimination fights. If you waste them all using me as a crutch, you're going to get crushed in the early rounds of the one-on-one fights and that removes a bunch of our chances to get first place in the tournament."

He was right, and honestly I didn't feel like sitting around the whole fight for the next few rounds anyway. I shrugged. "I was mostly kidding. Anyway, maybe we should go and check on the pirates. We never got an introduction, and they were actually about as impressive as the mop team."

I expected him to snap or get pissed, but Abel nodded. "True." At our surprised looks he just shook his head. "You assumed I'd be too pissed to talk to them? I was annoyed when they almost hurt my partner, but I already got my revenge, so now we're even. They actually did better than I expected, so I'm not against introducing ourselves."

The match was over, but it would be a while until the exhibition matches anyway, not that it really mattered. We would leave when we were done. As we approached, the redhead saw us coming from where she was healing the metal guy (who was no longer metal) and reached for her weapon subconsciously.

The captain, who was already healed and conscious again, rubbed his chin gingerly. "Ok," the captain said sheepishly, "I probably deserved that, but dear gods man, you took that a bit personally didn't you?" Abel just raised an eyebrow at the man, who put up both hands. "Right, right, my apologies. That gas isn't normally quite so flammable, or rather, it combusts at absurdly high temperatures. G-rank fire abilities aren't usually enough to set it off like that." He reached out a hand to bandage guy, who had already been healed, and let the smaller man pull him to his feet.

Mel rolled her eyes. "It's fine. No one got seriously hurt." Her tone was annoyed, though the trace of a smile on her face told me she wasn't exactly unhappy with Abel's extreme reaction to her injuries.

I stepped over, putting a hand on Mel and Abel and releasing a heal burst. They weren't too damaged, but it didn't make sense to leave them hurt for no reason when I could help. Mel in particular seemed like she might be more banged up than she was letting on based on the way she was carrying herself.

The captain nodded. "Glad to hear it. Fighting dirty is what we do, but we aren't lunatics. No one wants bodies dropping in a tournament." He held out a hand to Abel, who was the closest. "Teague Cromwell. The one in the bandages is Rum, the jumbo lad turning a lovely shade of plum from his teammate's own poison is Ruffle, and the fetching lass with the blood-colored hair keeping our sorry arses alive is Mallory. I know you lot are the Starchaser Pavilion, but I'm afraid I haven't heard any more than that." He said the last bit leadingly, obviously curious about who we were.

Callie smiled at that. "I'm Nightstrike, team leader. The terrifying thug in the silver mask who totaled your whole team single handedly is Apollyon, our resident hothead is Starbreaker, and the big lovable goon looming over me is my partner Solomon. Not a surprise you haven't heard of us. We're a local team, and a recent one at that. We were impressed how you handled yourselves though, and we were hoping you might want to grab something to eat and share information, given you're already out of the tournament and have nothing to hide anymore."

Teague burst out laughing. "Well, you're certainly an optimistic bunch, I'll grant you that. Not wrong though. Sure, we would be happy to tag along. We don't really have anything on after this anyway. We were planning a little celebration dinner later tonight with just the team, but I suppose we can move it up to a lunch."

That struck me as a bit odd. "What do you guys have celebrate? You lost?" Everyone looked at me, and it took me a second to replay that in my head and realize how dickish it sounded. "Um. Sorry, did I say that out loud? I meant you… experienced an important growth opportunity?"

The grin on the scruffy blonde man's face told me he didn't have any hard feelings. "Right you are, mate. Lose we did. But it was a good fight. Maybe not the most impressive showing we've put on, but we hardly embarrassed ourselves did we? No reason to sulk about not making it. Only one participant of the ten thousand teams will win the grand prize, so our odds weren't exactly great. No shame in doing your best."

"Besides," Mallory said as she approached with a now healed, albeit still limping, Ruffle (whose name made literally no sense to me). "We weren't the favorites in this by any means. My money is on those girls from Final Frost Heaven personally. Those ice queens are scary. Anyway, someone said something about food? Healing really takes it out of me."

That was interesting. I hadn't really contextualized Jessie's eating habits with her energy expenditure for healing and taming, but it made a lot of sense in retrospect. Callie seemed interested in the comment as well, but as the leader her focus was on the bigger picture and she was less prone to drifting off on tangents (admittedly most people were less prone to that, I was a fairly flighty person).

"We should get out of the pit," my girlfriend said wryly. "I imagine they want to get another team in here, or at least clean this place up."

It should be noted that the sand pit was definitely a bit of a mess. Teague grimaced and nodded, waving his teammates over as we all filed out of the pit through the exit gate on our side. I wasn't sure if they were supposed to do that, but again, not really our problem.

As we walked, Abel sidled up next to Teague. "So, I'm interested in your combat style, it felt sort of… haphazard, but in an unpredictable way."

His comment got a laugh from the pirate captain. "Because it's supposed to be. Scallywag is a combat style designed to take advantage of a variety of environmental and situational factors to create openings in the enemy's form. The handful of powder, the variety of bullets—those make things easier, but natural dust and sand or improvised local weapons work just as well. Our Admiral created the style himself over centuries of traveling the Cluster and getting in fights in all sorts of different locations."

Abel nodded thoughtfully. "Sacrifice power for versatility. It isn't a bad idea. The pit wasn't exactly your ideal fighting location then. Would have been better for the lot of you if we fought in the wild."

"Somewhat," Teague said with a shrug. "But *any* location means even ones where there isn't much around. Hence the prepared armaments and tricks. I'm more impressed with your style. I'd heard there were Master Candidates in this thing, but I hadn't done much research into them. I didn't know one of you was local. Getting to that level of Skill on a pseudo D-rank planet is pretty monstrous."

There wasn't much to say to that. It was monstrous, so Abel just gave a shrug of his own and changed the subject. "So, what's the deal with the bullets—they enchanted?"

I'd been wondering about that myself. It was almost similar to how I used my stored attacks, albeit less versatile and more cumbersome. I wouldn't be switching to a flintlock, no matter how badass it looked.

Teague drew said flintlock in a smooth motion, laying it across a forearm and aiming it at the wall as he closed one eye to sight down the barrel. "Yup. We have a dedicated Bulletteer in the Armada. His whole ability is a synergy between Enchanting and Ammo Creation, and he even experiments with Inventing and Alchemy for some of his formulas. It's amazing what you can accomplish when you dedicate yourself to a craft. Especially once you reach the Master ranks."

It certainly sounded like it. I couldn't wait to see what kind of things Benny would be making at C or even D-rank. Teague filled us in on some of the history of the Seven Seas Armada, which had one of the largest standing navies in the System and employed most of the highest-ranking engineers who worked on ships at all. I'd have loved to be able to afford a ship that could take us off world, but I knew there was zero chance the money I had on hand was even approaching enough, so I filed that information away for later use.

Mallory had a suggestion for a local steak house, and we decided to eat there at her suggestion. As we emerged from the underbelly of the arena we met up with Rime and the others and introduced them. Benny gave me a subtle nod of approval—apparently making friends with pirates was a win in his book.

As we headed out to the car, I felt a buzz on my finger and told everyone I'd catch up. I opened the call from my cousin, seeing her looking worried. "Shane, you're okay—thank the gods." Her relief was not encouraging. "You need to be careful. There were attacks on six of the major faction teams within the last hour. Someone is making moves they really shouldn't be. I don't see what anyone gets from moving this early, but there's been huge bounties offered on several promising teams including yours and mine. They all went out around the same time."

My eyes snapped to my friends, who were heading for the car. Melinda and Alexander weren't there, nor was Zeke—they figured having high rankers around would ruin the vibe for lunch. The four and Rime were still with us though, so when the vortex of whirling grey mist slammed down on the group, they weren't completely helpless. I barely had time to see the dome of fractal ice form over them all before they were swallowed by the mist.

Without a second of hesitation I bolted at the mist, triggering Seek Hidden on Callie and harmonizing it with our bond to enhance the effect. I could see a glowing form a few dozen feet away and focused on that, trusting her to recognize I was coming and tell Rime so she could let me through the dome.

As I drew closer I detected movement behind me and without even pausing I used Leaf on the Wind and Cloud Step to send myself flashing up diagonally in a way that almost no one would be able to account for in an attack. A wave of acidic purple sludge hit the ice, hissing even as it came down. I thought for a second it had melted, but I saw Rime looking my way and realized she was opening the dome for me. I Cloud Stepped again and landed inside as she closed it up. Sadly though, ice wasn't exactly opaque, which meant we could still see the dark forms emerging from the mist. We were surrounded.

Chapter Twenty-Eight

THERE WERE a lot of people here. More than I'd been expecting, and more than a few of them were F-rank. I don't think they had taken the Silent Dagger quadruplets into account, probably because their addition to the party had been last minute, so there were only five F-rankers total. I was pretty sure those were prepared specifically for Rime, based on the way they efficiently spread out to surround and begin to take down the dome.

G-rankers were much more numerous. Easily twenty of them. This lineup would have been a death sentence for us if we hadn't taken the precautions we had, but even so it was damn dangerous. I thought back to what Natalie had said. This was a concerted attack and would have taken massive resources. What was the point of this?

Callie grabbed me in a hug when I landed. "Oh thank the gods. I was about to come out and get you."

"I'm fine," I said with a smile. "Is everyone here okay?" I looked around to check on everyone. Benny and Jessie were still here, presumably because while in existential danger, they hadn't been placed in direct life-threatening trouble yet, and as such hadn't triggered their emergency escape wishes. Those had really been a good idea, even if they hadn't seen use yet.

Abel, who was looking around in annoyance, spoke up. "We're fine, though I can't help but notice that all our E-rankers are gone."

That was Zeke, most likely. I wasn't sure why though. I knew he couldn't interfere, but the only reason to actively draw off our protection would be if he thought that letting these people attack us would be useful for some reason. I doubted it was training, which implied that they might have some sort of information we could use. Or he just wanted me to be ready for assassins. Who fucking knew?

Callie looked surprisingly furious, but I could feel her reign in her temper through the bond, forcing herself to calm down as she closed her eyes and took a deep breath. "We don't need them," she said, her voice level and her eyes still shut. "We'll be fine." She raised her voice. "Don't suppose any of you shadowy asshats feels like talking?"

To our surprise, a figure slipped from the fog, a short man in a dapper suit and top hat, complete with mantle, cane and monocle. His mustache looked a little thin, like he wasn't quite old enough to grow a proper one, which sort of ruined the effect, but he gave us a perfunctory smile. "I suppose I might be open to a dialogue. I have to admit, we were led to believe your force would be less... formidable."

Which meant whoever had given them our information had been working on out-of-date intel, though they had also been watching us, otherwise they wouldn't have waited until the E-rankers left. Had they not been able to tell the quadruplets were F-ranked until they engaged us? Maybe their scout couldn't differentiate Impact from a distance and they were working from photos, or maybe Silent Dagger had ways of keeping that information hidden at range.

Callie nodded. "What's your name? If you're going to threaten us, we should at least know who we're talking to."

The man smiled. "Miles. My name is Miles Blakely."

"Well, what's your offer? Going to say you'll let half of us go if we stay out of the way?"

"I've been hired to...dissuade you, from taking part in the remainder of the tournament. Violence isn't an inevitability, simply one of our options. Though I caution you, we are not unaccustomed to such methods."

I thought back to what Natalie had said. She'd said the other teams were attacked, not killed. Of course, I somehow doubted that these people were as reasonable as they portrayed themselves. If we hadn't been such a tough nut to crack I was pretty sure they'd have just crushed us.

146

Still, I understood what Callie's next move would be. We'd already talked this over, and I told her I'd understand if things got too dicey and we needed to back out of the tournament. Which why I was shocked when my usually rational and cool-headed girlfriend fucking spat at the guy.

"Fuck you!"

I... blinked at her in shock. What was she doing?

Miles seemed thrown as well. "You realize you're throwing away any chances for a peaceful resolution?" If he was trying to talk her down, he fucking sucked at it. Nobody liked being patronized, and his tone was pretty condescending.

Callie just sneered at him. "You assholes just attacked my boyfriend right in front of me. It wasn't a tournament match—you sucker punched him. If he wasn't as good as he was he'd never have made it in here and would probably be out there as a hostage, or worse, a corpse. So no, I won't reconsider or rephrase. Fuck. You. If you'd made the offer before attacking I might have accepted—gods know I've considered pulling out of this mess —but if you think I'm going to let some bullying assholes tell me how to live my life, your intelligence is as pathetic and minimal as your wispy little mustache."

I burst out laughing, and everyone turned to look at me, but I just shrugged, ignoring them all to turn and grin at Callie. "I'm so proud of you right now I can't even stand it. You really took that whole 'do stupid shit because you feel like it' thing to heart, huh?"

She rolled her eyes. "Honey, if you aren't going to be helpful, please shut up." I snickered but didn't say anything else.

"Excuse me," Benny said in an offended tone. "Shouldn't *we* have a say in this too?" We both looked at him and he stuck out his chin. "I mean, I don't think we should surrender, but it would be nice to be asked."

I scoffed at him. "You aren't even on the team. Abel and Mel might have a say, but let's be honest, it'll be a cold day in hell before Abel walks away from a fight, and Mel won't let him run off and punch some random assassins on his own. You two won't even be targets."

Miles, who was looking annoyed at this point, cleared his throat. "If you are quite finished, I take it that your answer is no, and so we will move onto more… forceful methods of persuasion. I admit, I shall perhaps enjoy this more than is proper. You've all been quite rude."

"Oh kiss my ass," I said indignantly. "You came here to fucking attack us." I looked around. "Dibs on top hat. I want to light him on fire a little bit."

Surprisingly, that seemed to annoy Teague. "Can he just call dibs like that?" Everyone looked at him, and he said defensively. "It seems a bit childish is all."

Callie clicked her tongue reproachfully. "Doesn't even respect dibs. Pirates. You all have no sense of honor. If we don't submit to dibs we're no better than animals. It's like ignoring when someone calls shotgun. Some things just aren't done."

Miles had apparently had enough, because he made a sharp motion with his cane and the figures surrounding Rime's dome of ice all moved at once, each condensing a different kind of energy. I saw a few flashes of fire, that same acidic purple sludge, and a few others, all collecting above one guy holding up what looked like some kind of empty glass hammer.

As they channeled the energy to him, he siphoned it into the hammer, which began to fill with a riotous cascade of all the colors from the different energy types. I'd assumed they encircled us for some sort of joint strike, but it looked like they were just trying to block us off as this one guy built up his attack.

When the hammer was full he stepped forward and, with a heave, slammed it down on the dome. Rime had been watching it grimly and was preparing to tank it, but at the last minute I saw a warping in the air. Abel manifested a massive palm outside the dome, space warping as it waved through the intervening area. I expected a slipstream like usual to guide the hammer out of the way, but to my shock the F-ranked hammer slammed into the hand manifestation and *shattered* it.

Abel grunted in pain, and I saw his hand flash and begin to blacken and crack. Jessie hurried forward, laying hands on him as Mallory took up his other side, the two of them treating his hand together. Still, despite the breakage, he'd managed to divert the hammer enough that it hit at an angle and skittered off, only cracking the dome instead of shattering it like I suspected would have happened.

There was a cavernous boom as the hammer hit the ground off to one side of the dome, shattering the pavement of the parking lot and creating a massive crater beside us. As the dust and debris slowly cleared away, we all braced for a second attack, but the guy who conjured the hammer looked completely wiped out by the move.

Miles glared in irritation as Abel stood back up, flexing his now repaired hand. I was amazed to see that the water-based healing energy had fed into Jessie's life force and compounded the effect, knitting Abel's hand back together despite it having been damaged by a higher ranked enemy.

"Fine," Miles spat. "Your little shield is still up. But we'll have it demolished within the next ten minutes even without Samuel's ability. What are you going to do, just sit inside and wait for us to come get you?"

Callie actually started laughing. "Oh we won't need to do that—I know something you don't seem to be aware of." Her tone was smug, and I felt her brutal amusement over the bond, though I had no clue what it pertained to.

The monocled man jeered. "And what, pray tell, might that be?"

Callie's grin got sharper. "I know that there were thirteen people inside this dome a minute ago." My eyes widened even as Miles's did, and I quickly looked around, checking the number of people nearby, only to realize that the quadruplets had vanished, each using the cover of the dust to exit the dome.

Miles spun to scream a warning, but it was too late. Four dark forms appeared behind the encircling F-rankers, each one landing a textbook perfect sneak attack with either a small blade or some kind of power. Seizing on the moment, Rime dropped the shield, and the rest of us blurred forward, Rime engaging the last remaining F-ranked as I went for Miles.

Everything became a blur of motion, violence, and power. Abel and Mel joined up with Teague and his people as they hit the small crowd of G-rankers. I cast poison fire on my cane and triggered a fire attack through it, creating a massive wave of green flame that headed right for Miles.

Callie circled around behind him to attack from his blind spot, and I smirked behind my mask where it wouldn't give anything away. She was technically honoring my dibs, but I would definitely be complaining about the interference later. For now I just focused on the battle. We needed to capture a few of these bastards. I had questions.

Chapter Twenty-Nine

"WELL THAT WAS ANTICLIMACTIC," Teague said with a frown. "I was expecting this to be some huge ruckus, but someone"—he glared at Abel—"wasn't leaving any enemies for the rest of us."

My mentor snickered, and the rest of us just rolled our eyes. None of us were surprised by that observation. Abel was a Master Candidate. If they had someone below F-rank that could take him out, they wouldn't be hired assassins—they would be their own faction and probably *in* the tournament. The more pertinent information was that Teague and the others were willing to throw in with us without blinking, which was pretty cool of them.

Callie cleared her throat and turned to the captain. "We still have to thank you for standing with us. This would have been harder on our own, though the most credit belongs to the four." She looked at the black robed quadruplets. "I realize your strike looked easy, but as someone who fights with a partner, I know how difficult it is to execute a four person stealth attack like that. If any of you had been even a split second off you'd have alerted the enemy and one or two might have gotten away. Thank you."

The four nodded. They rarely spoke in front of other people, so that was probably the best she would get. Some kind of edgy assassin mystique thing probably. I looked down at Miles, who was moaning weakly on the ground. We'd taken him apart without much trouble. I'd expected him to be strong, but Callie and I together could take down a new F-ranker, which put us in the odd position of being much too strong as a duo for most G-rankers, but not good enough to fight up ranks individually.

I walked over to the burned but already healing mercenary and kicked him in the most damaged spot I could find. He whined and jerked, eyes opening blearily as he glared up at me. I grinned at him—not that he could see it behind my mask, but I'm sure my voice conveyed my amusement. "Aww, don't look so mad. I stopped you from bleeding too much, you should be thanking me."

He practically snarled as he climbed to his hands and knees. "You *cauterized* them. With *poison*. And your stab-happy harlot was the one who—"

I swung my cane down sharply, smashing it into the ground close enough to his head to send chunks of rock at his face. He squealed and backpedaled, looking up at me in fear.

"You," I said calmly, "should watch your mouth when you talk about my partner. We might need information from you, but we can always hire a necromancer to get it out of your corpse." That was a bluff. I wouldn't kill someone for bad mouthing my girlfriend. I would kick the living shit out of him if he didn't watch his tone, though, and putting the fear of me in him might make this whole thing go faster.

He seemed almost… offended. "Fine. I'll be polite then. Honestly, no one has any etiquette anymore. Can't even let a man bemoan his own capture." He snorted, waving me off. "Well, go ahead. Ask what you want. Not that it'll do you much good, I'm on contract, and my NDA is nearly ironclad. Unless you have an Oathbreaker on staff you're out of luck."

I looked at Callie, sending my impressions through the bond so she knew what I wanted. She nodded, trusting me to take the lead. Good. I had ways of handling this.

I turned back to the man. "See, I believe you. I believe that you can't tell me a single thing about your client. Anyone with common sense would have made damn sure of that. I *also* believe that you would have known that going in, and that you wouldn't be so naive as to trust your client completely."

The smug amusement that had been bubbling up after he deflected me with the NDA comment was replaced with wariness. "I don't know what you're talking about," he said flatly.

"Sure you do," I responded with a grin. "I'm talking about insurance. You're a local boy, I can tell, and you might work with local forces based on their credibility. But this mess is ass deep in tournament politics, which means some of the parties involved are decidedly not local. A smart guy such as yourself wouldn't trust strangers as far as he could throw them. Maybe not even that far."

I crouched down next to him, chucking him under the chin with a finger. "See, I know a thing or two about contracts, and one of the biggest flaws in a contract is that it only covers as much as the author can think to add. That's what loopholes are, things people forget to mention. That NDA for instance, would prevent you from talking about your client, but if, say, you were a very paranoid person and followed that client and happened to see who they might be meeting with, *that* person wouldn't be covered under contractual confidentiality, since the client would have no reason to add them."

Despite our involvement in political messes, I had no desire to expand my political toolbox—politics annoyed me. But dealing with sneaky shit like this was becoming second nature. Spending so much time in the WCP was helping me expand my worldview, and combined with my contracts skill, I was figuring out all sorts of new ways to deal with people.

Miles's face paled noticeably, which meant I had hit the nail on the head.

"If," he said quietly, "and I do mean *if* I had done such a thing, that information would simply be insurance in case of difficulties with the client. It wouldn't be for sale. If it got out that I was collecting and passing information on clients, the mercenary union would have my head."

I paused. "Mercenary union?"

Abel piped up from off to one side. "Mercs traditionally don't get to E-rank and when they do, they tend to join a faction because of the offered terms. A few decades ago, though, a particularly dangerous mercenary who called himself Rattling Bones established an organization for mercenaries in the city, topside and bottom. Over the years, six more E-rankers have joined the union. It's nowhere near enough to be on the same level as the major factions, but very few of the subfactions have the muscle to make trouble with the union."

Which meant Melinda and Alexander didn't. I hadn't expected that, but it wasn't like I didn't have an answer for it. "The same logic applies. The information isn't covered in the contract, and the insurance was only necessary because you were misinformed of our capabilities. Your client screwed you, simple as that. Did they tell you that one of your targets was directly representing the Wish Curse Palace as a Candidate?"

Telling him that was a calculated risk. Now that we were working with Frostbite, word would spread up here soon enough anyway—might as well get something out of it. His face paled even further at the words, so clearly they hadn't mentioned that. Hell, I wasn't even sure whoever hired him had known, but it was enough of an excuse that he could tell us without compromising his reputation.

"You'll let me go if I tell you?" His voice wasn't confident or even resigned anymore. He sounded scared. Like someone who had just found out the pool they were swimming in connected to the ocean, and there were sharks in the water.

I looked at Callie, and she nodded. She didn't want to kill some random mercenary either. This guy had come at us to injure, even if he'd been a dick about it. I genuinely believed that he wasn't trying to kill us.

"Yes," I said reassuringly. "We'll let you go if you tell us." He started to relax but I cut in sharply. "Assuming you have actual information. If you're stringing us along we'll hand you over to the Unity and let them deal with you."

That was the furthest I was willing to take the threat, and it seemed like it was enough. "I was approached by... a certain party." He said carefully. "A few days ago. The job was quick and easy, but I knew that a lot of other mercs in the city had been contacted. Outsiders showing up and then a massive operation going down? That stank of trouble. So I did what I do. I reached out to an associate of mine and arranged to have my client followed discretely. I didn't tell him what he was doing, obviously—that would have violated the NDA—but we've worked together on jobs like this before."

He groaned in pain as he sat up but settled down after a second. Callie gestured to Jessie and she stepped forward, Benny at her side, to start patching him up a bit. "They were paranoid, of course," he continued after he got a bit of relief. "Most people I work with are. But the big trap about paranoia is that it's self-congratulating. If someone thinks they're being followed and takes precautions, once that's done their own bias tells them they must be safe. We've been at this a while. My guy stuck to them, and eventually they led us to who we needed."

I groaned. "What are you, hourly? This glimpse into the inner workings of the life of a mercenary is fascinating, but I don't need all the set up. Get to the point."

He chuckled. "Sorry. Right. Anyway, I put my guy on their trail and he followed them for a bit. He eventually ended up following the target back to a meeting at the Academy. He met with one of the students and exchanged an envelope, then chatted for a while and left. My guy couldn't hear what they said, they used Stealth Skills, but the client didn't go anywhere else until our next meeting."

"Ok," I said slowly, "that helps a bit, but there are a million students at the academy. Plus we know that the faction behind this is most likely one of the five, since any smaller group would be insane to try to bully a bunch of representatives from the largest forces in the universe. Must be someone else." I sighed. "It's fine though, you gave us what you had. You can go."

He shook his head. "No. That's just it. The person my client met with wasn't a member of the Unity at all. They were a student at the academy, but they were there on some kind of diplomatic mission or something."

I felt the bottom drop out of my stomach as he said that, and desperately hoped his answer to my next question wasn't what I was pretty sure it would be. My voice was rough with shock as I forced myself to ask. "Did... did he give you a description of this contact by any chance? Maybe some distinguishing features that could be used to identify them if we run into them later?"

"Oh sure," he said casually, unaware he was throwing a lit stick of dynamite into the morale of my entire team. "He was actually pretty excited about it. There aren't many of her kind around Callus after all, and definitely almost none at the Academy. Like I said, diplomatic mission or something. Guess you don't forget the first time you see an elf."

We all turned to look at Benny, and even with his mask I could see my friend's face paling. We only knew one elf at the academy, and she was indeed on a diplomatic mission. So the question was, why had Celine just arranged to have us attacked by mercenaries?

154

Chapter Thirty

BENNY WAS, understandably, not at all thrilled to find out his girlfriend hired people to assault and possibly murder us. I was still shaky on what their orders had been, but regardless of whether the intent was to take our lives, it had clearly been to at least screw us over, and my best friend was devastated.

We debated over what to do for a short while, but in the end, we only really had one option. We headed for the Academy to talk to Celine. I wasn't sure what she might have to say, but in the end, she deserved a chance to speak her piece, and Benny deserved a chance to hear it.

Jessie, to my surprise, was livid. She and Celine had bonded during the siege, and she and Benny had gotten closer waiting for us during our time in Doomtown. For her own sake I hoped the elf had a good explanation for all this.

We were all unusually quiet during the ride, arranging to meet up with Teague and the others later while we went and handled what could only be described as personal business.

I expected Benny to hang back when we arrived and let Callie and I take the lead since this would already be hard on him, but my friend was the first one out of the car. We had to hurry to catch up as he purposefully strode through the campus, ignoring everyone as he approached the dorm where Grimmengap lived. When he arrived, he pounded on the door calmly, still and cold as he waited for someone to answer.

Sarah was the one who opened the door. "Oh!" she said happily. "Hey guys. I thought you had your match today? How did it go?" The soft spoken blonde was as happy and upbeat as usual, but when she saw our faces, her smile wilted a bit. "Ah, not so good then?"

That was a reasonable conclusion to come to, but Benny just shook his head. "They did fine. Is Cel here? I need to talk to her."

"Sure..." Sarah said slowly, seeming unsure what to make of this sudden and apparently unpleasant visit. "She's in her room. She's not feeling well today. Guess she had some trouble sleeping last night."

Benny seemed to almost react to that, his eyes flickering with a bit of hope before he squashed it down. "She'll want to see me. It's important. Tell her we met some friends of hers outside the arena and wanted to talk about them." His voice was thick and raspy, as if he was slightly sick, and I felt my heart clench for him, knowing how awful this must be.

Benny hadn't been in Doomtown with us, hadn't been in the tournament or involved in our dueling training. He'd been doing his own training some of that time sure, but he'd also been spending most of his time with Celine, getting closer to her and getting to know and care about her. I tried to imagine how I would feel knowing that Callie had potentially been planning to stab me in the back for our whole relationship, and I just... couldn't.

Clearly sensing my best friend's seriousness, Sarah nodded and turned, hurrying back inside to ask her team leader what to do. She came back a minute later looking worried. "She says you guys can come back." She paused. "Are you sure it needs to be right now? She looks really bad."

I bet she did. But we just shook our heads and pushed past. Abel and Mel hung back, since this wasn't really their deal. Mel intercepted Sarah, asking the girl about the wolves they had sleeping around the dorm, while Abel started chatting up Martin, much to my relief and gratitude.

We headed back to Celine's room, and when we knocked on the door, a faint voice told us to come in. Celine was sitting at the mirror, brushing her hair. Sarah hadn't been kidding—she looked... *bad.* Dark circles under her eyes, sunken cheeks, and a dull expression somehow different from her normally placid countenance. Her eyes stayed locked on the mirror for a second when we entered, before dragging dazedly over to us.

"Oh," she said in a quavering voice. "Hello everyone. I was glad to hear about your match going well. Sarah said you met some friends of mine?" Her tone was high and kind of unsteady, like she was trying not to cry, and I noted that this was probably the most emotional I'd ever seen her. Benny had been coldly furious this whole time, but I could see real concern on his face, and I didn't blame him.

He didn't let it deter him though, forcing himself to focus on the pain he was feeling. "Yeah," he said lightly. "We met some people who mentioned knowing you. Guy named Miles, and a few people from the mercenary guild. They're friends of a friend apparently."

She swallowed hard. "Ah. Those friends." She closed her eyes, taking a shaky breath. "That's… unfortunate."

"Unfortunate?" said Benny calmly. "Why is it unfortunate Celine? Is it unfortunate that you betrayed all your friends and had us attacked? Is it unfortunate that we found out? Or is it unfortunate that you had to waste all your time pretending to give a shit about me to accomplish your mission? Maybe it's unfortunate we didn't just die and save you from this conversation."

Her eyes snapped open as she whirled to stare at him frantically. "No!" I was shocked by the vehemence in her voice, and from their reactions so were the others. She was… well I wasn't sure what she was, but it was certainly dramatic. "No one was supposed to die. No one was supposed to even get seriously hurt. I was *very* clear about that. I hired *five* F-rankers to counter your minder, made sure that they would strike when you were in a small group and overwhelm you."

She was almost pleading as she said it. "There were so many of them so they could handle you without any danger. You weren't in harm's way at all. I made sure of it. I know that doesn't make it better, but I did my best to make sure you would be as safe as possible."

Benny laughed coldly. "Oh, I guess I should be grateful. My girlfriend hired a bunch of thugs to beat me and my friends, but only a *little* bit." He threw his hands up. "All better! That fixes things."

The groan of frustration that came out of her mouth was almost animalistic in intensity. "I didn't *want* to do it. But if I didn't, one of the others would have handled the hiring and they might have sent people to actually kill you. I was *trying* to keep you safe." Her eyes frantically scanned over all of us. "Please. I didn't want anyone to get hurt. I was trying to protect you all. I *do* care about you Benicio. That's why I made my sister give me this assignment."

"Ok," he said casually. "So you care. Not enough to be loyal to me. Not enough to pick me over your family, but sure, let's say you care. How long have you been planning this?"

Callie cut in. "From the beginning," she said solemnly. "That was why they sent you here. For this tournament. You enrolled here at the academy to wait for this. Is it really that big of a deal? Like Impact is important, but a few points of it can't make that much of a difference."

Celine just shook her head sadly. "You're wrong. The competition between the younger generation in the galactic centers is horrifying. A few points of Impact could be the difference between one of the faction heirs claiming glory and resources in several of the major competitions. There's almost nothing the Queen wouldn't do to get even a small advantage for one of her grandsons or granddaughters. It's the same for any of the major factions."

Her eyes pleaded with us almost as fiercely as her voice did. "This isn't going to get better. It's going to get worse. This was the best thing for all of you. If you had agreed to drop out of the tournament early they never would have paid any attention to you." She looked at Callie. "You were thinking about it already. You *told* me that. It would have been so much safer."

"The Faerieland was preparing for this for a while, to invest so much manpower," I said slowly. "They set things up so they could attack all the major factions and weed out as much competition as possible. You mentioned your sister. Is she the higher-up that's responsible for all this?"

Celine's eyes were filling with tears. "Yes," she whispered. "My sister Nalia has been here for quite some time. She has special equipment to prevent herself from being noticed—it suppresses her aura constantly."

Benny snorted. "Well, guess that explains why I never met your mom. She didn't need to meet me not to approve. Bet your sister told you to dump me as soon as you stuck the knife in, huh?"

"I wouldn't!" she snapped. "She told me to end things weeks ago. She said I had enough information, that I'd made inroads with your other friends. She said your training was enough of an excuse to break things off without alienating me, but I wouldn't do it." Her tears were flowing now, but she wasn't sniffling or anything. Celine was a quiet crier.

"I feel so flattered," he said woodenly. "I meant enough to you that you wanted to really drag things out before you threw me under the bus. Glad to know I was at least a good distraction."

Celine looked like she wanted to pull her hair out. I reminded myself not to feel bad for her. This could all be bullshit. She was a courtier—putting on the waterworks and pretending to be upset was her bread and butter. Her shoulders slumped as her eyes dropped to the ground, and I found myself struck by how... defeated she looked.

"I know. I know I can't fix it. I know it's too late. But I am sorry. I just... I thought it would all work out." The desperation leaked away, leaving only hollow emptiness and shame. "I thought I could keep you safe and do my job at the same time. I just... I've never had friends before. Not really. Martin and Sarah, maybe, but it's not the same, they work for me. I wanted to keep you. All of you, but especially you Benicio. I realize that was selfish and stupid."

Her eyes snapped up, emotion filling them again as she forced herself to look him in the eyes. "But if you ever cared enough to listen. Listen now. You don't understand how bad this will get. The Faerieland tried to make the first attack as devastating as possible, but if you drove off your attackers then the less effective groups will have failed as well. Retaliation will be swift and brutal, and it will not be targeted. Please. *Please* drop out of the tournament." She aimed that comment at Callie, obviously. "Please don't get yourselves killed playing above your paygrade."

Benny just shook his head in disgust. "How am I supposed to trust that? How are any of us? How am I supposed to be sure you aren't manipulating us, *again?*"

"Because I love you," she whispered. "Because I don't want you to die. I don't want you to lose your best friend, or to see Shane lose Callie, or to see Jessie die. Because I care," she sighed brokenly. "But you have no reason to believe that. Or anything I say." Her eyes never left his though. "But... do you?"

The anger went out of Benny, and he just looked… tired. Just as tired and sickly as she did. "I don't know what I believe anymore Celine. Thanks for that." Then he turned and walked out of the room, and the elf lost her composure and finally broke down into wracking sobs.

We all left then. As much as we might be angry at her, some things shouldn't be seen by other people.

Chapter Thirty-One

BENNY DIDN'T LOOK SO good. That was to be expected. I left Callie to talk to the others about what we'd learned and deal with the next steps (sometimes it was really nice not to be in charge) and pulled my best friend aside to talk. Since we'd left the dorm he'd been quiet and almost listless. I hated seeing him like that, and I knew if it was me, he would have been right there to talk me through it, so I did the same.

Or rather, I didn't talk. I just sat and waited. We were out behind the house, sitting down and staring off through the yards of the places nearby, and he wasn't saying a word. That was fine, I could do quiet too. I'd leave him to his thoughts until he was ready to say something.

He sat there, staring off into space for a while, before finally saying, "I want to just ignore it."

I shrugged. "Then do that—it's your relationship."

He scowled at me. "What are you? Stupid? She lied to me and almost got us both killed, or at least seriously messed up. I can't just forgive that!"

I looked at him levelly, and his shoulders slumped with a sigh. "Which was your point. So, what? I never talk to her again? I can't even imagine that. I miss her already you know? It's been like an hour since we left and I want to call and hear her voice again."

That I could understand. "I don't think you should just never talk to her again," I said carefully. "Hell, I won't tell you not to forgive her. She was thinking of you at least a bit during all this. But she's also way too subservient to her family and that's going to go badly for you long term." I shrugged. "Which is to say... I don't know? This isn't exactly my area of expertise. I've been in one relationship and I basically won the lottery."

He nodded. "Yeah. I know. I want to forgive her. But I don't want to forgive her because I want to forgive her, you know?" I cocked an eyebrow at him (I'd taken off my mask when I sat down) and he rolled his eyes. "I *mean* that I want to decide based on the merits of her actions, and not be influenced by how much I care about her."

It took real effort to hold back the snickers, and when he looked at me I just lost it and burst out laughing. He just glared at me.

"Are you stupid?" I asked incredulously once I finally stopped cackling. "It's a relationship. How much you care about her is all that matters. You're not a robot, Benny, even if you sometimes swap your parts like one."

"You're a dick," he said flatly. "But... you're not wrong. So what the fuck do I do man? Do I call her up and try to make things work? Do I cut all ties?" He sounded a bit scared.

"I'd say you wait," I said with a shrug. "Give it time. Let yourself cool off, let her think things through. If things are going to work out, you both need to approach it from a place that isn't so... fraught."

"That," came a voice from behind us, "is actually surprisingly good advice." We turned to see Zeke leaning against the wall casually. "Better than I'd have expected from you. That girl of yours really is good for you. Color me surprised—I thought you'd never grow up."

I stuck my tongue out at him, not at all proving his point.

Benny looked up at him calmly. "What are you doing out here Zeke?"

My uncle shrugged. "Heard about your bad news. Wanted to offer my condolences. Also wanted to say not to hold it against her too much. From the sound of it, she tried to shield you more than most would. It can be hard to ignore a family like that when you grow up in it." He sighed. "I dated an elf girl once. Fucking nobility get their claws in deep. They have a long time to practice."

Benny looked troubled. "If it was just me, I could probably get past it. But it wasn't me, was it? I'm not on the team for the tournament. She tried to hurt Shane and Callie. I don't know if I can get over that."

Zeke nodded, walking over to sit down next to us, leaning back against the wall. "You know, I've known you almost your whole life. You were just a little thing when you and Shane became friends. And I've always thought you were good for him, getting him out of his comfort zone. But I never really thought you had what it took to stick it out once he got his ability. I thought he'd leave you behind—that you wouldn't be able to keep up."

"Gee," Benny said sullenly. "Thanks."

"My point," said Zeke firmly as he rolled his eyes, "is that what you just said was probably the first time I've considered you an actual companion rather than a freeloader. Not that I'm saying it was right or wrong. But it makes me think you're the kind of person who might make it out of all this alive."

I looked at him oddly. "I always figured you thought of Benny like my version of you. Dad was raised outside the family, so the two of you were friends before you became the scary badass you are today, right?"

He stared off into the distance, nodding slowly. "Yeah. Yeah we were. But do you think we were the only ones?" he asked sadly. "All the Candidates have friends, kid. They all consider bringing them along. Hell, the whole Candidate process is aimed at cultivating strong allies over time. It's natural to make sure that your earliest and staunchest allies are the ones who come along with you."

That made sense to me, but Zeke wasn't done. "But it usually doesn't happen. Most of them can't keep up. They get left behind, or just decide not to follow. I'm the exception, not the rule. It takes… a certain kind of person to abandon everything they have to follow a friend into the unknown. It's not an easy life." He looked down. "I don't recognize myself some days. The prices I paid weren't on Eli, but they were steep. Some-times I'm not sure if they were worth it."

I looked at him in concern. "So you regret it then? Leaving your planet? Following Dad back to the clan?"

"No," he said thoughtfully. "I guess I don't. If I had regrets I wouldn't have made it this far. Most of them were diluted as I became what I am, if they ever really existed." He looked at Benny. "My point is that you're going to have to make sacrifices for this if you want it. I did. I wasn't sure you could do that before. Now I'm a little more convinced. That said, it might be wise to consider what's going through your head as I say all this. Consider the attachment you feel to your family and your reluctance to leave, and then consider that Celine might be feeling the same things."

Benny's eyes widened as he realized what Zeke was saying in a roundabout way. "What happened to making sacrifices?" he asked wryly.

Zeke shrugged again. "Giving some things up is one thing, but you don't need to give up everything. I'm not saying to get over it or anything, I'm just saying if it's this hard for you to let go of your family, imagine how it must be for her. The fact that she did as much as she did is pretty damn impressive."

That got a thoughtful nod from my best friend, and he drifted off into silence, but I felt the need to ask another question, one that didn't have to do with any of the drama with Celine. "What about you, do you still have a family? You said you had to give up a lot. Have you seen them since? What were they like?"

A wistful smile crossed his face. "I was part of a small clan on a C-ranked planet called Rossus. Elijah's guardian was a crabby old bastard named Edgar, one of his uncles. Malachai always took care of his kids, and Eli and his brother and sister are among his favorites. Edgar was B-rank, like I am now, though much less personable. He ignored Eli mostly, and Eli grew up at my place."

His tone was somehow sad and happy at the same time. Like he missed those days, but thinking about them hurt him. "I lived with my parents, two sisters and three brothers. I was the only one close to Eli. My mother stopped talking to me when I told her I was leaving. My younger sister cried. My older sister told me she understood. My brothers said they hated me."

He chuckled glumly. "I checked in on them a few decades later. Cassia, my older sister, became the matriarch of our clan and reached C-rank. Olena, my younger sister, got married and had three children. My youngest brother Cyrus became an elder in the clan. Cassia boosted the two of them to peak E-rank with pills, and the other two died in a border dispute with a rival family."

164

I was stunned. Zeke, my uncle Zeke, had nieces and nephews. "I'd like to meet them sometime maybe," I said quietly. "If you're interested in letting me."

Chuckling, he patted my back. "Maybe someday, kid. But probably not soon. I stay away from them. You know how Fantasy works. Draws us toward things that are… interesting. I'm real interesting, and having me around might draw them into something more interesting than they can deal with."

Benny was still quiet, but he was looking at Zeke a bit differently.

My uncle smiled at him. "Thank you," he said sincerely. "For being there for him when I can't. And for being a better friend than I gave you credit for." He stood up. "Anyway. I won't bother you all. I'll just leave you with a bit of advice. I don't have any regrets about leaving home, but I *do* have regrets. I can tell you one thing for sure. I regret the people I *didn't* give chances to a hell of a lot more than the ones I did, even when it didn't turn out well."

With that uncharacteristic bit of seriousness Zeke turned and strolled away, leaving Benny to stare thoughtfully off into the distance. I clapped him on the shoulder and got up to go inside. He'd talked, he'd listened, and now he needed to process. Benny had always been like that. Once he heard what he needed to hear he needed time for it to sink in.

I headed back in to meet up with Callie, who was talking to the others, and slipped my hand into hers, twining our fingers together. She didn't stop talking, though I caught a flash of a smile at the corners of her mouth as she squeezed back. Seeing how bad Benny was feeling over Celine did one good thing at least—it reminded me how lucky I was.

Sadly being romantically lucky didn't make me lucky in other ways. We knew more about this mess now. The main antagonist from the Faerieland was a female E-ranked elf named Nalia, and she didn't seem to know I was a Candidate though she almost definitely knew about Mom given Grimmengap had been there for Aiden's explanation about that.

Which meant she didn't know about Zeke. We still had advantages, but we had to move fast. First step was figuring out where the hell she was.

Chapter Thirty-Two

I WISHED we could have taken the next day off so I could keep Benny company while he thought things through. Sadly, that wasn't in the cards. We had to start looking into our next opponent immediately. We only had the day to prepare for the fifth round, and after the next fight we wouldn't even have that. With three hundred arenas in the city, the fifth round would take place in a single day, as would every round until the eighth. Which meant our downtime was officially gone.

After granting Rime her wishes and passing the elixirs to Benny (all Focus-based, bringing him up to one hundred eighty-three), we headed out to meet up with the other teams we knew in the tournament. Since we had no leads on a new source for the tournament, our best bet was to talk to the other teams, especially the ones who lost, so we could start compiling information on the groups that were still in.

Since the winning groups would only have information on defeated enemies, talking to people like Lament would be pointless. But Silent Dagger's team and Beast Lord Garden would be easily able to share some info. We had them meet us at Deva again because the food there was fantastic. Rime decided to wait outside, not feeling up to a big social event, so it was just Callie and I after Jessie headed off to do some errands.

When we arrived, Sloane and Abigail were sitting on one side of the table, and their teams were mingling on the other. They'd saved seats for Callie and I, and we both plopped down next to them, stopping to order our meals before pleasantries. Once we'd done that Callie gave the other girl a hug. "Hey, Sloane, good to see you. I was sorry to hear you guys got dinged out."

The Beast Lord Initiate frowned, sighing deeply. "Not just me. All of our teams got bounced. Mine was the strongest and with us losing the other three didn't have much chance."

Callie made a sympathetic sound. "I'm sure you guys did great. Winning isn't everything—you'll definitely get some stat points out of the match for putting on a good show." Her tone wasn't conciliatory, more upbeat and positive, and despite seeming to appreciate it I didn't think Sloane was buying.

"No," said the other girl, "we didn't. We got crushed. The Burning Heaven Abyss is one of the factions with a Master Candidate. Their gunner absolutely destroyed us. From what I can tell they built their whole team around him. Two augmenters and a heavy to play defense up close. Their defender is tough too. My teammates double teamed him and couldn't leave a scratch."

Abigail grimaced. "I can sympathize with such sentiments. My own heart grows dark with sorrow as my mortality eclipses my hopes for the future. Curses and malaise on the heads of the swine who divert the paths of our bright destinies, leading us down the road to ruination."

I stared at the Silent Dagger team leader blankly. "I... have absolutely no idea what the hell you just said."

Sloane snickered. "Don't sweat it. You pick up Abby speak pretty fast when you're around her long enough. She basically said 'sucks to be you, I'm pretty pissed at the assholes who beat us too.'"

Callie raised an eyebrow. "Is the whole super-formal-archaic-speech thing really useful? Or is it just a preference thing?"

Abigail smiled serenely. "Tales fly swiftly on wings of whispers of the maiden with the transcendent speech. Worthwhile? Who can say, but the paths we take lead ever to the same peaks, naught a one walks them with less alacrity as can be managed at their utmost."

I tried to puzzle that out, but Callie picked it up first. "Translation: we all do crazy shit to get stronger." She smiled. "Fair point. So what about you guys? Who did you lose to?"

Sloane cut in before Abigail could respond. "Whoa there. Sorry sweetie, but I don't think any of us will get a word of that. They fought the Night Demon Throne. Super creepy group of berserker nutcases. I was actually at their fight. Those weirdos attack each other to boost their power before the fight. They have some kind of ramping ability that makes them stronger the more injured they get."

That didn't sound great. I was about to ask more about them when the scan ring on my finger vibrated. I left Callie to talk things out with the others as I stepped away, answering the call to find a surprising face.

"Celine," I said calmly. "Wasn't expecting to hear from you any time soon. Anything I can help you with?"

The elf girl looked awful. Her eyes were bloodshot and the dark circles around them were deeper, her skin was sallow and waxy, and her gaze was hazy like she was too tired to really function. Her voice was a rasp when she answered. "Benny wouldn't answer my call."

"Can you blame him?" I asked gently. I was at least slightly pissed at her myself, but being an asshole to someone clearly in this much pain seemed like beating a dead horse. That did not mean I was going to humor her. "I don't have anything much to say to you either Celine, so if you don't have anything you need to talk about I'm going to go."

Her eyes cleared, focusing on me as they widened. "No!" she yelped desperately. "Please. No. Wait. I have information. I checked with some of my sources and found out..." She paused, looking around. "Information you can use. I can't talk about it over an unsecured line. It's important though. If you can meet me I can give it to you. I promise it'll be worth your while."

I could only think of one obvious bit of information we could use on short notice—our next opponent. The question was why she would give that information to us when it would be directly counter to the interests of the Faerieland. That very question made this extremely suspicious. "Why would I trust you enough to meet?" I asked blandly.

She sighed. "You shouldn't. I know that. But I had to offer. I used all my resources getting this information. If you are going to use it, you need to do so quickly." The look of frustrated agony on her face was kind of heart rending, especially from the normally taciturn elf. "I... I just want to make things right. I wanted to use the resources I had to do something to help all of you."

"I believe you," came a voice from behind me. I jumped, whirling to find Callie. She shot me a warm smile. "I felt your shock through the bond. This seemed important so I excused myself." She looked back to Celine. "I believe you," she repeated. "But we aren't coming to you. That would be pure idiocy. Coming to see you on campus was a calculated risk because you wouldn't have had time to hear about us finding out and you were in Unity territory, but with prep time I absolutely won't bring my people to a place you'll have an advantage."

Celine's head drooped. "It's fine," she said quietly. "I'll come to you. I can meet you at your place to hand over the info. That way you'll be under the protection of your strongest backers and all your defenses. Is that acceptable?" Her tone was formal in a way that reminded me of the old Celine.

Smiling, Callie nodded, her tone gentler than I'd have expected. "It is. We'll meet you there immediately." I looked at her sharply, but she just ignored me, saying goodbye. Once I shut off the screen her smile dropped and she gave me a worried look. "I know. He might not be ready to see her. He can wait inside. But we need this information. Not to mention this is a good chance for her to show him that she wants to make amends."

I pulled her into my arms happily. "You big softie. You just wanted to give them the chance to start reconciling." She shrugged coolly. Smiling, I let her go and stepped back. "Alright, we should go then. We don't want her to beat us there."

I texted Jessie who was looking at plants nearby to come pick us up, and then Benny to fill him in on the situation as Callie went to say goodbye to the others and apologize for cutting things short. She also paid for the meal, since it had been our invite.

Once Jessie showed up we headed back to the house, filling her in on the way. She was a bit suspicious, having taken Celine's betrayal to heart more than any of us, but when we explained everything she seemed to come around. "Well," she said tightly, "if she's coming to the house where Zeke and the ice queen over there are waiting, I doubt she can cause much trouble." She nodded to Rime, who was in the back seat either pretending to sleep or just ignoring us. "I'm sure you already told Benny about all this?"

"Of course," I said. "He wants to sit in on the meeting actually." She glanced at me in the mirror with concern and I shrugged. "I don't like the idea either, but it's his decision. It's not my place to tell him how to handle his life."

She sighed. "I guess. I don't know. I'm not happy about all this of course, but based on some of our conversations maybe I'm not *totally* surprised." Catching our glances in the mirror she gave a guilty shrug. "Looking back, some of the things we talked about back when we were working on the perimeter for the siege might have hinted a bit at how beholden she was to her family. I just didn't notice it."

She snarled, slapping the steering wheel. "Which is my fault. I'm the one who is supposed to puzzle out stuff like that. The one who gets people to say too much and listens when they do. I dropped the ball, and now Benny is hurting and it's all my fault."

Her voice was raw, and I felt a pang of sympathy. We hadn't really checked in with her about this because Benny was so much more affected. Seemed like she's taken it to heart more than we'd thought she would. Callie leaned forward and squeezed her shoulder.

"Hey," my girlfriend said softly. "Stop that. This is not your fault. It isn't Benny's. This is Celine's mess, and further up the blame chain it's her sister and mother's fault."

I nodded sagely. "It's true. You mess up more than enough. No need to take credit for someone else's mistakes on top of that."

Jessie giggled, rolling her eyes as she flipped me off in the rear-view mirror. As she did that, we finally turned the corner heading back to the house, and we all braced ourselves for the upcoming mess. Regardless of intentions, there was a lot of raw emotion involved here, and this was going to be dramatic and painful for somebody.

As we pulled up, we could see Celine standing outside the house across from Benny. Annoyed we hadn't beaten her here, we hopped out of the car and made our way over to where they were talking.

Benny's face was closed off, but not cold, and as we approached he nodded to us solemnly. "Hey guys, glad you're back. Celine stopped by. She says she has information we can use." He turned back to her, saying flatly, "Go ahead."

She swallowed hard before turning to us. "I've been digging into it, and I've discovered the identity of your next enemy. I wanted to tell you as soon as possible so you can prepare for the fight." She took a deep breath. "Your next battle will be against the Burning Heaven Abyss."

Ah. Well. I could understand why she would think that was urgent. Shit.

Chapter Thirty-Three

AFTER DOING Rime's wishes and handing over the elixirs to Benny (officially maxing out his elixir cap and bringing his Might up to one eighty-nine and his stat total to five hundred and three) we headed for the arena to wait for the match to start, and we went over our various strategies for the fight in the waiting area.

The plan for going up against the Burning Heaven Abyss was pretty much "Abel fights the Master Candidate" again. I had zero delusions that I could beat most Master Candidates, but even less of a hope of taking down a fucking gunslinger who could use the terrifying abilities I'd seen from Abel and Lament. Which left us going up against the other three that Sloane had mentioned.

Two augmenters. Callie and I should be able to take them, but it would be stupid to assume they didn't know that. More likely than not at least one of them would probably be buffing the defender, who was apparently already a total monster. Hell, both augmenters might be doing that, you don't really need more raw power than being a Master Candidate in a tourney like this. Either way, the defender would definitely be sticking close enough to protect those two as well as the gunner.

Unfortunately we had no idea what the gunner's ability was since Sloane hadn't been able to push him to use it. When they finally called us out we moved into the arena slowly and with extreme caution. I was half expecting to be ambushed, but when we stepped onto the sand we found the other team waiting for us calmly.

Burning Heaven Abyss were... impressive. They wore what looked like black leather armor accented with gold and hoods over their heads, with the top halves of their faces hidden by black metal masks that glinted almost like mercury. The cloaks themselves were lined with bright red silk, and a few tassels of red were strategically placed along the armor. They each wore a mantle over their shoulders and gloves, leaving their arms bare from mid bicep to mid forearm, and lined with black tattoos that matched the golden traceries of symbols on the armor.

There were two women and two men, the women almost identical short brunettes, and the two men being a study in contrasts, one tall and muscular with olive skin and one incredibly short and pale with pitch black hair. Based on the holsters on his hips the shorter one was the Master Candidate, but it was jarring to see them standing so orderly and relaxed waiting for us.

The tall man was the one who spoke when we stepped out. Based on the *massive* F-ranked shield on his back he was the defender, and I was kind of annoyed that shields counted as defensive equipment because I was sure he could (and would) smash us over the fucking head with that thing. "Greetings," he said in a resonant baritone.

Callie nodded. "Hello. I'm Nightstrike from the Starchaser Pavilion. These are my teammates, Apollyon, Starbreaker, and Solomon."

"Of course," the said man politely. "I am Raka. These are Sult, Truva, and Forn. We represent the Burning Heaven Abyss." He had an undefinable accent I'd never heard before, something crisp and formal. It brought to mind nobility of some kind.

Forn, the gunner, smirked. "I doubt they know what that is Rak. Remember we're talking to hicks here. Admirable they made it this far, but even among the wider-scale forces we're tougher than most." He sighed, as if he was being given a chore of some kind. "Tell you what. How about you all just concede. No reason for us to slap you around just to be mean. This way you save some face and we don't have to waste the energy stomping your teeth in."

Raka put a hand to his face with a sigh. "Forn, I've told you that making offers like that is counterproductive. They won't be saving face now because you just put it like that and will be almost obligated to fight us. Not to mention your antagonistic and condescending tone."

"Oh," said the smaller man conversationally. Then he shrugged. "My bad." And his hands blurred as he drew both guns and leveled them at us.

The bark of firing pistols filled the air as he unloaded them at us, though I noted he mostly aimed at limbs and other nonlethal spots. Regardless, it didn't matter that much because Abel was just as fast and his own hands blurred. My eyes widened in shock as my mentor pressed his fingers in the air and created a series of finger width spatial slipstreams, one in front of each bullet.

Watching each of the bullets slide around us like that was shocking, especially since something in those guns was propelling them at *absurd* speeds. Forn looked genuinely shocked at the response, telling me he hadn't done much research on us. He calmly ejected the magazines, letting them slip to the ground, and, letting go of his guns midair, withdrew a pair of new ones and calmly reached up to grab one gun after another to reload them.

Abel, not one to let an opening pass him by, stepped forward, vanishing in a blur of warping space to appear in front of the group, throwing a punch at the gunner. Instead of throwing a bus sized punch this time though, he stopped right before he reached them and raised both arms. Space warped and a series of smaller images of his arms were left behind, and when he punched out, the six blows overlapped in a way I'd never seen him do before.

Raka reacted *fast*, managing to get his shield out and slam it into the sand in front of his teammate. There was a catastrophic *boom* as Abel's superimposed blow smashed into the shield and the fucking F-rank artifact *cracked*. Granted, it was a really small crack, but still. The explosion of sand and force would probably have blown the defender away if Sult and Truva, the twins, hadn't lashed out a hand each to augment his power.

Still, even with the boost, the explosive pressure of that single punch hurled the team apart. Raka was forced to dive for the twins, who were the much weaker part of their party, leaving Forn open as he brought his now reloaded guns back up to bear on Abel.

A pair of train sized barrels appeared in the air, and Forn blitzed a series of shots at Abel, absolutely monstrous bullets tearing through the air at my teacher. Abel raised both hands and manifested a pair of palm images that neatly redirected the flurry of bullets, taking a step closer with each movement.

Sadly I wasn't able to watch too closely because I had to back up Mel, who was in the midst of attacking Raka as buffed by the two girls. The big bastard was strong enough to tank what I was pretty sure was the first serious punch I'd seen Abel ever throw, and sure enough, when we got in close we realized he was much stronger than any of us individually.

Mel, being a fire user, was monstrously stacked on Might, so she wasn't exactly helpless, and combined with the flames themselves was able to at least get his attention, but he'd condensed the sand around him into some kind of earthen battle form and the heat wasn't getting to him.

He swung the shield forward at her like a club, and I lashed out with my cane, touching Mel's shoulder and focusing as I triggered my strongest defensive ability over her whole body. The strain of using Stone Limb across a whole person and triggering a density-shifted triple-strength attack and a Mercy Kill, along with Consecration of Flame just for the boost, was almost too much for me on such short notice. But I felt the bond flex as Callie took on some of the strain, allowing me to get away with the move with only a quick burst of head pain.

Even with the huge increase in power from the gala training, that had been rough. It was enough, though—the powerful shield blow stopped, only slamming Mel back instead of seriously injuring her. As she caught her footing again, she roared with effort, and a massive wave of flames appeared behind her before condensing into a huge fiery avatar of herself. She snarled and slammed her palms together and the avatar condensed, layering over her body and turning the magma-covered figure into a living statue of flame.

She hauled back with a roar of rage and, driving her fist forward with almost as much power as I'd seen from Abel, smashed it into the cracked shield.

There was a tortured groan from the metal as the already fractured artifact was superheated and the crack widened. Before the man could adjust, a massive hammer of shadow slammed into him, sending him sprawling. I triggered Double Trouble, appearing behind him, and swung my cane (which I'd spent all of yesterday charging up a blow for) at the shield. I triggered another triple-strength density-shifted blow and a Mercy Kill as I released all that stored up power.

Two things happened when I did that. First. The still fragile shield finally broke under the immense amount of power I'd had stored in my cane. Second. My cane fucking *exploded*. Without even thinking I released the thing and triggered Double Trouble as fast as I could, just in time to *mostly* avoid the fucking conflagration of toxic flame as the shattering cane released not only the stored force, but all the power inside it at once.

I cursed, dropping to my knees and holding my currently charred arm, which had been flash fried even under my armor, though the F-rank defensive item had mostly spared me from the poison aspect of the flame. I triggered a healing burst and scan heal, and when that wasn't enough did two more for good measure. I almost groaned with relief as my skin started the repair itself.

Once I attended to my injuries I looked up and around, trying to figure out what had happened. Raka... looked bad. He wasn't dead, and I dropped the poison fire skill instantly so he wouldn't die, but he looked like a melted action figure. I winced at the twisted rock armor that had warped onto his very badly burned flesh.

The twins were staring in horror, and at my glance immediately dropped to their knees, putting their hands behind their heads. I felt kind of bad. I could hear the booms of Abel dealing with the other Master Candidate but I didn't have the spare attention for it as I sprinted over to where our opponent was. Kneeling down, I started peeling off the rock as quickly as possible.

There was... a lot of skin and muscle that came up with it, but I used scan heal again and started dumping in healing bursts. I couldn't do more than five apparently, because his body just wouldn't accept more life energy at that point, but that seemed to be enough.

It took me a few minutes, but I got all the rock off him and his skin had healed enough to cover all the exposed muscle. Knowing he was going to live I exhaled in relief and found a hand on my shoulder. I looked up to see the others around us. Forn was beaten pretty badly but he looked more focused on his teammate. I couldn't imagine what this must look like to them, but I was just glad I hadn't accidentally killed someone.

Still... I guess this was a win. Gods I hoped the prize was worth all this.

Chapter Thirty-Four

THE FIRST THING the other team did was check on Raka. Which was completely reasonable given how terrible that had to have been. "I am so sorry," I said quickly. "I don't know what the hell happened there. I wanted to win but I wouldn't have done... *that*. Hell, I couldn't have done that. I have no idea how or why that even happened."

Abel sighed. "Not your fault. I was going to tell you to get a new weapon, but I didn't expect it to be an issue. Figured you'd make the jump after rank up. Wear and tear are inevitable, but it was the combination of that cane having a *massive* amount of power stockpiled and slamming it into a higher-ranking artifact. It was a freak accident." He looked down at Raka. "You okay?"

The big man had woken up and one of the twins was helping him sit up. He nodded. "I'm fine. That was... truly unpleasant. But it was clear it was unintentional and the healing you gave me is helping immensely. I'm not exactly in perfect shape now, but I'm on the mend."

Forn looked relieved. "Good. And don't feel too bad about it. That was pretty brutal, but we wouldn't have won anyway." He nodded to Abel. "Their boy over there is a straight up monster. I didn't even know planets this low level could *have* Master Candidates."

Helping Raka up, he waved us over to their waiting area, and we followed them in.

"So," Callie said as we trailed behind them, giving Raka some time to walk a bit slower. "I'm guessing the lot of you got attacked before this round, same as we did? Not that I know which faction you're with, but it seems pretty universal."

I missed the days when I could just assume we were dealing with the Unity or WCP. This whole tournament had become a mess of epic proportions.

Raka nodded. "We were. As for our interests... Well that isn't a secret anymore I suppose. We were representing the Black Sorrow Cult. They contacted several rim factions about contracts to sign over the spots if they won. They might be lunatics, but they're well-funded lunatics."

I grimaced. "They can afford that? Blowing a sizable bribe on presumably dozens of teams to stack the deck just in the event one of them wins?" I really didn't like when my enemies showed themselves to be competent. Competent and wealthy seemed like an even worse combo. They were a massive faction, but their border outpost should have been the main force behind this push. I wouldn't have expected them to have that much cash to throw around.

The big man snorted. "You don't get the stakes here. These resources are rare on a universal scale. Regional power games aren't the only thing at play. The Moonglow Dew will be funneled to their main heirs and will be a huge benefit during the coming years. The major factions are constantly at odds—anything that will put them ahead for a generation is a new benefit. This tournament could very well be the deciding factor for the lineup of the next Unlucky Thirteen."

I hadn't considered that. It made a lot of sense though. The Wishmaster was an automatic pass to the Unlucky Thirteen, but knowing what I knew about cultivation I imagined those other slots were fiercely fought over. Universal infamy would skyrocket the cultivation of anyone on that list.

"Well damn," Callie said with a grimace. "That makes this a bit wider scale than expected. How is this planet not crawling with ringers then?"

"Because it's one of many," I said slowly. "This is the smallest most back-water System in the Cluster. With that many points of attack it's no wonder most of the larger forces didn't bother with us. They went for the bigger Systems where they would be able to exert more pressure."

Internal System politics were one thing, but there was no way that the Black Sorrow Cult could have sent, say, a B-ranker like Zeke, to put direct pressure on the proceedings. The stratification of power was an important factor of how the universe ran. Pushing and bending rules was one thing, but the only real reason Zeke was able to move into his spot in Callus was the unique neutral reputation of the WCP.

Callie sighed. "This is just going to get worse. This round is only going to have three hundred teams, which means we're at the point where we'll be fighting every day. The closer we get to the endgame, the more frantic the other factions will get. We'll definitely see some kind of attack tonight."

"We have Rime and Frostbite already involved though," I pointed out. "Can we arrange for them to meet us? Our enemies haven't attacked yet, so clearly they have some kind of limit on what they'll do." I didn't relish the thought of trying to fight another hit squad with my head thumping like a bass drum.

To my surprise, Raka cut in. "They can't ambush you again. Not so soon. Rajak is a major metropolis with a huge Unity presence. They would have needed to make arrangements for the attack on us the other day. People would have needed to be bribed to ignore signs and leave gaps in security. There's no way anyone can pull something like that off again a few days later. There will be too many eyes on it."

Callie nodded thoughtfully. "That's… probably true. But it means we're going to have to deal with an attack later tonight or tomorrow morning. Probably tonight." She stared at him curiously. "The next round of attacks might very well be from the Black Sorrow Cult themselves. Wouldn't tipping us off probably be a violation of the terms of your contract? Why help us?"

He shrugged. "Our contract only lasted until we got booted. Plus I'm not a fan of the lunatics. We took their money because it was beneficial—that doesn't mean we're loyal to them."

We talked for a bit longer before they all said goodbye and left, getting their scan ring numbers to keep in contact.

After we headed outside, we met up with Rime and filled her in on what might be coming down the pipe. She grimaced at the news. "An assassination attempt? Are we going to be seeing them attack the house tonight? We might want to invite your E-rank friends over just in case."

I shook my head, making sure my Stealth Skill was keeping my voice from spreading past our little circle. "No. The house isn't just my place—Zeke lives there. The geas prevents him from helping in most circumstances, but attacking the house involves him directly and opens them up to his direct intervention. They might as well kill themselves and save us the trouble at that point."

"So the question is," Abel said in annoyance, "how are they going to hit us? Because it doesn't seem likely they'll ignore us given the Black Sorrow Cult's... contentious relationship with you. If they can't attack at the house or outside the arena, then what are their options?"

"What if they could?" Callie murmured. We all looked at her, and I saw a contemplative look on her face as she went over options. "What if we let them attack us, lined up a trap and used it to sweep up as many of them as possible? We could potentially take out a bunch of their teams before the next round."

I made an uncertain sound. "Assuming we could set it up so we had no chance of losing, what's to say they would even attack us directly? Taking out a bunch more mercenaries isn't likely to affect the outcome of the tournament one way or another."

She shook her head. "No—they'll send their own people. Mercenaries are A, less likely to take the job after we beat the last ones, and B, not going to take this as seriously. Especially after taking out Pietro. This is personal. They'll take the shot if we give it to them, we just need some way to make sure they go down when they do."

That was easier said than done. Without Zeke, we still had some serious firepower, but there was no way they wouldn't be expecting our E-rankers. They'd have counters in place for them, and assuming the dumb assholes weren't stupid enough to jump me personally we'd have no way to counter if they tried to drown us in bodies.

Then I got an idea. "What if they couldn't send anyone above G-rank?" The others looked at me quizzically and I grinned. "Abel, when the guardian enchantment on the labyrinth under the Cavalcade faded, did the place collapse?" I didn't remember if Cicero had mentioned that or not, and honestly even if he had it might have been bullshit—I didn't trust that asshole as far as I could throw the Unity building.

My mentor looked thoughtful. "It... shouldn't have. But that's a dangerous thing to try. It can't take any F-rankers. Our E-ranked backup can prevent

180

them from entering, but it isn't impossible that a bunch of E-rankers might gang up and collapse the thing to kill us all."

I shook my head. "They can't. Being inside means my health is tied to the labyrinth being whole. That means if they try to collapse it with me inside Zeke will need to step in directly. Even if they wouldn't know that, he'd warn them like he did with the cultist."

"That isn't a bad plan at all," Callie said with interest. "We might even be able to talk Raka and the others into leaking the information before they sever ties. The Cult wouldn't even question it. They would need to jump on the chance to get in an attack. We might be able to take out a bunch of teams."

I had to point out the obvious. "How would that affect the tournament? Would they condense the rounds? Also, we need some way to keep them locked up. The teams directly from the Cult will be murderous assholes, but they won't come at us light either. Some of them will probably be the local teams under contract with them. I don't want to kill some faction like the Burning Heaven Abyss."

"I can help with that," Rime said. "Attacking outside the matches is a direct violation of tournament policy. In my capacity as a local executive, or at least the representative of one, I can order their arrest. You'd need to knock them out and hold them until the authorities arrived, but it's more than feasible."

That sounded complicated, but I knew that the Unity could operate in WCP territory unless they were intercepted, and I could make sure that didn't happen. Shadowthorn had come down to save us when we almost got murdered in the underground arena in G-district after all. The labyrinth would keep the big fish off us until the local muscle arrived, and even the Cult wouldn't be stupid enough to engage in a full-on war. They would need to run or get dragged into a huge conflict.

Callie nodded to Abel. "Alright. I know you aren't exactly on good terms with him, but give your brother a call and see if he can give us access. You had that thing built in the first place, right? So it should be within your rights to use it. Unless you think he'll give you trouble?"

Our mentor snorted. "He won't if he knows what's good for him. He's caused enough trouble—he can be a little generous for once."

With that settled, we headed home to get in touch with anyone we thought would be able to help both in or out of the Labyrinth. It was nice to be the ones luring someone *else* into a trap this time.

Chapter Thirty-Five

"So," Mel said to Abel, her tone dripping with relish as we walked into the Cavalcade's entrance. "Did you have to threaten him to get him to cave? Because I loved seeing you do that last time, and watching him get all whiny and stomp his feet would make me smile."

My mentor smirked at that. "No, I didn't threaten him—I just reminded him that it was my labyrinth and that he threw you two in there and I doubt you were the first. Once I implied I might charge him for damages if I found any, he decided pretty quick to help out."

We hadn't been attacked yet, though it was only a matter of time. It had been hours since the match, and we'd gathered most of our G-rank friends here to help out, as well as Rime, Frostbite, Melinda, and Alexander to wait outside and prevent any F-rankers from just shattering the labyrinth with us inside.

The rest of our team was Cark, Lament, Teague, Abigail, and a few other former competitors we had managed to get on board. When we arrived at the tent, Cicero wasn't around. Apparently he'd decided discretion was the better part of valor and had chosen to have his assistant let us in. Probably smart given Mel's extreme dislike of him. Barring intervention from Abel I had no doubt she could easily set him on fire.

Once we arrived, we hopped down into the labyrinth, and I breathed a sigh of relief at the lack of pressure once we did. This team was more than overkill for a bunch of cultists, or even powerful G-rank mercenaries. We were basically untouchable in our level, and I was really hoping to take some of the enemy out ahead of time.

"Wow," Cark said with a whistle. "This place is a dump. Look at all the damage." He kicked a small rock across the hallway, and we could all see the burns, scrapes, and holes from all the traps we'd set off.

"Imagine actually *being* in it," I said in annoyance. "This place was a giant unnecessary pain in the ass. Shame we triggered all the traps though. We might've been able to use some of them." It would be pretty convenient to be able to take some of them out without any effort. We'd picked this place clean for the traps when we'd built up the trap alleys during the siege from the Sanctuary Hall, though, so there wasn't anything to reset.

Abel shrugged. "I designed it to be too annoying for a normal G-ranker to get through. Otherwise Cicero would have just kept sending people in. Honestly if you didn't have a Trap Skill there's no way you'd have made it. Most people would have needed to run it cold, and they'd have died."

Which made me wonder something. "What about Mel?" I asked hesitantly. "Not to bring up a bad time, but she was here when you weren't. For years. Why didn't she run it herself and get the deed?"

"Because she knew I wouldn't want her to," he said with a smile. "She also knew it was safe down there. Without anyone to run the maze, Cicero wasn't going to advertise where it was because he didn't want someone stealing it. He guarded the place and kept an eye out so she didn't have to."

Mel chimed in. "Plus I had no desire to be in charge until much later. I only started making moves to oust that asshole once I felt he'd taken things too far."

"This is a really interesting design," Teague interjected from off to one side. "Who designed this place? I'd love to get them under contract."

Abel chuckled at that. "Mad Madigan built it. He isn't around anymore. Fun fact, designing unstable pocket spaces that can fall into the void at the slightest touch doesn't do much for your life expectancy." He paused. "Well, I mean people assume. No one was there when he died for obvious reasons."

Cark shook his head ruefully. "Crafters. All of them are nuts." He glanced over at Callie and I. "Speaking of crafters with a screw loose, where are Clockwork and Agria? I'd have figured they would be all over this."

I shook my head. "Too dangerous. They're not high enough into G-rank. If this were a few weeks from now it would be a different story, but as they are now, Clockwork is only halfway into G and Agria isn't even that. If not for the nature of this place we might have brought them anyway and let them work with Randall, but since F-rankers are a no-go, they wouldn't be safe down here in the middle of this mess. I expect to never hear the end of it, but we convinced them to watch Cass."

Which was unnecessary since Zeke was there, but we'd cheated and had Cass ask them herself, and Jessie had melted instantly. Benny had pretended not to care, but he'd also caved way easier than I'd expected. Guess it had been long enough since Maria was a kid for him to lose some of his puppy-dog-eye resistance. She'd been a menace when she was younger, and those eyes got her out of a fair amount of trouble with both of us.

Lament looked bored. "When are the enemies going to show up? I want to see what I can do in this kind of place. With such small corridors I bet I won't have space for manifestations. Not in most of it anyway." She turned to Abel with an intrigued look. "Want to have a fight in here? Might be interesting without full use of our disciplines."

"No he does *not*," Mel snapped. "I don't know what your teammates will let you do, but he isn't fighting a Master Candidate in the middle of the tournament outside a match. If you want to fight him you'd better make it to the later rounds so you can get matched up with him."

Lament rolled her eyes, but didn't comment. She took a few steps and then froze. I'd have assumed she took a second to think of a comeback, but Callie had frozen too, and I had enough knowledge of her stats to realize what was going on. I clenched my fists, wishing I had my damn cane, but all I could do was plan to pick something up with the money I'd been saving. I'd hoped to let Jessie and Benny pay me out a bit more before I bought one, but I guessed it wasn't in the cards.

Callie's eyes were scanning the hallway, and the bond was telling me exactly what she was looking for. As I felt a twinge of panic I reacted seamlessly, spinning and releasing a burst of fire from my stockpile behind me, stacked with a Mercy Kill to boost it.

My flames revealed a dark robed form. He roared in pain, distracted just long enough for Abel's fist (only the size of an engine rather than a bus) to smash into him and send him hurtling into the wall. Callie's shadows leapt from the ground as she raised a shield to protect the rest of us. We'd all been on the lookout so there was no chance of serious injury, but that one had been sneakier than expected. I was glad we caught him early.

I cast a dispassionate glance at the robed figures appearing along the hallway. The hoods cast a shadow so deep I couldn't see their faces, sort of like I'd seen from Natalie when I first spotted her. I guessed that kind of disguise was common in larger forces.

"You all look like idiots," I said. "It's like ninety degrees out. You must be sweating like pigs."

Callie snorted out a laugh. She turned to Abigail. "Is the secondary force in position?"

The Silent Dagger Initiate's eyes glowed for a second before she nodded. "They have the way blocked off. No one is getting out of here. Our backup has already started pinning down the others and the authorities have been called. Their choices are either abandon the ones in here or fight the entire Unity security team for the planet."

Frostbite being able to call up Unity forces was a big win for us, since she could get local security to head down here. Just because they were capable didn't mean they'd do so easily, even with us smoothing things over. When an executive of their faction said jump, though, the only answer was how high.

The closest figure, the one who seemed to be in the lead, snarled. "You seek to detain us? No name trash. We alone will be more than a match for you, and your strategy will prove fruitless if we kill you all and remove ourselves from the situation before the local Unity branch can arrive."

Another figure snorted at that. "The fuck you say." The first looked at him. "We're out. We came on contract with you guys, but the stipulations were only for the tournament. I'll return the bonus you paid for this little operation, but I categorically refuse to stick around and get arrested. We'll take our chances with their rear guards."

He turned to leave and the first figure flicked a hand and hurled a wave of pitch-black flame at him. A figure to the side of the target waved a hand and a cascade of purple bubbles filled the hall. The flame hit the bubbles and the black fire tore them apart, but the water inside created steam, blocking the passage from view. When it cleared, the target and seven others were gone.

I wasn't too worried about it. Either the rear guard would catch them, or they'd get outside and probably get picked up by our backup. I turned to face black flame guy. He spun back to us and barked, "Kill them all!" before throwing out his hands again and coating the whole hallway in a sea of dark fire.

Cark roared and hurled a wall of blue flame back at him, but the black fire clearly wasn't your run of the mill flame. I didn't have time to engage though as the golden fist of one of the other figures flashed toward me. I flicked on the overlay, sidestepping as Callie swept in at his feet. He stumbled and fell forward, right into a stomping kick to the head reinforced by Mercy Kill. He was down in one shot and we moved on to the next.

I saw Abel clash against three other fighters while Lament took on four, and Mel joined Cark in pushing back the black flame guy. Callie and I closed on another man, whose hood had fallen back to reveal some sort of man-zebra. I prepared for an attack, but was interrupted by a bang as a howling purple jackal head smashed into the animalistic man, driving him off his feet.

Teague tipped his hat to us as he reloaded and we were free to move on. Between the bond, the overlay, and Balam, me and Callie wove through the crowd of hooded figures like striking cobras, taking them down wherever we hit. I used Touch of Tears sparingly, given my lack of a focus, but it was devastatingly effective.

Finally, we finished off the last one, turning to see Mel and Cark subduing the black flame wielder. Once we finished, we pushed his hood back, and Teague confirmed he was one of the Cult's team leaders, which meant we'd taken out at least some of the competition.

I sighed in relief as we started to cart them out. Callie sidled up next to me, raising an eyebrow. "Everything okay?"

Shaking my head, I stared off after the others. "Not really," I said. "This will get worse before it gets better. We need to fight another team tomorrow and we have no idea who."

She just took my hand and squeezed it. She didn't need to say anything— we'd been here before. All we could do was move forward best we could.

Chapter Thirty-Six

WE MADE it home earlier than expected all things considered, but it was still relatively late. Since we had a battle tomorrow we decided to knock out early, but before we did, I went to go check on Benny. My friend was sitting outside staring up at the stars, and I sat down next to him.

"So, want to talk to me about your meeting with Celine the other day?" I said casually. "I didn't ask because I wanted to respect your privacy."

His lips quirked up in a small smile. "So my privacy isn't important anymore?"

"Nah," I said solemnly. "It was never important—I just forgot that for a minute. Now I remembered that I don't really give a shit when you don't want to talk about stuff so I figured I'd check in." I shot him a smile to let him know I was messing with him, but I didn't offer him an out. If he actually didn't want to talk about it, he'd just tell me to get lost. We were close enough not to need to walk on eggshells.

He snorted. "Thanks for that, dick." He went silent for a bit, obviously choosing his words, but I didn't rush him. "It was... weird. I know we weren't you and Callie with your constant affection and PDA, but I got used to us being... close, in our own way. Seeing her right there and acting like she was a stranger sucked."

"Then why do it?" I said seriously. "You know she wants you back. She turned on her family to help us out for you. Why not just… treat her like you always do?"

Shaking his head, he let out a long sigh. "Because it wouldn't be fair. I don't know if I can get over what she did. I want to. But I don't know if that's going to be enough yet. If I start being affectionate and acting like nothing has changed it'll make her think that I'm already over it all. That'll hurt her more. I may not be happy with her but I still care about her. I don't want to make her suffer for no reason."

I reached out to put my hand on his shoulder. "That's… Shit man, that's so much more mature than I would ever be. When the fuck did you get so much more adult than I am?"

My best friend put on a profound expression. "One such as yourself can never understand my journey. Don't beat yourself up over your failure, someday you too will be as wise and farsighted as I." His faux condescending tone made me snicker, and I flipped him off.

"I've heard people shrink as they get older," I said with an annoying smirk. "Maybe there's some inverse correlation between wisdom and height. Did this new maturity start to show up once you noticed I was taller than you?" My tone was saccharine, and it was my turn to get flipped off.

We talked a bit longer about how he was feeling, and I helped him work through a few things, but mostly it was just an excuse to vent. A lot of feelings had bubbled up for him when he saw her and he needed to let them out. Banter and venting both played a big part in that process. Finally, we said goodnight and I headed off to my room. Callie welcomed me with open arms (literally, the woman clung like a python in her sleep and I'm fairly sure she would have long since choked me to death if I wasn't so much bigger than her) and I finally drifted off to bed.

The next morning everyone seemed quite a bit more relaxed. Sure, we had a fight today, but we'd managed to take out three full teams from the tournament, which wouldn't change the round numbers, but *did* mean that there would be three potential automatic wins available next round. Who knew, maybe we would get one of them.

I granted Rime's wishes, and she paid in Vitality Elixirs that I passed to Jessie, since Benny had hit his cap last time. That brought her Vitality up to a whopping two hundred sixty-three. She also had twenty-five spare points of Might, presumably from her bond with Randall, allowing her physical strength to somewhat keep up with her stamina. At four hundred twenty-eight stat points total, she was closer to the midway point of G-rank than I'd expected.

Once that was out of the way we headed into the arena. We had a wait once we got to the ready room under the stands so I decided to ask something I'd been wondering about. "Once we get through round eight we're starting individual matches. Are they going to be the rapid-fire daily setup like these are starting to be? Because with forty teams breaking down to one hundred sixty contestants, there are more than enough arenas to hammer them out one day at a time."

Callie, who of course had done her homework on the tournament, shook her head. "No. They'll be using four arenas for the early rounds. Ten matches per arena per day. Helps concentrate the audiences in preparation for the finals and semifinals. That means there'll be a four-day break between the ninth and tenth rounds, assuming we get sent out at the beginning which seems likely."

I sighed in relief. I needed to get Jessie and Benny as close to the cap as possible before the tournament ended, since that final month wasn't going to be nearly enough on its own. I'd be able to get them close, and with Randall helping Jessie an extra week or two might get me over the edge. Especially since once I ranked up again I'd have another daily wish. They were already taking jobs together to try to save up for the stats, and that was convenient since I needed cash for my new weapon.

Which I didn't have yet. Unfortunately. I had a few stockpiled contingencies that could help out here, but without my cane to act as a focus, my combat capability had dropped drastically.

Finally they called us out, and all of us filed through the gate, walking out onto the sand to find a familiar face.

The blonde-haired, blue-eyed captain of the Heavensong Tower gave us a friendly smile as we stepped out. "Oh. Hello all! Good to see you. I have to say I wasn't expecting to meet up with your lot so early."

I froze at the sight of him, my veins filling with a cold sense of dread. I had no idea why, honestly. Alec wasn't particularly tall or intimidating, and I doubted he was a Master Candidate or we'd have heard about it by now. Something about him was just... terrifying, though. He reminded me of Abel the few times I'd seen him upset, this sort of predatory edge to his amused gaze that made it seem like he could kill me without blinking.

Behind him stood the rest of his team, who I'd made the mistake of ignoring up to this point. A smaller blue-eyed blonde girl with pigtails, a tall dark-haired girl with olive skin and serious brown eyes, and a dark-skinned man with a shaved head and an intense green stare, who was about the same height as Alec, but twice as wide at the shoulders.

Callie kept her cool (despite me feeling through the bond that she was just as wary as I was) and smiled back. "It'll be an experience, I'll tell you that. Anyone who made it this far must be strong. I'm looking forward to our match. Hope you all don't disappoint us."

The blonde girl with the twin tails giggled. "Oh I doubt that'll be a problem. I bet this match won't last long enough for you to be disappointed."

"Lena," Alec scolded lazily enough to make it clear he wasn't really scolding at all. "There's no need to antagonize our friends here. I'm sure they're very strong. I've heard of some of the teams they've beaten. I have no doubt that they can give us a decent work out." His tone was dripping with sincerity, and despite being almost sure he was mocking us, I couldn't really prove it. Alec was just one of those people that always sounded like they were making fun of you.

The taller woman snorted. "Doubt it. Some backwater Master Candidate isn't enough to stop us. Besides, we can't lose any face for the Church. We've kept ourselves out of the political nonsense so far, but if we don't make an example, we'll bring shame on the faction."

I grimaced at that. Fuck. The Church was involved here too. I'd been wondering where the last of the five factions was in all this, but I'd hoped we were lucky enough to miss them. Apparently not. I looked at Callie, using the bond to ask her if we should share about my mom.

There was no way to be sure that my mother's position would buy us any good will, but it certainly bought us bad will amongst their opposition. She shook her head in a short, sharp motion. Which was fair—there were still cultists here, and finding out I was a "heretic" was sure to make me a target. Though it made me curious. "If you're with the Church, why haven't the Cult members targeted you more specifically?"

I was sure they'd been attacked when we all had, but that wasn't the same as being hunted down like me. Granted, a Saintess was pretty damn high up in the hierarchy of the Church, but still.

Alec shrugged. "The lunatics do what they will. If I had to guess it would be because the Heavensong Tower's affiliation with the Church is distant. We're raised to its tenets, but we're nominally in the Unity's sphere of influence. They probably don't count us. The Church doesn't have many teams here either because we don't work with mercenaries, and there aren't many legacy factions like ours in this System."

Yeah, that sounded about right. Shame—I'd been hoping we could get some backup. Even if sharing in public like this wouldn't work, I was sure Callie and I could find a way to tip them off to my bloodline without everyone and their mother finding out.

The muscular guy with the green eyes sighed. "Can we just start this? I don't feel like sitting around bantering. I didn't get nearly enough sleep last night. Having to do these every day is such a drag." His complaint was said with such soul-crushing boredom that I felt tired just listening to it.

The others rolled their eyes. Lena, the blonde, pointed a finger at him. "Damn it Carlos. Can't you play along? We're supposed to be making an impression here. We'll never be taken seriously if everyone thinks we're lazy bums like you!"

Before he could respond, Alec cut them off. "Enough." The edge of amusement faded for a moment, replaced with a sharp edge. "We're in public. Deal with your nonsense later." He nodded solemnly to Callie. "Sorry about that. They can get carried away sometimes." He smiled menacingly. "To make it up to you, I'll end this quickly so we can all go home."

He tensed and was clearly about to move, when Abel's fist smashed straight out at him. He snarled, and a tornado condensed around his own hand as he lashed out with a four-fingered chop. The wind formed a massive blade and as it did, his hand ignited, creating a slashing wave of golden fire.

It didn't look like peak Intermediate, more like he was using wind and fire manipulation at the same time, but something was off about those flames. Whatever was going on, it split Abel's fist manifestation in half.

Wow. Guess I was right—this was going to be a tough fight.

Chapter Thirty-Seven

I was in shock that Alec had managed to break one of Abel's punches. Seeing as Abel was a Master Candidate with an extremely complimentary ability (albeit one he hadn't really been using just then), it was crazy to me that someone who definitely *wasn't* a Master Candidate had countered his attack.

That giant flame chop had just been a wide scale wind burst that he'd somehow set on fire. The really weird thing was that he was using wind *and* fire. Either he had two abilities (extremely unlikely since my dad's cousin Aiden, the current Wishmaster, was the only person I'd heard of with that distinction) or that had been a Skill that he'd combined with his ability. Or two Skills, since it also seemed like some kind of martial art had been used.

"Hey Starbreaker," I said seriously, "any feedback on that attack? You're our resident firestarter." Something about the flames just then had seemed... different. Not the color (Mel's flames were golden too), but something about the energy that made them up struck me as odd. They looked weird, like I could see a strange shimmer in them.

She sighed. "Those aren't pure flames. I can't tell you what kind of flames they are, but they're mixed with something. Maybe a unique Skill."

Abel nodded. "That was impressive. I think the wind is his ability, but whatever that Skill is synergizes well with it, and it's *really* strong." He cocked his head. "He isn't a Master Candidate, but he's amazingly skilled at using that Skill and his ability in conjunction." Abel reached up and fluidly stripped off his coat, letting the fabric flutter to the ground as he lashed out with a flurry of massive fist images. He didn't use his spatial ability this time either, but it was clear he was being much more serious about his Ragam.

Alec clapped his hands together, and when he drew them apart he was holding a sphere of warped air. Inside the sphere was a single flower made of golden flame. Alec spun the sphere up onto the tip of his finger and then blew on it lightly. It floated up like a soap bubble until it came in contact with one of the descending fist images and then the whole thing destabilized.

The bubble warped, and the flower inside followed suit, becoming unstable and then exploding. The wave of golden flames fluctuated inside the bubble for a second before it popped, and a colossal burst of fire swallowed the air in front of the Heavensong Tower team, consuming the fist images before they got close enough to do damage.

My eyes widened in shock, but Abel just nodded. "Purification." I looked at him quizzically. "The fire purified my fist energy from the blows. My manifestations use a Fantasy base with a heavy Might percentage. It makes them easier to control. The fire eroded the Fantasy, and the Might was consumed to fuel the flames, since fire is almost entirely Might. Annoying."

I stared at him. That explained a few things I'd been interested in knowing. I knew Master Candidates could create manifestations, though he'd implied those were just the most common form that high Intermediate Skills took. Still, those manifestations were standardized, and Intermediate was about branching out and making a technique your own. Finding out the manifestations were created custom from various stat mixtures made a lot of sense.

It also wasn't really important right now. Purification fire wasn't ideal, but I did have a counter for it. I cracked my neck, stepping forward. "Hold on, I'll try next."

I wasn't sure why they were letting us attack, but it felt like a provocation. It didn't matter in the end. We just needed to beat them and it would be fine. Closing my eyes, I pulled up a triple-strength density-shifted flame attack and activated Mercy Kill, Touch of Tears, and Consecration of Flame. The blast hit Alec in a massive burst of dark green fire.

I'd never tried density shifting an actual fireball before, and apparently it was really effective, because the flames seemed to have become ten times more toxic when condensed like that. Combined with all the boosts even Abel looked impressed.

Alec's previously casual expression turned stoic and annoyed and he lashed out with a quick series of punches. Each punch created a wind-based explosion of air that fueled a bigger golden explosion of fire. The series of attacks eroded my fireball, eating away at it until it dispersed, but it took him dozens of attacks, and the blast got much closer than I think he was comfortable with.

Callie gaped at me, and even Abel seemed surprised, but Mel nodded. "Smart. Purification flame is diametrically opposed to something like toxic fire. It's like trying to burn water. It's possible to turn it into steam, but it isn't an efficient process. How many more times can you do that?"

I grimaced. "Myself? Not nearly enough, but I can imbue that skill into your orb so you can throw toxic fire like that." She nodded and held it out, and I placed a hand on the orb, triggering a second Touch of Tears and Consecration of Flame. That should increase her actual flame power too, which would be a big help.

Sadly, showing that we could counter his attack without just relying on Abel meant the spectator sport portion of this was at an end. Lena, the blonde girl, inhaled and then let out a scream of challenge. A deluge of angry red mist spewed forth from her mouth right at us. Abel reacted immediately, cupping his hands in a dome to create a shielding hand manifestation over us.

The red mist hit the shield and stopped, but Abel hissed in pain, and I could see his hands starting to burn under the touch of the corrosive mist. I closed my eyes, using Mistwalking for the first time in a while, and I triggered *another* triple-strength density shift, creating a hyper-dense, extra-powerful mist.

As my mist manifested outside the shield, it began to mix with and disperse the red stuff, both types of mist dissipating as they consumed each other, just like I'd been hoping they would. Lena looked enraged. She screamed again, louder, and vomited another wave of red mist. The tall dark-haired woman clapped her hands and the mist condensed into a rain of sharpened red ice spikes.

The last member of the team, Carlos, snapped his fingers, and the spikes all randomly changed direction. He snapped again and they shifted back after traveling some distance. That trick had spread the spikes across a wide area and then reoriented them on us, and the momentum never stopped, so we had a hundred plus acidic ice shards heading right for us, attempting to turn us into pincushions.

I reached out and grabbed Abel, using triple-strength density shifting and Stone Limb on him, focusing it through the medium of my mentor's skill, or at least trying. He could have obviously resisted (soul manipulation of another person's skill is really easy to counter, especially when your soul is much stronger), but he didn't because we were on the same side.

The folded hand manifestations shielding us (which were touching the sand of the pit) became covered in reinforced earth. It was a really weird thing to see, because for some reason, between the sand and the intangible nature of the manifestations, the stone versions weren't actually opaque. I was able to see as Alec deployed another huge attack.

As the ice spikes hit the manifestations and stopped (though based on Abel's grunt it was painful for him to experience), Alec lashed out with a hundred plus punches. Each punch created another one of those flame flower wind orbs, and they spread along the arena on an unseen wind, circling around to bear down on us.

Though he couldn't use manifestations or create giant versions of that attack, using it a hundred times would accomplish similar things. I knew he wasn't at the peak of Intermediate since he couldn't manifest, but I'd be shocked if the Skill he was using wasn't early Intermediate at least.

Mel snarled, having been focusing her fire energy into the orb for a while for some reason. I was pretty sure she was charging an attack or something, but since she usually used shapes or bursts I wasn't sure why she didn't just launch the attacks directly instead of saving them.

To my shock though, when she made that snarling sound and I turned to watch, I saw her inhale, sucking all the fire energy she'd been condensing into the orb back into her body. She reinforced her physical body with the flames (which made sense since they were technically Might I guess) and her whole form turned green gold. She hissed in pain and I started, realizing she wasn't immune to my poisoned fire.

"Why are you—" I started to ask, but I was cut off when she turned to Abel with a nod. He unfolded his hands, letting the shield around us dissipate, and closed his eyes to concentrate. It took me a second to realize what he was doing, but I finally figured it out as *he* began to glow green gold.

It was their bond—he was using it like Callie and I could to channel a Skill or ability. I was pretty sure he couldn't just *use* her fire, but he *could* use a single attack, which happened to be what she'd stored. She had internalized it despite the pain because otherwise he wouldn't have had access, since the orb was a tool and not an innate part of her.

The air around us filled with hundreds of floating golden flowers in soap bubbles, gently bobbing through the air down toward us. Abel clenched his fists, condensing his spatial energy along the lengths of his arms, and then shot out a few dozen rapid punches. The manifestations in the air were green flaming fists the size of busses, but as they began to move they touched off the flower spheres, which detonated in a chain of explosions.

Callie slammed her hands into the sand, a dome of shadow raising above us as I triggered another density shift and Stone Limb again, reinforcing the shadow dome to withstand the chain reaction.

The area shook as Abel's massive fist images clashed with hundreds of golden flame flower spheres, and while I expected them to be extinguished fast, I hadn't realized how much the poison fire would help with that until the dome came down.

The other team was standing, barely, and the arena was torn to shreds. Based on the area around them, Lena had used her acid mist and the taller woman, whose name I hadn't gotten, had condensed a shield of ice. There was a ton of shrapnel from where the dome had been busted before melting, but from what I could see Carlos had interfered with that weird, momentum shifting power and prevented them from getting pincushioned by their own protections.

Alec looked pretty dead on his feet, and when he saw that we were all completely unharmed, his smug smile became bitter. "Ah." He paused for a beat. "Fine. We concede."

He sounded unhappy, but I respected him for making the call. In their current condition there was no chance of them beating us. Based on the way he was swaying, Alec had nothing left in him to use, anyway.

197

As the match ended I headed forward, deciding to heal them up like I had the last group. Since they were in the Church they might be allies once I mentioned my mom, and if not... we beat them once, and we could do it again.

I could feel Callie's pride as I approached. Seemed like she was happy with how this went. I was too, but I also had a lot of questions. Once they were healed, we'd need to meet with them and clear some things up.

Chapter Thirty-Eight

WE DIDN'T GET ATTACKED after the fifth match, which I attributed to how many of the Cult got cleaned up in the raid last night. Since the other forces were busy recovering (or trying to exploit the Cult's weakness) it was safe enough to bring Alec and crew back to the house with us. Zeke was already gone when we'd come out, as were most of the others, so I assumed they'd beaten us home.

With Rime along I wasn't worried about an attack and the house seemed like the safest place to discuss my mother. I was kind of excited honestly. I knew very little about my mom, and these people were actual *members* of the Church. Granted they were external members, but any A-ranker should be more than well known, and they definitely had some idea about what she was like.

As for why I was so enthusiastic? I guessed deep down I didn't blame my mom as much as my dad for leaving. Seeing what happened to Zeke made me suspect my dad had forced the issue, plus I spent a long while thinking she was dead, so there was a part of me that was still in shock that I even had the chance to meet her someday. I tried to temper that excitement with pragmatism, though—she was an A-ranker, and that meant not really a human with an understandable mindset. What that meant for her specific case wasn't clear, but it would mean something.

We texted Zeke on the way, and he confirmed that he was back at the house waiting. It was skirting the rules to bring them where Zeke could intervene, but since I left things up in the air it shouldn't matter. You could never be too careful—even if they seemed like potential allies, it never hurt to have some insurance. I'd recently learned that the hard way.

"I appreciate the heals," Alec said as we sat in the backseat of the car. "Where exactly is this place?"

All of us easily fit, but the atmosphere was a little weird. None of them knew exactly what was happening. We'd invited them over, but they weren't exactly close to us. I think the only real reason he'd accepted was that we'd already said yes to his party invite and gone in blind, plus we'd healed him.

I was pretty sure he'd warned his own faction before leaving, but coming was still a gutsy move, and I liked him a bit more for it.

"Not far," I said. "We should be there in a few minutes. Can I get you guys something to eat or drink when we get there?"

Callie beamed. "Solomon is a fantastic cook—you should take him up on it. He can whip something up pretty fast."

They waved us off, thanking us but saying they weren't hungry. We chatted a bit about earlier matches in the tournament and just general facts about the planet before finally arriving and going inside. I was glad they seemed to know that we wouldn't speak about private matters until we were somewhere more protected.

Once we were inside, I took off my coat, though I left the mask on for now. I wanted to relax a bit, but I wasn't comfortable showing my face, even if that was stupid because dozens of powerful people saw it in Doomtown. Cass and Cark weren't here, having vacated when we texted just in case, and the animals were in their own building, so it was just us and Zeke, who wasn't visible despite me knowing he was here.

"So, what's all this about?" Alec asked. "We appreciate the heal, but if you're hoping to question us or something we'll have to shut that idea down. You did us a favor, but we're not like those mercenaries the other factions have hired." He seemed on his guard, like we would attack them and force them to tell us their secrets.

I wasn't planning that, and I knew Callie would follow my lead here, since this was my story to tell. I considered how to explain and decided to start by easing their fears. "No—we aren't trying to force you to tell us anything. In fact, I'm hoping you'll listen while I tell *you* something."

Alec raised an eyebrow but didn't say anything, waiting for me to continue. I decided to give him a bit of background. "Did you know," I asked conversationally, "that I had all my stats when I awakened? I was told that's uncommon, and the main reason it happens is that the Ascendant in question had powerful parents. Now I know my dad is powerful, but he isn't someone you should care about. My mother, though—she's A-rank from what I know. And she might be of interest to you all."

"How so?" he said calmly, but I could tell he had at least an idea where this was going. He wasn't an idiot, and for them to care about who my mom was, she'd either need to be a total monster or someone from their faction.

"My mother is a Saintess of the Red Revenant Church," I said matter-of-factly. "It's something that's brought me into conflict with the Cult at least once or twice. I figured if they cared enough to try to murder me over it, you might care enough to be willing to be friends?"

Alec's eyes widened, and his pupils narrowed to pinpricks. He was standing very still, though whether out of fear or some other emotion I had no idea. "There are several hundred Saintesses," he said, his voice radiating an obviously forced calm. "Which one, might I ask, are you related to?"

I shrugged. "My mom's name is Sasha. I'm not sure how many Sasha's might be in the higher ranks of the Church, but one of the crazies who tried to kill me mentioned she was the youngest Saint the Church had, if that helps."

Lena, who had been letting her captain do the talking, *squealed* in glee. "Sasha the *Star Queen?* The Fist of the Radiant Pope herself? Oh my Revenant, are you serious? Can you introduce us? Can I get an autograph? Do you have any pictures?"

She was gushing like I'd told her my mom was her favorite pop singer, which given we were all Ascendants might not be too far off the mark. "Maybe one or two," I said. "She left when I was young, and I'm not sure why. Can you tell me more about her? What do you mean the Star Queen, and who is the Radiant Pope?"

Alec held up a hand to stop her, giving the excited blonde a disapproving frown. "Sorry, Solomon—Lena can't always read the room. I can tell your relationship with your mother isn't exactly close, and I apologize if my teammate was insensitive. I can answer your questions for you, if you'd like. Since *someone* has the social skills of a blunt battle axe."

Lena pouted at him. "Shut up. Just because Mom likes you better doesn't mean you can be mean to me. Daddy says that as the oldest it's your job to help guide me and teach me when I do something wrong. Scolding me in front of new friends isn't very teacher-y of you."

He rolled his eyes. "That isn't a word. And Dad cuts you too much slack because you inherited his ability."

Huh. Guess they were siblings.

Alec turned back to me. "Ignore Lena. I can answer your questions since I'm the *captain of my team,*" he said loudly, clearly aiming that at his sister. "The Radiant Pope is one of the S-ranked Popes of the Red Revenant Church. Most of them are the original disciples the Revenant took in as he was rising to power millennia ago." He paused. "Anyone who hits S-rank attains the Pope Job, but the current Popes are his personal disciples, and they inherited some of his powerful Skills. The Radiant Pope is the youngest of the original disciples."

Lena nodded enthusiastically. "He's also the Star Queen's *dad.* She inherited his ability, the flames of purification, but she altered it as she progressed. When she fights, she glows like a star and her physical power is unparalleled. It's crazy, and some people claim it's an entirely separate *ability,* like she might have two, which almost never happens."

She sounded… terrifying. And amazing. I wondered what she was like as a person. I didn't remember her at all. Maybe she was intense and driven? Or maybe she was kind and had a core of steel underneath? Maybe she had a temper, like I did sometimes. Gods knew I didn't get it from dad. The idea that she had two abilities like the current Wishmaster just made her seem even more mysterious.

I paused, looking at Alec as I processed all that. "Speaking of which, do *you* have two abilities? Because I saw you using wind and fire in that fight. Was one of them a Skill?" I was pretty sure it was, but he must have been using a bunch of different Skills to get those effects, which made me curious how strong his soul actually was, because that would be exhausting.

To my surprise, Zeke answered. "He was using the Fist of the Red God."

Everyone jumped as my uncle appeared on one of the couches. I wondered why he'd waited, but maybe he'd stayed out of the conversation until they told me more about my mom so he didn't risk being involved.

Whatever the reasoning, I was pretty curious about his comment. "What is the Fist of the Red God?"

"It's a martial art the Red Revenant created personally when he was younger." At our shock he snickered a bit. "That doesn't mean he taught it personally. It's a unique Skill but he took it far enough to make a systematic training regimen. Still, it's overcomplicated and notoriously annoying to learn. I'm surprised you bothered," he said to Alec with a nod of approval.

The shorter guy sighed. "My personal ability is too weak. The Fist is extremely powerful and synergizes shockingly well with wind abilities. I could achieve power with it using only one Skill that I'd have needed several to accomplish with normal synergies."

Zeke shrugged. "Not a bad idea, and it clearly worked for you." He looked at the other team, clearly searching for something in their faces. "That said, I didn't come meet you all because I wanted to compliment your fighting style. I came because I have another question."

That didn't seem to be a surprise to Alec. "You want to know if we'll support him because of his parentage." I'd been wondering that too, and not having to ask was helpful.

To my surprise though, Zeke shook his head with a small smile. "Children. Always so quick to jump to conclusions. No, kid. I don't want to know if you're going to back him. I want to know if you have the qualifications to do so." Alec looked confused, but I understood what Zeke was doing. It skirted the edge of what was allowed because it showed more than they knew, but if he put it that way I was pretty sure it was allowed by the geas.

Callie must have felt it through the bond, because she braced herself as I did, grabbing my hand because I was sure we weren't going to be excluded. Looking Alec right in the eye, Zeke released his aura, letting it smash us all down into the cushions. I felt like I was drowning, being crushed by a million tons of rubble.

As I lay there looking at the other team I smiled a bit internally. If they passed this test, they'd remember this. Remember what Zeke really was. My uncle really did do the best he could to help where he was able.

Chapter Thirty-Nine

I'D BEEN under Zeke's aura before, but this felt... different. Of course, I'd know that he hadn't been trying last time. Given that an E-ranker's unleashed aura had been able to seriously pressure a whole crowd of us in the scavenger hunt, I was pretty sure if he felt like it Zeke could have crushed us all to death with this kind of attack.

Instead, it felt *just* strong enough to overpower us, and his extreme precision and power made it easy enough for me to figure out what exactly I was feeling. This was soul weight. It was more direct than what we went through when using Skills, but it was definitely the same thing. I wondered if this was what it felt like for your soul to shatter under the weight of your own stats when trying to rank up.

As expected, none of us were immune, but Abel was doing surprisingly well resisting the aura, managing to come partway to his feet against the massive force being exerted on all of us.

What I didn't expect was that Zeke wasn't sparing any of us, nor was he letting up. This test wasn't just for them, it was for me, and I could feel that resisting the soul weight, while exhausting, was also viable training. Since he was putting as much weight as my soul could take (no more and no less) at all times, it was wearing me out fast, but I felt like it was also helping my soul improve at a much faster pace than just sporadic Skills would.

"Why..." Alec gritted out. "Why is someone like you in this place? This level of control over your soul isn't something an E-ranker could have. Manipulating the weight across all of us individually at the same time. You're a monster. There's no way you're less than D-ranked." His voice was rough and his face pale, he looked genuinely terrified. "Are you some bodyguard the Saintess left with him?"

It took me all of ten seconds to realize the point of him doing this. He was setting the stage for me to tell them about my dad. Zeke looked at me inscrutably, clearly leaving the choice in my hands. I could see why he'd do it this way too. The combination of me getting them out of this, me healing them already, and my own potential strength down the road made this whole thing a perfect combo of carrot and stick, and one only possible for him to even do because I'd brought them into his space like this.

"Not my mother," I gritted out, making my decision. I mentally rolled my eyes at the fact that Zeke didn't bother to exclude me from this bullshit. "My father. Specifically, Elijah Wyndham, an A-ranked former member of the Wish Curse Palace. The person I inherited my own ability from."

Even under the pressure, I saw Alec flinch back in shock. "What? That's... I mean I wondered what your ability was, since you used such a crazy variety of attacks. But if it's *that* ability... I mean, I know Wishmaster Candidates are known to gather a variety of Skills. It explains all the variety. I'd just assumed you made some really crazy unique Skill that did all of that, kind of like my Fist of the Red God."

"I have questions about that actually," I admitted. "But first I need to know what you plan to do with this information. I admit, I wasn't expecting the test, but I *was* hoping to recruit you all to work with me. Unless that's against your arrangement with the Church. I'm not asking you to join the WCP of course—just my personal faction. If you agree you could become members of my Starchaser Pavilion if you want, or we could just make a personal alliance."

Alec made a pondering sound. "I... I'm not sure. It isn't against our vows to the Church. The Wish Curse Palace isn't a rival to the five-faction alliance—they exist among and around us. That position makes dual employment possible in a way it wouldn't be with other factions. Granted, the Church isn't the closest faction to the WCP, but we still use their services and have a decent relationship. None of the higher-ups are stupid enough to alienate the only source of wishes in the universe."

That didn't sound like a no, but it also wasn't a yes. It took me a second to figure out what he was saying and I rolled my eyes when I did. "Really? You're being crushed under the weight of a B-rank soul and you're trying to negotiate for compensation?" I said it derisively, but honestly I kind of respected the hustle.

It was still hilarious seeing the even more severe flinch from Alec when I mentioned Zeke's rank. "I-I'm just looking out for my team. Even if he's B-B-rank that doesn't mean we'll be bullied. You wouldn't want to work with us if you thought we'd fold so easily anyway."

With a chuckle, I looked at my uncle. "Hey Zeke, ease up on them? I don't know if that's a pass in your book but it's definitely one in mine. Any longer would just hurt our negotiations going forward." My uncle raised a brow, but fast as it had descended, the pressure vanished. When it did, we all gasped and our bodies went limp. While there wasn't really a physical aspect to the pressure, the way our bodies reacted to the soul weight was another story.

Abel, who had been trying to stand up, fell over when his muscles went limp and crashed through a flimsy table next to the couch he'd been sitting on. We all stared at him in shock for a second before he groaned out, "Ow." And that opened the floodgates. He wasn't hurt, couldn't be from something like that, and seeing our brutal mentor make a fool of himself set me and Callie off into a storm of mad giggles. The others stared at us for a second, but they needed to release all the tension, and one by one they started laughing too.

Our mentor just lay there in the wreckage of the table, sulking, until our bodies started working again. I groaned as I sat up from where I'd slumped. It was extremely uncomfortable—all my muscles felt like they were cramping at the same time. I triggered a heal burst, bringing me to fifteen total stockpiled including my reserves. Since the damage was done by a G-ranked source (me tensing up) it healed straight away.

I considered healing the others, but their Vitality should patch them up soon, and I didn't want to waste the heals on minor annoyances.

"Thanks," I said to my uncle. "Can you give us the room?" It was a useless gesture since he could eavesdrop on things happening across the planet, but I thought it would at least make us all more comfortable.

Callie was glaring at Zeke and flipped him off as he left, something that made me smile and the members of the Heavensong Tower's team blanch. Abel had gotten back up on the couch and was doing what I could only describe as pouting while Mel sat next to him, trying to suppress the giggles the rest of us had gotten past already, which I imagined didn't help his irritation.

Turning back to Alec, I gave him a smile. "Now, I figure we can talk a bit more openly without all the threats. Don't mind Zeke. He's my guardian and he tends to be a bit protective." I neglected to mention his complete inability to actually act on that protectiveness most of the time, but it wasn't like they needed to know everything. Since talking shop when they were sore and shaky seemed stupid, I figured I'd let them recover a bit by finally asking something I'd been wondering about. "I was curious by the way, can you tell me more about the Fist of the Red God?"

He nodded slowly, seemingly happy to have something to focus on other than just being in the presence of someone who could casually destroy his home planet with a disapproving look. "I... yeah. Of course. It's not a secret or anything. Fist of the Red God is a true martial art. The high-level ones don't just include movements and themes—they incorporate other Skills that give the techniques direct effects. Like my peace blossom barrage. That's one of the lower-level techniques in the Fist repertoire. Of course, the wind spheres are my own twist that make it more effective, but still."

That... that was interesting. I briefly wondered why Callie hadn't gotten some high level shadow art, but then I realized she'd wished for the 'best martial art for her' in that situation, and presumably the inability to learn something like that due to a weak soul and the complexity of progressing had made stronger martial arts a bad fit, not to mention the inability to teach it to me since she'd intended it for both of us.

It at least opened up some interesting new options, specifically for Jessie and Benny, who were much lower in G-rank. I supposed a Minor Skill would work for Callie too, but given our bond and its connection to Balam, I doubted my girlfriend would upgrade like that. She might try to synergize the Skill with her Shadow Embodiment or whatever came after it to make her own version, though.

I refocused on the opposing captain, but before I could bring it up, Lena spoke. "So... you can really grant wishes?" She sounded uncharacteristically somber, based on what I'd seen of her. "Like, you can give us anything we want?"

Shaking my head, I decided to clarify. "No. Not anytime soon. If you want Skills or items or other things around our rank then sure, but big wishes require big stat pools. The crazier the wish is the longer you'll need to wait to have it granted. I take it you have something in mind?"

Alec cut her off. "We don't. Not in the short term if that's the case. But it's something we'd like to address later on, if you're willing to commit to that eventuality."

Based on their demeanor, I was pretty sure this was a Jessie scenario. They'd lost someone, or someone they loved was ill or something. Whoever it was must be strong if they didn't think it would be anything I could help with soon. Future consideration wasn't a problem for me though.

"I can do that," I said carefully. "I can't make any promises without finding out what the wish is in terms of *when*, but it shouldn't be too long from now. A few years at the current rate. Is that okay?"

Lena exhaled in relief, looking at her tall, dark-haired friend. "See Ella, I told you they weren't so bad." She winked at her. "I have a great eye for people. You should listen to me more often instead of always acting like I'm a total airhead." She leveled a finger at the taller girl. "Respect your elders!"

Ella rolled her eyes, but she was smiling slightly. "Whatever you say Lena."

The smaller blonde puffed up her cheeks. "That wasn't even remotely sincere! Call me big sis! I don't think you take me seriously enough as the older member of this team."

Alec pinched the bridge of his nose, sighing heavily, and I smirked under my mask. I liked all of them so far.

I walked out of the room to grab a piece of paper, then started writing up a contract that would benefit both sides, letting the captain give his input as I worked.

I was thrilled with how this had gone down. These guys were strong and tons of fun to be around. This round couldn't have worked out better for us. Only three left in the team matches though, and I had a feeling things would only get harder. I didn't mind. All I could do was be ready for anything.

Chapter Forty

THE NEXT DAY saw another round of wishes for Rime and another batch of elixirs for Jessie. Our healer was up to two hundred seventy-eight Vitality with only half of her elixir limit used up. She hadn't quite made it to the halfway point of G-rank, but it was close. Sadly that was the easy part of the day. After, we headed to the arena for our now daily match.

This was the sixth round, meaning we had two more after it before we switched to the solo fights. Upon arrival, we made our way down to the room under the stands to wait to be called out into the pit.

We sat for about twenty minutes before approaching the guy who was assigned to wait with us for a hint, but got shot down and told to just wait. Eventually we were called out into the arena, and on reaching the sand pit, were greeted by our next opponent.

"Greetings!" said a short man in a huge hat with kelp green hair. "My name is Albai! I am the current representative of the Magnificent Fable Forest. You must be the team from the Starchaser Pavilion! We were warned about you all, so we won't be taking you too lightly."

Callie froze. "Oh shit." I looked at her quizzically, and she swallowed hard. "They have Fable in their name, and they were warned about us. I'm guessing this is one of the teams sent in by the Faerieland. Probably a legacy team like the Heavensong Tower." She turned back to Albai. "I take it Celine's sister was the one who warned you, and that warning came with instructions to show no mercy?"

He nodded cheerfully. "Of course. Lady Nalia was most displeased at her sister's defiance. She's instructed me to be extremely rough on you to prevent such an affront from occurring again. Lady Celine has been refusing to respond to meeting requests, and Lady Nalia's ability to punish her while under the purview of the Unity is unfortunately curtailed, so you'll be the instrument of her discipline, as it were."

A tiny red-haired girl wearing a blue dress and a ponytail scowled at us. "I don't see what's so impressive about them that the Lady would be willing to forsake her family. They seem pathetic to me."

Another woman to her side, one with literal metallic gold skin and bronze hair, clicked her tongue. "Don't underestimate them Roxy. They must have something going for them to get this far. I hear one of them is even a Master Candidate." I was a bit surprised they didn't have any up-to-date information, but then I remembered that we'd been befriending the teams we went up against.

Sure you could watch the matches from the stands, but experiencing an attack was much different than seeing it. Alec's Fist of the Red God used golden fire, and so did Mel, but the two flames were radically different in effect and application.

Roxy snorted. "I call bullshit. You're just too cautious Fiona. If they had a Master Candidate who was any good, we'd have heard of him before the tournament. I bet they're just hyping him up for the reputation."

"Enough, you two," said the last team member, a huge rotund man with a bald spot so large he only had tufts of hair on either side of his head. "We're here to beat them, not insult them. Lady Nalia wants them used as a lesson, but that doesn't make them less worthy of our respect."

Albai nodded. "Right you are, Garret. They've shown extreme talent and skill to get this far. We'll do them the courtesy of demolishing them with our full power." He spread his arms wide. "Now, to begin the match—I dislike this dreary sand. Let's change the scenery a little bit." He tilted his head back a bit and whistled.

As the sound split the air, there was a ripple behind him, and the air around him started to swirl. As it eddied, color began to mix into the nothingness, green specifically. The whirlpool of color and space accelerated, dragging more space into it, and the entire field around us blurred momentarily before returning to normal again after a second of disturbance.

Well… not normal. Returning to being clear. The area around us was unrecognizable. The whole sand pit had been replaced by what looked like a giant forest clearing full of colossal mushrooms.

Roxy giggled. "Welcome to Wonderland," she said maliciously. Her eyes, which were shining with ruthless glee, began to *actually* shine, and they transformed into a deep gold from their original hazel. As they did, her body shifted, taking on the form of a massive wolf creature that bounded into the surrounding tree line (mushroom line?), somehow vanishing into the shadows.

Garret reached out and snapped his fingers, calling up a humongous caterpillar beast, and Fiona laid a hand on the monster, coating it in a casing of solid gold armor that looked much tougher than normal gold.

Abel snorted, stepped forward, and cocked back a fist. He lashed out at the caterpillar monster and… nothing happened.

We all froze. "What's wrong?" Callie asked quickly. "Why aren't you attacking?" She sounded nervous, which I didn't blame her for given the circumstances.

Abel growled. "I can't. My ability isn't working and neither is my manifestation. The space here is being… restrained. I think this is a Domain ability. I've never actually seen one before. They're much more common in the Faerieland. This guy's Fantasy stat must be *high* for it to restrain me like this. Probably a few boosting Skills between them too."

Cursing, Callie started looking around. I triggered Seek Hidden, expanding it to her through the bond, and looked for the wolf girl. As we searched, she grilled our mentor. "What is a Domain ability exactly? What does it do? Aside from"—she gestured around us—"this."

"No clue," he said flatly. "I only know a bit about it. It's not a common style of cultivation here. It's not even a universal thing *there*. As I'm sure you remember, your elf friend uses something closer to the Empire's nobility cultivation. All I know about it is that it can lock down space in a way that makes it effective against Master Candidates and that to take it down, you need to take out the caster or overwhelm it in some other way similar to a Domain."

I scowled. "Well how are we supposed to do that? If you can't use your ability or your martial art how the hell are we supposed to beat *that?*" I gestured wildly at the massive metal caterpillar. "Never mind the wolf thing Roxy turned into." I was still scanning the forest. "Speaking of— Nightstrike, do you see her yet?"

"I didn't say my Ragam wouldn't work," Abel interjected calmly. "I said I can't make manifestations right now. I'm still a Master Candidate, I'm just more limited in my range. Starbreaker, take care of the wolf girl—I'll handle the metal bug. Nightstrike, you and Solomon can handle Albai, just be careful. I have no clue what he can do in here."

One of my favorite things about Callie's leadership style was that she had zero compunctions about letting other people take charge if it was needed. Abel was by far the more rational choice to come up with a plan since he knew even a tiny bit more than us, and she had no issues letting him.

Albai and the others seemed content to play defense, with one exception. I felt a buzz through the bond as Callie noticed an incoming attack from behind me and spun to finally catch sight of Roxy, who had been hiding but was uncovered by Seek Hidden. She'd already committed to her assault, so she only slowed down for a second before barreling toward me despite losing the element of surprise.

Callie and I turned and moved even as Mel appeared in front of her, propelled forward by her flames like a damn rocket booster in a move so fast I could barely track it. I *did* notice her seeming to tense up when she got there, presumably unable to handle the strain, but she quickly moved into a hand-to-hand fight, mobilizing her massive Might and coating her punches with flame.

As we headed for Albai, we were shocked to see the massive caterpillar in a crater with Abel already on top of it, fists driving into the plated shell like drop hammers as the summoner and metal woman tried to interfere in a panic. Grinning, I activated Leaf on the Wind, grabbed Callie, and hurled us forward with a long, low leap—right at the captain of the enemy team.

We came in fast, and I once again wished I had a weapon, because this bastard had somehow used his Domain to expand himself into a series of illusions, surrounding us and staying just out of reach. Callie lashed out with a hand, trying to pincushion all of them with her shadows, but nothing came of it.

I dismissed and retriggered Seek Hidden and was pleasantly surprised to see the glow of a locked-on target on one of the bodies. I alerted Callie through the bond without needing to say anything.

My girlfriend, well-practiced at deception in battle, created another wave of shadow blades, and I triggered Flurry of Blows, funneling it into her attack to speed up the stabbing shadows. Since it was an area of effect attack, Albai didn't notice we were onto him, and I watched him use his Domain to somehow swap places with one of the illusions.

Once he did, Callie redirected *all* her shadow spears at him at the last second.

Albai snarled, agitated for the first time. He clicked his fingers and Roxy appeared in front of him, the wolf girl seemingly unsurprised at being summoned as she braced for the blades. She took them head on, the shadows tearing her apart.

I planted a foot, activating Stone Limb as casually as possible, and stacked a triple density-shifted blow with Consecration of Flames and Touch of Tears to make a poisoned version of my Magma Leg.

I waited for Callie to launch an attack again to force Albai to swap out. As soon as he did, I triggered Double Trouble. I was already whirling off my back foot and swinging my leg around with the full rotation of my body when I appeared behind him. Apparently his spatial bullshit didn't prevent a Skill as weird or obscure as my DS Mastery.

Using my Balam Skill, I'd built up the strongest kick I could manage, and a Mercy Kill at the last second made it even stronger. I aimed for his lower back instead of his head because I had no desire to kill someone over some stupid tournament, especially not someone who had made a point of mentioning he wasn't aiming for my life (even if he did it by telling me he wanted to kick my teeth in).

When the kick landed, Albai let out a low scream as I felt a crack, and he toppled forward, the domain shattering as the poison fire and damage to what I was pretty sure was his spine completely destroyed his concentration.

Roxy turned on me to attack, but was unable to do anything due to the train-sized fist manifestation that straight up smashed her into the ground like a bug on a windshield.

I looked around to confirm the match was over, and once I saw everyone subdued, I released Touch of Tears and used a heal burst to fix Albai's spinal damage. The team captain shuddered, finally going limp as his pain ended.

I sighed. That had been a rough one, but we'd come out on top. Only two more to go.

Chapter Forty-One

WE DIDN'T TRY to recruit the Magnificent Fable Forest, mostly because they were working for a faction that was currently actively pissed at us. While technically most teams could be part of the WCP or the Starchaser Pavilion and whatever faction they were in at the same time, Callie and I didn't see any upside to trying to recruit someone who had already admitted they had orders to teach us a lesson.

So once I finished fixing up Albai's spine, we just left, heading home to talk without any meetings or networking for a change. Which was a good thing, because as soon as I got there my first order of business was tracking down Zeke to find out what the fuck had just happened, and everyone else came with us.

Zeke, of course, had been there to watch the match, but had come home right after on his own, bypassing the hour of travel time with what I assumed was either an artifact or some stupid broken Skill. Well, or he just flew home. I knew that traditionally once your Impact passed one hundred (D-rank in other words) you could literally step on air and fly by manifesting the Impact onto the air under your feet. At Zeke's level he could probably fly insanely fast.

Either way, when I found him he was in the kitchen eating... enchiladas. I glanced down at the takeout container on the counter and raised an eyebrow. "Did you somehow get down to Doomtown, order enchiladas from the Raving Baby, and then come back in the time it took us to get home?"

He stared at me for a second, taking a bite, and pushed the bag off the counter into the trash. "No," he said through a mouthful of food.

Mel actually giggled at that, while Abel was glaring at my uncle with the white-hot intensity of a thousand suns for picking up his favorite food and not bringing enough for him (not that I blamed Zeke, given the amount of enchiladas my mentor could pack away).

Callie sighed loudly. "Right. Moving on. You saw that fight, so what exactly happened? We have a basic understanding since Abel knows that Domains can nullify abilities like his, but it isn't exactly something we've seen before. Are you allowed to tell us about them?"

He looked at her with narrowed eyes, chewing as he hummed speculatively, then swallowed loudly and burped, making all of us grimace. "Sure," he said casually. "This is considered common knowledge, since so many people have Domains in some parts of the universe. What do you want to know?"

I rolled my eyes. "Everything?" I had to hold back a sigh, because of *course* he had to make things difficult.

"No," he said firmly. "*That* would be interference. I'll give you the crash course. Domains are a special type of Skill or Ability that allows a person to impose their power around themselves in a radius. They're kind of the opposite of a high-level Intermediate combat skill, since you're offloading a large portion of the stress onto the space around you, so they don't require quite as much in the way of soul strength."

I blinked at that. "Wait… then why doesn't everyone use them? If they can counter a Master Candidate they must be really strong. Shouldn't they be way more common?"

Zeke shook his head, taking another bite and talking as he chewed. "Nope. There are downsides. Domains are kind of complicated, but basically there are two kinds—Personal and Fable Domains. Fable Domains are based on stories like that Wonderland Domain. They're well explored, but that comes with its own issues."

"Oh," Callie said in understanding. "Fable Domains aren't unique, so they would be pretty boring to anyone who knew how they worked. Especially if there's a lot of overlap. That means you would rank up really slow right?"

He pointed his fork at her. "Give the girl a cookie. You guessed it. Fable Domains are incredibly standardized, and unlike the cultivation system the Empire uses, which is mostly just a twist on the Job System, there are enough variations that it dilutes the mass renown that they might have as a singular concept."

That made sense. I'd wondered why, say, a Count could funnel belief from the entire concept of that rank of nobility and it didn't work the same for Fable Domains. "Okay," I said, "what about the other kind, Personal Domains? I'm assuming that's a less well-known story suited to the user?"

"Yup," he said cheerfully. "But much like Unique Skills those are monstrously hard to rank up. They're still based on stories, but lesser-known ones." He paused. "There's… other ways to apply the concept, but that's higher-level stuff. Regardless. Domains are the nemesis of spatial Skills and abilities, and manifestations count. It isn't something you'll often come across."

That was vague, but pretty much meant I wasn't getting any more. Luckily I had another question this whole thing had brought up that I hadn't had a chance to ask. "I'm curious though. Do you use Heroic Cultivation? I've never asked, but I know the Unity is the youngest god, and I don't know how old you are. Did you come from the Conglomerate?"

He actually stopped eating to look up at me coolly. "I was wondering when you would get around to asking that. No. I was born in the Empire, though I won't tell you how old I am. I use the Job system. I'm currently a Legendary Voltomancer. That's Volto like the style of mask, not Volt as in electricity."

I nodded thoughtfully. "Like how some people in the Faerieland use the Job system, but others use Domains? I guess there's more variety in the other factions."

"Of course," he agreed. "Heroic Cultivation is considered fairly new and untested. It has limitations and benefits like anything, but Ascendant culture is old, as are most Ascendants who are in charge of it. Most of them are taking a wait-and-see approach and consider the Unity's whole guild and this entire faction as an experiment."

"An… experiment?" I said blankly. "The Conglomerate as a whole and the Unity guild has to be centuries old at this point—how the hell does anyone consider that a passing trend?"

He just shrugged. "High-end Ascendants have more than three or four hundred Impact, and you know that high Vitality keeps you in good health for long into the natural lifespan, while a person only ages a single biological year for the number of chronological years that equals their current Impact. Since people can live a hundred to a hundred and twenty or so natural years, multiplying that by Impact means high ranking Ascendants can live for tens of thousands of years. On that timescale, a few centuries isn't anything much."

When he put it like that I could see his point, but it was still a staggering thing to think about. It also kind of explained why he didn't want to talk about his own age. Who knew exactly how long he'd been around? I'd probably avoid thinking about it too. "Do… do you think we should switch to the Job system? Would that cause me to lose my modifier for the Wish power?"

"Short answer is no. You *can* switch over if you want—your Job would just need to use Wish as your Base Skill. It's not something I really want to get into unless you actually go through with it. But the Wishmaster position has existed since well before this particular cultivation system, and obviously the original Wishmaster didn't use it. He created the Wish Skill and then used it to create the Wishmaster Job."

That said some interesting things about how the Job system worked to me, not least of which that the Base Skill probably worked at least a bit like an inborn ability. I didn't know much about Jobs, though from what I did know they insulated you somewhat from recursion at the expense of some of the speed you got from Heroic Cultivation.

I had no real desire to change my cultivation style though. It might be a bit safer, but it would also be slower, which would draw attention. Maybe I'd change my mind later, but at the moment I was fine with the way I was doing things. Plus I was pretty sure that making Wish my Base Skill would end up giving me the same limitations as I currently had, so there wasn't really a point, with the added problem of needing to somehow *train* my Wish Skill, and gods only knew how I'd do that.

This was the naturals vs. Martial Arts Skill user argument, and I had no desire to get rid of my free rank ups in Wish out of some misguided faith in my ability to understand the damn Skill well enough to grind it past where I currently was.

Zeke didn't seem interested in talking more since he put his head down and focused on his enchiladas. I knew him well enough not to expect any more from him. I could see a faint glow from his forehead under his hair, so I suspected *something* he'd just told me or been about to tell me had been counter to the geas.

Callie must have felt my guilt and also backed off, turning to Abel. "Did you have fun during the match? I didn't get a chance to see what you did, but clearly that caterpillar thing wasn't able to take it."

The grin that split his face was one of the most ferocious I'd seen on anyone in my life. "Nope. They made the mistake of assuming hamstringing my reach made me useless. But Ragam is about pinpoint precision and focusing force into a small area. Bigger opponents aren't a weakness, they're a strength. Took me a few dozen blows on the same spot but I punched through the armor on that summon like an awl. When you dropped the Domain I was finishing up with the summoner and the metal girl."

Mel piped up. "The werewolf was surprisingly fun in a fight. Her regeneration was nuts, some kind of racial trait thing I think. Even cauterizing the wounds as I made them wasn't enough. Good thing I was strong enough to muscle her with all my Might. Though she was definitely a marathon runner and not a sprinter, so the help from Abel at the end there saved me some serious time."

"What do you think we'll have to deal with tomorrow?" I asked hesitantly. "Seems like they're getting tougher and tougher every round as people are eliminated. Only two more left, so our next opponent will probably be a monster."

Abel just shrugged. "Who cares. You got me don't you? You shouldn't worry about the next two rounds." His grin took on an edge. "You should worry about the five rounds after that." He paused. "At least unless you get one of the bye spots. But somehow I don't think you have the luck for that."

I just shook my head with a laugh. "Well, good to see you don't have confidence issues." I turned to walk past where Zeke was still eating quietly.

"Now, why don't I make us all something for lunch, since *someone* didn't think to bring enough for everyone else."

Zeke just flipped me off without stopping his food rampage and I rolled my eyes as I took out a pan. I would have asked what they wanted, but given Abel was here I didn't need to. He always picked the same thing if he had the option, and honestly the enchiladas smelled good anyway. Now, I just had to find out if I could make them as good as the ones at the Raving Baby. Probably not, but it never hurt to try.

Chapter Forty-Two

THE MORNING of the seventh match was the same as the ones before it. Five wishes for Rime, five elixirs for Jessie, and she officially reached two thirds of her elixir limit as her Vitality broke past three hundred. On top of that Jessie got another ten points of Might from her bond, bringing that to eighty-seven on top of the insane three hundred and three Vitality. Specializing definitely had upsides, since her entire skillset was based on Vitality and compounding it brought *insane* returns on her stats.

I could see now why people with my power usually had bodyguards. Funneling all of someone's stats to one point could create absurd levels of power in compatible abilities. Like Cark having almost all his points in Might. Sure, he already had most of them as a fire user, but that was *most*. Having almost a hundred percent stat allocation reinforcing your main skillset was incredibly broken, and not something that happened naturally even to people with heavily skewed powers.

The further behind a stat was, the easier it got to raise, and the other stats started to climb quicker when you got too focused on one, unless of course you cheated and did it like I did with wishes. Given how strong Jessie's healing already was, not to mention the enhancement abilities of her energy infusion on her animals, I was terrified to see what that power would be able to do at next rank.

Once again we found ourselves back at the same arena. Rime was waiting in the stands with Zeke, who would as usual be gone by the time we came out. By this point everyone had other things to do, and no one but them had time to go to every single one of our matches, not that we would ask them to.

Stepping out onto the sand, I was prepared for anything. From what I'd seen, we usually got one of two situations when facing new groups—either a widely varied set of enemies, or four people in a uniform or some sort of identical concealment attire.

This particular group of opponents were the latter. "So," I said musingly, "exactly how many factions use the whole shapeless dark robes ensemble? This is what, the third we've seen? You'd figure it would be counterproductive given how big a role attention plays in cultivation. Like, doesn't the uniform defeat the purpose?"

Callie shook her head as we made our way into the pit towards the other team. "No. I asked The Nothing about that. He said they're usually limited within a region, and they make enough of an impact as a group to justify the choice. Being members of that faction gives each person a similar amount of prestige, sort of like Raleigh's Raiders back in the scavenger hunt."

One of the figures nodded slowly. "She is correct," they said with a voice like a creaking door in a haunted house.

"Yes," said another in a voice like claws scraping over a dead tree, "most correct. The Hate Demon Convergence is indeed such an organization."

I sighed. Wonderful, they were total creeps. Callie remained calm as ever as she said, "That's a... nice name. Any chance you could give us some sort of individual moniker we could use to identify each of you? I respect the whole... group mentality thing you have going on, but it would be nice to put a name to the lack of face."

Because the hoods were completely dark, full of nothing but bottomless shadow... of course. One of them nodded. "We are Skell. We are also Veck, Stang, and Ruk." It announced this with a voice like metal screaming as it shattered, clearly a different one than the other two.

"Right." Callie said flatly. "Very helpful, thank you." Apparently the Hate Demon Convergence didn't teach sarcasm, because the figure nodded again despite her clear implication that announcing the names of the… *convergers*, while using the collective "we," made the introductions functionally pointless. "You haven't attacked yet—are you waiting for us to start things off?"

The four of them shook their heads in unison. "It begins," the fourth one said in a voice like cold water hitting hot stone.

I was a bit confused as to what that meant… until I looked up. Four circles of red symbols, all slightly different but close enough to be recognizable as a similar or identical Skill or ability, floated above us in a square. Red light connected the four circles, and through that square of darkness I could see a giant red hand manifesting.

"Fuck," Abel spat. He threw out a punch, a massive manifestation of his hand slamming into the demonic appendage.

The red hand clenched into its own fist, meeting the blow with a similar punch, and the explosion dispersed the manifestation, causing Abel to stumble back with a growl of pain. I stepped over and put a hand on his shoulder, triggering a heal burst, and he muttered a thanks.

As we watched, another hand came down through the square, the two of them latching onto either side of the square and beginning to tear the space wider with brute force. Through the hole I could see a massive red face with glaring yellow eyes and a huge mouth packed with razor sharp teeth. Ram horns curled back from a brutal looking face as the monster grinned down at us.

"What the actual fuck is *that?*" I yelped in terror. Whatever the demon was, it was F-rank, which shouldn't be possible here.

Abel groaned as he flexed his fist. "That," he said distastefully, "is a cooperative invocation. Looks like they're summoners. Most invocations have a primary caster, and they modify the Skill and offload the power and soul requirements onto others. Cooperatives are what happen when multiple people use an invocation when they all have the same Skill or ability."

The monster's foot smashed down on the sand as it finally crawled free, a pair of giant red wings spreading out behind it as it threw back its head and roared in triumph.

Only to have its roar cut off by another massive fist as Abel slammed a huge punch into its jaw. The beast reeled back as my mentor shook out his hand. "Ok, this is going to be rough." Despite the grim words, his face was plastered with a massive grin as he stripped off his coat and started to limber up. "Mel, an F-rank enemy is going to be a mess, especially one that size. Mind if I borrow a bit of your power?"

Mel shook her head. "Of course not, but be careful. You know the bond has limits at our rank."

He just waved her off, then closed his eyes. The summoners all seemed pretty much motionless but they were behind the damn demon so no way were we getting to them fast. Callie still nodded for me to circle around and we started moving slowly, letting Abel and Mel keep the monster's attention.

I'd never seen them use their bond for anything like Callie and I did. Abel was the main attacker and had never needed to tap into her powers. As I stared in awe, a massive avatar of Abel's fists manifested above us, condensed from golden fire. I'd seen Mel use that ability before, taking advantage of the physical aspects of Might to enhance her body with her condensed flames, but seeing it on this scale was... terrifying.

More than just the size, the sheer presence of those fists was staggering. There was a shift in the air and the space began to warp around the hands as Abel moved them through the air, warping the space to leave behind afterimages until there were six distinct manifestations in the air. The left fist flashed forward, the other two images condensing on it, then the right followed, each blow coming down with triple the force.

The demon roared, hurling its own fists out in a flurry of punches, but unlike last time Abel didn't budge. His blows met the punches from the demon head-on and the beast reared back in pain, but the damage to its hands healed almost as soon as it happened. Summons were a bitch to take out if you couldn't one shot them, since the summoners could repair them.

I had no doubt Abel would get the demon eventually, and seeing him get serious and actively work with Mel for the first time in the tournament I was blown away, but this was a team match, which meant he didn't *have* to do that. Callie and I had circled around within range for me to use Double Trouble, but I held back, kneeling down to condense Stone Limbs on both my hands, as well as poison fire, just in case.

Waiting for the perfect timing, I stood stock still, staring at the nearby figures as the giant demonic summon and Abel's massive flaming fists boxed it out above us. Finally, there was a shift near the summoners' feet. Callie had flooded the ground with shadows, triggering a Sucking Mud through the bond. The distracted figures had no chance as they all got snagged by the shadow tendrils of the Dark Swamp combination technique, slowly being dragged into the mud.

That alone didn't end the summon, so I activated Double Trouble. A Cloud Step to prevent me from sinking allowed me to lash out with a pair of Mercy Kill boosted punches and then spin off to slam both hands down on the third one's head and drop an elbow on the last, all imbued with a triple-strength tranq blow, using four from my stockpile.

The figures all slumped, obviously unprepared for a random teleport into their midst. The unconscious bodies were dragged into the muck, but Callie cancelled the skill, leaving them all buried in the now solid sand. I felt a shudder in the air as the massive summon dispersed, showing the major weakness of summoners in general better than any other example I'd ever seen.

Flaming hands faded from the air as Abel released the fire empowerment Skill. I checked on the hooded figures, and they were all breathing, unharmed mostly since the poison fire had faded when I released the skill. Seeing they didn't need any healing I turned to check on Abel, who was nursing a pair of seriously damaged hands.

I put a hand on his shoulder and used a heal burst, hearing my mentor's sigh of relief as I did. "Ok. Ow. Haven't pushed that far in a while. Bit bummed you ended it so early though—that was the best fight I've had in ages." He shrugged. "Oh well, I guess I'll have to hope someone better comes along in the solo matches."

Mel snorted. "You would have been hard pressed to beat that thing without me. If someone better than that comes along when you're alone you're screwed. Though I guess the damn thing *was* F-rank, so who knows." She glanced at the unconscious figures. "We going to do the meeting thing?"

Callie shook her head. "No. They give me the creeps, I don't really want them hanging around the Pavilion. I'm sure we can find some other people who can do cooperative invocations. That summon was scary, but Rime would crush it. They just aren't worth the investment."

I agreed, though more for the first reason than anything else. I found them all pretty unsettling. With a sigh, I turned to make my way out of the arena with the others following behind.

The next match was the last one in the team segment, and assuming we got through that, we might be forced to fight each other. I was going to have to do some work on my **DS** Mastery to prepare for fighting alone. I had a feeling things would only get harder from here.

Chapter Forty-Three

AFTER THE MATCH we went straight home again and I secluded myself. This next part was going to be an important step, and I wasn't willing to have anyone sitting in. Even Callie might be a competitor later in the tournament, and as much as I loved my girlfriend, I wasn't going to make it easy on her. We were finally on even footing, and unlike our sparring up till now, this tournament had real stakes.

Granted, it would be fine if either of us won, but we both had our reasons for wanting to advance, so if we ended up fighting I wasn't going to do any less than my level best to win. She knew it too, could sense my resolve, even if she couldn't sense what I was going to do about it.

Which was, of course, get stronger. My stats were maxed, but I had plenty of room to grow, and my DS Mastery was my best chance to do that. I had ten or more subskills to upgrade still, and I needed to make sure to grow them in a way that would let me fight one on one without relying on backup from Callie, Abel, or even Mel. I had to use my room to grow to make myself a legitimate threat, and the best way to do that was to get back to my roots a bit. It was time to min-max my build.

Or at least the aspects of it I could. The Fatewalker build was fantastic for DS, but it was less than ideal for a frontline combatant. Specifically, my diviner subclass, while useful, had yet to unlock any of the combat applicable skills I could get later in the tree, and as such was much less of a priority. I had a few tricks like the overlay, but that wasn't really even a skill so much as an interface. Seek Hidden was useful but wouldn't be combat applicable in most situations.

Which meant my upgrades should be aimed at the most compatible of my subclasses—the monk. Granted, the rogue subskills were hugely useful, but I'd upgraded most of them already, and I had no weapon anymore, at least for the moment. After tomorrow I would finally have some breathing time to get a new one made, but until then leaning into the monk abilities and their synergy with martial arts was going to be the key to making me stronger. Even after I got my weapon this would be a useful path to take.

Now, I'd upgraded several of my monk skills already. Consecration of Flame, Stone Limb, and Afterburner. Which meant I had five more left. Mistwalking, Sucking Mud, Boiling Cloud, Cloud Step, and Leaf on the Wind. Two water skills, an earth skill, and two wind skills.

Four skills didn't give me any groundbreaking options exactly, but it gave me some, especially if I used them in conjunction with each other. Which meant I needed to figure out ways to alter each of the skills so they would work in harmony with each other, or at least a few of them. I was pretty sure I couldn't jail break them completely, but by making multiple skills different enough to work as part of an overarching whole I should be able to manage... something.

Then I stopped. Skills could be used in conjunction. Part of a whole. They could also be *synergized*. While I wasn't sure if I could synergize full Skills into my subskills, I didn't see why not. I had plenty of bullshit Skills that did nothing, and combining them into aspects of DS Mastery could improve its function.

I considered my options. First up was Stealth. It was still at Lesser, which meant it was well within tolerance for synergy. Mistwalking was designed to help me hide in a cloud of mist, but there was viability for something much more powerful. I might lose Stealth by doing this (I didn't know since it was my first synergy) but even if I did I had stored charges and I could use it through the bond.

So I closed my eyes and reached down into myself. I used Mistwalking, filling the room with mist that would let me move more sneakily. It was a pretty basic and uninspiring ability. But I focused on a specific part of it. The hiding aspect. I focused on the stealth element of the skill, trying my best to shift the skill as I did with any skill, using my soul to sort of highlight a path for it.

Instead of just altering it over and over until it became effortless, I altered it as far as I could and *held* it. My head started to pound, but I ignored it as I focused on my Stealth Skill, and holding the Mistwalking skill, I resonated Stealth as hard as I could. I felt something catch, felt the two skills begin to harmonize as my skills did sometimes, but instead of letting it go, I focused on the harmonization.

It felt... simple. Not easy mind you. My head was throbbing, but simple. Like it was meant to happen. I held it like that, letting the resonance get stronger and stronger, and in the same way a skill eventually became different when I upgraded it, there was a sort of... click inside me as the two skills blended together.

I fell over, letting myself breathe as I tried to tamp down on the pain. It took a few minutes for my head to clear, but it eventually did, and when it was done, I mentally checked over my Skills. They were mostly the same, except two small differences.

First, Stealth was gone. I hadn't been sure that would happen, but this was a Skill and not an ability so it didn't shock me. I knew most Skills that synergized with an ability didn't vanish since you had to keep ranking them up to progress, but it looked like Skills synergized with other Skills did.

Second was what I saw under my DS Mastery skill. It listed my subskills, and Mistwalking was no longer one of them. In its place was an entirely new skill, Moonlit Night. My subskills and skills didn't have descriptions or anything, but I didn't need them. It was *my* skill. I knew what it did, and this one was pretty fucking amazing.

Moonlit Night did what Mistwalking had done, filled the area with fog, but with Stealth included that fog did a few new things. Aside from obscuring sight, it also obscured me specifically from other senses, like hearing and smell. On top of that, because Stealth was doing a lot of heavy lifting, the Mistwalking skill was able to get back to its roots as a monk skill, which meant it amplified the force of my blows when I was hidden by the fog. In other words, I got a fucking sneak attack bonus. Every blow I made undetected inside the fog caused double the damage.

I wanted to do more, honestly—I couldn't wait to find some new way to improve my DS Mastery. I could feel it becoming... more. Evolving as a

Skill not only because I had upgraded a portion, but because I had included more Skills in it. What that would do, I had no idea. Maybe it would change the Skill when it upgraded (that was certainly how abilities worked) but either way I was excited to become more powerful.

For now, my head was still throbbing and I decided the best move here was to test out my new ability. I headed down to the training room, making sure it was empty before starting my practice. I closed my eyes, triggering Moonlit Night. When I opened them… I could see.

I hadn't considered why it would be called Moonlit Night, but standing in the fog I could understand perfectly. Light. The fog itself wasn't opaque. Rather, to my eyes it looked like softly glowing phosphorescent liquid. That was interesting. I had a full understanding of the mechanics of my new skill, but apparently not how it would physically manifest.

Other people, based on what I knew about the skill's function, wouldn't be able to see or hear or smell me. Granted some special tricks like my Seek Hidden would make it possible to detect me anyway, but detection abilities weren't exactly universal, especially among the enemies I'd be facing. They would all be pure combat types.

As I strode forward in the fog, silent as a ghost, it was amazing, like being inside a giant Stealth Skill. I couldn't wait to do this with my last few subskills and make DS Mastery really mine. I shifted into my Balam stance, moving undetected among the targets on the edge of the training room. As I got within range of one I spun off my back foot, scything out with a kick at the nearest target.

There was a bang as my kick fulfilled the condition of a sneak attack, namely, that no one was perceiving me actively within the fog. Double the force was expressed through the blow. I triggered Mercy Kill, inflicting three blows at half again the strength, a grand total of two hundred fifty percent damage. I'd been hoping those would stack instead of combining but I supposed it kind of made sense since they both came from the same skill.

Looking at the target, I didn't see any particular damage, but that was fine. These were peak G-rank targets, and my Might was two hundred and twenty. Five hundred and fifty points of Might wasn't anything to scoff at, but it wasn't peak or anything. Then again, it didn't need to be. I could deliver these all day, and this was without any enhancement at all. Stack this with some of my triple-strength punches and I was throwing blows hard enough to be F-rank.

Now I knew, of course, that it didn't really translate exactly like that because of the way Impact worked, but against someone my own rank I'd be able to do some serious damage, and everyone in the tournament was G-rank, even if some of them would have F-rank defensive gear like I did. I got back in position again, readying myself for another attack, and proceeded to spend a few hours focused on utilizing every speck of Might I had perfectly, finding the optimum usage for my Balam Mastery for sneak attacks and mist-based combat. I kept going until I could barely stand, ignoring the pain in my head as I practiced.

Finishing up my training I slumped down, head still pounding, and closed my eyes. Sadly the pain didn't fade quickly, but that was okay. I hadn't strained my soul too much—this was within my tolerance, it was just at the high end of it. I would be right as rain tomorrow before the big match. Not that it would matter because there was no way I was going to show this new skill off in the team battle. I'd save it for when I needed it.

Once I stopped feeling like a pack of boot-wearing rat kings were playing hop scotch on the inside of my brain, I climbed to my feet and headed upstairs. I shuffled into the shower and slumped down on the bench, letting the boiling water wash away the soreness and sweat from the hard workout. I wasn't exactly invincible now, but I still had another four monk skills and at least one rogue skill to upgrade before the solo fights. I was going to make sure that I was a completely different fighter by the time that all came around.

As I stumbled into bed and dozed off, I felt Callie climb in after me, and I drifted off to sleep, happy with the progress I'd made. Tomorrow was the finals of the group matches, and I couldn't help but be excited to find out who we would be facing. Whoever it was, I was sure this would be a hell of a fight.

Chapter Forty-Four

"So," I said as we arrived in the waiting room below the arena. "Last team battle." I swallowed hard, trying to ignore the pounding of my pulse in my ears. "Who do you think we'll be up against?" Not that it mattered—I was barely thinking about this fight. I was more worried about the next five. Because any one of them could be against one of my own teammates.

On the one hand that was exciting. I was almost positive if I fought Abel I would lose, but I had a decent chance against Callie and possibly even Mel if I pulled out all the stops. But still, I'd gotten so used to us all moving as a unit. Especially Callie. She was my partner. Fighting with her at my side was almost like breathing at this point. It was going to be jarring switching from that mindset, never mind actually fighting against her.

Which… was what Abel had told us during training. That we would need to be able to keep that mindset separate from our normal outlook so we could turn it off. In some ways I was pretty sure that was the point of making Paired Dueling a Skill. By doing it that way we kept it as a separate part of our lives, which made it easier to do without. As opposed to making every aspect of us codependent.

Callie sighed, and I could feel through the bond she was just as hesitant. I couldn't feel the *reasons* for that, but I knew her well enough to assume they were similar to my own. "No idea," she said. "But if they made it this far they must be tough. Each of the teams has been pulling out some crazy trick that we've never seen, so we should assume the same of this one. Whatever it is though, I'm sure we can hang with whatever they've got."

Abel seemed pretty much at ease with everything, but that wasn't surprising. I'd yet to see him go all out for real. Sure, he'd tapped his bond with Mel in that demon fight, but that was just a raw power thing. Given Mel's comment that he only ever got serious when he took off his mask, I was positive that Abel had other tricks. The rest of us weren't as… invincible.

Mel was pretty calm too though, and while I didn't think I was as strong as she was, I was closer to her in power than my mentor, especially now. Strangely, hearing Callie's fear about what was coming in her voice made mine seem inconsequential. I stepped forward and wrapped my arms around her, pulling her into a hug.

"I know you're not worried about this fight. Not really. And neither am I." I felt her stiffen against me as I touched on something she hadn't brought up. The bond was useful and positive a lot of the time, but empathy was a tough thing to get used to. "We're going to kick ass in the solo rounds. We've been training constantly, and we've learned a ton. We can do this."

She nodded against me. "Yeah. You're right. I'm just letting this get to me. Besides, even if I lose it isn't the end of the world. Four of us means four times the chance of victory. And that isn't even counting your cousin."

I'd almost forgotten Natalie was taking part in this. I wondered who her fourth team member was.

Callie sighed, stepping back. "Alright, well for this to matter we need to win the current match. Like you said, I'm not worried, but we should focus."

"Oh definitely," I agreed. "Being confident doesn't mean being stupid." I heard the call from outside as we were summoned for our match. "Speak of the devil. That'll be us. Whoever it is, I'm sure we can figure something out. We just need to make sure to take our time and work out what they can do, right?"

She grinned at me. "Of course. I'll come up with a plan as soon as we know what they can—" She stepped out of the gate onto the sand and stopped. "Oh. Well shit."

I was a bit confused as to what had stopped her, but when I stepped out myself, I realized what it was. "Sanctuary Hall." I cursed. Beat, Sever, Carl, and Serenity. Four of our old enemies who were strong enough to be a serious threat. I turned to Abel. "I don't suppose you discovered some secret weakness of hers in battle and will be able to shut Serenity down quickly?"

"Nope," said my mentor. "And with Carl added on this is going to be tough. Neither of you are a match for Beat or Sever one-on-one, and Mel can't handle them two-on-one either. We beat them all last time because of our distribution, but with one more person this is going to suck." He scowled. "I hate fighting her. It's like punching cotton. There's no fun if she just no-sell's everything I do." Because almost everything Abel did was brute force, and Serenity was the closest we'd seen to a hard counter to him.

We stepped forward, and the calm looking girl nodded to us. "Well now," she said lightly. "I wasn't expecting you to be our last group opponent. But maybe I should have." She smiled warmly. "I have to say I don't dislike the symmetry. We'll make sure to pay you back for last time."

Seeing that banter would be pointless, and not wanting to deal with Carl's bullshit, I knelt down, triggering Stone Limb on both arms as well as my poison fire, coating them in toxic acidic magma. "So, who am I up against?" Ironically, despite being unarmed and therefore more vulnerable to Sever, my armor was better at tanking sharp force trauma, so Beat would be the bigger threat.

"Carl," Callie said firmly. "We can handle the other two, but Carl has who knows how many tricks up his sleeve. We need our most versatile fighter on him. I'll deal with Beat, Starbreaker is on Sever, and Apollyon will handle Serenity as planned. Go."

She moved as soon as she finished talking, clearly planning to overwhelm them with surprise as a wave of crushing shadow smashed down at Beat. Mel expelled a burst of golden flame, appearing in front of Sever in a flash and then releasing a burst of fire right in his face. I sighed and triggered Double Trouble, appearing behind Carl and launching a flurry of magma infused punches.

To my shock, when I arrived my punches were countered as a pair of huge hairy arms pulled free of the ape tattoo on Carl to slap them aside. Despite the knowledge that he would have tattoos that could protect him courtesy of his dad, I had no idea where the things were until now. They should have been obvious since Carl didn't wear a shirt.

Now I saw where they came from though—I could see the tattoos fading into existence, not from nothing, but as if they were coming from a great distance, a trick of perspective as his skin was flooded with colorful images that he hadn't had a second ago. I backed off, watching him closely as the writhing images adjusted themselves across his skin.

Behind him, I saw a massive golden shield form in the air, defending against a storm of massive punches as Serenity channeled her ability through what I was pretty sure was an F-ranked artifact, nullifying them with her pacifying power on impact. I could hear my mentor's groan of frustration as he accelerated the punches, weaving them in from new angles only to have the shield intercept them all.

I could feel Callie was tense but safe, and I didn't have time to look over everyone as I prepared for Carl. I triggered Flurry of Blows and Mercy Kill, three augmented super speed punches to test out what Carl had going on. Another tattoo, this one a small monkey, dashed off his skin and split into a chain of monkeys, each throwing one of the others into the path of one of my punches and exploding into fucking confetti of all things, though luckily this stuff didn't cut me.

Seemed like the tattoos had individual abilities, though I wasn't sure about how varied they were. Carl grinned at me, flexing his muscles ridiculously. "First stage of my tattoo boom, Primate Parade! You think your stupid lava punches can hang with my monkey madness, Solomon? Punchin' Carl spits on pathetic hand-to-hand bullshit! Only nerds throw hands."

It took all my effort not to literally groan aloud in pain at how stupid he was. "Your name is *Punchin'* Carl. You're saying you think punching is beneath you?"

Carl snarled at me, flicking his hands to hurl a pair of snakes at me. "Shut up! Real men don't punch with their fists, they punch with their brains! I have the most badass bare-knuckle brain in the world, so I don't need hands to punch!"

I just... stared at him as I easily sidestepped the snakes with the help of my now active overlay. That wasn't how *anything* worked. At all. "That... made no godsdamned sense, you lunatic."

Rather than hurl more snakes, Carl reached behind him with both hands. He let out a grunt and hauled up what looked like a fucking boar made of rocks, holding it over his head like a championship belt as he roared, "I'll punch sense in the *face!*" and hurled it at me in an overhand toss.

Activating Leaf on the Wind, I pushed off the sand, my foot coming down on the boar as it arched through the air. I pushed off it, hurling myself further up. Glaring down at the crazy gangster, I triggered one of Benny's spider leg attacks, pointing both legs above my head to form a sort of arrowhead. Using Cloud Step to reorient myself, I aimed the point down at Carl, triggering a gravity attack, a triple-strength density-shifted attack, and Mercy Kill as I plummeted down at him point first.

I aimed for the shoulder and arm, because I didn't want to murder Carl for being a fucking idiot, but limbs could be regrown. Sadly, it didn't really matter. Carl saw me coming and knelt down to slap the ground. As he did a shape erupted from his back, an absolutely huge grey form. It took me a moment to figure out it was a literal steel elephant, and it crouched over him to tank the attack before it had a chance to hit him.

The pointed spider legs propelled by their enhanced density and the gravity attack slammed into the back of the elephant, and there was a thump as the tattoo beast's body proved too dense for the spider legs to punch through.

I dismissed them, kicking off a Cloud Step platform to hurl me out of the way of the wounded elephant (which bled mercury apparently) as it lashed out with its trunk, trying to break me in two. I touched down lightly, Leaf on the Wind preventing my impact from being too rough. I'd had to strain the skill a bit to prevent it from stopping my attack altogether, but I'd managed, even if my head was twinging a bit. I stood up and looked over at a glaring Carl. Behind him I could see Abel coming up blank against Serenity, and I growled with annoyance.

This was the last fight of the team section, it should have been easy fighting people we'd beaten before. But from what I could see someone (probably not Carl) had done quite a bit of research. They knew what to expect from us and had covered all their bases.

I cracked my neck as I took up a Balam stance. That was fine. I'd just need a home run.

Chapter Forty-Five

Carl was scowling as he put his hand on the metal elephant. "Hey! How dare you hurt McRuffles. He's one of the best tattoos my old man gave me." Looking up at the elephant I actually did feel a little bad, but I didn't believe that the tattoos being harmed damaged them long term. I was, however, concerned about another part of that statement.

"Your old man?" I said dubiously. "M-Jack's tattoos have to be above G-rank—how are you even using those? If they're F or higher then they would be illegal in the tournament because they would count as offensive weapons." I wasn't actually sure they would, but I'd at least bring it up. Honestly I couldn't tell what rank the tats were. Their Impact came from Carl, so the manifestations of the tattoos didn't give it away.

Carl snorted. "Nuh-uh. They're G-rank for sure. My old man isn't just a tattoo user, he's a tattoo artist, and he can tailor his work to the person he's working on." He made another ridiculous flexing motion. "And with an awesome canvas like this he made some badass tattoos. You're just trying to confuse me with your rules bullshit. Do you think I'm stupid?"

I stared at him for a second. "Oh! That wasn't rhetorical." I paused. "I feel like the answer you're looking for is... no?"

My condescending tone was obvious enough that even Carl couldn't miss it. The shirtless man roared in rage and reached up to slap the bottom of the elephant. The massive metal form dissolved, shrinking down and recovering Carl, except this time it didn't imprint itself onto his skin. It covered him like some kind of armor, giving him a metal suit with an elephant head helmet and a long hanging trunk, as well as gleaming metal plates along his arms, back, and shoulders, though it left his chest and stomach bare.

His arms, hulking with muscle and metal, started lashing out at me in a series of punches, and between my overlay and Balam Mastery, avoiding those blows was completely feasible. Roaring with outrage, Carl started flinging his head around, trying to smash me with the metal trunk.

Gritting my teeth, I triggered a triple stack density shift on my arms, which were still coated with toxic magma. I got them in front of my face, tanking the trunk whips with my armored forearms as I waited. It sucked. A lot. I triggered a heal burst to begin healing the damage and to overclock my energy reserves as I weathered the storm.

Despite the pain and constant barrage of attacks from both arms and the trunk, I had to admit Carl was holding back. He could have tried to gore me on those tusks, and he didn't. He obviously didn't want to kill me any more than I wanted to kill him, though apparently he had no such compunctions about tenderizing me.

Waiting for a gap, I took the punishment, finally seeing an opening via the overlay. I triggered Flurry of Blows, enhancing my speed as I slipped through the gap, letting my armor tank the hits (though since they were blunt force I felt a rib crack, only to be healed up by my still surging life force) and hit Carl with the heaviest right cross I could manage, using my Minor Boxing Mastery along with Balam and Mercy Kill to land the best punch I could.

The elephant armor dissolved as Carl staggered back, head spinning from the punch, which I followed up. I had two more hits with Mercy Kill of the three, and I triggered a tranq punch with each hand as I used them. As that happened, I tagged him with a gravity attack from Alden, making sure he could feel the obvious change.

Seemingly convinced that the sluggishness from the tranq punch was the increased gravity, Carl started flailing around, not bothering to try to resist or counter the tranquilizer or even the poison fire that was still spreading from all of my strikes.

As I kept up the punches, his own arms came up to try to stop them, but they couldn't do shit about the spider legs raining down short sharp stabbing blows from above. Granted they weren't imbued with poison fire, but they were G-ranked metal spikes stabbing into bare flesh which I didn't imagine was fun.

Despite the advantage, I waited. I could see him getting more and more dizzy and unstable. Finally the overlay tipped me off on an opening, and I triggered Double Trouble, appearing behind him and leaving behind a fake image of me as usual. When I did that though, I decided to try something new.

I had tranq blows, but I'd imbued other kinds of attacks with certain abilities before. Feeling my head split open I used a tranq blow, but instead of a punch I slipped past his guard from behind and locked him into a sleeper hold, imbuing the choke with the tranquilizer attack.

Carl stiffened, slapping my arm and struggling, but I could feel the tranq working with the stuff already in his system. After about twenty seconds he was out, and I let him go, dropping him to the sand as I doubled over, hands on my knees, to process the intense head pain. I'd strained my soul with that little trick—it had been a big change very quickly.

That had me down to four tranq blows and three density-shifted ones. I needed to top up soon. Luckily Jessie was almost at her elixir limit and I'd be back to buffing Benny. I waited for my head to clear and then stood, turning to look around at the rest of the battle.

Abel was still stalled fighting Serenity, but I doubted I'd be either useful or appreciated there. Mel was dealing with Sever and Callie with Beat, so I decided to go help my girlfriend with the blunt force user. Without waiting I spun and triggered Double Trouble again, appearing behind Beat mid-rotation, bringing my elbow around into the side of his head with another Flurry of Blows.

Callie, who had been barely keeping up with the powerful force user, felt a surge of relief that I could clock through the bond, but it turned to horror when the hoodie-wearing younger man bent at the knees, leaning back to let my blow pass over his head and planting his hands on the sand behind him, feet coming up to smash into me.

His lead foot slammed into my chest, and the other hit the back of his first shoe, smashing his initial kick into me like a chisel driven into stone. The energy from his punches gathered on his feet and hammered into my chest like a car going full speed, and I felt my sternum crack as I was sent sailing off into the distance, my head blurry with pain as I hit the sand and rolled like a stringless puppet.

I used a healing burst, then another just in case, and I felt the bones in my chest begin to knit together, though my head didn't stop spinning. I rolled over, propping myself up on my elbow, and panted with pain as I tried to right myself. I could feel Callie's rage through the bond and heard her roar as several of my abilities were funneled through it—Touch of Tears, Consecration of Flame, and Stone Limb, all channeled through my girl-friend and the soul weight borne solely by her.

I raised my head, seeing the massive shadow magma dragon construct bear down on Beat, who was hurling explosive bursts of concussive force to keep the monster from reaching him. Staggering up to my feet, I nearly fell over, having to catch myself with the spider legs before limping towards to the spot I'd been at before.

That had been my bad. I'd tried to engage a fucking member of the Titan Twenty in close combat, one who almost definitively specialized in Might. I'd gotten cocky after beating Carl and fucked up, but I couldn't let Callie lose this. As I tried to step forward and almost fell again, I felt a hand on my shoulder. "Enough, kid."

I looked up to see Abel standing next to me. Serenity's golden shield was nowhere to be seen, though the woman herself was lying in the sand near where they'd been fighting. "I have to help."

"No," he said firmly. "You had your fight. I'll mop up the rest of this. She was only supposed to slow him down, anyway. It was my fault this took so long. The two of you are pretty good, but handling someone like him is still a little ways off. Sit your ass down and let me handle it. Might as well take advantage while you can."

Of course, right at that minute, the spider legs finally gave out, the attack collapsing and my body going with it, falling back into the sand. "Okay," I said calmly, ignoring my spinning head. "You go ahead and take care of that. I'm just going to rest here for a second."

He laughed at that, grinning down at me. "Good work on taking out Carl, kid. For future reference, you are *not* a frontline combatant, even if you're physically inclined. Next time pick your moment better if you need to take on someone like that in close quarters."

I already knew that, so I just gave a grunt as he vanished, appearing behind the distracted form of Beat. He didn't bother with manifestations, he just got in close and started throwing hands. Callie let the construct drop, sagging herself as she did, but her soul had clearly grown since the last time, because she didn't pass out, just seeming exhausted.

Beat... he lost. Bad. I'd forgotten after seeing Abel fight how brutal he could be, and I guess he was annoyed at the force user for hurting me so bad too, because he fucking *dismantled* the guy. Every blow Beat threw was turned aside or minimally dodged, and every blow he took was brutal and aimed at the worst possible spot.

I had to give Beat credit, he lasted much longer than the F-ranker had, though admittedly Abel was much less driven this time. Still, he actually landed a few punches in return, though my mentor mostly diverted them with his ability.

Finally, the younger brawler couldn't take it anymore and missed Abel slipping around with spatial lubrication to nail him in the kidney. He gasped in shock, and my teacher wrapped an arm around his neck in the same sleeper hold I'd used on Carl and choked him out, waiting until he wasn't moving and dropping him in the sand.

He turned to where Mel was still fighting and cleared his throat. Sever, who was burned in several places, looked up to see the rest of his team totaled and sighed before dropping his knife and folding his hands behind his head, getting down on his knees.

And just like that... it was over. The fight had ended, and now we were officially past the team matches. From here on out, it wasn't us versus them, it was *me* versus them. I had a few more upgrades to make to my abilities before my first round, and after. My major plan was to make sure I got to Intermediate in DS Mastery before I hit anyone scary, because I had a few incredible skills coming next rank.

Callie staggered over, dropping into the sand next to me, too tired to leave but not too tired to get over to me to make sure I was okay. I smiled at her and pulled her close, dropping a heal burst on both of us to combat the side effects of a hard battle. Then I leaned back and sighed in relief. We were one step closer. That alone was worth celebrating.

Chapter Forty-Six

"So," I said as I slumped back onto the couch, "how long exactly until the next round starts? I know there's going to be a few days between rounds nine and ten, but I didn't bother asking how long until nine actually starts." I was sitting with the others—Jessie, Benny, Abel, Mel, and Callie. We'd decided to have one last team meeting before this whole thing became a mess of conflict.

Callie, who was leaning against me on the couch, gave a groan of despair. "Three days. They only gave us three days off. I'm so tired, and my head is killing me. My damn eyelashes hurt."

I chuckled and pulled her against me. "Well that's what happens when you go ape shit on your opponent without caring what it takes."

She glared at me. "I did that because he hit you so hard I was afraid he killed you for a second. The bond sort of... fizzed out. I couldn't sense anything but pain and fear and I was terrified."

"I..." I stared at her. "I didn't know. I swear. It's a low-level bond—I guess the feedback from the attack was too much for the empathy portion of it. Or maybe I was in shock and you felt that. Either way I'm sorry. I didn't know how scared you were."

Abel groaned. "Can you please save your soulful staring into each other's eyes for later when we *aren't* having a meeting? Because if this is just going to be you mooning over each other like usual I don't think we need to really have this one. What exactly are we doing here?"

Callie groaned again and sat up. "We're here to discuss what happens if we end up fighting each other, and exactly how soon that might be coming. They won't be pitting people against their own teams first round, but after that we could easily run into one of our own at any time after."

"She's right," I said grimly. "Granted, early game it probably won't happen. There are one hundred and sixty fighters left in the final bracket. Five rounds will bring us to the top five, which they'll be handling as a separate issue from the current lineups, a big main tournament competition in front of the whole city. Until then our odds for running into each other are slim to start with, but with each round it becomes more and more likely."

"I hope you two aren't expecting me to take it easy on you," Abel said with a smirk. "Because it would be a disservice to my training not to come at you as hard as I can. If we win, you get the slots to distribute like we said—as long as the two of us can come along—but which of us actually gets the win depends on who is stronger."

Callie grinned at him. "Which is what I wanted to confirm. We're a team, and we're friends, but from this point on, we're all competitors. Don't share your new abilities, don't share your plans, don't tell us about your tricks." She looked at Benny and Jessie. "And that means no help from you two for any of us. If we're keeping this confined to the tournament we need to do it fair and square. No outside assistance."

Abel's smile couldn't have been prouder. "Well, well, well. Looks like the kids are finally growing up. Agreed. This is going to be one-on-one. Anything else?"

Shaking her head, Callie called the meeting to a close, and we all headed off on our own. As I walked, I considered what she'd just done. Some might think that little meeting was pointless, but I knew that doing it that way was not only intentional, it was important.

This tournament wasn't just sparring—it would be our first time up against friends in a battle with stakes, and because of that all of us had our own ideas about how it would go. By setting the standard now, she was confirming that none of us were going to hold it against the others if they won and set combat expectations so no one would feel taken advantage of.

That said, now that that was all taken care of, we were well and truly on our own. As a fighter who was used to working with people, and one with a support-based ability, I was at a disadvantage here, which meant I needed to take the next step on creating my cohesive combat style.

I stepped into the training room and considered my options. First up were the skills I'd get on my next rank in DS Mastery. I'd have three new abilities, one in each of my subclasses, and they were all pretty impressive.

Danger sense was an extremely useful divination ability that did exactly what it said on the tin. For my rogue ability I was getting a finishing move, which I only got every other rank. This one was called Marked for Death and gave me a single un-dodgeable hit that landed with twice the damage. Finally, my monk ability was called Mountain Stance and tripled my defense as long as I was standing still on solid ground.

For now though, I needed something to get me through the *next* fight until my rank up. With Moonlit Night, I had my concealment and some of my combat taken care of, but within that fog, I still had plenty of things to improve on. So with attack and concealment handled, my next big move was going to be mobility.

My main mobility skill was Leaf on the Wind, and since I'd had so much success with my last attempt to merge in an outside Skill, I decided to do it again. I closed my eyes and crossed my legs, breathing in deeply as I triggered Leaf on the Wind. I felt my body... lighten. Like I was soaring through the air despite being landbound. Focusing on that sensation I tried to envision moving with Leaf on the Wind. The unbound motion, the speed.

I held that image in my head, and as I did, I began to resonate my Minor Gymnastics Skill. It was weak, but it was also something I associated with motion, something that would let me move about as I wished. I felt the two skills begin to blur as my head started to ache. Strain just like last time (though not as bad since I had the practice now) began to pound through my brain.

Pushing through, I focused on recreating what I did with Moonlit Night. Suddenly, I felt the skills give, and then there was that same click and the skill just... changed. Checking my Skill list to make sure, I confirmed that yes, the Gymnastics Skill was officially gone.

Focusing on my DS Mastery, I searched for the subskills and found the one I was looking for. State of Grace. I grinned widely as I felt what it did, and understood I'd gotten exactly what I needed from this one. State of Grace freed me from the bonds of gravity, but it also freed me from my natural limitations. It enhanced my speed to double what it was during the five minutes I spent under the skill, allowing me both weightlessness and enhanced movement speed during that time.

It was perfect. With this I would be able to move around inside the mist perfectly and deliver incredibly fast, incredibly powerful strikes. It also meant I only had three more upgrades until I reached Intermediate, and no one else had a clue. I hadn't been keeping anyone up to date on my alterations to this Skill since it had so many parts, and not one of them would see this coming.

I sighed and slumped to the ground, exhausted and in pain. Again. I maybe should have waited until I recovered from the fight to do this, but I'd gotten so fired up by Callie's proclamation. I wanted to win through the tournament and get to the point where I'd be fighting all of them. I wanted to make myself strong enough to beat them all. To beat Abel.

For the first time since I'd started this, I felt like I might actually manage to go all the way. I not only had my new powerful subskills, I had stored attacks and the power to use them alongside my skills. If I could create a synergistic system of powers, I could win this. Or at the very least show everyone that I had what it took to get close.

I hadn't realized how much the assumption that Abel would crush me had colored my perception of this whole tournament, because knowing I might possibly be able to win this made my already decent amount of anticipation explode into a bonfire of excitement and restlessness.

Reaching down for my scan ring, I spun it up and called my cousin. Since we couldn't have outside help, I wanted to check and make sure that she and her team actually got in before this all started. After all, they were supplying part of our forces here, since if they won we'd get to go too.

Natalie picked up with a smile, her face appearing with no hood or mask in the floating screen above my ring. "Shane! Judging by the slight smile I'm guessing you made it, and judging by the wince I'm guessing you already started training for the big show."

I laughed. "Good guesses. I was calling to let you know my team made the cut, and to let you know that we decided on a non-interference pact, so I won't be able to be in contact much. Aside from being shady I'm going to need all the time I can get to train if I'm going to make it very far on my own."

"I feel that," she said, blowing out a heavy breath. "I have tricks of my own, but I'm not very confident in myself for this. My teammates, however, are definitely going to be strong contenders. You better watch out if you fight any of my people. They don't play around."

I laughed at that, and we spent the next few hours just chatting, relaxing and discussing family business and our histories, and just generally getting to know each other better. Aside from time spent with Callie, it was hands down the most fulfilling time I'd spent in a while. Actually bonding with my family, getting to know one of the few people who could understand me.

All good things must end though—I had to say goodbye, and since the call had been to inform her I wouldn't be in contact, I might not speak to her again anytime soon. My best shot would be during the Moonsong Glade trip if we made it, and I made a note to get to know her better when that happened, and maybe to let Callie get to know her too if there was time. It couldn't hurt.

My head, thankfully, had already stopped pounding because of the down time. I climbed to my feet and headed over to the track on one side of the training room, ready to get back to work. Moonlit Night might be conspicuous to train, but State of Grace would just look like Leaf on the Wind to an outsider, and I needed to be as prepared as possible.

Using my new skill, I felt my body free itself from the bindings that kept me slow and chained to the earth, and I grinned as I blurred forward, beginning a mad dash around the track, bouncing off every possible nearby surface as I tried to acclimate myself to high-speed three-dimensional movement. This was going to be so much fun.

Chapter Forty-Seven

THREE DAYS WASN'T NEARLY AS LONG as it sounded. Each of the days was its own project and exhausting in its own right. The first day I finished granting Rime's wishes and got Jessie her last twenty-five Vitality worth of elixirs. She also got another eight Might, bringing her Might to ninety-five, her Vitality to three twenty-eight, and her total points to five hundred and eleven.

The same day I also managed to upgrade my Cloud Step to Ripple Running by synergizing it with my Minor Swimming Mastery Skill. One step became ten, and combined with State of Grace, I became a much more mobile and dangerous combatant.

Day two saw me going back to working with Benny. He traded me five triple-strength density-shifted attacks for twenty points of Focus, bringing himself up to two hundred and three. I also managed to upgrade Kidney Blow to Heavy Hands, my first passive subskill. I sacrificed my Minor Boxing Mastery to add armor penetration to every single one of my blows (albeit not very much of it).

On the third day Benny paid five triple-strength tranq blows for twenty points of Might, bringing it up to two hundred and nine and his total up to five hundred forty-three. My final ability was created by merging Boiling Cloud (which I barely ever even used) with Minor Archery Mastery (another Skill I almost never touched) to create Steam Arrow. It gave me a ranged attack, something I was sorely lacking up to this point. That only left upgrading my divination skills and Sucking Mud before I could rank up the Skill to Intermediate.

Training with these new abilities took up the rest of my time over my three days off, and by the time the morning of the ninth match came along, I'd officially gotten as far as possible, even scheduling in some downtime the night before to allow myself to enter the match at my absolute best.

Jessie drove me to the arena again, though it was strange going without Callie. Rime tagged along, as she would when Callie had her own match (we were at different times). As I entered the waiting room under the new arena, I couldn't help but stop and take stock of what was happening.

It felt... weird, being here alone. Knowing I had an opponent coming up who I would have to deal with all on my own, and that said opponent would be a member of a team that made it just as far as we did. When they called me out onto the sand, I stepped out of the tunnel and groaned aloud at the person I found there.

Of course my first round would be against someone I knew who was strong as hell. Wren grinned wryly at me, offering me a cheerful wave as his giant bone spear sat over one shoulder. "Morning Solomon. Lovely day we're having, don't you think?" My friend's amber eyes were twinkling with amusement, but they were also twinkling with something else. Eagerness.

I felt my pulse pick up. I wanted this rematch as bad as he did, and I'd put in a lot of work in my training. I'd beaten him last time, but that was with Callie, and I hadn't forced him to use his ability. "Seems like it," I replied cheerfully. "You must be pretty confident. You know what I can do."

He waggled his free hand. "Yes and no. Logically I know you're much less of a threat without your partner, but you have a habit of doing the impossible. I'm not stupid enough to go into this underestimating you." He started to spin his spear slowly, passing it back and forth hand-over-hand, letting the metal coated tooth atop it drag in the sand. As he did, I could see water start to gather from the air around him, coating his palms and flowing down the bone haft of the spear.

"Fair enough," I said casually. "I won't hold back either." The water thing wasn't ideal. It meant even if I was willing to expose my Moonlit Night skill, the option was off the table. That said, I'd made plenty of other preparations. I triggered Ripple Running and State of Grace, then knelt down to coat my arms in toxic magma. I half expected him to come at me while I prepared, but he didn't—he just kept spinning up his spear.

As he passed it back and forth, the water accumulated along the spear, turning it from a wet stick to a pillar of liquid. I could sense some extreme power from it, and I was looking forward to seeing what it could do.

Knowing any more talking would be pointless, I used Double Trouble, appearing behind Wren and triggering Flurry of Blows, increasing the rate of my already massively enhanced movement speed as I unleashed a barrage of sharp punches at his back.

The spear, which was still being passed slowly, sped up. The water shifted around it, and suddenly I was faced with a fucking shark made of water bearing down on me, its gaping jaws surrounding the head of the spear as it chopped down on my arm. I used a triple-strength density shift on my left arm without thinking, massively enhancing the density and power of the magma.

There was a loud clang and I bounced backwards, skipping off the air like a rock across a pond, using the mobility of State of Grace to enhance the speed and distance I was able to travel with Ripple Running so I could withdraw nearly instantly.

I sucked my teeth and shook out my left arm, which hadn't been cut, but had been smashed pretty heavily by the damn spear. My armor was probably the only thing that had saved me from being disarmed in a much more literal sense than when I lost my cane.

"Impressive—you're faster than I remember," Wren said as he went back to spinning the spear. The longer that went on the more water was condensed. I was pretty sure that shark would get bigger and nastier as it did, which meant I needed to break that buildup. The burden of initiative was on me, not on him. Joy.

I shrugged, trying not to let him see me sweat. "I'll be honest, I thought I'd have to earn that ability. I'm honored I impressed you enough to pull out all the stops."

His smile was predatory. "Did you think you were the only one who went to see a friend's match? I've seen what you can do, Shane. I came here to win, and I'm not holding back. Seems like you're not either. I'm curious though—exactly how many tricks do you have up your sleeve? Are they enough to make up for not having your partner? Your teammates? You're a scary guy, but I'm not exactly a pushover myself."

I gave him a knowing grin and unleashed a series of techniques. Double Trouble, a shadow clone, and a stored Stealth attack from Callie. I stepped back and vanished as a doppelganger took my place and a dark copy appeared behind Wren. As I did, I bounced off the air with Ripple Running and circled around to the side as Wren seemed to detect the clone. I wasn't sure how he was doing that, but it was something I'd counted on.

I triggered Double Trouble again on myself, and I saw Wren's shoulder stiffen as the shark spear tore apart the clone, dispersing it into darkness as I appeared behind him. Before he could attack me directly, I triggered my new Steam Arrow skill, spitting a boiling steaming jet of water right at his face. His eyes widened and he stumbled back, bringing up his spear defensively to deflect the attack.

With all the water concentrated in one place, I triggered Afterburner to massively increase my power. Then Mercy Kill, then a gravity attack to slow him down before finally releasing a fire attack combined with a Balam empowered punch right at the water around the spear.

A massive roaring cloud of toxic fire enveloped my punch and when it hit the water, steam exploded out. I kept up the assault, using up both fire attacks the same way to take advantage of Afterburner. Seven attacks left, I grabbed the spear in both hands and channeled a gravity attack directly into it, combined with a density shift as I jerked it out of his grip and sent to spinning away.

Continuing that whirling motion I lashed out with a series of punches, all six of them imbued with triple-strength tranq attacks. Wren grimaced, arms coming up to tank the punches, and winced as my magma coated arms imbued with tranquilizing poison smashed into his forearms.

Which he *did* tank, unfortunately. Even with all the tricks, his Might was much higher than mine, and I was forced to rely on Ripple Running again to disengage, two more steps ending the skill and forcing me to recast it. I was about twenty feet from him now, and I was panting as Afterburner faded, sapping my strength. My head was pounding from the massive repeated skill and attack usage, but I wasn't the only one who was unsteady.

Wren was wearing a hauberk from what I could see but he hadn't been protecting his arms, probably to prevent anything from slowing down his spear. His arms were coated in poisonous cracks as the toxic fire burned away at him and sent the tranquilizer into his system even faster. He was barely standing, eyes starting to flutter, but I saw him haul back and slap himself hard across the face, which seemed to temporarily stave off the effects.

We were both weakened by that last flurry of attacks, and as he spat his blood on the sand he gave me a wide grin. "That... was sneaky. A double decoy. And you'll have to tell me how the hell you disarmed me after this is over." He shot a glance at his spear, but I'd tossed it across the arena pretty hard. He wouldn't be able to reach it before I could reach him. The water had been boiled away, and though I saw him try to condense some more, the droplets wouldn't stick for some reason. Maybe the lack of concentration.

I didn't respond, waiting for any sign of weakness. His eyes fluttered again, and when they were closed for a second I triggered Double Trouble, then blitzed him with another barrage of punches from behind. He spun and put his arms up, somehow detecting me again, but I dipped back, allowing the punches to peter out as I put a bit of distance between us and kicked a cloud of sand right up into his face.

Unlike the Steam Arrow, there was no way to block a cloud of sand. He panicked and inhaled, sending himself into a coughing fit, and as he dissolved into hacks and wheezes I dove forward and ducked under his flailing arms, smashing a right cross into his jaw and sending him stumbling back before I followed it up with a stomping kick to the face, finally laying him out flat on his back as the damage combined with the tranqs to knock him out cold.

I doubled over, panting, head blazing with pain, but I grinned down at my friend as I let the skills fade. Leaning down, I put a hand on him and triggered a heal burst before turning to stagger out of the arena. No way I would be able to carry him in my condition. Besides, I wanted to look cool after my first victory. I couldn't be more pleased with how it went down. I couldn't wait to see who I'd be fighting next.

Chapter Forty-Eight

"So," Callie said with a grin as I walked into the house. "You made it through, huh?" Despite her light tone, I could feel through the bond that she was happy for me. "Who did you end up against?" We'd agreed not to come watch each other's matches because it would tip our hands if we revealed any new tricks.

I slumped down on the couch, peeling off my mask and dropping my head in her lap, barely giving her time to move the book she'd been reading. She rolled her eyes at that, but smiled, reaching down to run her fingers through my hair. She was wearing sweatpants and a tank top, and her face looked almost surreal without the mask.

I smirked at her. "Wren."

She whistled at that. "Well damn, no wonder you look so tired. I can't believe you won. If I hadn't felt your excitement through the bond I'd never have believed it. That's pretty impressive. I remember how hard to beat he was when we fought him together." She paused. "What was his ability anyway? Since he's out it won't affect the tournament if you let me know, and that was driving me nuts."

I snickered a bit at what a nerd she could be. "Water manipulation of some kind. Conjured up a giant shark. I handled it. He was no pushover though. When is your first solo match?"

She sighed in annoyance. "I'm up on day three. I'm going stir crazy sitting here alone." She held up her book. "This is the owner's manual for our car."

I gave her a flat look. "You realize you aren't allowed to drive no matter how well you know how the car works, right? The tournament is enough life-threatening danger, thanks."

"You don't drive either," she said with a pout. "You don't need to act like I'm some kind of monster."

Deciding it was best to change the subject, I made a noncommittal noise and then said, "Oh, by the way—granting wishes for attacks doesn't count as outside interference does it? It *is* my ability."

I was pretty sure it didn't, but I had wishes to grant today so asking would be a good distraction. Sure enough she waved the question off easily. "Of course not. The point of this is not to make people feel like they're being cheated no matter who wins. You're behind us all in raw stats and that's how you keep up."

Sighing in relief, I sat up with a groan. "Fair enough. Then I'll get that out of the way. You should have a day out with Jessie or something. You can't just sit around and worry for two days."

She gave me a soft smile. "Pot and kettle. But as long as we don't work on training it shouldn't be a big deal. In fact, it's such a good idea that as team leader I order you to spend the day with Benny tomorrow after you get your wishes done. Assuming he's free."

"Free?" I said with a snort. "If he was any more prone to brooding alone we'd need to build him a bell tower. I wouldn't describe him as free of anything except the compulsion to bathe regularly."

"That rings a bit hollow from the guy who feels the need to shower three times a day," she said with an eye roll. "How your hair isn't basically straw at this point I'll never know. If you weren't an Ascendant your skin would be parchment by now. Regardless, his brooding is kind of the point I was trying to make. He needs to get out. I get you want to give him space to figure out things with Celine, but at this point he's just spiraling."

I let out a long sigh. "I know, Cal. Trust me. But I also know Benny. He needs time in his own head. If I don't let him sort through this himself, he's going to second guess the decision fifty times after he makes it and neither of them deserve that. He doesn't let much get to him, but when things do he needs to wallow in them." At her arched brow I held up both hands as I sat up. "Fine. Tomorrow. But only for an hour or two. Nothing that'll take away from his thinking time for too long."

"Fine," she said with a sigh. "You know him best. Not like Jessie hasn't been trying and failing anyway, so I might as well listen to the expert. I just feel... responsible. I'm the leader—I'm supposed to vet our allies. Celine completely fooled me and Benny had to pay for it."

Leaning down to press a kiss against her forehead, I leaned mine against it right after. "Contrary to your own warped worldview, being leader doesn't make you responsible for everything. Benny decided to pursue her, and she was the one who went through with it. I hope they work things out, but even if they don't, it's no one's responsibility but theirs and Celine's sister's. Feel free to tell her off when we meet her. I'll get in her way if she tries to murder you."

Standing up, I let go of her hands, which I'd been holding. "Sadly, if tomorrow is a day off, today is a training day as usual, which means I'd better go get started." Not to mention I needed a re-up on some of Benny's attacks badly. At least it meant he could keep his money for the moment.

"Whatever," she said in a faux-condescending tone. "Some of us have important and interesting work to do. Off with you. You're distracting me while I'm trying to learn."

I chuckled at that and rolled my eyes, heading out like she said and leaving her to her weird reading choice. We still wouldn't be letting her drive. The only one of us anyone trusted behind the wheel was Jessie.

With that done, I decided to head off in search of my best friend. It wasn't a long search—Benny spent most of his time outside staring dramatically off into the middle distance these days. I didn't mess with him about it. I was pretty sure that if I found out Callie had been lying to me our whole relationship, I'd be equally miserable.

"So," I said, dropping down next to him, "you ready for your wishes today? Because I'm pretty much tapped on density-shifted attacks again. Wren is a bitch and a half to fight. Not that it stopped me."

He chuckled at that. "You won? Nice. Only four more rounds to go, huh? You realize every round you fight after this is one round closer to having to fight one of our own?"

I grimaced. He was right, and I was pretty damn sure it would happen sooner than later. Fantasy tended to push us toward dramatic and unusual situations, and that wasn't just me. The person who drew the names would have a high Fantasy too.

Seeing I wasn't enjoying the conversation, Benny smiled and changed the subject, making his wishes for the day without much fuss. Four density-shifted attacks and a tranq blow, bringing me up to ten of the first and four of the latter. Benny's Focus jumped to two hundred twenty-three, and his overall stats hit five hundred sixty-three, after which I made plans with him for the next day and left him to his brooding, heading downstairs for the training room.

With only Sucking Mud and my divination abilities still needing to be upgraded, I technically had four to go. Earthseeking, an old skill I almost never used that let me find things like mines and ore. Pulse of Life, which let me find rare plants, and which I also never used, and Seek Hidden, which I used all the time and would need to make sure remained useful, if not making sure to give it a flat upgrade.

It would have been useful if I could synergize Sucking Mud with Earth-seeking, but sadly it wasn't in the cards. They were both subskills of DS Mastery, and you couldn't synergize a skill with itself. I could use two charges to use multiple abilities, and even use them in conjunction, but that wasn't the same thing.

Though that made me wonder if to finally upgrade the DS Mastery Skill I might need to synergize it with Enchanting once I finally finished upgrading all the components. It was something to think about at least. That might be what I needed to push it to a completely new level, and since DS Mastery was my most powerful offensive ability and I barely used Enchanting anymore, I could think of worse options.

For now though, I decided to focus on synergizing another skill. My head wasn't exactly up to anything crazy. I'd rested but this fight had taken a lot out of me in terms of soul strength, so there was no reason to push things past where they needed to go. I'd do a small Skill, and I had just the one in mind.

Focusing on Pulse of Life, I felt barely any strain. It was a first level divination ability and not one I almost ever used, so it wasn't much strain on my soul. Neither was the other Skill I decided to synergize with it, Minor Herbalism Mastery. The combination was so obvious that I couldn't see a reason NOT to use it, and even clicking them together took almost no effort relative to my last two synergies. Both skills were designed to do similar things, so I barely had to push them.

The resulting skill was... stupidly useful. Rhythm of the Wild was a new ability that let me not only find rare plants but identify them through the interface as long as they were my rank or lower. The utility of a skill like that somewhere like the Moonsong Glade was staggering, and it made me seriously think about how skill synergy worked. While I could make amazing and unusual abilities when synergizing off the wall combos, I could make powerful and useful ones when the two skills in question were of a similar nature.

Power vs. utility was an interesting conundrum, though utility still mostly won out considering my stockpiled attacks and how the meta abilities of DS Mastery affected them. Sadly, based on how much thought I had to put into this one, I was running out of easy synergies, and I needed to come up with a basic idea for a skill before making it. I probably wouldn't hit Intermediate before the tenth round, though I might before the eleventh, depending on if I even made it there.

Slumping back on the ground, I realized that with plans made, a new skill done, and wishes finished, not to mention the fight over, I was officially free for the day. No more responsibilities that needed to be taken care of. Just me and some much-needed downtime. I could work with that.

I let my eyes drift closed as I pushed worry about my next match out of my mind. My fight with Wren had been an immense amount of fun, and I was sure the next one would be just as great, whoever it might be against.

We were so close to the end. I wasn't sure how they were going to handle the last five people standing (Benny insisted it would be a free for all but that just seemed like a mess to me), but whatever the format, I'd be ready.

As I surrendered to sleep, my last thoughts for the day weren't about combat, Benny, or even Callie. They were about me, and how happy I was with how far I'd come. I was standing on my own two feet now and had proved to myself I could do that. I had to admit, it felt damn good.

Chapter Forty-Nine

I SLEPT for like nine hours. It was amazing. I didn't even tweak my back sleeping on the training room floor because of my high Vitality. The luxury of just slumping down and sawing logs like a layabout was just... perfect. It felt so good to have some downtime that I decided not to work on my wishes or training until later in the day so I could ride the relaxation wave through the morning.

Hopping to my feet, I set off for the kitchen, shooting Benny a text to tell him we'd be doing breakfast here before we went out for the day, and starting the process of making eggs benedict. I was feeling fancy this morning, and I was going to show off a bit.

Callie, of course, basically floated into the kitchen on cartoon smell illustrations, and when she saw what I was making she squealed and tackled me. "You're making breakfast! You've been so busy lately it's been cereal and premade meals. Real eggs benedict. I think I'm in love."

"With me or the eggs?" I said with mock concern. "Because the former has been established, and the latter might give me a complex. I refuse to share your affections with breakfast food."

She gave an exaggerated wince. "Oooh, sorry. Breakfast had me first. You're pretty decent, but if I have to choose I'm afraid breakfast and I have too much history to ignore." She winked at me. "Besides, are you telling me I don't have to compete with long hot showers for your affections?"

I shot her a grin. "I'm happy to share any time." I looked around for Cass before I said it, because I absolutely didn't want another "why Callie and Shane do things you can't know about" discussion.

Sadly, it wasn't to be. She just patted my cheek fondly, resting her head against my back and putting her arms around me. "Sorry love, you shower for way too long. It would ruin my hair. Even Vitality can only prevent so much dehydration. Maybe if you can cut down your shower time a bit." At my appalled look she just giggled. "I thought so. Anyway, what's the big plan for today? You're having a guys' day out with Benny right? Because Jessie and I are hitting a flower nursery and a swap meet."

"One thing for each of you huh?" I said wryly. "Does she know the very concept of loot turns you into a drooling lunatic? Because if I were her I'd keep you on a leash." She opened her mouth to give an undoubtedly suggestive response, but Cass barreled into the room excitedly, cutting her off.

"Shane is cooking!" she cheered. "I love your food! I'm so sick of eating cereal all the time. What are we having?" The little girl was practically bouncing in place as she grilled me on what I was making, but she too was interrupted as her brother strolled in behind her and pushed her lightly toward the table.

He gave her a stern look. "Cassidy, let Shane cook. I'm sure you'll like whatever it is we're having. It's not nice to bother him while he's in the middle of cooking."

"But Callie is doing it!" she whined loudly. "She's giving him a hug and he doesn't even care. My questions are probably way less distracting than that." I snickered at the comment as Callie groaned and let me go, turning to walk over and plop down in a seat next to Cass.

She gave the younger girl a warm smile. "I was just saying good morning. We should let him cook for now. He's making eggs benedict, and that's really good—I think you're gonna love it. I didn't see you yesterday—did you do anything fun with Tony and your Uncle Zeke?"

The girl gave a put-upon sigh, informing her that Zeke had been busy and that Cark wasn't nearly as fun, and then giving a thorough if slightly disjointed account of her entire day, skipping around to different parts when they were more entertaining. By the time Benny made it to the kitchen, she was telling us about the new episode of her favorite cartoon for the third time, this time from the point of view of a side character with a cute dog that she really liked.

My best friend wandered in but didn't interrupt, yawning and dropping into a chair before resting his head on the table and starting to snore. Sadly for him, I finished cooking about then, so I woke him up by slamming a plate down in front of him, startling him so much he fell out of his chair with a shout of alarm, sending Cass and Callie both into a fit of giggles, though my girlfriend had the decency to try to hide it at least.

"Thought we could hit a couple local markets to look for some stuff for your Inventing," I said as he picked himself up, glaring at me. "You haven't made anything new in a while, and I know you still have some cash from working that job to pay me." Since he'd been paying off wishes with attacks when I needed them, he had a small stockpile of unused cash which would work well for buying Inventing materials.

He took a bite of the benedict, mollified by the delicious taste, and nodded thoughtfully before swallowing. "Yeah, I could probably use some new gear. Some of my merged artifacts are losing their punch. Some of them are great and plenty useful still, but stuff like the gut rope are pretty far past their best buy date. Plus with my Inventing at Intermediate, I have a bit more influence on what I get, and I can work with much better materials. Where are we going to look around?"

I shrugged. "Not sure, but I asked around and heard about a few places. Maybe Junk Island would be fun. It sounds like an interesting place."

We chatted a bit longer. Cass finished eating and got bored, wandering away. Cark trailed behind and lectured her about not saying "thank you" while she ignored him as usual. Jessie had shown up and grabbed a plate, presumably after a bad night, because her face looked haggard and her eyes were ringed with dark circles. She ate quickly and then went to go get ready.

Callie finished last, having taken her time to enjoy the meal, as well as having seconds. As she finished she rinsed her plate and gave me a quick kiss on the cheek. "Have fun on your day off. Try to relax a bit. I know I can't convince you not to train later, and I wouldn't if I could, but rest is an important part of improvement, even Abel admits that."

I grinned at her. "I know. I promise we'll waste tons of time and do many things that are pointless and unnecessary today."

"Well," she said wryly, "as long as you're sure." She turned to Benny. "Look out for him for me? You know how he tends to get into trouble. I swear he can't leave the house without getting wrapped up in some kind of dark conspiracy." She giggled at my affronted look and bolted from the room before I could protest, leaving me to sulk as I finished my own food.

Benny looked… sad. I cursed at myself, because us being affectionate probably made his own situation harder. Not that it was something I did on purpose. It just… kind of happened. Shoveling my food in I stood up abruptly, announcing while still chewing, "Alright. Time for us to go. We need to get to the bus stop since Jessie is going with Callie."

My best friend half grimaced half laughed at me talking with a full mouth and started teasing me as we took off. We walked to the bus like we had as kids, talking about anything but his relationship or cultivation, which admittedly didn't leave many options in our current lives.

When we arrived at Junk Island, I had to admit the place was interesting. It was an entire closed off island on a lake, full of hundreds of run down shacks and buildings piled with random junk.

There were weapons, tires, machines, appliances, furniture, and dozens of other things. Some of it was old and looked valuable; some was just trash. Some of it was heavy in the way that let me know it had Impact, even though visually it looked so destroyed as to be completely worthless.

Benny dove into the shopping with gusto, picking up items and exclaiming excitedly what they were, or trying to puzzle it out based on context. His Inventing Mastery was a wish granted Skill, so he had an absurd foundation, but that only went up to Beginner, because you had to tweak skills in Intermediate to your own use to progress them, so wishing for Intermediate Skills did more harm than good.

"Any ideas on what you're hoping for?" I asked as we sifted through random junk. "I know you can only really do so much to predict what the outcome will be, but you have to have something in mind for what would help you most." Inventing was annoying to deal with, but even if he couldn't control much about what he made, I was pretty sure he could predict what certain things would do based on the attributes of the material.

He shrugged. "If I could pick, I'd probably go with some kind of mobility artifact. I'm thinking I'll try using this." He held up what looked like a corroded dark-yellow metal wrench. "I'm almost positive this is a gravity artifact of some kind. It's so busted and rotted through it probably won't ever function again, but the best thing about Inventing is almost anything can be used in production."

I reached out and took it, noting that it was heavier than expected. "So what? Just melt it down and throw it in with some other stuff? I'm not sure if I love the randomness of Inventing or hate it."

"Tell me about it," my friend chuckled. "But there's something… amazing about it. Mad Science is just pure chaos. Sure, you can make something useless or even dangerous, but really, that's the fun. You're offering your fate up to the universe, putting yourself at the mercy of the whims of random chance. Isn't that what being an Ascendant is about? Seeing where the future takes you? Getting swept along by the current?"

I nodded contemplatively. "That's a decent point. I can see the appeal, and I know you can make some pretty crazy stuff. Stuff that Enchanting wouldn't be able to make at anywhere near the same level. The randomness is balanced out by power. Risk and reward. I guess that is kind of a microcosm of what it means to be a cultivator."

He pocketed the wrench, paying the stall owner a few chits, and then we moved on. We spent hours there, combing through garbage to find a few worthwhile items. Benny spent a surprisingly small amount of money. Given how hard some of the stuff was to find, the people selling it didn't always know what it was worth. They were here to bulk sell random trash —if some people got lucky that was on them.

Once we finished shopping we went out for dinner, eating somewhere relaxing and then heading home to begin training and working for the day. We'd let ourselves recharge, and now it was time to get back to the grind. With the downtime behind us it was almost exciting to get back to training, and I couldn't wait to see what my next skill would be.

Once we got back Benny did his wishes, five tranq blows for twenty points of Might, bringing him up to two hundred twenty-nine Might and five hundred eighty-three total stats. With that out of the way we each set off to do our own thing. I was happy for Benny especially. Seeing him so excited about Inventing instead of worrying about Celine was a nice change. Plus it would be cool to see what he came up with.

Chapter Fifty

THE NEXT TWO days passed without much incident barring a missing dessert I'd picked up for myself. I kept up training, but between my daily improvements I made a point to relax and spend some time with my friends. Jessie and Benny weren't in the tournament and had been left mainly to their own devices, but seeing how dangerous things were and how much work we were doing had them worried.

Benny I mostly tried to distract. Callie might have had a point about letting him stew. I'd wanted to leave him to think things through, based on personal experience, but the reason that had always worked was that we were usually inseparable. I'd neglected to note that this time was different because I wasn't around, and our time hanging out had seemed to help a lot, so I decided to spend more of my time being around my friend to give him a bit of relief from the constant soul searching.

Between outings, we did his wishes. Twenty Might, twenty Focus. He paid mainly in chits, bringing my personal stockpile to one hundred thirty-six chits, as well as topping up my tranq blows to ten. I'd considered stockpiling some extra attacks, but honestly with the tournament ending soon I really needed to save for my weapon. Hell, even not being able to use it I would have still probably bought it if I hadn't been waiting for the new skills I was developing.

For now though, it was the last night before the second round, and I hadn't been able to come up with a proper Skill yesterday, being stuck on Earth-seeking. I'd tossed it around for a while, trying to come up with a proper synergy, but had ended up wasting two days on it. Today, I decided to try something else and was planning to officially switch to a different skill. Specifically, I would try to tweak Seek Hidden.

Seek Hidden occupied a strange place in my arsenal, being both extremely useful and extremely useless. When it made a difference it made a big one, but because of the nature of the skill I didn't find much use for it as it was meant to be wielded. Seek Hidden was meant to be used on large objects over great distances. It could be used on smaller ones up close, but that wasn't its real purpose.

Not to mention it only picked up one thing at a time, which was a huge downside to a skill like that. What I needed was the ability to look at everything around me and see the hidden and concealed. I also used it for investigation, so I needed to be able to pick up small clues with this ability.

It took me quite a while to puzzle out exactly what Skill I needed to mix it with to get what I needed, but after spending some time on it, I made the connection that was obvious if you were paying attention. Poker.

So I went through the process of combining my Minor Poker Mastery with Seek Hidden, to create the skill that I needed. Unlike the last couple times, where I kind of guided them to the point they were close to what I wanted and then smashed them together and let them do as they would, this time I decided to try to guide the formation of the new skill more carefully.

In the spirit of that, I decided to define the skill as I wanted it to be. A new skill to let me see what was hidden, to find what was lost, to discover the traces of that which would conceal. I resonated the two skills, doing my best to use the aspects of both that I wanted to see.

Despite being prepared, I almost passed out. Micromanaging skill synergies was apparently *extremely* soul intensive. I felt like I was trying to lift an engine block with the power of my mind, focusing so hard I was worried I'd burst a blood vessel or something. It hurt. A lot. More than any other skill merge, but I pushed on. This was exactly what I wanted, exactly what I was hoping for.

Finally, after what seemed like forever, I felt the click that I'd been waiting for and the burden vanished. I slumped over backwards, shaking and sweating as I tried to get my heart to calm down. I breathed heavily for a few minutes until I finally had the strength to check my Skills.

Minor Poker Mastery was gone, as expected, and when I checked on my subskills I noticed the new one I wanted. Eye of Revelation.

Eye of Revelation was perfect. It wasn't a passive, only lasting for five minutes, but while it was active it allowed me to find the hidden and disguised, as well as discover traces of things missing. The tradeoff was that Eye of Revelation had an extremely low radius of effect, only being able to see things within twenty feet or so. Still, what it lost in distance it made up for in versatility, and it would be ten times more useful as it was.

I grinned, forcing myself to my feet, and staggered over to the track where I'd been training. I prepared to start… and then realized that I had nothing to actually find. I considered what to do with this, and then decided that I might as well have some fun with it. I headed upstairs, opening the refrigerator and peered inside at an empty spot. I'd picked up a slice of cheesecake on the way back from Junk Island, and someone had eaten it. I didn't know who, but with my new skill I could find out.

Triggering Eye of Revelation, I watched as the world kind of… darkened. Everything got kind of dim, with the exception of a few brightly lit items that I was pretty sure were hidden or clues. I could see some candy hidden in the cabinet behind the fridge, a bag of cookies shoved into the back of a cutlery drawer, and what looked like a plastic monkey under the oven mitts, the last one presumably belonging to Cass.

Along with that, I could also see footprints, leading off into the distance. Well, twenty feet into the distance. I stepped forward and picked up the next set, following them down the hall. I stopped, to my complete lack of surprise, outside my girlfriend's door.

Rolling my eyes, I rapped on the wood, and she opened it, looking out at me with a pleasant smile. I smiled back, then slipped around her into her room. She looked confused, until I followed the trail to the back of the room, dug around in a drawer, and pulled out a styrofoam container.

She giggled nervously. "That's… not mine?" I just looked at her for a beat, and then she pouted and looked away. "You didn't get me anything. That was rude. It looked really good so I ate it. It's not like you put your name on it or anything." I opened the container, showing her the inside, where my name was printed in black marker. She clicked her tongue. "Yeah, okay I don't know why I even tried that."

"No cooking," I said flatly, "for a month." I didn't actually care that much, but I liked cheesecake, and I wanted to make an impression so she didn't do it again.

Her eyes widened in shock. "Wait. What?" She crossed the room in a blink, clinging to me. "That's not fair. Come on, I'll buy you another slice. I can't go back to eating materializer meals and I don't have the money to pay for takeout. I spent it all on wishes!"

"Want to make it two months?" She jerked back, sulking but unwilling to risk it. I actually felt a little bad but if I caved every time she gave me puppy dog eyes I'd never stick up for myself.

I flopped down on the bed. "So, you already had your round right? When was it, yesterday?" It had been day three of the first round which would mean two days after my own match.

Snorting a laugh at the subject change she thumped down next to me. "Yup. Next match is tomorrow. I won, in case you were wondering."

"I wasn't," I said with a smile. "But I'm curious why you're up again so soon. Shouldn't you be in a later round?"

She shrugged. "Guess not. Since there are so few people left, the rounds won't be as consistent. Not everyone will fight at the same point in the rotation. I don't know who I'm fighting this time, or even where yet. They're sending out locations the morning of."

"Makes sense." I admitted. "If they told us where we would be fighting it would be easy to figure out our opponents by process of elimination. This way the surprise is fresh." I was still worried as hell about who I'd be fighting, but I had to admit that the first round had been a blast.

She rolled over to cuddle up next to me. "I guess. I'm just worried one of us will run into someone really scary. I know there are safety measures, but this is still battle. If someone like Abel decided to kill you, do you really think you would survive? And now we have Celine's asshole sister putting bounties on us—which, granted, she was nice enough to specify shouldn't cause our deaths—but…"

"But," I agreed. "But there's still the Cult. But we have enemies here. But

265

the tournament is the perfect opportunity to kill us without allowing for interference."

"Do you really think that would work?" she asked cautiously. "Like… Zeke is bound not to interfere, but if you died…" She sounded uncomfortable bringing it up, but I got her point. Hell I couldn't argue it because I'd asked him the same thing once.

I mulled over my wording. "I think that the person who kills me is going to have a bad day. Or century. But I also think that won't mean much to me since I'll be dead. If it makes you feel better, I'm not planning on dying, and I've made some serious preparations for the next round."

She looked up at me, raising an eyebrow. "Oh really? And what would those be? Inquiring minds want to know." She fluttered her eyelashes at me so fast it looked like she was trying to blink morse code, and I cracked up at her, which earned me a poke in the ribs and another pout. She didn't push for my answer though—she knew I wouldn't give it. After all, we might be up against each other at some point.

We chattered for a bit about nothing, not wanting to give away anything about our preparations but still wanting to spend time together. She tried to convince me to cook for her early, and I resisted, leading to lots of bargaining for one or two weeks taken off despite my steadfast refusal.

Eventually, we drifted off to sleep, and I couldn't help but smile as I dozed off, loving that we were still able to relax together even though we might be enemies if things went a certain way.

I was woken the next morning by my scan ring, and Callie by hers. I groaned and sat up, flicking open the screen. Callie was yawning and doing the same, and as the screens came up, we each noticed what the other person's said and we froze, staring at the information. Nothing too complicated, mind you. A simple address. Very simple, in fact, because it was the exact same address on both screens.

I glanced up to find Callie looking at me in worry. We'd both gotten our assignments. Our tenth-round fights would be against each other.

Chapter Fifty-One

WE DIDN'T FREAK OUT, though we did kind of shut up for a while. We both got ready and Jessie drove us to the arena. We didn't say much on the ride, and I admitted to being a bit nervous. My emotions were a jumble, really. I was excited for a good fight, upset I had to fight Callie, scared she would resent me if I won, scared I would resent her if I lost. My head was swirling with all these different thoughts, and I had no idea what to do.

Then she reached out and took my hand. I looked up into her eyes and she gave me that dazzling smile I only ever saw on her face when we were alone, and... I felt better. My worries weren't gone—I could still feel them, both mine and hers because the bond was open. But I could also feel how much she cared about me, and that in the end this fight wasn't going to mean anything we didn't want it to.

I squeezed her hand back and then turned to look out the window until we arrived at the arena. Jessie wished us both good luck as we climbed out of the car, and then we were on our own.

We headed for our respective waiting rooms below the arena, which was another new one I hadn't seen. There would be two matches here today, ours being the first. One hundred and sixty fighters over ten arenas. Four per day for four days for the first round, and two per day for four days for the second.

Sadly for Callie, I'd gotten lucky. I'd had my first match at the beginning of the rotation, so I'd gotten the full four days off. Since she had hers midway through she only got a day or two of downtime before her second match with me. I wasn't going to go easy on her because of that though.

Despite my worries about her resenting me or me resenting her, I'd never considered softballing it. She deserved better than that, and so did I. We were competitive people, and we both had a lot to prove. Holding back would be an insult to both each other and the audience, and I could feel through the bond that neither of us had any intention of doing so.

The wait before the match felt much shorter than normal, but that was probably just distraction. The guy watching the waiting room ushered me out when it was time, and I walked out onto the sand to stand across from Callie. She looked back at me, and I got ready to shut down the bond. Before I did though, I *really* looked at her.

Seeing her like this, like an enemy, was strange for me. The mask, the flowing black hair, the doll like features, the coat, the leotard, the boots—I got so used to the sight of her in costume as my partner that I lost track of what it felt like to take her in all at once like this. As a threat. Because she was a threat—maybe one of the biggest I'd ever faced.

Callie wasn't an F-ranker, or some kind of combat genius like Abel. But she *knew* me. Knew me in ways most people never would. We had a fucking Skill that proved that. Even without the bond active she wouldn't be easy to beat. Not least because she was the one who trained me in close quarters combat.

Speaking of the bond, I decided to take one last glimpse at it. I focused hard on the connection, and found her doing the same, and for a split second, before it shut, I saw myself. I saw me through her eyes and felt her own trepidation. She was seeing me the same way as I saw her, as a threat for the first time pretty much. And it was jarring to see myself like that. Despite the tinge of affection, there was a sense of wariness, but more than that, a sense of pride at how far I'd come. What I'd turned into.

Then the bond snapped off, and it was just me, looking at her, seeing myself in her eyes more literally now as I looked at the reflection off her irises. The whole experience had felt endless, but it took us about thirty seconds tops.

She grinned at me. "You ready? Because I'm not holding back. I'm gonna kick your ass. Not that it'll be hard considering the size of you."

I bit back a little trash talk of my own, because if I got sucked into banter, I wasn't sure I'd be able to commit to fighting at my best. So without responding, I triggered Moonlit Night. Fog billowed around us, filling the arena with dense mist that occluded the sight. At least, it occluded *her* sight. Mine was fine, since the fog was luminescent and partially translucent, just like last time, making it easier to see, if anything.

Next I triggered State of Grace, giving myself the ability to move more freely and quickly, then Ripple Running, so I had three dimensional mobility. With that done I knelt down, planting my hands on the sand and using Stone Limb along with Touch of Tears and Consecration of Flames to coat my arms in toxic magma.

Callie was standing in the middle of the arena, not moving, eyes fixed forward. I grinned, and without delay triggered Double Trouble. Appearing directly behind her, my eyes widened as one of her boots flashed up at my head. I ducked back as she dashed forward, blitzing me with attacks so fast I couldn't figure out how to counter.

I blocked them easily enough. Between the speed boost and my magma limbs, I was more than up to defending, but she was launching attacks so quickly that I couldn't find time to respond. Cursing, I triggered Double Trouble again, but instead of attacking I dashed forward, Ripple Running allowing me to avoid impacting the sand until I reached twenty or so feet away. Shaking out my arms, I gnashed my teeth.

Callie giggled. "You use that Double Trouble skill too much. It's predictable. I knew you wouldn't want to come at me head on, so I just listened for the displaced air. Don't forget how much higher my Perception is."

Which was probably how she'd been able to siege me down. She could hear my movements and use them to detect me, even without seeing, especially at close range. Moonlit Night made me harder to detect, so further out I should be fine, but her Perception was so much higher that the Stealth aspects of the ability couldn't keep up when I was right next to her. Joy.

I had other options, but before I could employ them, a massive wall of shadow spikes erupted from underneath me. Ripple Running was still active, so a quick step on the air and State of Grace let me blast upwards. I planted my foot midair, kicking off to the side, and touched down warily, waiting for another attack. This time she didn't speak to me, and I cursed internally when I realized what she'd done.

Callie had figured out I used Double Trouble, which made me appear right behind her, and then she'd attacked in a straight line. She'd probably used the damn shadows to burrow under the ground, and then told me how she'd beaten my attack to distract me while she felt around for my weight.

The stealth aspects of Moonlit Night would keep her from hearing me touch down, but they didn't prevent me from putting weight on the sand. Ripple Running could do that, but without a heading finding her would be near impossible, and I wasn't wasting the soul power to create a platform that would hold me the whole fight.

I did, however, have other options.

I triggered Sucking Mud (which would normally be too slow) and then used a stored shadow attack with it, forming a Dark Swamp that used grasping tendrils to drag enemies down. The darkness spread across the sand, but as it closed in and the tendrils lashed out, Callie narrowed her eyes and darted back and up. I saw the tendrils move slightly, changing direction in midair, and I hissed in annoyance as I figured out what had happened.

Callie had shadow manipulation, and the Dark Swamp used her very own shadows. She'd detected the attack and overridden it slightly. She couldn't use it against me or anything, but I was damn sure not going to catch her with it. Close combat would bring me within range of her Perception, which was strong enough to override my stealth.

The Dark Swamp was out.

I triggered Sucking Mud again but followed it up with a gravity attack. Callie buckled, looking surprised as the crushing force started mashing her into the sand. She snarled, hands lashing out as a wave of shadow tore through the ground below her, pushing the Sucking Mud aside as she dropped into the hole. Sand wasn't hard to move for people our level, and I'd seen her do the underground thing before.

Without any hesitation, I triggered Eye of Revelation, just in time to see a dozen forms erupt from the ground and rush out in all directions. She'd used the time out of my sight to spam those damn clones. Unfortunately for her, my Eye of Revelation told me which ones were clones and which was real.

I dashed forward again, hoping that all the noise from the clones and exploding sand would keep her from detecting me once I got close enough. As I came in I bounced off the air with Ripple Running, spinning off into a switchback kick aimed right at her head. Her eyes widened as she picked up the sound and hit the ground, which was what I'd wanted. I stepped on air again, redirecting myself as I used Touch of Tears and a tranq blow on my leg, slamming myself down on her back and triggering another gravity attack to pin her.

My fists slammed down on her coat, and the blunt force traveled through. It wouldn't have done anything, except Heavy Hands allowed partial armor piercing, which let the effect of the poison fire bypass her coat. Not completely, but enough that a few dozen blows made within a split second stacked enough of it up to hurt, and it combined with the similarly small percentage of the tranq poison that bypassed her coat.

She groaned, but kept her head, reacting with a shredding blitz of shadows aimed over her back where I was standing. I jumped straight up to avoid it and stepped on air as I waited for the blades to retract. Then I triggered a second gravity attack and smashed the same leg down on her back again with another tranq attack.

I missed—she rolled aside, having anticipated the attack. I could have grabbed for her, but grappling was the worst possible decision when she was stronger than I was, even with the poison. So I just backed off. She staggered to her feet, looking unsteady, and I remembered the boost from Moonlit Night, which would have improved the amount of the poison that penetrated her defenses.

The rest of the fight was just wearing her down. Using my Steam Arrows to pick at her, mixing them with poison and tranq attacks. I used half my tranquilizer stockpile, but finally, she couldn't hold out anymore and dropped to the sand, unconscious.

I let Moonlit Night fade, the fog rolling away, and walked over to her tiredly. This had been an intense fight, even with me having most of the momentum. I knelt down, dismissing the poison, and triggered a heal burst on her, patching up all of her wounds.

As she woke up, I was somewhat worried about how she'd react, but she gave me that same big dazzling smile and I laughed. I picked her up in a princess carry and walked out my own entrance. She just rolled her eyes and leaned against me, and I felt grudging acceptance through the bond, which was now active again.

Only three more rounds to go.

Chapter Fifty-Two

"YOU MADE me work for that one," I grunted as I slumped down on the couch. We hadn't talked much on the drive home. "I was worried a few times there. Your main stats are so much higher than mine. Can't believe you could see through my Moonlit Night. Even close range."

She shook her head. "Not see. Sight was gone. I was going off hearing. You almost got me with that. Some kind of Stealth element I'd guess? But you forgot that Stealth is about using Perception to erase all trace of yourself. Someone with a high enough Perception can overpower someone else's Stealth. Even with nearly triple yours though, I could only pick you up when you got close."

I winced, pressing on my ribs. "Being able to read and react to every move was pretty impressive. Fighting me blind must have been tough, even with your Balam Skill. Honestly, I'm shocked I even won with your advantages. I kept expecting to get pincushioned."

That got a laugh from Callie. "Honestly, you just have too many options. Especially with the new tricks, you were able to counter everything I tried. Several of those were new right? Stuff you've been working on during the tournament? I was on the back foot the whole time. I had no clue how to react."

"I guess that's the downside to us knowing each other's fighting style so well," I said with a shrug. "Changes are harder to keep up with, though you made a damn good effort."

I massaged my side. I could have healed it up, but I didn't want to. I'd earned the bruises in that fight. Callie had earned them. Plus they were light and they would be gone by the time I woke up tomorrow. No use wasting a healing charge.

She sighed. "So, with that out of the way, I guess we can talk about the tournament now. If you want. The closer we get to the end, the more likely you'll be fighting Mel or Abel. What do you think your chances are?"

I could see she didn't want to talk about her loss anymore and was trying to move on to discussing the tourney like someone who was just a bystander. She couldn't give me tips (because while she was out, I wasn't, and we still had an agreement with the others), but getting my opinion on it wasn't too much of a problem.

"Honestly," I said with a frown, "they're not great. I have more options for possible upgrades, and I might be able to take Mel if I prepare for it right, but I have no clue which one of them I'll face, if either. As for Abel... I'll do what I can. I'm not sure I can beat him, but at this point, even if I can't, that still means someone from our team will probably enter the finals. That's enough for me."

Not that I wasn't going to give my all to beat Abel, but I just... couldn't think of anything that would get it done. He was too strong. Too versatile. Too... Abel. If he did beat me though, I was going to make him work for it. I wouldn't be just another crushed enemy. He was going to remember our fight, even if he won the whole damn tournament.

The chances of me fighting him next round weren't high, though. Statistically, running into two teammates in as many battles wasn't exactly likely. Knowing that she still needed time to process, and that being under foot wasn't helping, I took off my mask and leaned down to press a kiss against Callie's forehead. "I have to go check in with Benny about today's wishes. Especially since *somebody* needed half my stockpile of tranq blows to take down."

That got a smug grin from my girlfriend. "Well, you didn't think it would be easy did you?"

Rolling my eyes, I headed off to find my best friend, but internally, I was happy to know she wasn't too upset. She'd put up a hell of a fight. It had taken me finally utilizing my stockpile of Skills to their utmost to have a chance at winning. If nothing else, Heavy Hands had been a hell of a weight on the scales. The passive ability was the only way I'd managed to do anything with her armor in the way.

Honestly, the way that worked out in combination with my other abilities was amazing. The augmentation from Moonlit Night boosted the force enough that even ten percent of it could have a real effect, and I hadn't even used Mercy kill during this fight. Or Afterburner. I'd be keeping those in reserve for dealing with Abel.

When I found Benny, he was sitting in the kitchen eating cereal. He gave me a mute nod as I came in, shoving another spoonful of sugar-coated corn flakes into his mouth and chewing. I always thought it was funny seeing Benny eat while tired. It was so... bovine. Staring off into the distance, jaw moving in a circular motion as his teeth ground up the food, the sound of it like a metronome. Crunch, crunch, crunch.

"Stop comparing me to a cow," he said without looking up, mouth full. I grinned, about to ask why he thought that, but he cut me off. "You always do it when I eat tired. I'm not in the mood this morning. So tell me how your match went or get with the wishes. Either way, shut up about my breakfast."

I scoffed. "Buzzkill. But fine. I won. It wasn't easy though. My match was against Callie." He stopped chewing, swallowing his food as he looked at me sharply.

"You okay?" he asked slowly. I smiled at the fact that he knew me well enough to ask, but... I was. I hadn't expected it myself, but Callie and I were in a good place. This hadn't hurt us. My smile must have made that obvious, because he nodded. "Good. Could have got messy."

I knew he didn't want to talk about this because it reminded him too much of his own situation, so I changed the subject. "Well, if it helps, I need another five stored tranq blows. Callie didn't go down without a fight, and I blew through half my stockpile. That's today's wishes paid up if you want to get them out of the way. It's a Focus day today, right?"

He chuckled. "They're even so either works, but sure, Focus is usually first on the rotation. I wish for four Focus, in exchange for a triple-strength tranquilizer attack."

Wish detected. Grant wish?

275

Confirming, I reached out to put my hand on his shoulder, ignoring the list of necessary stats because I'd seen it dozens of times. A growing charge of electricity broke over me and poured into my friend, our eyes both glowing purple, though I could only actually see his.

I couldn't help think back to that first wish all those months ago for a steak dinner in a park. This used to be so difficult for me. The effects of the power had drained me every time I used them, and it had felt insane doing it. Now… big wishes still hit me hard, but stuff like this didn't even wind me. A side effect of having such a high Vitality probably.

Benny wished for his next four wishes, topping up my tranq blows again as he got the last of his twenty points of Focus for the day. Two hundred and sixty-three Focus, and six hundred and forty-three total stat points. Not bad for someone who had hit G-rank so recently. At this rate, I'd just barely manage to get him and Jessie both to F-rank before we left. My healer friend was stockpiling cash for it as we spoke, so when I finished up with Benny I'd have a nice influx of money and I could buy a much nicer weapon before we actually left.

Once that was done, Benny slumped back with a sigh. "Man. That never stops feeling weird, you know? Not the wish itself, though… that too. But the sensation of just being… different, one moment to the next. Twenty points in a minute or two is just nuts, as I'm sure you remember. Like, yeah it's a smaller percentage now, but having my brain work that much faster and better out of nowhere is still jarring."

I nodded. "The huge stat dump after the scavenger hunt was nuts. Glad we don't need to go through that again anytime soon. Even big events in the future won't hit us as hard without that insane ratio." I paused. "Does it ever bother you?" He looked at me quizzically. "The feeling that this is eating away who we are. I don't think it ever bothered me really—I wasn't too attached to my humanity. But I've always been a bit weird that way. Looking back, I think I might have been raised with that disassociated view on purpose. But you…"

He shrugged. "Maybe? A bit. The idea of something external changing me like that was certainly weird for a while. But in the end… it's for the better right? Like I can mark notable improvements as my stats go up. Sure, I'm changing, but so is everyone else. I'm not becoming another person, just… more of myself. Recursion makes it a bit worrying, but in the end, don't we all change because of the world around us? It's a bit more literal for you and me, but it's not like *not* becoming an Ascendant will mean I get to freeze the person I was in time forever and never be anyone different."

"True," I said, slumping back on the couch as I mulled things over. "I guess for me, it just never mattered in the first place. My sense of self has always been a bit weird. Physical alterations, mental ones—none of it feels like it's changing me. Just making me into the person I want to become. I guess it's the same thing in the end. More of myself. That's a good way to put it."

"What about Callie?" he asked quietly. "Do you feel like your relationship with her is changing who you are? Making you different in a way the stats aren't?"

I could tell the question meant a lot to him. "Of course," I said immediately. He seemed... thrown. "I'm different because I'm with her. But like you said, everything changes us. The changes from being with her are ones I like. Is this about your recent training mindset?" He'd been very focused, and while a lot of that was us being gone and him worrying, at least some of it had been inspired by Celine.

"Yeah," he murmured. "It is. How much of that was because of her? Do I want to undo that? Does *not* wanting to undo it mean I want her back?"

"Nope," I said. He looked up in surprise. "It doesn't. I'm not saying you don't want her back, or that you shouldn't, that's not my call. But even if she inspired the changes in you, that doesn't mean that she's necessary for them to stay. We're all made up of nothing but constant changes. The people in our lives, both the ones who stay and the ones we leave behind, bring about most of them. And they don't go away, even when the people do."

His eyes cleared, the haze of doubt I hadn't even really registered lifting. He appeared pensive. "Yeah, you're right—that's a good way to look at it." He shook his head. "I'm dwelling on this too much. Let's go watch something stupid on the scan box. I want to decompress."

I nodded, clapping him on the shoulder. "Of course. There's a new reality show where they make people with poor balance try to walk down a long beam with a wedding cake as a hat. I haven't seen it yet, but it sounds just stupid enough to numb our brains for a while."

Benny laughed as we headed for the living room. He'd given me a lot to think about, but that was for another time. For now, I just wanted to be dumb with my best friend.

Chapter Fifty-Three

THE NEXT THREE days passed relatively quickly. While fighting on the first day of each bracket was a pain because I had to be one of the first in the round, which was nerve-wracking as hell, it was also a benefit because I got the full four days off for each round.

For the eleventh round it would be another four days, though there would only be one fight per day instead of two. That said, there would only be two days off before round twelve. Over the last few days I'd gotten another fifteen G-ranked chits from Benny in exchange for twenty Might and forty Focus, meaning my friend had broken the three hundred mark for Focus and the seven hundred mark for total points.

I still needed to upgrade Earthseeking and Sucking Mud and was having trouble coming up with a good combination for either of them. While I could just upgrade them normally without synergizing, now that I'd realized how to make DS Mastery stronger I was loath to leave power on the table. I couldn't be sure, but I had a decent guess that this process was similar to how my Wish ability had been created. Maybe not exactly the same, but I was betting the resulting power when I got DS Mastery to the peak would be absolutely amazing.

Despite not having any real ideas for my last two skill upgrades, I was relatively happy with the results so far. Which meant I was in a pretty good mood... that was completely ruined when I left the training room to find an agitatedly pacing Benny. When he saw me, he let out a sigh of relief and rushed forward to shove his hand in my face.

"I don't know if anyone told you," I said dryly, "but that 'talk to the hand' thing went out of style years ago. I hear these kinds of trends are cyclical though, so maybe you can bring it back if you try hard enough." I smirked at him, but the expression melted into concern when I saw his face remain twisted in worry. "What's wrong?"

He seemed to realize that he wasn't being clear, and spun up his scan ring, shifting it from the normal dormant mode to the screen. As he did that, I realized that the ring had been what he was showing me. Texts circled the band when it was dormant. Once he had the display up though, I was able to more easily read the message from Celine.

Things are going wrong, get somewhere safe. I love you.

"Well that's… ominous," I said as my stomach began to tighten with sympathetic anxiety. "Did you call her back?" I knew he had, but I had to make sure. He wasn't in a good place right now, so overlooking options wasn't beyond the realm of possibility.

He ran a hair through his messy brown hair. "Yes. Obviously. Nothing. I tried six times and got no answer." He started pacing again. "What the hell, man? What's going on? Celine isn't in the tournament herself. Did one of the other factions jump her? Is this a trap? Do I care?"

It said a lot about how far Benny had come that the idea of this being a trap occurred to him. But it didn't feel right to me. Celine had been trying to make amends, even put herself in a bad situation with her family to do it. A trap felt out of place, which just left some kind of attack… which wasn't much better.

"Come on," I said to my friend, grabbing his shoulders to stop him in place. "We need to go talk to Callie and the others. We'll figure out what to do as a team, okay?"

His eyes were shimmering with fear as he looked back at me, and it tore me up to see the panic and agony in his expression. "What if…" His voice broke. "What if she's dead? What if the last thing I ever said to her was that it was her fault I couldn't trust anyone? What if she's lying somewhere in a ditch with no head like those sleepers Aiden killed down in G-district."

He was shaking, and voicing that possibility seemed to be too much for him. He blurred down the hall, smashing open the door to the bathroom.

I could hear him puking from where I stood, and honestly I didn't blame him. That had been gruesome, and I tried not to think about it, but the idea that one of those bodies could be someone I knew— Just imagining Callie's head exploding like that made me want to vomit myself.

Following him into the bathroom, I ran the sink and then passed him a cup of water to rinse out his mouth. He swished and spat, then downed the rest of it, eyes still vacant and his breathing shallow. That wasn't just fear. That was a panic attack. Which made sense in this situation but told me that some of what we'd been through had affected Benny more than he liked to let on.

I clapped him on the shoulder. "Hey," I said, getting his attention. "She'll be fine. I can feel it. She texted you. That's not something people can do easily from captivity. She's probably on the run. Let's go check with the others and make a plan so we can find her and help her. Don't forget we have Rime around—she goes where we go. Whoever is after her, if anyone still is, will be in for a rude awakening."

He swallowed hard but seemed to cling to my words. "On the run. Right. We can help." He grabbed a bottle of mouth wash and swished a few times so no one would be able to tell he'd just puked his guts out.

I stepped out of the bathroom while he washed his face with cold water and tried to breathe for a bit. After he was stable, we headed to the living room to loop in Callie, Jessie, Abel, Mel, and Rime. Cass and Cark were out at the park... thankfully. I didn't want to explain to the little girl what was going on.

After Callie heard everything that we knew, she grimaced. "That... that's bad." She bit her lip, gnawing at it in a way I only saw her do when she was really nervous. "This could be a trap. And even if it isn't... I'm not sure I can risk us for Celine after what she did."

Benny looked ready to attack her. "What she did? You mean when she leaked our next opponent to us so you could prepare for your match? Or when she helped us learn about information gathering at the academy, compromising her own advantage so we could get access to information?" Callie looked at him sadly, and he closed his eyes, taking a long, slow breath. "Look. I'm sorry. I get it. This is risky. I can't ask you to put yourself in danger."

He turned to walk away. Callie stood up, grabbing his arm. "Oh stop being a drama queen." She huffed. "I'm not letting you run off to do this by yourself. And you aren't wrong. Celine helped us plenty of times. We might have died during Aiden's siege if it wasn't for her. If it means that much to you… we can help."

My friend's relieved smile was cut off as she shoved a finger in his face, continuing. "But," she said sharply, "if we're doing this, you need to listen to my orders. You're way too emotional right now. We can help her, but the person doing it needs to be making smart calls. You have to follow the chain of command here. If you don't, then I'm going to have Abel knock you out and lock you in a room, no matter how much you hate me for it. I'm not letting you get yourself or any of the rest of us killed."

Benny looked uncertain, but finally, he sighed and nodded. "Ok," he said dully. "I can agree to that. But you need to help me. Help her. Do *something*. Because if that was one long way of telling me to sit tight and wait it out or something you can fuck right off."

She smiled wryly and turned to Rime. "I need you to get in touch with Frostbite. Find out what's going on. No way there was an attack at the academy or even in the city proper involving an active diplomatic attaché and she doesn't know about it. We need to know what's happening and where before we can decide our next move."

The blue haired F-ranker nodded. "Seems like a good start. I'll need somewhere private to reach out—you have any quiet rooms I can use? My scan ring is untraceable but Frostbite isn't a fan of being overheard."

Jessie stood up. "I know a place. This orange eyesore is bigger than you can imagine, and I wander around here sometimes. I still don't know why we can't paint the place, but either way, there's a room I have in mind." She waved the ice user after her, stopping before she left to wrap Benny in a bone crushing hug. As my friend grunted in discomfort, she buried her face in his shoulder. "She's gonna be okay, Ben. Just have faith."

He smiled tensely down at her, resting a hand on her head, and then she let him go and headed off with Rime. Callie, still in the zone, turned to Abel and Mel. "I need you two to reach out to the Magnificent Fable Forest.

They're the only real connection we have to Celine's faction and are the best bet for getting information from anyone we actually know."

The two of them nodded. I wasn't sure how they would manage it since we didn't get a number from the Faerieland team, but they didn't seem worried. They just headed out of the room, presumably to start getting in touch with some of their own contacts to try to find a lead.

Callie turned to Benny. "Did you call Sarah or Martin?"

My friend looked stunned for a second, but then shook his head. Callie nodded understandingly. "Alright, well that'll be your next move. Reach out to her team, see if they know anything. Once we've heard back from all our sources we'll head for the Academy."

"What?" Benny snapped. "Why the hell wouldn't we leave now? She could be in danger, or hurt, or even dying!"

"Which is why we wait," my girlfriend said calmly. "The Academy is a protected and secure place. While it's possible she might be there, the chances of her being under threat while she's that defended are low. That means if we head there, we might be moving further away from where she actually is, and not find out until we're already there. So yes, we sit tight, and once we know more we decide what to do."

Benny deflated, but he seemed to accept her explanation, slumping down on the couch like the bones had gone out of him and staring worriedly off into the distance, completely oblivious to anything else but the storm of pain and fear I was sure was in his chest.

It was funny. If it had been any other situation I might have pointed out that they were fighting, that he was angry at her, or a dozen other things. But now... it didn't matter. Because seeing him like that was the best answer to any question I could ask about how he felt, or any question he could ask either.

He would forgive her. I knew he would.

I just hoped to the gods that his forgiveness would still be possible. Because if it wasn't, I was pretty sure he wouldn't be extending that same mercy to himself.

Chapter Fifty-Four

RIME CAME THROUGH. Or rather, Frostbite did. Upon receiving the call, our ally combed through the local information sources and got us a location for a recent fight matching the parameters we gave her. She wasn't able to actually locate Celine, but she told us where the elf girl *had* been, and that was more than enough for me. Eye of Revelation would let me track her if I had a place to start.

Just as she said, Callie wasn't pulling punches either. Aside from Rime, she also called her uncle to ask him to lend us the Four, and with Randall thrown in that gave us *six* F-rankers. Which was good, because when we arrived at the address we'd been given... there was a lot of damage. Like, someone blew up the house levels of damage, except instead of craters and ash, there were mostly trees. Branches and roots had torn the place apart, and I saw the twisted forms of huge tree golems, though the ones around the house were dead and partially rotted away.

"Um..." I looked at Jessie, who was currently sitting on Randall's back, her F-ranked green cloak drawn around her for protection. "Can Celine do this? Because I feel like I'd have noticed."

Benny shook his head from my other side. "No. Cel is more on the political side of things. A lot of her Skills are aimed at reading tells and remaining composed. She does have some nature manipulation stuff, but it's all either small scale or very slow. This... this is not slow." He looked at Jessie.

"Could you do this? Even just in terms of growth rate? I know that you can't really control plants like this given the direction your power has gone."

She shook her head. "This isn't G-rank plant manipulation. I don't know if it's closer to F or E, but this kind of power is way beyond what I can do within any reasonable period of time. But that's not what's bothering me. There isn't any life in these plants. At least, not much. It seems like whatever killed the golems sucked it out maybe? Or the plants were depleted trying to defend themselves. The plant user wasn't the only powerful person here."

That gave me an idea of what we were dealing with, and it wasn't one I liked. I walked up to the nearest damaged tree and used Eye of Revelation. Under the view of my new gaze I could see a few clues I hadn't before. Enough to confirm my guess.

"Cultists," I spat. "This was Black Sorrow. Pietro used something like this, some weird kind of conceptual darkness that twists the world around it."

Callie made an angry noise. "I remember. This is a clear lead—now we just need to find them."

If Celine was being chased by cultists, we definitely needed to help. "The question is, where do we start?" I asked sheepishly. "The plant stuff isn't Celine, so I can't use it to track her. I can only track over short distances, so I need a location to begin my search." Twenty feet wasn't a short distance in battle, but for tracking, it seriously limited my options.

"Here," Benny said from off the side. I turned to find my friend kneeling next to one of the trees, pointing to something I couldn't see. "This is an earring I gave her. I have a matching ring that heats up a little when it gets close. I bought it for her as a joke because she told me she didn't like surprises. I figured she'd like it, since she'd always know I was coming. I... I'm surprised she's still wearing them."

That was a surprisingly touching story, and it made me realize that Benny and Celine probably had a lot of those. Just because I only saw them around each other for a little bit didn't mean they didn't have a whole relationship that none of us were aware of. This was the first real clue to exactly how much my friend had been mourning, and despite having no option to learn more without him telling me, I felt bad that I hadn't understood how much Celine meant to him.

Well, the only way to fix that would be to help find her. I approached the earring, which Benny was smart enough not to pick up, and flexed Eye of Revelation again. The earring glowed a soft green, and beside it, a set of footprints shone the exact same shade. "Got her. I can't really see who might have been with her or following her, but I can tell you which way she went."

I started to track her. The residential area around us was shockingly quiet and unruffled for a place with a giant tree tearing apart one of its locations. I ignored it all though, following the footsteps behind the house and past a small lake to a strip of woods. "I think this was a safehouse or something." I said as we entered the trees. "No way the cultists are stupid enough to bring them somewhere this close to the woods. The elves had to have picked this spot."

Callie made a noise of agreement. "That was my guess too. Based on the amount of power thrown around, I think this might have been where Celine's sister Nalia was staying. That means the cultist around here is at least E-rank. Which is… less than ideal."

I could try to get in the way of whoever it was, but if they attacked anyone but me we were screwed. The E-rankers seemed to be gone at least, but I made sure to take the lead anyway. For one thing, I was tracking so I kind of had to, but for another, if some E-rank asshole was waiting in the wings to attack, I'd be the one to get tagged.

We followed the footsteps into the trees, then down a narrow gully and through a stream. As we crossed the river the footprints got *really* faint and almost flickered out, but I managed to keep with them by slowing down and shrinking the radius of my Eye of Revelation.

I hadn't had much chance to train this one in the field, and the knowledge that I could condense the twenty-foot radius to increase effect was damn helpful. It was also a minor change in the skill, which meant my soul was barely taxed by keeping it up. Something that would be necessary on long tracking missions if that became necessary.

"This is weird," I murmured, using the bond to tap into Callie's Stealth Skill to keep my voice from carrying. I still had stored charges of Stealth too, but it didn't seem smart to use them when I had other options. "The tracks are fading out. I'm keeping up, but I can't really figure out why they would be doing that."

"Because," said a pained voice from up ahead, "I was trying to make them disappear as I left them." We all looked up to see Celine propped up against a tree, hand on her side, and blood leaking between her fingers. She had a black eye and her hair was matted to her scalp with dark fluid on one side. The biggest problem, though, would have to be her other hand. The flesh was black, like she'd been frostbitten, and it hung limply off to one side.

"Cel!" Shouted Benny, practically blurring across the space between them. It was jarring to realize that his Might was way higher than mine because of his specialization, something I knew but hadn't internalized really. He stopped just short of grabbing her, looking on anxiously. "Are you alright? What happened?" He looked over his shoulder. "Agria, can you come help patch her up?"

Jessie hopped down from the bear, zipping over to lay glowing green hands on the elf. She winced. "These were made by an F-ranker. This will take a while, Celine—sorry."

The elf shook her head mutely, sighing in relief after a minute. "No, it's more than enough," she said with a hoarse voice. "Thanks. Nalia and her guards drew most of them off. The F-ranker that was left behind was extremely injured. I was barely able to finish him off."

Reaching down to touch the blackened arm, Jessie winced. "This… I can't fix this." Benny's head snapped up. "This isn't damage—it's some kind of persistent effect, like a curse or something. If it was damaged or even dead I could probably do something about it with enough time, but whatever the force that made this wound is, it's still active, and it's not something I can work against directly."

Celine chuckled. "It's fine. The wound in my side is already feeling much better. I can find a solution to the arm later. We need to get out of the open. There's a cave near here. I've been slipping out to watch for rein-forcements, trying to use my Woodcraft Skill to stay out of sight. It's only at Beginner, but my Perception is relatively high." She shot me a wry look. "Though apparently it isn't useful on whatever it is Solomon was doing."

I just shrugged. "I don't play by the rules—it's a character defect." Drop-ping the joking tone, I frowned at her worriedly as Benny and Jessie helped her stand up. Jessie needed to keep a hand on her to heal, and Benny was clearly reluctant to let her out of his sight. "You sure you're going to be okay? That hole in your side looks nasty."

She just smiled. "I appreciate your concern. I admit it feels... nice, to know you all care." Her smile wilted as she looked at Benny. "I didn't... I didn't mean for you to come. I just wanted to say goodbye, and say..." Her cheeks darkened. "That."

Benny's smile could have split his face in two, it was so wide. "Of course I came." He pressed a kiss to her forehead. "I love you too." He hesitated before murmuring, "I'm not saying we're good. You really hurt me. I'm not over that. But... it's less important right now than making sure you're safe. We can work on things later. If you still want to."

Leaning her head against him, she nodded, her smile still in place, though more solemn and filled with pain. We got into the cave and helped her sit down so Jessie could have better access, and I stepped up to use a combo heal and scan heal. Jessie's ability (being the source of my heal burst) was much more powerful, but scan heal could help target injuries better, and might even be able to do something about her arm.

Sadly, that didn't turn out to be the case. When I apologized she waved me off again. Benny looked concerned, but Jessie had an idea on how to help her. She said she needed to check on a few things but she knew someone whose ability could help.

"Alright," Callie said after we'd mostly gotten Celine patched up. "As glad as we are all to see you okay, we need to know what happened. Who did this?" We had a general idea, but we needed confirmation.

Sure enough, Celine immediately responded, "The Black Sorrow Cult. They snuck many more people onto this planet than we expected. They lured me here with a fake information leak and showed up in force. Three E-rankers and ten F-rankers. Nalia stalled the other E-rankers—my sister has always been the most martially inclined member of our family—but there were just so many..." She trailed off. "I don't think this was an isolated attack. If they hit us, they probably hit the other factions."

I was already sprinting out of the cave for a signal, calling Natalie. If they had F-rankers in those numbers, she was in danger even with her guardian. I just hoped my cousin was okay.

Chapter Fifty-Five

I HADN'T VISITED the location where my cousin and her guards were living. With the tournament ongoing and my team's deal not to seek outside help, it seemed smart to minimize contact, but I had at least gotten an address from her in one of our conversations, so I was able to direct Jessie to the location. Luckily the expanded space came with an expandable entrance, or we'd never have fit Randall in the car.

Natalie had been in a hotel for a while but had moved into semi-permanent lodging after confirming my team's strength in the first round, since between us we had a decent chance to make it all the way. When we arrived at the rented house, I grimaced. It was dark and silent, but looking close I could see a few issues. The lock on the door was snapped and it hung slightly ajar, and some of the windows were cracked.

I tried calling again. No response. Shit.

I turned to Callie, who was standing close, offering support silently with her presence and through our bond. "Someone's been here. But it seems weird there wouldn't be more mess. Nat is a Candidate. She's not going to go down easy."

There was a loud crack behind us, and we all spun to stare at Jessie, or rather, Randall, whose back she was on. He had stepped on a curbside bench and smashed it to kindling by accident. We all glared, and she just shrugged, saying in a soft tone, "Well, he's a bear. They aren't made to be stealthy."

Rolling my eyes, I turned back to the house, my tension pretty much shattered. I was still worried, but it's hard to feel stifled by the gravitas of a situation when you're walking around with a big clumsy teddy bear on your team. I looked at Callie. "Do the Four have a higher Perception than you? I know out of the G-rankers present, you're our best stealth agent, but I don't really know what they can do."

She glanced at them questioningly and when one of them nodded, she pointed at him. "That one does, apparently." At my snicker, she just shrugged. "What? It's not like I lunch with them. When would I even have the time? We're together almost any time I'm not working or training. They're acquaintances through my uncle." She turned to the indistinguishable-from-their-siblings hooded figure. "Check the house, report back if you run into anything we need to know about, and be careful in there."

The only real upside to this was that we knew there was no one over F-rank inside. With Rime and the rest of our crew along there was very little chance they'd be able to overpower us. I hoped. No matter how many times I repeated that to myself, a part of me was pretty terrified we were kicking an anthill and about to be ass deep in F-rankers we couldn't beat.

Speaking of which, I looked at Rime. "Is Frostbite coming to meet us here?"

I'd asked her to tell our ally we needed her on hand after we found Celine. The blue-haired ice user nodded. "She's on her way. This isn't exactly a central location, which I imagine is the point."

That was the best we could ask for. Callie, hearing the confirmation, dispatched whichever of the Four had been pointed out, and one of the figures vanished. I'd seen them use that trick in the fight with the mercenaries, but I hadn't been sure how much of that was taking advantage of my lapsed attention. This time they just blinked out of existence right in front of me, and I recognized that they'd used Perception to erase all traces of themselves from my sight.

The door to the inside shook slightly as it creaked a smidgen more open, but it didn't make any sound or anything, and if I hadn't been looking right at it I'd have missed the motion. Callie put a hand on my arm. "She's fine, Shane," she said softly, her voice being run through Stealth to prevent it from carrying. "Your family is tough, and if her guardian is anything like yours, in the very unlikely circumstance that something happened to her, they'd have burned down half the planet in retribution."

I snickered at that, but it actually did make me feel better. If there was anyone I trusted to have my back it was Zeke, and remembering that Natalie had someone like that really helped. Not to mention her two guards, whose names I'd forgotten if I ever heard them. She had plenty of backup even without my team coming to help.

After two minutes the hooded form reappeared in front of us among the other three. The weirdest part was that somehow even knowing where there hadn't been one of them before, I somehow couldn't figure out *which* of the figures had just appeared and which had been there for the entire time we'd been waiting.

"The house is empty," the F-ranker reported. "Signs of a struggle. The inside is bigger than the outside, and the fighting was mainly in the middle of the top floor, so none of it spilled onto the exterior."

I cursed and stalked through the door, letting it bang open as I strode into the house. Near the exterior it looked like a nice normal house, but the further in I got, the more signs I saw of combat. Acid burns, fire, purple crystal and some strange blue glowing slime that had stuck at least two literal lightning bolts to the wall, suspending them harmlessly inside the gel in an extremely disturbing way.

I saw splatters of blood in a few places, none of them too big, so I was pretty sure no one bled out here, but in and of itself the fact that Nat and her people hadn't managed to kill any of their attackers was jarring. I also wasn't sure how they'd attacked this place. Was Nat's guardian not living with her like Zeke was with me? The whole loophole of protecting their own residence should have applied. Though maybe that was a liberty Zeke took with his contract to help as best he could.

Looking around, I shouted. "Hey, if Natalie's guardian is here, I'd like to talk. It's not interference—I just want to confirm a few things. Even if you aren't living here you should be keeping an eye out right?" My voice carried into the depths of the empty house, but I got no response.

Callie shook her head. "They probably followed Natalie. We need to figure out where she went. What about your tracking skill? You have a starting point here, so you can follow her trail right?"

That... was a good idea. I should have thought of that. I was off my game. My stomach roiled and my chest was tight. I had exactly one biological family member who I was aware of in this entire damn star Cluster, and she was on the run from insane cultists who had tried to kill me multiple times. Nat and I weren't close (we barely knew each other), but what she represented... was a member of my family I could talk to. Could learn about.

"Shane," snapped Callie, and my head came up. I'd frozen for a few seconds, lost in my panic. Callie knew about my tendency to drift off, but she usually left me to my thoughts. This time she was looking at me sternly. "I know how scary this is. How confused you are. I can *feel* it, and it breaks my heart. But if you spiral and let her die it's going to break *your* heart, and that will hurt me a million times more. I need you to focus up. Okay?"

I took a long, deep breath. "Yeah. Yeah I'm good. Thanks Cal. I'm okay."

I turned to the destroyed room and triggered Eye of Revelation. There was... a lot. Footprints were all over, and some of the attacks were glowing, showing me they'd been Nat's. I had to stop for a second, not because I didn't have a trail, but because I had like seventeen of them. Nat had lived here, there were traces of her everywhere.

It took me a few minutes to sift through the traces, figuring out how the passage of time affected them, and using that to date the most recent trail. Once I got it, I set off down the hall, following several passages back further into the house. We stopped in the kitchen, and everyone looked at me quizzically until I reached up and put a hand on the refrigerator and shoved to one side.

The large metal machine slid aside easily, smashing into the wall because I was way too strong to do something like that without paying attention. Behind it was a small closet full of cleaning supplies, and I stomped down on the floor of that closet, crumpling a well-hidden trapped door that led down into a cement passageway.

It was a huge relief that they'd managed to re-hide this place behind them, but the blood smeared across the cement as we climbed down the metal ladder into the tunnel was... less encouraging. It wasn't enough that I was sure someone was dead, but it wasn't a little bit either. Handprints on the wall showed where someone had tried to hold themselves up, and the prints were lower to the ground and smaller than they would be from a man or even a reasonably tall woman. Natalie was small like that.

Callie stepped up next to me as she came down the ladder. "This keeps going, and it's not a huge amount." She squeezed my arm. "I know it doesn't feel like it, but this is a good sign. I sent Jessie with Rime to take Randall around the back of the house to look around. Mel went back to let them know which direction the tunnel is going, so they know which way to head."

I nodded silently, not trusting myself to speak right now. I was… angry. Irrationally pissed off at everything. This was taking too long, my cousin was hurt, possibly dying and I couldn't help and everything was getting in my way and I just wanted to punch something and throw up and possibly strangle a Cult member. The cocktail of unpleasant emotions and feelings was not helping my composure at all.

Callie just smiled at me reassuringly and then set off down the tunnel. She could feel what I was, and she knew I needed a minute to clear my head. But I also needed to keep moving, so once they pulled ahead I followed. The tunnel went on for an unusually long time, the blood smears getting more and more fresh as well as having less blood on them, which I took as a good sign.

About three quarters of the way down we started hearing noises and felt shaking. We reached the end of the tunnel and opened up a hatch at the top of a ladder, pushing aside a bunch of leaves to reveal our position at the edge of a massive clearing. In the center of that clearing, glaring at a series of hooded figures, were Nat and her two guards.

One of them was cracking whips made of blue gelatinous material like the stuff from the house. There were dozens of types of energy caught along the whips, and the taller hooded figure, whose face had been revealed as a red-bearded giant of a man with a shaved head, was bringing them down to ward off the other forms.

The smaller hooded figure, who turned out to be a muscular blonde girl with her hair in a pair of braids, had a huge axe coated in green smoke that she was lashing out with in short, sharp chops.

Surrounding them was a huge construct made of some kind of red energy in the shape of a wall of briars, and I could see that while it was F-rank, some of the cultists were hard at work tearing through it. Off in the distance, I could see Jessie on Randall's back with Rime bringing up the rear.

Without hesitation, I dropped to my knees to condense my poison lava fists. I needed to help.

Chapter Fifty-Six

STATE OF GRACE flowed through me as I dropped to a knee, planting my hands on the ground to trigger my usual magma limb and introduce poison into the mix. I was about to charge forward to help, but a hand caught my shoulder. I turned to see Abel frowning at me.

"No," he said bluntly.

"What do you mean, no? My cousin is fighting for her life here!" I tried to shake him off, but even boosted, his Might was much higher. His hand remained locked around me, and probably would be unless I took a swing.

He pointed at the red wall of briars. "No. She isn't. She's under a defensive enchantment or something. It's holding, even if her guards seem to be dipping out of it to engage. We aren't rushed, as much as it feels like it. You need to wait for the others to engage first. A crowd of F-rankers mainly focused on you would be fatal. Once Rime and Randall arrive we can engage with our full forces."

He sounded... weird. Serious and efficient. I'd seen him pissed, seen him casual, but Abel when he was operating in a serious manner was weird to me. It was jarring enough to make me stop and think. With the red barrier still up, I was willing to give him the benefit of the doubt.

Sadly, just because I agreed to wait, didn't mean the figures would. We'd been noticed, and while most of them stuck with trying to chip through the red barrier and take pot shots at the guards, two of the F-rankers turned and started heading toward us. Both of their black fathomless hoods pointed at me, and when they spoke, they didn't bother to keep it down.

"It's him," said the muffled voice of one of the figures. "He killed Pietro. But not just Pietro. Can we fight someone who killed an E-ranker?"

The other shook his head. "He's like the girl, another of the wish spawn. His protection doesn't cover us." He looked over a shoulder as the others arrived—the Four, Randall, Rime, Mel, and Jessie all rushed the crowd of F-rankers around Natalie. There were seven hooded figures, not counting the two before me, but Rime engaged two of them so I wasn't worried.

I *was* worried about being up against a pair of F-rankers (even admittedly weak ones) with just a group of G-rank backup. I felt Callie step up next to me. On this side of the clearing it was just me, Benny, Celine, Callie, and Abel. I considered using Moonlit Night, but it would hamstring my allies, so I stuck with my current boosts.

As they drew closer, I got more and more angry, my hands almost shaking. These fucking lunatics. Attack my family, kidnap children, try to murder my loved ones—they just wouldn't stop. Just wouldn't give up. Why couldn't they just leave us alone? They were fucking poison, a toxic rot pervading the whole planet.

I stalked forward, yanking my arm from the grip of a distracted Abel, and strode toward them. The closest figure, the weaker one, chuckled softly under their robe and flicked a finger casually. A dozen spears of bone erupted from the ground, and I triggered Double Trouble, appearing behind him. He was already turning lazily to meet me when I triggered Steam Arrow. Buffed with Touch of Tears, Consecration of Flame, and Mercy Kill, and with my speed enhanced by State of Grace, the arrow of boiling, toxic liquid smashed into his face.

Despite the hood, there must have been no face covering, because the figure reared back with a roar. Or maybe there was, but Heavy Hands pierced some of the defenses. Either way, the hood fell back, revealing an olive-skinned woman with close cropped hair, one side of her head shaved.

Her face was being chewed away by acidic boiling steam. Though the damage was already starting to heal, her eyes had been right in front of me and received the worst of it. I thanked the gods that Steam Arrow worked through my mask since, despite the spitting motion to manifest it, it condensed right in front of my face.

I triggered another arrow, and she screamed, clawing at her face. When Callie appeared behind her and slammed a leg into the back of her knees, I turned my attention on the second figure.

He was pretty distracted. Mel had circled around with her flame movement and joined Abel in assaulting him. They shredded his cloak, revealing a tall bald man with glowing veins covering his unnaturally distended body. He was trying to punch holes in Abel, who was never where the man thought he was, and was tanking a ton of very scary blows.

Deciding that wasn't something to worry about I dipped down and triggered Sucking Mud along with a shadow attack, activating the Dark Swamp. The tendrils lashed out to grip bone girl, dragging her down. She screamed, and a torrent of dark bones ripped the ground around her to shreds. Each bone was gleaming with a black sheen, like they were coated in oil. They split apart the Dark Swamp with sheer numbers, displacing all the earth within that ten-foot radius.

Callie lashed out with a hand and a palm of shadow smacked me aside as a grasping claw of black bone formed from the spikes and tried to grab me. Apparently we now warranted being taken seriously.

Making sure Benny, Mel, and Abel were out of range, I used Moonlit Night, shrouding the area nearby in fog. I felt Callie reach through the bond and I let her connect to the skill, allowing her to see inside the fog like I did. She didn't get the boost to attacks that I did, but mobility in a fathomless fog bank imbued with Stealth was a hell of a useful advantage. I triggered Ripple Running, bouncing off three separate spaces to land next to her.

I grimaced as I saw the slash on her thigh. One of the bones had slipped between her leotard and boots and through the gap in her jacket. I put a hand on her shoulder and triggered a heal burst. "Alright," I grunted. "Really don't like her. Any ideas?" Inside the mist Stealth was all pervading, which meant we could talk openly without being overheard by a third party, though it was a trick that would only work with Callie due to our bond allowing her to bypass the concealment.

She scowled at the hooded form still climbing out of the hole left in the muck. "Not sure. That bone power is annoyingly versatile. Not sure if it has a range limit, but she seems to be able to use it in close proximity to herself as well as far away. I'm *pretty* sure she can't just pincushion the entire clearing, since she hasn't yet. But if we get close we need to put her down hard or she's going to skewer us before she drops. Any chance the poison will take her down?"

"No," I growled. "And tranqing is out too. My tranq attacks aren't strong enough to take down an F-ranker—even with poison as a carrier—without some serious damage to soften them up and compromise their healing factor. Kind of wishing Benny kept that big-ass hammer. Any chance the shadow dragon might be able to get things done? We could have it attack from the fog."

Shaking her head, Callie sighed as we watched the bone woman spin blindly in circles. "No. The dragon is only as strong as the combined power of our skills. The shadows are G-ranked and my Might isn't high enough to hurt someone cross rank. Even Stone Limb reinforcing it wouldn't bridge the gap. Maybe with a density shift and a few bonuses stacked up, but I'd have to support most of the soul weight myself since I'd be holding the construct. That's too much for me to handle."

I let out a frustrated huff. "Okay, so, we need a single powerful attack, something that can smash her defenses before she can react and spear us." I paused. "I've got nothing. I have a few single-shot finishing blows but nothing that can cross ranks with any certainty. You don't either." I turned and strode out of the fog, Callie following as we left the hooded figure thrashing around. Once we were out I bellowed over to Abel. "Hey! Apollyon. We need a finishing blow for this F-ranker. Want to switch?"

Abel gracefully slid through space, avoiding a blow from the big guy before smashing a right cross into his jaw. "Can you guys take this one? He's mostly softened up but he's an ornery fucker, just won't stay down." The cultist was snarling in rage and hate, glowing green blood dripping from his malformed and battered face. Guess his blood was a carrier for whatever was boosting him.

I triggered Double Trouble, then dismissed and retriggered Moonlit Night, letting the fog disperse from around the bone girl and condense around the big guy. "Yeah, go ahead," I said before the fog closed around us. Abel had seen the direction needed and booked it out of the fog as soon as it came up, and I turned my attention to the big guy.

He was bruised and bleeding and seriously damaged. Abel had to have used that weird multi-blow stacking ability to beat him this badly. My arms were still covered in magma, and with the bonuses from State of Grace and Moonlit Night, Mercy Kill was able to boost me enough to take advantage of the tranq blows.

Since the tranquilizer punches were triple strength, all the power added up was enough to chip away at this guy, since his Vitality was too busy healing Abel's beating to counter my poison. And so began the slow and steady process of beating the asshole into the dirt. Without the ability to see and with my own boosted speed, I was able to avoid him easily, especially with Eye of Revelation helping me predict his punches. I rabbit punched him with a tranq blow and then spent the rest of the time making sure the poison was dense enough to carry it.

Callie joined in once the poison had permeated most of his body, counter-acting the healing. Together, we wore him down. The guy was tenacious as hell, but after what felt like a small eternity, I put him down with a tranq punch to the temple. I let the fog fade as I stumbled over to slump down on the ground (out of range for if he somehow woke up).

Pointing at him, I groaned. "Restraints, please."

There was a *thump* and I looked over to see Abel toss the other cultist right next to her glowing companion. "Her too," he said. He didn't seem partic-ularly winded, and while I'd have loved to take credit for softening bone girl up, I was pretty sure this was all him.

Callie made her way over and started wrapping them in so many layers of chains that if they did wake up, they wouldn't be able to exert much force. The restraints wouldn't hold if the cultists were in peak form, but with them unconscious and horribly beaten, they should be fine.

As we turned to see the others finishing their fights, a hole opened in the red barrier, but no one came out. I smiled and hauled myself to my feet, trudging over to speak to my cousin. Guess I was supposed to come to her. Nice to know she was okay enough to be a pain in my ass still.

Chapter Fifty-Seven

NAT WAS GRINNING at me as I entered the barrier, but I ignored that and yanked her into a tight hug. She eeped in surprise before tapping on my back. "Ribs," she wheezed, "breaking."

I flinched and pulled back, grabbing her by the shoulders to look her over for any injuries I hadn't apparently just caused. "Are you okay?" I asked frantically. Natalie just rubbed her ribs as she chuckled at my panic. I flushed. "I mean like... other than possible rib fractures from me being an enthusiastic hugger."

She rolled her eyes. "I'm fine, Shane. I appreciate the backup, by the way. Perit and Valk wouldn't have been near enough to handle this many F-rankers. They definitely came prepared for me." She shook my hands off her shoulders. "I appreciate the worry though, cuz—it's sweet that you care so much. I kind of assumed we were just allies of convenience." Her smile became warmer. "You came to bail me out when you didn't have to. I won't forget it."

I had no real idea how to deal with being thanked like that by a family member—best to just move on. "Speaking of which," I said, clearing my throat and looking around uncomfortably. "How the hell did they get this many people on world without being noticed? This wasn't the only attack —they jumped all the other factions too. How are they fielding these kinds of numbers and why didn't anyone know about it?"

Seemingly aware of how out of my depth I was, Nat chuckled and turned to look at the subdued F-rankers. "Neighboring System. I'm guessing they've been slipping people onto the planet since the tournament was announced. Traffic among F and G-rankers is much less likely to be monitored than E-rank entry. Getting foot soldiers in would prove far less of a challenge. Not to mention alternate routes like smuggling. Still, this couldn't have been easy."

I growled with frustration. "But what's the point? I get wanting to win the tournament but this ridiculous shadow war between the factions seems like a huge overreaction. Why do any of this? It can't *just* be about the damn dungeon."

Nat laughed a bit louder, reaching over to pat me on the shoulder as she stared unblinkingly at the enemy. "Politics, little cousin, politics. Don't think too much about it—if you understood it, you wouldn't be sane enough to ask questions like that." She shot a side eye slyly at the rest of my team. "No offense to future cousin-in-law, of course." I heard a coughing sputter from Callie and felt a surge of embarrassed shock through the bond.

Deciding to take pity on my girlfriend, I gestured to Nat's backup. "So. You never did introduce me to your guards. I assume they're the beneficiaries of most of your wishes. Being able to hold off a crowd of F-rankers, even with that barrier to help, is no small feat. They must be boosted pretty hard."

That got a wide grin. "Yup. That's my crew. Perit and Valk. Most of us try to confine our direct subordinates to between two and five people. Single guardians work better if they're dramatically higher ranked, and anything past five means less than a wish a day at our rank. Two is considered a pretty safe amount. They can watch each other's backs. Though three is popular too, because it gives you the possibility of ranged support."

I considered my own mess of backup and grinned wryly behind my mask. I could see how that could get complicated. "So... what do they do? If it's cool to ask? Because I get that... Perit—if that's her name—uses an axe, and based on the cloud of green mist around it, probably some kind of acid? But I'm drawing a blank about the blue stuff that guy is whipping around, other than some kind of power trap."

She paused for a second before nodding. "Yeah. Okay I'll tell you, as a sign of trust. Valk's ability is called Vector Gel. It's a sort of spatiotemporal thickening. Think of it like suspending something in amber, but less rigid and more weird. When energy comes into contact with the gel it becomes stuck in it. Only raw energy mind you, nothing with physical mass. It's an odd power, but he's managed to make it work for him."

I could see that. The whips were a brilliant use of a power like that. He could create a chain of effects and slam them into something over and over until the energy dissipated. Since the gel suspended energy, most of the attacks seemed to be stuck halfway, so there was some sticking out, though I wasn't sure what would happen if you just brought a completely ensconced attack down on a person. I knew they wouldn't stick, but did the gel just pass through them?

Abel seemed intrigued. I hadn't realized he was listening, probably because he was giving me space for my reunion, but he had no problem butting in to comment. "That's interesting. It's the closest power to my own I've seen in ages." He narrowed his eyes at Nat. "But you're all still in the tournament. Aren't you worried about Shane using that information against you in the arena?"

Natalie snickered. "No offense little cousin, but Valk is a monster. Just because you know what he can do doesn't mean you can stop it. I trust my guy to be able to take you on." She shot Abel a challenging smirk. "You or any of your little buddies. You've got a knack for this kind of thing, but you're still from a backwater. Valk has traveled the Cluster with me. He can take anything you have to throw at him."

I wasn't offended. I had just as much faith in my own crew. It sounded like Valk was her version of Abel, though probably not as scary. That said, I didn't want to fight him. Like, at all. The big burly red-bearded man had that same feeling of barely suppressed gleeful violence that my silver masked teammate gave off when he was excited and I wanted no part of it.

That wasn't important now though. What was important was my cousin's safety. "Okay, well, you should come stay with us until you find a place," I said. I hadn't brought this up with anyone, but seeing Nat in so much danger worried me. The safest place around was my place. I wasn't sure why her guardian hadn't stepped in, but if they got attacked at my place, I knew mine would.

Natalie, however, had no such understanding. "Shane, no," she said firmly. "I appreciate the worry, like I said, but I have my own guardian. She's a C-ranker. If she can't take care of me then neither can you and yours. This incident proves that guardians aren't there to protect us from threats at our own level. I'll take more precautions with my living arrangements next time."

"But my guardian is B-rank," I wheedled. I wasn't willing to sell Zeke out for helping, since if he wasn't supposed to then telling Nat was a bad idea, but claiming that the extra rank made him scary enough not to mess with would work fine. And it would give her a reason to stay somewhere safe.

To my surprise, Natalie's head snapped up. "See, I feel like I might have heard you say that before and brushed it off, because it's not possible. B-rankers are real powerhouses. They aren't at the level of branch clan founders obviously, but you can start a family of your own within a branch at B-rank. Having a Legendary ability is no small thing. No way a B-ranker agreed to play babysitter. Especially not for Elijah. He's not exactly popular."

I shrugged. "Couldn't say, but Zeke has known my dad since they were kids. They're best friends. From back in the day when Dad was a Candidate himself."

"Janus?" she asked incredulously. "Your guardian is Janus? Fucking *how?* How do you get someone at that level to agree to vanish for decades and raise a kid? Because that's what happened based on what you're saying. No way he could reach A-rank in hiding like that. If he ever was at all. B to A is a qualitative leap. At that level the sheer number of stats you need becomes nearly unmanageable. Plus the… other requirements."

I wanted to ask about that, but it didn't seem like the time. "He asked nicely," I said flatly. "The point is my uncle is a scary guy, and you'd be safe staying with us. So will you please do it? With so few rounds left, no way they aren't going to be getting desperate. It'll get worse before it gets better and you know it. I want to make sure everyone is safe, especially you."

She just shook her head. "I'm sorry Shane. I get the intent, I do, and I appreciate it. I'd be more than happy to hang out sometime after the tournament, have some family time and just try to bond. But I'm not going to hole up in your place like a coward. Being a Candidate requires a decent amount of discretion and sneakiness, but you need a backbone. If I hide behind you no one would respect me, and honestly I wouldn't respect myself."

I groaned in frustration, rubbing my temples. "This isn't about self-respect Natalie, it's about your safety. You can't just—" I was cut off by a hand on my arm, and I turned to see Callie smiling up at me softly.

"It's her call Shane," she said quietly. "I know it sucks, but you can't force her." Her soft smile turned wry. "In my experience, Wyndham family members are insufferable stubborn oxen who don't know what's good for them, so changing her mind seems like a long shot to me."

I heard the unspoken commentary. That since she wouldn't recant, I should accept it. That trying to force her to do something she didn't want to do was just going to alienate my only nearby family member. I wanted to punch something. A tree, a wall, my dad for getting me involved in all this. Dealer's choice.

Ultimately, I just sighed. "Alright," I said, my shoulders slumping. "It's your choice. But can we at least keep in contact? I was doing the whole training maniac thing up to now, but I don't want to leave you hanging. Can we do like... nightly check-in calls?"

Nat burst into giggles. "Oh, my god. How are you such a mom? My actual mother isn't half this neurotic. But fine, little cousin. If it'll make you feel better." She glanced over at the F-rankers on the ground again. "You proved you have my best interests at heart... for some reason. I'll make time to call and check in." She raised an eyebrow at me. "Now, since I'm not crashing with you, you ought to get home. After all, you have a fight tomorrow, as do we. Gotta be rested up."

I wasn't likely to have a problem with that, given my Vitality, not to mention Jessie's healing, but I wasn't going to argue. We'd helped, and I imagined her guardian would be coming to pick them up now that things were over. "Alright," I said grudgingly. Leaning down to hug her again, this time less tightly, I murmured. "Stay safe, okay? I'll call when I get home."

She rolled her eyes again, but was still smiling as she hugged me back. Stepping away, she said, "You too. Can't have you getting crushed by cultists before you face us." With that, she turned and gestured for her guards to follow, vanishing into the darkness of the forest around us.

I turned back to my friends, drained, and gestured toward the car. It was finally time to go home. Just a shame I had another fight in the morning.

Chapter Fifty-Eight

I WAS able to get a bit of sleep before my match. Not as much as usual, but enough that I wasn't really tired or jumpy. Despite that, I was at least a little nervous. The chances of me fighting a team member again, even with the smaller pool to draw from, were low. For the eleventh round I'd probably be up against a stranger. Whoever it was had made it almost to the end of the solo rounds, which meant they were terrifyingly strong. Whether it was someone I knew or not, I could almost guarantee that my next match would be a tough one.

When I arrived at the arena, Rime headed for the stands while I made my way down to the waiting area to get ready, and I couldn't help but fidget a bit with worry. When they finally called the match to start, I strode out onto the sand on my own. Hardly my first solo fight, but the closer I got to the end the more intimidating this became.

When I saw my next opponent though, I calmed down a bit. He wasn't intimidating. Just a scruffy looking teenager with brown hair and brown eyes. He wore a green shirt, red baggy pants, and a relaxed, peaceful smile. "Like, hey man. It's nice to meetcha." He waved lazily. "Pretty far out we managed to get almost to the end, right? My best pal got bounced out last round but I think it's pretty legit that I get the chance to keep tryin'."

His voice was a lazy, happy drawl, and it made me chuckle a bit in response, my shoulders relaxing. I didn't let my guard down, mind you, but

I felt less worried. Hard to fear for your life against someone that mellow. "Yeah, it is neat. My girlfriend was in the solo rounds until last fight, when we went up against each other. Carrying on for her is pretty cool. I'm Solomon by the way, if it matters. From the Starchaser Pavilion."

The shrug he gave was nonchalant. "Matters to you, man. That's like... good enough right? I'm Norman from the Enigma Corporation." I cocked my head at him, not seeing anything corporate about him, and he gave a low laugh. "It's like, an ironic name man. We're just pals who like to travel around helping people out with weird stuff. We get that reaction a lot though, don't worry."

I laughed at his wry tone. Norman was a pretty interesting guy. "Alright," I said as my laugh ended. "Well, may the best man win, but I'm not holding back."

He gave me a laconic nod, and then I triggered Moonlit Night. The whole arena filled with fog only I could see through, and I activated State of Grace and Ripple Running alongside it. Kneeling down, I coated my arms in magma, triggering Touch of Tears after that, then stood up and started to circle.

Norman did... nothing. Like at all. He just stood there, though I could vaguely see a silver glow coalesce around him, not that it was easy to spot in the glowing backdrop of the fog. I waited, but he didn't engage at all, just waiting and completely at ease.

I realized I'd run out the clock on my skills if I didn't attack first. Pushing off the ground, I bounced up into the air, then planted my foot on nothing with Ripple Running and shot toward his back. I spun in a tight rotation midair as I came in, bringing my hand down at the back of his head in a spinning backfist as I flew straight at him. Norman leaned ever so slightly forward, and my fist passed within inches of his skull as he stepped aside casually to avoid the rest of my body impacting him. I hit the sand at a skid and slid for a few feet, before turning to stare at him in confusion.

He didn't look flustered, or even aware of my presence. I triggered my overlay, checking to see how I should attack next, and got... red. All the arrows were red. That made no sense. Triggering Eye of Revelation next I tried my best to observe anything, but nothing happened. He just stood there, glowing slightly silver at the edges and staring blandly ahead. I closed in slow, keeping Eye of Revelation active, and then used Steam Arrow, spitting an arrow of boiling water at him.

Adjusting himself so slightly it was barely perceptible, he leaned back diagonally, letting the arrow pass within a hair of his skin yet again. Fuck. I tweaked the Moonlit Night skill, allowing my voice to pass through. "You have some kind of prediction ability," I said flatly. Nothing I had would hit him, at least not according to my overlay. The Eye was more reactive, but it didn't spot any weaknesses in his form or anything.

Shrugging again, he smiled. "Like, I don't know man. I just move before stuff hits me. It's all instinct." His voice was placid and cheerful as ever, and unlike before, it kind of annoyed me. Being taken so lightly was bound to irritate anyone, even if I was pretty sure it was nothing personal.

I narrowed my eyes at him, then triggered Sucking Mud and used up a shadow attack to create the Dark Swamp. The sand beneath him started to darken, but before it fully manifested he hopped casually back. Unfortunately for him, Dark Swamp wasn't just a quicksand trap—it could respond. He tried to shift in midair to avoid the tentacles of earth, but since the attack had been launched while he was midair, and by something that didn't actually think, he hadn't seen it coming.

With no leverage his legs were dragged back into the dark sand, and he started to sink. I charged in, attacking again with a flurry of punches and kicks to see how his defense was holding up.

Despite his immobile legs being secured from the shin down, he swayed and moved out of the way with lazy graceful ease. But this time, he also attacked back. His fist shot out at a weakness in my guard I hadn't even known was there, and I tried to get my arms in the way of the blow, barely managing thanks to the speed boosts.

There was a loud crack as the blow landed on my encased arms, crossed in front of me, and even through my armor and the magma I felt the bones rattle as I was blown backwards. I skidded over the sand, my arms barely working after the impact of that one punch.

Of course the instinctual fighter who could dodge without thinking was a Might focus. Because that would be where the fucking speed to dodge came from. I'd have guessed Perception before he explained it, but if he had no actual input, then he wouldn't be perceiving, his power would. There was probably some of that because of his reputation, but since he was so physical he probably just came across as a bruiser.

"Like, careful man," said the relaxed monster in front of me. "I punch pretty hard. Don't want you to get hurt too bad."

I grimaced, triggering a heal burst to patch my arms up as I circled. Blunt force was a bad match for my armor, but anything helped. I felt the surge of energy flood me, slowly relieving the pain in my limbs as I circled.

Norman was still sinking into the sand, but not fast. He seemed unbothered by the trap, sitting eerily still and ignoring it, which of course made it slower. The Dark Swamp was reactionary at heart. Even with the shadow attack, once it captured you it didn't keep dragging unless you tried to escape.

I needed some angle. Coming at him directly wouldn't work. Without a Perception focus, his reactions to my attacks were either ignoring the stealth completely or he was reacting at the last possible instant. Either option wasn't good for me. I was wracking my brain for what to do, when it finally dawned on me.

Triggering Mercy Kill, I used a gravity attack. The ability, boosted by Moonlit Night and Mercy Kill, landed heavily on Norman. Then I did it again, and again, and again. I stopped at four, since I only had eight of those, and then blitzed forward again to attack. State of Grace allowed me to bypass the field around him easily, and when I attacked this time, I got much closer to hitting him.

I still missed, because he was *fast*, even under the pressure, but he dodged by a much narrower margin. His placid expression finally cracked, his brow furrowing a bit. When my next attack came in at him he dodged and tried to counter, but I used Afterburner to increase my next ten attacks.

With the existing boost of speed from State of Grace added to the attacks, my fist was a blur as it raced in at his face. He dodged the first, but the second he had to divert his counter to deflect. I grunted in pain as my arm creaked under the pressure, but I ignored it. Redoubling my attacking efforts.

Norman seemed to get serious this time, his hands flying up to deflect my blows. I grimaced, because I was running out of attacks on Afterburner. I tried Steam Arrow, and the explosion of steam was much more powerful when enhanced. He tried to avoid it, but because of the slowing effect of the gravity and the increased power of the arrow it scored him across the face, leaving a thin burn on his cheek.

He was so stunned by the injury he froze up, and I used my tranq blows on the three punches I managed to get in on him before he had a chance to react. I tried one more, but didn't manage to land it, and my Afterburner ran out, forcing me to retreat to avoid being hit.

I panted in exhaustion as I stared at him, having gone all out even with all the stacked debuffs to keep up with this absolute beast. I was damn lucky his only trick seemed to be close combat. If he had a ranged attack he might be able to keep up with Abel.

I circled slowly, waiting to see what he would do, but he just waited, unmoving, patient to the end as he let his power prepare.

And I did nothing. I was weakened because of Afterburner, and exhausted from the fight, and there was no need for me to attack. Norman's weakness was his strength. The ability to sit still and remain unconcerned while he trusted his power to predict any attacks.

A minute passed, then two, he kept sinking, but only got to mid-thigh. I just waited. I'd won this already, and it was only proven when I heard the first faint snore. I grinned. Those tranq blows were supercharged by a bunch of buffs as well as stacked, and I'd known they would do the job.

I raised a hand to signal the end of the match, and when he didn't move or respond for a minute they called it. I groaned, debating healing him but realizing I'd only managed a few glancing blows anyway so it wasn't needed. As he stirred awake, I held out a hand and let Dark Swamp fade, pulling him up out of the sand.

He grinned at me. "Like, wow man, that was a pretty cool nap. Shame I lost, but nice moves."

Laughing, I returned the sentiment and we traded numbers, Norman saying he could use the occasional knock out to get some rest since the nap had been so peaceful. I was happy to make a connection with such a badass.

Turning to leave, I felt a pang of fear, knowing the next fight would be even worse. I'd need to bring my A game to win. I had two more days—it was time to finally rank up my DS Mastery.

Chapter Fifty-Nine

TIME. Something I'd had plenty of in the last few rounds, but not enough of to accomplish a goal I was now planning to accomplish in just a few days. I needed to finish my last two upgrades, then synergize DS Mastery with Enchanting permanently to hopefully eliminate the whole charges thing completely. It would be nice not to have to count my attacks during combat.

But to do that, I needed to figure out a possible synergy for Earthseeking and Sucking Mud. Which gave me an idea. Well, I had an idea for Sucking Mud. I decided to go track down Callie to ask her for some advice.

I found her lying on the couch, watching the scan box with Cass, looking bored and amused in equal measure as the younger girl cheered at the cartoon currently displayed on the screen. The wolves were inside, the four of them sprawled about the living room, with Jin acting as a pillow for my girlfriend while Rellia played the same role for Cass.

Slumping down next to her, I smirked at her boredom. "So, not much to do? I figured you would have work today."

She just shook her head with a sigh. "Nope. With so many visitors in town jobs have gotten thin. I can pick up a decent bit of work every few days, but since I don't have any crafting skills or anything, jobs are hard to come by. Benny's been getting a ton of work as a crafter, even if Inventing is less useful and precise. So, what brings you down here so close to the next fight?"

I'd been excited to share my idea, and when she asked I jumped on the chance to mention it. "I want to talk about traps," I announced grandly. I had a bad habit of waiting for my turn to talk when I was excited, rather than really listening, and I had definitely been doing that. In defense of my enthusiasm, this idea would solve a lot of my problems.

She gave me an amused smirk. "Is this your way of telling me that I'm smothering you? Because I thought things were going pretty well."

I rolled my eyes. "Only in the literal sense that you sometimes choke the life out of me in your sleep, but that's why I'm the big spoon. No, I mean I want you to teach me about traps. Like… the Minor Trap Mastery Skill. I've seen enough of how it works to be close—I just need some basic lessons. Even though you wished for it you can still teach me manually, and I've been around for a *lot* of your trap making."

Mulling it over, she nodded. "I could see how you might have an easy time picking it up. It is just a Minor Skill, and with your Focus you wouldn't have any trouble with the knowledge. I'm guessing this plays into your prep for next round somehow?"

The whole noninterference thing was kind of out the window since the last two people in the tournament besides me were Mel and Abel, who didn't care. Still, I wanted to play things close to the vest, so I just nodded. Callie slumped back in annoyance, groaning loudly, only to be shushed by Cass. "Sorry sweetie," she told the younger girl with a wince before turning her gaze to me. "This is going to be annoying, but fine, meet me in the training room—I need to get a few things."

She hopped to her feet, strolling off, and Jin sat up, glaring at me for taking away the warm person he was cuddling with. I raised an eyebrow. "Yeah, I've been there. But I have training to do. Some of us don't just get to become house dogs after a little while. Watch your show." He snorted dismissively at me before refocusing on the cartoon.

When I reached the training room, I had to wait a few minutes for Callie to show up. She was carrying a large black bag with a strap that hung over one shoulder. Slipping it off, she let the bag fall to the ground and unzipped it, taking out various odds and ends—wire, spikes, springs, rope. The bag was quickly emptied as she gestured proudly at her collection. "Boom. Beginner trap maker kit."

"Okay," I drawled. "Glossing over the fact that you have a bag full of restraints that I didn't know about, which is weird since we basically share a room at this point, shouldn't you set up the traps... first? Then show me how to disarm them?" I knew a bit about traps, but not much—Callie's Skill did most of the heavy lifting in the labyrinth.

She shook her head firmly. "No. You've seen plenty of traps disarmed and made. Now you need to make some yourself. If you can't construct them, all the theoretical knowledge in the world is pointless."

"Alright," I said with a shrug. "You're the expert. I should be able to do this —like you said, I've seen plenty of traps. Here, turn around for a minute." She gave me an amused look, but with a quiet snort, she turned her back to me. I grabbed a few supplies, some rope, a small pulley, and a net, and walked over to where the obstacle course was situated.

Cracking my knuckles, I started to rig up an expertly arranged trap... then stopped. I knew the basics, but that was mostly just reactions—cause and effect stuff. I didn't know *how* a lot of traps worked. I held up the rope, mulling over my options, before looping it between two posts. I tied one side down, then looped the other up around the pole and over the top, tying it loosely around the net.

Nodding happily, I stepped over my makeshift trip wire and whistled to Callie. "Alright, all done." It wasn't pretty, but it should work.

Turning around, she looked right at me, then scanned over the trap, and subsequently burst into gales of laughter. I glared at her, which made her laugh harder, and I spent the next minute seething as she almost fell over in fits of hysterical giggles.

When she finally got a hold of herself she wiped her eyes mirthfully. "Oh. Wow. Sorry. It's just... You were solid when we started training in Balam, and you have so many varied skillsets. You seem to pick up everything fast, so I was expecting you to be... at least competent."

"You're not making this better," I complained. "What exactly is wrong with it?" I gestured to the trap. "Sure, it's simple, but at least it's functional right? When you trip the line it tugs the rope off the net and it falls on you."

She giggled again, getting it under control faster this time. "No, Shane. That's a slipknot. The jerk on the line will tighten the knot and then fling the whole thing off the side of the structure." She paused. "What is this anyway? Just a pair of posts next to a climbing wall with a protruding arm?"

I shrugged. "Salmon ladder—at least the posts are. The protruding arm is for hanging a harness when climbing I think, but who knows."

Honestly the training room was weird. Half of this stuff wasn't really that useful, and I was almost positive some of it wasn't always here. Zeke said it was a side effect of the last owner's reputation, and since he wasn't worried about it I just ignored the whole issue.

Callie chuckled, then started actually teaching. While I'd watched her process directly, there were lots of small details I didn't note just from observing. Types of knots, angles, tensile strength of certain materials and a dozen other little tricks of the trade. We worked for hours, with her filling me in on little bits of knowledge I didn't have that put things I did know into context better.

By the time we finished, she had taught me enough to make my own traps, albeit not great ones, and with my Focus and Perception, not to mention the time I'd put in, I officially got enough information figured out to officially have a Minor Trap Mastery Skill.

I slumped back against the wall with a groan. I wasn't physically tired, obviously, but doing the same menial task for hours was boring and annoying. Callie just smirked at me. "Well, seems like my work here is done, I'm going to go watch mindless cartoons and leave you to your training." She leaned down and gave me a quick peck on the lips. "Good luck on your match. I'll be there watching this time, so you'd better kick ass." She pouted at me. "If you beat me and then lose to some nobody I'm not speaking to you for a week."

She was bluffing, and we both knew it, courtesy of the bond, but it was her way of cheering me on, and I smiled softly at her as she strolled away. With her gone, I was officially done with prep work and sat up to cross my legs. An unnecessary step but one that would at least help clear my head.

This next upgrade had a solid amount of synergy. Not as much as the herbalism skill had, but enough that I thought I'd get something pretty good if I focused on the right method of combination. I'd already seen proof that there was some better and some worse ways to combine things.

I used Sucking Mud, focusing on the space in front of me as I did my best to synergize it with Minor Trap Mastery. I'd only just gotten the Skill, but I'd spent hours practicing so I was in a good headspace. I considered the possible methods of combining them and decided to focus on increasing the trap capability of Sucking Mud, instead of something like time delay that might lean more toward the trapping aspect.

Imagining my Sucking Mud, I focused on the mental image of a pitfall trap. Instead of something slow and plodding, the pitfall trap was a single sharp drop, but I didn't want to lose the earth aspect that made the skill what it was. Instead, I focused on making the sand thinner and decreasing friction, creating more of a silt material from the skill use.

With the strong mental image and the recent practice, not to mention my experience tweaking Sucking Mud, it clicked into place pretty quickly, and I felt Minor Trap Mastery vanish just as soon as it arrived. Focusing on my DS Mastery and feeling out subskills, I confirmed the new addition with a smile as I made sure Sucking Mud was gone.

Pit of Despair, a control skill that created a pit of silt that swallowed up anyone standing on top of it nearly instantly. Fast, deadly, and a distinct upgrade to Sucking Mud. I grinned happily to myself as I checked to confirm my last subskill. Earthseeking was all I needed to finish it.

Intermediate DS Mastery was so close I could taste it. I couldn't wait to use it on whoever I was fighting for the last round. I was so excited I wished I could upgrade the last Skill now, but I knew that wasn't on the table. The soul weight of the one upgrade after learning a new Skill was already hard on me.

Standing up to stretch, I decided to take a small break before going to find Benny for his wishes. This was good progress, and I knew that I was well on my way to reaching the finals, but everyone needed a break now and then.

I headed for the kitchen, pondering what I should make for dinner. I was hungry, and I was in the mood for something complicated. Maybe chicken and dumplings as a thank you to Callie for helping (I suppose I could forgive her for stealing my dessert).

Chapter Sixty

TODAY WAS THE DAY. Round twelve. I got up early so I could finish my goal of ranking up DS Mastery and was just finishing up the last step of that. Yesterday I'd ranked up Earthseeking to "Song of the Soil," which increased the range and specificity of my seeking ability by using my Minor Singing Skill to boost it. I'd also considered using piano and guitar, but realistically there were accessibility issues there. I wasn't carrying around a whole piano for one skill.

Aside from finishing up that last skill, I'd also done Benny's wishes for the last two days. He'd paid me in G-rank chits from his jobs this time, bringing me up to a hundred and sixty total, which would make buying my new weapon after rank up so much easier. Twenty points each to Might and Focus brought Focus to three hundred twenty-three, and Might to two hundred eighty-nine. At seven hundred forty-three total points he was incredibly close to three quarters done.

With all that done and out of the way, I was officially at a point where I could do what I'd been dreaming of for months now. Get my first Intermediate Skill. Sitting down and crossing my knees, I closed my eyes and breathed in deeply. Deep breath in, deep breath out. Then I reached into myself and flicked on my overlay.

The overlay was the most basic ability of my DS Mastery Skill, and the first I'd gotten. It was also completely unchanged. I could probably have ranked up the Skill just by upgrading this one aspect, but I didn't want to do it that way. I wanted to make DS Mastery a complete system, a unique Skill all on its own that didn't need any other abilities to function.

Feeling DS Mastery resonate as I tapped into it, I reached out and found the connection I always used, one that I'd begun to internalize so much it was almost like it didn't exist. I pushed the connection between Beginner Enchanting Mastery and Beginner Doom Sovereign Mastery. I'd never merged two actual Skills of the same power like this, but I felt in my bones it was the right call.

The two of them resonated easily and quickly, having both been shaped around each other. I reached into the resonance and *pulled*. The two Skills began to blur, and so did my brain as I felt a massive strain on my soul. It hurt. A lot. But I kept at it. This wasn't great, but I'd already started, and taxing myself before my match without accomplishing my goal was the stupidest thing I could imagine doing.

It felt like trying to drag an engine through a tunnel full of hot coals and broken glass, but finally, after what seemed like hours but was probably a minute or two, I felt that same click as the last few times. Unlike the last few times though, there was a massive shift in my brain, like someone turning over a car key, and then things just... changed.

I didn't know if the sensations were from ranking up my first Intermediate, from combining two huge Skills, from the change of losing one of my foundational Skills, or some combination of the three, but my body felt different—better. More. It wasn't Impact, or stats, or any of that stuff. It was more like I'd gotten over a cold, or cleaned out something gunking up my body.

Bringing up my Skills, I looked at what I'd created. Intermediate Path of the Doom Sovereign. I didn't know what the lack of the word mastery meant, but it didn't seem like a bad thing. I was pretty sure it had to do with this being a unique Skill. A *real* unique Skill now. Other people could theoretically have DS Mastery, but with all my additions and this final shift, this Skill was something that was only mine now.

I could also actually bring up the subskills directly and read them by focusing on the Skill itself. Which allowed me to see the three new ones I had available. Mountain Stance, Danger Sense, and Marked for Death. My soul also felt... stronger. Like I'd gotten a burst of power when I did whatever I did. I'd have to ask Zeke about that later, but for now... I hopped to my feet with a grin.

Only an hour or so until my second to last match of the solo tournament. I had no clue who I was fighting but I was sure I could take them on as I was now. I was salivating thinking of possible synergies, attacks I had stored, my new powers, all of it.

Finished up, I headed to my room to knock, and the door opened to reveal Callie. I just... stared. My girlfriend was wearing a dark blue sundress with a black jean jacket over it. Her hair was in a long ponytail and she had on a hint of lip gloss, which was rare because frankly, she didn't need makeup. She wasn't wearing her mask, and she gave me a beaming smile when she saw me. "Here," she said cheerfully, shoving a bag the size of my chest into my arms. "Hold my purse."

I just stared, dumbstruck by both the beauty and the audacity, and then I burst out laughing. She pouted at me. "What? I just mean until we get to the car. It's not like you're driving." She grabbed my arm, dragging me behind her as she headed for the vehicle. Jessie was already outside waiting, listening to music. The arena was far enough that we would need to leave soon to get there on time.

Callie and I climbed in, and I dumped her monstrosity of a purse on the seat, earning a glare. I just shrugged. "You said carry it to the car."

She growled at me, sifting through the bag to make sure everything was unharmed. "You know," she said testily, "I went out of my way to dress up and be supportive today. This will be a big fight for you. The least you could do is appreciate my hard work."

I took off my mask, giving her a soft smile. "You don't need to put in any hard work to be beautiful Cal. But the fact that you decided to is sweeter than I can say. Thank you." She blushed at the comment, clearing her throat and going back to rooting around in her purse. I could feel her pride and embarrassment through the bond, and knew she was just trying to distract herself.

Jessie giggled from up front. "I don't know if the two of you are relationship goals or the biggest cautionary tale for cringey sweetness ever. Either way, I think you're pretty adorable. Plus I think it's sweet you're trying so hard to distract him from being nervous, even if we both know it isn't going to work."

Callie glared at her. "It might have worked—if you didn't have such a big mouth."

I put a hand on hers, squeezing gently. "Sorry love, I can feel your emotions. I knew what you were doing. And it *is* working. I can't help but be distracted by you." She blushed again, rolling her eyes dismissively as she tried to hide her small smirk.

We spent the rest of the trip like that. Cuddled close and chattering about nonsense and flirting to try to keep my mind off the fight.

I was... afraid. Norman had been a monster, and realistically, whoever I was fighting next would be worse. I was about to take on someone truly terrifying and even though I felt invincible with my new Skill, I was also worried as hell.

If I lost, it would all be on Mel and Abel. I'd be cutting our chances down even more, and that would be after making them worse by beating Callie. It was just the same old thing all over. The excitement of a great fight tempered with the knowledge of what was riding on it.

Callie, sensing that confusing mix of emotions, tried her hardest to distract me, and did a better job than anyone reasonably should have been able to. Sadly, all good things must end, and we eventually reached the arena. Callie hopped out, stopping to press a firm kiss to my lips before shoving my mask back on with a wink. "For luck." Then she took off into the area to find seating so she could watch my match.

Jessie just giggled, shaking her head at me. "I don't even have to see your poleaxed expression to know what it looks like. You'd better win I guess—can't go disappointing the lady of the house."

I just chuckled. "Nah, can't do that. But thanks for the well wishes, Jess. I'll give it my all."

Her smile became affectionate. "Oh I know you'll do that. You always do. I'll be up there cheering you on. Don't... don't put too much pressure on yourself, okay? You're not in this alone. I know how prone you are to taking on too much, and so does she. She'd have told you that herself, but she was pretty sure you'd get all guilty about making her worry and over-compensate. You're not the best listener."

I put my hand to my chest with an offended gasp. "I am an amazing..." I trailed off jokingly. "Sorry what was that last bit? I wasn't paying attention."

"That was a bad joke," she said flatly, "and you should feel bad for making it."

Grinning, I rolled my eyes. "Nag, nag, nag. Poor Maria. I wonder if she knows what she's getting into. Go sit in your comfortable stadium seat and watch my match."

She turned for the arena with another giggle, muttering to herself about idiots who thought they were funnier than they were. I chose to ignore her hurtful and clearly spurious remarks and headed into the arena myself. I walked down to the waiting room, excitedly warming up for my match. Stretches, bit of cardio—I didn't really need it, but it helped me get in the zone.

I also started mixing and matching possible combos for my match. I'd need to evaluate my opponent and figure out exactly what I needed to do, but some canned combinations like Dark Swamp and Magma Leg were always helpful, and with my three new tricks I was sure I'd be able to do even better.

Finally, I got the call to head out to the pit to meet my opponent. Giving the attendant a nod of goodbye, I strolled out onto the sand, having mostly gotten over my nerves from spending time with Callie. I felt ready to take on anything. It's not like I'd be fighting…

I froze. The smile dropped off my lips and my eyes widened in horror at my opponent. His own reaction was slightly less dramatic. He just offered me his usual toothy smile, eyes twinkling with sadistic amusement behind his silver mask.

"Well, looks like I'm going to get a chance to put all that training to the test, huh kid?" said Abel Castleton casually.

I just stared at him, feeling one of my new abilities trigger passively before the match even started. I wasn't even remotely amused by the occurrence. After all, Danger Sense warned me when I was in a position where I was vulnerable to extreme harm, so it wasn't a shock it would be going off right now. Telling me Abel was dangerous was far from useful.

I tuned it out and considered my next move as he stood there, hands in his pockets, and waited. This… was going to suck.

Chapter Sixty-One

MY FIRST MOVE was to immediately trigger Moonlit Night. Danger Sense wouldn't stop trilling in my head, but it at least dimmed. I'd need to learn how to adapt it to any situation so it would actually work—sensing that you were *always* in danger wasn't actually a warning of anything.

Abel, meanwhile, stared into the fog with amusement. I'd moved out of the way immediately, making sure he couldn't see or hear me well enough to aim. He could probably cover the whole arena with his manifestations and a couple flurries of punches, but that would be sloppy and desperate, which were things Abel wasn't. I knew my teacher well enough to be aware that he was genuinely excited about this fight.

I'd sparred with him before, so I knew that none of my old tricks would work, but I had new abilities now, new tricks I could use. I needed to time this though—Abel's instincts were insane, and if I got close enough to attack he *would* sense it. I wasn't sure if it was Perception, Fantasy, or some sort of combat sense from years of constant attacking but he was tough to sneak up on.

"Smokescreen," he said lazily. "Mediocre idea. Interesting execution though. My Perception should be enough to pierce a veil like this, which means that you somehow mixed Stealth into the fog. Fascinating. I take it this is a new trick? Or were you sandbagging during training?"

Deciding to buy some time, I triggered Pit of Despair, creating a silt trap under his feet that sucked him right in. He vanished into the ultra-thin particles in an instant.

Knowing it wouldn't hold for more than a second, I dropped to my knees, triggering my Magma Limbs. I barely had time to apply Touch of Tears before Abel came shooting out of the ground like a rocket, somehow arcing down right towards me.

My eyes widened in shock and alarm, and I saw his hands move, the images of other arms condensing on his right as he wound up for one of those layered punches. Without waiting I triggered Stone Limb from where my feet touched the ground, coating my whole body, then used Mountain Stance for the first time, as well as a triple-strength density shift. I was stacking every defensive move I could possibly think of.

Abel hit me at speed, smashing a fist directly into my chest... and stopping cold. His feet landed, and he just gaped for a second, unable to see me, but having felt that a full force punch from him had stopped when it hit me. Don't get me wrong, it *hurt.* I think he slightly cracked my sternum. But with the massive defensive bonus of Mountain Stance (triple defense when my feet were firmly planted on the ground) enhanced by the density shift *and* Stone Limb, not to mention the bleed off from my armor, I'd actually tanked the punch.

I didn't waste the opportunity. I triggered Steam Arrow, and when Abel's non-punching hand flew up to bat away the attack with his spatial lubrication, I triggered State of Grace and laid into his ribs with the strongest punches I could manage. I pummeled his midsection as hard as I could, but his armor wasn't bad either, and he somehow absorbed the blows as they made contact by clenching his abs. Some martial arts trick probably.

He stepped into a trail of lubricated space and slid effortlessly away from me, stopping about five feet back. "Okay." He grunted in amusement. "That was pretty good. I didn't know you had that kind of durability, kid. Must be new. I can't believe you took a serious punch from me head on." Reaching up, he shucked off his jacket, cracking his neck as he went about limbering up his shoulders.

I swallowed hard. That... wasn't comforting. Taking off his jacket was the first sign that Abel was getting serious. He still had his mask on, so he wasn't going all out, but it also meant he didn't think he *needed* to go all out, which wasn't at all reassuring to think about.

Letting Mountain Stance fade, I winced a bit as I felt the soul weight. Sitting still and taking hits was the exact worst way to handle Abel. He'd punch through any defense I put up once he had time to build up steam. I needed to go on the offense.

I triggered Double Trouble, and then once I arrived I used another new skill—Marked for Death. It was the newest finishing blow from my rogue class. I got one every other level, and this one was amazing. The actual damage increase was subpar, just double, but the real value of Marked for Death wasn't the damage increase. Once the Mark was applied, the next blow would land with perfect accuracy. Regardless of space, defenses, or anything else, Marked for Death was an unblockable sure-hit attack.

Probably. There were most likely high-ranking Ascendants who could avoid or stop it, but within the confines of reasonably close ranks to mine, it would work. I grinned as I leaned on State of Grace and triggered Ripple Running to bounce away from Abel's response to my appearance, because despite leaving fast, I could see the glowing purple mark of my sigil, the well of wishes, on Abel's shoulder as I slipped away.

My mentor spun slowly, waiting for the next attack, and I considered the best way to hit him to do as much damage as possible. "I have to say, Shane," He said warily, "you got lucky as hell with that Skill. It makes up for so many of your shortcomings."

He was right, though I frowned at the dismissal of my hard work. I'd built my Path of the Doom Sovereign Skill from the ground up. First in DS itself, and then with other Skills and hard work. It was unrecognizable from the original Skill, and the combination of it with my stored attacks gave me a ton of versatility. I was willing to bet I was leagues stronger than your average Candidate in a straight fight, and I didn't like the implication I'd just tripped and fallen into my powers.

But on second thought, I had definitely gotten a heaping helping of good fortune in more than a few ways. That thought was enough to deflate my ego a bit and let me clear my head. Once I did, I rolled my eyes. Of course Abel knew what buttons to press to piss me off.

Sadly for him, it wasn't going to matter. I was going to end this in a single blow. Afterburner, Steam Arrow. Touch of Tears, Consecration of Flame, triple stack density shift, triple stack tranq, a shadow attack for good measure, Mercy Kill. I piled my advantages and power ups so high I thought my brain was going to explode, and I barely managed to trigger the hit.

Marked for Death meant a certain hit attack, doubled the blow, further enhanced as a sneak attack inside Moonlit Night, sped up by State of Grace and stacked with Mercy Kill. It was the most devastating direct attack I'd ever made in my life, and I saw Abel roar in pain as the horrifying tranq fire shadow steam arrow abomination slammed into his fucking rotator cuff and tore right through it, bypassing all his defensive skills and armor.

Of course, I wasn't exactly in good shape myself. That had been *way* too much soul weight, and I was currently on my knees in agony as I gasped and clutched at my skull. I'd come *very* close to blacking out from shock with that one. I used a heal burst, hoping it would help, and staggered to my feet, swaying slightly as I stared at my currently blood-soaked mentor.

"Fuck," he spat, looking genuinely annoyed for the first time this match. "You took out my arm? Not cool." I closed my eyes, focusing on trying to recover at least a bit. He wasn't down, and I knew he was going to be coming at me hard. I was completely tapped, and I had no way to put him down. That attack had been everything I had. Hell, I had no clue how he was conscious, given all the boosts applied and the tranquilizer aspect of the attack.

At the very least, I could see lines of searing toxic magma radiating through the wound, though Abel wasn't showing what must have been the agonizing response to being eaten alive from your arm with poison. Contrary to his statement, his arm wasn't actually gone, though it was pretty much dead meat on his shoulder at the moment.

I didn't respond since I didn't want him to know where I was. Somehow he'd felt where the attack came from, anyway, because as he hauled back, my previously oscillating Danger Sense became a damned storm siren. A manifestation coalesced above his head—a fist the size of a bus. Then another and another. Six of them, all floating there before he compacted them down into one single fist and swung at me with everything he had.

I knew that fist would seriously injure me if it hit, and my immediate response was to try to turtle up. Mountain Stance, density shift, and luckily Stone Limb was still coating me. I hunched my shoulders and brought my arms in front of my face, trying to defense as best as I could from the coming attack. My head was pounding like a war drum, and I was about to pass out, but I held on, just for this one last move.

Afterburner was still in effect, and that had boosted both defensive abilities, though not Stone Limb, since it had already been active. As the fist landed I felt a crack, not just from the stone but from my arms and legs. I kept my feet planted because I had to or I'd lose Mountain Stance, but all four of my limbs fractured under the impact.

With the punch over, I barely managed to stay standing, mostly because of the still active heal burst patching me up, and as I watched the fog receded, Moonlit Night fading as I fought to stay upright and functional. To my shock, Abel was staring at me shakily, the tranq seeming to be wearing him down. He started thumping toward me, one foot in front of the other, almost dragging himself, his arm hanging limply.

I could hear the burning of the flesh as he approached, and I tried to pull back to throw another punch, but with my arms broken I couldn't move them, barely able to keep them up. Abel made it to the spot in front of me, wobbling on his feet as he grinned at me proudly.

He put a hand on my shoulder, something I couldn't resist at all in my current condition, and chuckled. "That was a hell of a fight kid. You almost had me." I wanted to reject the statement. To tell him it wasn't over. But I couldn't move. Couldn't speak. Could barely think. I was so close. I was almost there. But I just couldn't make it. I couldn't beat him.

He gave a gentle shove to my shoulder, and Mountain Stance broke as I tipped over backwards, toppling to the ground with a loud thump. The last thing I saw as my vision faded out into blackness was the crowd going wild. At least I put up a good fight.

Chapter Sixty-Two

I WAS SURPRISINGLY PAIN free when I came to. Well… my body was. My head was fuzzy, but that was to be expected with overtaxing my soul. Oh, and the yelling. The yelling wasn't helping. "Look at him!" screamed a voice. "How many bones did you break? Do you even know? Now he won't wake up even after healing. None of the rest of us were that badly hurt in any of our matches. Is there even an ounce of forethought it your head?"

Groaning slightly, I opened my eyes, taking in the situation. Callie was standing over me in the back of our car, bellowing at Abel like she was about to attack him. For his part, my mentor didn't look contrite, or afraid, or even guilty. Just patient, as if he was letting her get it out of her system. Which he was, since this little nap had been my fault not his.

Reaching out, I snagged her wrist, which was within arm's length. "Whoa," I said groggily. "Keep it down Cal, my skull is splitting. What's going on?" Sitting up, I saw my girlfriend's relieved expression as she hurled herself at me, her knee driving into my gut as I grunted at the impact. I laughed, putting my arms around her. "Whoa there, what's wrong? Actually, why didn't you feel it when I woke up? I'd have figured the bond would have tipped you."

She squeezed so hard I groaned, but when she noticed my discomfort she eased up, staring up at me tearily. "It shut down. As soon as that punch hit the bond fried. Maybe it was all the soul weight, or maybe just you passing out, but I saw you lying there and the bond stopped working and I thought you were dead."

"You weren't dead," Abel chipped in helpfully. "In case you were wondering. Half dead, at worst. I carried you out to Jessie and let her patch you up before she started the drive home." He rotated his arm stiffly. "Me too actually. Shit, kid, you don't fuck around. If you'd landed that weird mark thing on my neck or head I'd have been a corpse."

I snorted at that. "As if you'd let me. You reacted as soon as I appeared and shifted your body unconsciously. I was aiming for the middle of your back. You're the one who changed the spot where you were going to take that blow. That final punch was monstrous—I guess you were holding back in all your other matches." Hearing my tone seemed to calm some of Callie's anger, though she still looked upset.

Abel shrugged. "Is it holding back to open a soda by twisting off the top instead of smashing it in half with a hammer? I just do enough to do the job. You came close to pushing me into going all out though. That was a hell of a fight, especially for someone who started cultivating so recently."

"Don't patronize me." I said flatly. "Mel told us that you don't get serious unless you take your mask off. I might have pushed you, but you sure as hell weren't going all out."

That got an acknowledging nod. "Well, fair enough. But you were damned sure the hardest fight I've had so far. Even if I'm pretty sure that won't continue to be the case. I hear that the top ten are monsters, one and all." He grinned. "Even a few familiar faces in there. Helix made it, and so did Lament. Whether they're going to pass round thirteen and take part in the finals is anyone's guess, though a five-man free-for-all does sound like fun."

I looked over at Mel, who had been relaxing across from us, having been fighting at another of the arenas. Jessie had gone to pick her up after she dropped us off and had made it back just after the match. "You've been quiet. Did you make it through your round?" I hoped she had—if not we would be left with only one entrant on the team. I mean, sure, he was our strongest and the one with the best chance of winning, but going into the finals with two of the ten would be nice.

Sadly, she shook her head with a sigh. "Gods no. I got demolished. I ran into one of the tournament favorites. Roland Wilder. They call him the

Walking War. He uses this crazy weapon summoning ability, calls up swords and spears and axes of different sizes and materials." She looked at Abel. "Decent chance he'll be your next fight, or Helix, or Lament. With only ten people left the chances of meeting up with someone you know gets more and more likely."

He grinned at her. "I promise you'll be avenged if I meet him. I'll stomp his teeth in and wear his head like a shoe."

Mel giggled. "You say the sweetest things." Her tone flattened, becoming severe. "But don't underestimate him. He was one of the scariest people I've ever fought, and I've sparred with you plenty." She looked at Callie. "You looked into the people in the twelfth round right? Any educated guesses on who makes it to round thirteen?"

Rime, who I hadn't even noticed because she'd been so quiet, piped up. "Firn from Final Frost Heaven is almost a shoe in for the last round. She uses a weird mutated version of ice manipulation that makes extremely durable permafrost. Durable even for her rank, I mean. Her control is also insane."

Callie nodded. "Heard about her." Her voice was rough, still hoarse from crying earlier, though we all pretended it wasn't. "There's a teleporter named Lucas who seems to be doing well. Ambush fighter. Mixed his teleports with a nasty knack for Stealth. Not sure if he makes the top five, but you'll probably see him in the next round, even if you don't actually run into him. Other than him, Arrabus—from the Cult—is pretty scary. He uses that same dark corrosive energy we saw from Pietro, though it's not the same."

Mel nodded. "I saw him fight. He's Might focused. Makes the destructive aspects of the energy more apparent. Stat allocation has a strong influence on how abilities manifest, as I'm sure you know, since it's one of the ways to alter an ability without synergy."

None of this seemed to bother Abel. "I'll keep it in mind," he said casually. "We can worry about it when we find out who I'm actually going to be fighting. No use crying over being about to spill milk."

"That's… not a saying," Mel said in exasperation. "It doesn't even make any sense. Can you for once take it seriously when someone tells you to watch out for an enemy, instead of barreling right at them like some kind of demented five-year-old on a sugar high?"

Abel pursed his lips before shaking his head. "Nah, not my style. But thanks for worrying about me, love. You know I can take care of myself, but it's still sweet of you."

I groaned, and they all looked at me. "Sorry, not about you. Just realized I have to tell Nat I'm out of the running. Any of her team make it through?" I'd almost forgotten my cousin was in this with us. If she had team members entering round thirteen that would massively increase our chances.

Callie brightened a bit. "Oh, right. Yeah, Valk, that red-bearded guy with the weird gel powers. I guess he has a chance to make the finals too." She shot a stern look at Abel. "To be clear, if he makes it in, you're to team up with him until the other three are eliminated to maximize our chances. That means no free-for-all just to have some fun punching out a bunch of powerful warriors. Play it smart."

"Yes *Mom*," he said belligerently. Then grunted when Mel elbowed him in the ribs. He shot her a wounded look. "Hey be careful, I'm still in pain from my gruesome injury."

Her only response was a dismissive snort, which drew a smirk from my teacher. I rolled my eyes. "How did you beat me in a fight again?"

Abel's face smoothed out, his normally expressive features (so loud that it was easy to tell what he was thinking even under a mask) flattened as he stared at me intently. "With some effort. Seriously, kid. I don't think you get how much that means coming from me. You did good. I'm proud of you."

I froze. That... Wow, that caught me flat footed. It felt... weird. I mean sure, Zeke had said it before, though not often (he wasn't the type), but that kind of thing is something you expect to hear from your dad, and I really hadn't. Ever. My dad hadn't said he was proud of me once in my entire life. Not even when he left me his final message throwing me into the deep end.

Callie, who out of everyone got what I was feeling, grabbed my hand and squeezed it as I muttered out. "Thanks, Abel."

He nodded, effectively declaring the conversation closed, but I understood. Abel was a gregarious and outgoing guy, but that was mostly surface. He didn't share what was under it often. I appreciated him doing it now.

Finally, we came to a stop, and they helped me up to open the door. My brain had settled mostly. A bit of pain remained but the fuzz and discomfort I felt on waking was mostly faded.

As we made it inside, I heard cheering and turned to see Cass running up. "Happy losing day!" she said cheerfully. She was being so upbeat about it I couldn't even get mad, just laughing at the odd comment.

Cark, who came up behind her, rolled his eyes. "Cassidy, you're not supposed to point out when someone fails at something. It's rude."

She shot him an annoyed look. "Nuh-uh. You always tell me that trying your best is what matters. Uncle Zeke said he went to watch and that Shane tried his best and did really good. As long you try your hardest, losing isn't a big deal—it's even better than winning, because you learn something."

We all just stared at her, before Callie burst into laughter. At Cass's glare, she held up both hands. "Sorry sweetie, that's just a really smart way to look at it. I'm laughing because the rest of us were being dumb. Where did you hear that take on it though?"

Cass rolled her eyes, as if Callie had asked the dumbest question possible. "From cartoons, duh. Anyway, I wanted to wish Shane a happy losing day, because he tried his best and that means he got to learn something. Isn't that way better than winning?" Then she whispered to Callie and Mel, loud enough for us all to hear. "He needs it more than you did, because he's a boy. They get stupid about that kind of stuff."

Even I couldn't help but laugh at that, though I noted Cark shooting Callie and Jessie suspicious looks and muttering something about bad influences. I grinned, taking my mask off. "That's a good way to look at it. But if we're celebrating I guess I need to make something for dinner, maybe even a cake." I paused. "Is it arrogant to make your own congratulatory cake?"

It was hard not to crack up as everyone vehemently assured me it wasn't, choosing to interpret that as support and not the obvious desperate attempt to get me to make dessert for them that it was.

Turning to head for the kitchen, I heard the others trailing behind me, and I thought back to what Cass said. She was right, there was more than one way to look at a loss. Sure I wasn't thrilled, but I'd done better than most, and I'd really shown what I could do. This wasn't such a bad outcome really—at least I got to show Abel how strong I'd gotten.

Now I could just sit back, relax, and let him crush our enemies. Poor bastards.

Chapter Sixty-Three

I HAD to admit that the people running this tournament were smarter than I'd given them credit for. The next day was downtime before the semi-finals, and to get everyone pumped they released the names. At this point, everyone had fought enough times and there were few enough people left that anyone who wanted to be prepared (Abel didn't) would be. In light of that, all the matchups were trumpeted from the rooftops.

It had only taken me a second to realize why the five-way brawl was set up for the finals. Besides being big and flashy, it meant they could advertise ten different semi-final matches, maximizing the amount of attention each of the contestants got. Which was how we got the announcement that Abel was going to be fighting Lament for his match.

The grin on my mentor's face was so wide I expected his face to split when he found out. We were all gathered around the scan box in the living room, watching the coverage of the tournament so far. They'd been cherry-picking the best moments to play for everyone on Callus and all the surrounding worlds with champions involved.

When my own fights came up, I froze. "Wait... I had the whole fight under cover of Moonlit Night. How are there so many clips from my solo match-es?" I hadn't really watched any of the coverage, wanting to stay focused on training, but now that I was out I was free to enjoy the downtime, especially since Abel's match wasn't until tomorrow.

That got a snort from Abel. "Please, you think they don't have counters for Stealth effects? Those barriers that keep out audience sound act through Perception. Same basic principle as Stealth itself, erasing sounds as they go through, but it also acts as a sort of revealing lens for anyone or anything looking through from the outside. Nothing more boring than seeing two people vanish at the start of the fight and the pop-up after it's over."

Huh. That made sense. "Oh, well." I said with a shrug. "I knew some of my secrets would get out. Just a shame I won't be seeing the points from this tournament, since I'm at my cap."

Abel shook his head. "Nah, I told you there's a ceremony for rank up built into the tournament itself. That way the event doesn't end until the contestants have hit the next rank. Otherwise why waste all that time on promotion. Once it ends you'll get all the points at once, kind of like the scavenger hunt the academy does."

I tried to remember if someone had mentioned something like that. I remembered hearing about the ceremony but wasn't sure if I ever asked why they had it.

I turned back to the screen, where I saw a clip of Lament's insane lightning ability. "So, you think you can beat her?" I said seriously. "Because she's about as scary as you from what I saw. I know you were holding back on me, but by how much exactly?"

"Ah," he said with a grin. "But that would be telling. As for whether I can beat her... who knows. I look forward to finding out though. Don't worry kid—if I lose, it's not going to be because I was slacking off."

Cass, who had decided to watch with us, was staring at the screen with a serious expression. "Hey," she said solemnly. "Mr. Abel, can you teach me to fight?"

We all froze, turning to look at the small girl and her intent gaze as she took in the on-screen combat.

"Cassidy!" snapped Cark. "That's not something you just ask like that. Mr. Abel has things to do—he's still in the tournament and he doesn't have time to teach you combat."

My eyes were wide with panic. "Cass, that's not really a good idea. What even made you ask that?" Having been through Abel's training, I knew it wasn't at all something I would ever put a child through. I could sense Callie's shock and unease through the bond as well, so it wasn't just me.

She shrugged. "Mr. Abel is really strong. I want to learn to be strong like that too. In case someone tries to hurt me again."

Her voice was... flat. But too flat. And I detected a slight shudder at the end. She was trying her hardest to seem disaffected, but she was still obviously disturbed by what had happened to her, not that I blamed her at all. We all knew about her bad dreams, and as much as she repressed it most of the time and played the happy carefree little girl, there were other signs too.

We all went quiet at that, all of us except Abel. "Sorry kid. I won't teach you to fight—you're too young for my kind of training." Her face screwed up in anger. Before she could voice her complaint though, he held up a hand. "But I *can* teach you martial arts. At least until we leave for the Moonsong Glade. Nothing fancy or dangerous, just some low risk training and forms. To help build confidence."

That... was less objectionable. I knew that learning martial arts could help a person feel more in control and safe, and if he was planning to teach her just Ragam, and gently at that, it seemed fine to me. In the end it wasn't my call. We looked at Cark, who was scowling. He could see the benefits too, but I could tell he didn't want to admit it.

It must have been rough, knowing she needed help and not being able to give it. I mean, sure any of us could have taught her, but we didn't want to shove her into combat. She'd been through enough. Now she was asking though, and it clearly meant a lot to her.

Eventually, he sighed. "Alright. But I want to sit in on the lessons, and if I feel like you're being too harsh I reserve the right to end them at any time."

In an uncharacteristic show of seriousness, Abel nodded, his face set. "Of course." He turned to Cass, standing up only to kneel down in front of her. "I'm just going to teach you exercises, some of the forms I found in the book where I learned Ragam. Even so, this won't be easy. Our martial art is time consuming and difficult to master, and you may never make much progress in it. Even if you become an Ascendant, not everyone can learn Ragam."

Seeming to ignore that last part, Cass squealed with joy and hurled herself onto him, hugging his neck as he laughingly stood up. He nodded to Cark.

"Going to be swamped tomorrow—might as well start the lessons right away so she can work while I'm not around." He looked at Jessie. "Think you could come with? I think having a healer on hand in case she falls or something would be a good idea."

Jessie looked thrilled to be included. "Of *course!* I'd love to come watch her practice. Can we do it in the outside building so we can hang out with Randall and the puppies after?"

The building behind the house was... Well, we weren't sure of its original purpose. There were some hints of it being a garage, or maybe some kind of barn, and there was a swimming pool full of broken glass jars and multicolored twenty-sided dice out there. No one was willing to touch it because the whole mess was somehow F-ranked and Zeke thought it was too funny to get rid of.

That was in the back, though. There was a big empty hangar-type room in the front that Jessie had co-opted for the animals and had spent days decorating and sprucing up.

With an eye roll, Abel nodded, and the small group headed outside, with Rime deciding to tag along because we were in the house with Zeke and therefore safe, plus she seemed fascinated by seeing Abel fight, which I couldn't exactly blame her for given the battles she'd seen from him.

Once they were gone, I turned to Benny. "Alright, so I got yesterday's points traded. How about we get today's out of the way early?"

He shrugged. "I'm not against that. Yesterday was Might, and I'll do Might again today to even things up. Focus has been pulling ahead." He fished out a small bag, tossing it to me, and I heard the clink as I jingled it around. Chits. This would bring me up to one hundred seventy-one combined with the five from yesterday. He made his wish, pushing his Might up to three hundred and nine and his total points to seven hundred eighty-three.

Benny finished up his wishes and decided to go check in with Celine, who had been staying with us, though mostly keeping to her room. With him gone, I slumped back into the couch with a world-weary sigh. Callie frowned at me, having been letting us get the wishes done and enjoying the show until she felt my unease. "You okay babe? You seem out of it. Anything I can help with?"

"I… guess not?" I said contemplatively. "I was pretty down about losing until Cass's speech yesterday, and now I'm fine, but I'm also kind of lost. I've been going full tilt for so long, and now I have to just stop. The whole hurry up and wait thing is giving me whiplash. I know we have to wait for Abel to do his thing and leave it up to him, but at this point I can't sit still. I feel like I should be training or something."

She made a pensive sound. "Nope." I raised an eyebrow at the dismissal. "No training—that's an order from your team leader. Until the end of the tournament, wishes are the only Ascendant thing you're allowed to do. You need to find other things to occupy your time. Visit friends, get a hobby, whatever you want." She gave me a sly look. "Maybe lavish your adoring girlfriend with attention. Or even do two of those things at once."

"I'm not sure cooking for you counts as a hobby," I said wryly, "but I'm starting to think you only like me for my culinary skills."

She gave me wicked grin, leaning in for a kiss. "That's a lot of talking and not a lot of getting in the kitchen to make me a sandwich." When I chuckled, she squeezed me tight. "You know I love you. I love you because you're sweet, and kind, and loving, and brave, and you're a total beefcake. The fact that you're a gourmet chef and happen to be a treasure magnet is just icing on my absolute favorite kind of cake."

I nodded solemnly. "High praise, given how much you enjoyed the one I made last night. But fine, I see your point. I'll try to take some me time. I don't suppose watching matches counts?"

"It does not," she said firmly. "Though you can still go, because we need to support our team. It's the right thing to do as teammates. Plus, come on, you have to admit you want to see Lament and Abel face off. They're the two scariest G-rankers I've ever seen."

I laughed at the admission, and she snuggled up to me to get started on this whole downtime thing. Of course, that didn't mean she let me pick what we watched. She connected her scan ring and started flipping through the channels on the scan box until she got to a cooking channel. From her surreptitious glance at me it was clear she was hinting at something, but I just snorted and settled in to watch.

Though I had to admit, I'd never actually made stuffed peppers before… Maybe I actually would give that a shot.

Chapter Sixty-Four

FINDING a seat at the arena the next day was harder than expected. I don't know why I hadn't assumed it would be packed, maybe because it had been so sparsely populated all the other matches. People had watched from home or just ignored most of the lead-up fights, since there were so many happening. Even last round, the top twenty, hadn't really been a concern for most.

This one was different though. This match was one of the semi-finals, and everyone wanted to be here. I don't think it even mattered to them who was fighting, one of the matches being as good as the next—they just wanted to be part of the spectacle. Which made finding a seat annoying and difficult.

Luckily, Rime was with us, which made it at least possible. After thirty minutes of looking she finally approached a group of locals she knew and just literally kicked them out of their seats. They whined about it a bit, but she was annoyed at the wait, and once they knew she was being serious they lost most of their momentum, quietly vacating to join the throng of searchers.

Zeke had come along directly, bringing Cass with him. She wanted to see her new teacher fight, and Zeke was the only person she really felt safe with in a place like this. I wasn't sure the little girl *knew* how scary her "Uncle Zeke" was, but some part of her recognized that he was at least competent. Along with them were me and Callie (of course), Cark, Jessie, Benny, and Mel.

To my surprise, we all seemed to be in good spirits, almost as excited for this fight as Abel himself was. Mel was sitting closest to the aisle between the seats, just so she could reach the pit fastest if she needed to. I'd never seen anything close to uncertainty from her towards Abel before, so it was a bit jarring, but even she looked anticipatory. I decided to at least say something. "Hey, you okay?"

She jumped slightly, looking up at me. "Yeah, sorry. Just out of it. It's been years since I've seen him in a really big fight." She coughed lightly. "Uh, no offense. But this just reminds me of how things used to be. When we were younger he would challenge anyone except freaks he had no chance of beating. I just— Shit, there he is. Time to watch."

Sure enough, Abel was walking out onto the sand, looking so excited he was about to vibrate through the ground. On the other side Lament emerged, hefting her spear over her shoulder and staring intently at my mentor. They spoke for a minute, not that we could hear them, and then the two of them started to circle.

Lament lashed out with a spear thrust, and Abel clapped his hands together, massive manifestations halting the colossal spear head before it could reach him. He slapped the blade aside, driving forward with a flurry of punches, fist manifestations appearing and vanishing as he struck from a new angle with each blow.

It didn't faze Lament, who started to spin her spear, the haft manifesting in the air over her head, creating a whirling defensive manifestation that blocked all the blows. Shoving the haft forward, the whirling defense drove at Abel. My mentor stepped lightly aside, carried on a thin stream of lubricated space out of the path of the attack with his arms raised. I saw him use that space warping effect to manifest six afterimages of arms around him, then condense them and hurl out a barrage of punches with three times the power.

Using her spear as a pole vault, Lament shoved herself aside, dodging back and forth to avoid the punches. She called out for her power, manifesting lightning to her blade, and flashed forward in a driving charge faster than my eyes could track. A manifestation of the lightning-charged blade headed right for Abel.

My mentor tossed his jacket to the side, arms clenching as space seemed to shimmer and warp around them. Manifestations appeared above him, but these were somehow denser and more intimidating. Raising his arms, he brought them down, leaving a trail of afterimages, each one stacking behind the other over a dozen times to create a sort of dimensional overlap.

There was a clap of thunder even the sound wards couldn't suppress as Abel's phantom hands smashed into the spear, one at the head, and one halfway down the haft just over where the hand would be.

Lament's manifestation snapped, and with it the actual spear she was holding. It basically exploded in her hands, the spearwoman dodging back as quickly as possible, but not fast enough to avoid the shrapnel completely.

Abel shook out his arms, giving her an easy grin, and I saw the two of them start to argue. Or rather, Lament was arguing, seeming to get more and more agitated until... something changed. Literally, the weight of the spear user on my consciousness was altered as she...

"Is she fucking breaking through?" I asked.

My question was answered a moment later as I felt her stabilize at F-rank. Mel whistled. "Wow, she does *not* want to lose. They'll disqualify her for this, but I somehow don't think she cares. Looks like they'll continue the fight though. Probably waiting for Abel to call it." She was trying to sound casual, but there was an undercurrent of worry in her tone.

Lament raised a hand into the air, and another manifestation appeared above her. I stared at it in shock—how the hell was she doing that without a spear? As I gaped, lightning condensed on the spear image, coating it completely, and then she clenched her fist and the manifestation began to *contract.* The huge spear image started shrinking, becoming more solid and dense as it did, until a literal lightning spear was sitting in her hand, visibly physical and deadly.

"What the actual fuck?" I asked Mel, who was staring at the spear in horror. "How did she do that? Some kind of power synergy?"

She shook her head mutely. "No. That's a physically manifest Skill. Manifestations are physical, but only for a second or two during attacks. That's an actual solid object. Different people manifest things differently, but... I'm pretty sure she just ranked that Skill up to Expert."

337

I snapped back to watching the fight, terrified for my teacher, but to my shock he looked elated. Reaching up, he pulled off his mask and slipped it into a pocket, cracking his neck.

At the motion, Mel seemed to deflate, the pressure of her worry fading. "Okay, he's going to start taking things seriously."

I blinked at her. "But how much can he be holding back? I've seen him fight, and he's scary as hell, but if she's an F-ranker and an Expert now…"

To my surprise, Mel seemed to actually calm down at the words, starting to chuckle to herself. At my strange look, she jutted her chin down at the arena. "Let me ask you a question. We've talked about Ragam plenty right? Told you it's a striking art that allows you to condense force with pinpoint accuracy?"

I nodded, and her chuckle gained a wicked edge as she pointed to the arena. "Well, at any point during those explanations did we mention that Ragam only used *punching* techniques?"

My head snapped up, eyes widening as I saw a colossal phantom leg appear and sweep towards Lament from the side. Seeing it, she spun her lightning spear, turning to intercept. As she did, Abel stepped into the manifestation, which extended from where he was standing to where she was blocking. The limb had been coated in his spatial lubrication before manifesting, and Abel basically vanished at one end, appearing in front of his enemy.

Lament's eyes widened and she lashed out at Abel, who rolled in midair, leaving behind a warped space in the shape of his body that seemed to condense as a manifestation. He slipped around behind her, spinning off his back leg to scythe a kick at her head from behind as the manifestation of himself launched a flurry of attacks and faded into nothingness as it was struck by the spear.

She yanked the spear out, rolling it up over her arm to place it between her and Abel. As his foot landed, he pulled back, shedding another blurry manifestation of himself cobbled together from warped space. He spun on his toe, whirling around her in a complete circle, leaving copies behind, and then changed direction as she attacked the spot he'd just been in.

As he moved back through the warped copies of himself, he absorbed them, seeming to become denser and more powerful, not quite hitting the next point of Impact, but coming close. After absorbing ten clones he dashed forward and engaged her in a direct head-to-head fight.

Her spear lashed out like a glowing blue rainstorm, striking the air and creating explosions of thunder as it tore through the sound barrier, but Abel was always a step ahead, twisting and contorting his body in a strange movement style that was both fluid and ragged, always just an inch from being hit as his blows smashed into his opponent with brutal and punishing force.

Blow to the ribs, downward elbow to the collar bone, uppercut to the jaw, stomp the knee. Lament was getting frustrated, moving faster, attacking harder, and she even landed a few hits. Despite that, Abel didn't stop or slow. I'd see him get stabbed and think he was dead, only to realize it had been a glancing blow, or landed somewhere less vulnerable than intended.

Even with the new holes being poked in him, Abel was clearly in a frenzy of joy. Lament attacked again, driving the spear into his thigh, and I saw his smile turn feral as he used the second it was stuck in his leg to slam his head forward into her nose. Her eyes went hazy, head falling back as her nose fountained blood, and Abel's hand came up to grab her hair, holding it back as he drove a fist into her throat, knuckles first, in a brutal knifehand.

She doubled over as he backed up slightly, tearing his ragged and bloody shirt off to tie it around his thigh in a makeshift tourniquet. He then stepped in and grabbed her head, smashing his other, uninjured leg into her bloody face again, and again, and again.

It took ten blows before she slumped over, unconscious, and Abel threw a fist up in the air as the crowd erupted in cheers.

I stared, dumbstruck. Not because he won, but because of what he'd done to get there. The pain, the blood, the injuries he'd just shrugged off. I could see what Abel had wanted us to see. That fights weren't clean and orderly like the ones we'd been in so far. Even the bouts with assassins had been neat, tame. We tried not to get hurt while taking down the bad guys. That was what heroic cultivators did.

This wasn't that. This was brutal, bloody, and unfiltered. If we wanted to take down people stronger than us, we'd need to fight like this when it mattered. I made a mental note to take all of this to heart as I stood up, following Mel down the steps to the edge of the pit as I saw Abel keel over, probably from blood loss.

With both fighters out they dropped the shield. Mel and I jumped down, bolting for Abel to heal him up. After a heal burst and scan heal (both just to be safe) had him on the mend, we healed up Lament and carried them both out.

Our team was in the finals for real. Time to celebrate.

Chapter Sixty-Five

BY THE TIME we got home, Zeke was already there. He always beat us back, which was fine, but I had other things to address. Questions for Abel, more specifically.

Callie, Jessie, and Mel had gone out with Rime to get enchiladas from the Raving Baby (Abel's favorite). We'd gotten permission from Zeke for a quick trip from the F-ranker into Doomtown, and they should be back soon enough. Benny, Cark, and Cass had all gone back to their rooms, so until the food came, it was just me and Abel.

"Okay," I said heatedly, "what the actual fuck was that? I mean congrats on the win, but you were really holding back against me that much?"

My mentor was still healing, and I admit I wasn't gentle dropping his ass on the couch from the fireman's carry I had him in. He grunted as he hit the cushions, but didn't seem upset about it as he crawled to a sitting position with a chuckle. "Not exactly. My Cicada Stacking Steps is new. I've been working on the technique for the tournament. I had something... kind of like it before. But what you saw from me today was me going all out."

I noticed he dodged the question, but I didn't bother to point it out. "Cicada Stacking Steps? How does that even work?" I had been damned impressed by my mentor's fight, and some of what he pulled off made almost no sense to me.

His grin was proud as he adjusted himself on the couch. "Good question. Why not guess?"

Groaning at his insistence on making everything training, I gave my best guess. "Well, the actual clones were obviously spatial lubrication. But I'm not sure how you did the rest exactly. Something with manifestations?"

He nodded. "I can manifest any part of me used for Ragam, and at basically any size. Using my legs transitioned it to a full body art. I shed spatial lubrication behind me and then harmonized it with a quick full body manifestation, then used it to stack like my punches do, amplifying my strength multiple times over."

I whistled. I'd figured it was something like that, but the details… the complexity of something like that must be absurd. It wasn't just harmonizing several different instances of power use, but doing it with a Skill that already taxed the soul to the peak of G-rank. Speaking of which. "What happened to Lament by the way? I mean, she lost, so she was out anyway. Did they do anything to her for cheating?"

That drew a snort from my teacher. "Hardly. Like you said, she lost. If she'd beaten me they'd have had to fix it, but since she was bounced there was no reason. Plus her Master is a scary old man. Nobody wanted to pick a fight over a dead issue. I didn't throw a fit so why should they?"

"But aren't you…" I searched for the words. "Mad? Disappointed? She almost cost you all your hard work just because she was a sore loser."

He just chuckled, shaking his head. "See, this is why I think the Unity is a bad influence. It doesn't matter. It never mattered. Not just to me, because I wanted the fight to be as hard as possible, but at all. The world isn't about fairness or hard work. It's about doing what you want. Finding the thing that makes your heart pound. If someone crosses a line it's not an offense —it's an opportunity to take advantage of."

Rather than refute him, I sat and thought for a minute. "The way you were fighting…"

An approving nod accompanied his grin. "Exactly. People love to talk about the downsides of being an Ascendant. You have whiny romantics go on and on about losing themselves, and cautious people insisting they hone their force of will to resist recursion, but they ignore the best parts. The parts I love. To be Ascendant is to be a force of nature. A story made flesh.

Never ceasing, never ending. Even after you die, you *don't* because stories always live on as long as there are people to tell them."

I gaped at him. I'd never seen him so… philosophical. "But what if you *do* lose yourself? Who you are? Giving so many people control of you is just…"

"But you aren't!" he said passionately. "Renown is reactive, not active. It's a response. You're the one throwing the stone in the pool, creating the ripples. Your destiny is all on you. It can be hard to keep complete control, but it's still you driving. It's a snowball, kid—the more you show the world the person you want to be seen as, the more they push you to that ideal. You're the author of your own story."

I groaned in exasperation. "So what? What does that have to do with your fight? With how self-destructive you were being?"

"Because," he said, like it was obvious. "The story I was telling is one of overwhelming power. And you can't have overwhelming power without something to overwhelm. The blood, the injuries, the pain—they paved the road I wanted everyone to walk down, showed them my journey in a way deeper than words. They walked my path with me, and because of that, they'll *remember* it."

Which I couldn't argue, really. He'd left a hell of an impression. "But is it like that everywhere? Is that the new standard? Will I need to watch Callie bleed like that? Hurt like that?" I could take the pain—it would suck, but half the problem with injury was wondering if it would be the end of you, and with my abilities I'd be fine. But seeing Callie like that— hurting, tearing herself apart like an animal gnawing off its arm to escape a trap… It made me sick to think about it.

"Honestly, probably not," he said to my surprise. At my cocked head, he laughed. "There are more types of stories than stars in the sky, kid. Callie is a sneaky type. People like that walk a fine line. Gotta be scary enough to build a rep, but being all blatant and violent like me is counterproductive. Sneaky people aren't supposed to get pumped full of holes and get up. They're supposed to be a whisper that may or may not be true. It's a safer life, but a much more ruthless one in some ways."

That was surprisingly insightful, but I could tell from his drifting attention he'd said all he really wanted to say. So I changed topic. "Fair enough.

Speaking of safety, are you going to be okay to fight in the finals? They gave us three days, but your wounds were from an F-ranker. That's pretty nasty to heal."

The healing energy had prioritized the worst injuries because of the inclusion of a scan heal in my patch job. He would be fine, but there were still plenty of non-vital spots that were the human equivalent of swiss cheese.

"I'm fine," he said with a casual wave. "Plus we have full time access to one of the best G-rank healers on this planet. Jessie already has a higher Vitality than most F-rankers start with—she can help patch me up with plenty of time to spare. Even if she doesn't feel like it, I've fought hurt before. I'll be alright."

Seeing how little the idea bothered him brought me back to his little speech earlier about making yourself who you wanted to be. Abel had been trudging forward without flinching for decades, and this was definitely a result of that. The idea of that kind of determination shaping who I was... it was kind of nice.

It was also an angle someone like Zeke wouldn't even consider talking to me about. Zeke had been living it for longer than I'd been alive, probably *much* longer. It would be like trying to give someone breathing advice. The downsides of being an Ascendant would be obvious, but not this particular aspect of things.

My thoughts were interrupted as the front door slammed shut. "We're home!" Callie called. We got up to head to the kitchen. I gave Abel my shoulder for support, but he ignored it. I smirked a bit at how stubborn he was, but I respected it.

In the kitchen, Callie was coming in with several containers of enchiladas. She set them down as Rime and Jessie came in. Benny, who had been off with Celine, came in after, clearly summoned to help carry things in. Cass came running through the door with Cark and Zeke. The little girl sniffed the air. "That smells so good!" she crowed. "What is it? I want seconds!"

Callie giggled at the girl's appetite while Jessie set down the containers (metallic foil trays with crimped folding tops), scooping Cass up to get her out of the way. Cass squealed in surprise and joy as Jessie carried her out of the room to go watch cartoons again.

We all chuckled, and Mel dragged Abel to the table, fussing over her boyfriend. "Sit down you insufferable idiot. We got your favorite, so park

344

your ass and eat it before we decide to feed it to dogs. I bet they would love some enchiladas." Her voice was brusque, but the worry in it was clear, and Abel obviously got that too, since he gave her a solemn look and then sat with a nod.

It was weird to see her so worried about him given what he could do, but I could do plenty, and Callie still worried about me. I guessed it wasn't often someone you loved fought an F-ranked Master Candidate. The rest of us crowded around the counter once they got Abel his food, Jessie coming back in with Cass (though "with" was a bit of an overstatement—it was more like she got dragged).

Abel, of course, had a stack of trays next to him with dozens of the damned things in there, which I was assured would not only be delicious, but help him fuel the energy burn of Jessie spamming her power on him for days. Jessie's power supercharged the body, but it still *used* the body. Short term it acted like healing and a pure energy boost, but long term it needed nutrients to work with.

We gathered around the table, stuffing our faces and enjoying the food, listening to Cass talk about Abel's fight and the cartoons she'd watched after coming back.

It was nice.

I'd expected to be a bit bitter about losing to Abel, but honestly, seeing him so happy and just being part of the winning team washed any bitterness away. I'd never have won. I had known it deep down, even if I'd wanted it desperately. This, though—this was better. Friends. Family. Eating, laughing, spending time together—this was a damn good result for the tournament.

Even if Abel didn't win the finals, the current moment made this whole thing worth it. Challenges like the tournament made us stronger, brought us together, and showed us who we were. I could see why these things were so common—there was a lot to be said about learning from combat.

Looking back at how far we'd all come, I considered the next round. The finals. The last thing Abel needed to overcome. It wouldn't be easy, but at this point… I almost didn't feel the pressure. As a part of the team of course. I wasn't the one fighting, but even this round I had felt a drive for him to win.

Now though... we had made it to the end. It was insanely impressive. If we fumbled here, life would go on.

I shook the thought away, tucking back into my enchiladas as Cass started telling Callie all about how the main character in her cartoon had just gotten a power up. Like I'd said, it was all worth it.

Chapter Sixty-Six

THREE DAYS of downtime passed far more quietly than expected. Granted, it wasn't my downtime, it was Abel's, but still I'd figured I'd be more nervous about the last round. My odd sense of peace continued until the last minute. The morning of, I finished up my wishes with Benny. With another fifteen G-ranked chits in my bank for my weapon fund, I was free to give Benny another sixty points (forty in Focus and twenty in Might) over the break. Then I headed to talk to Abel about his final fight.

Getting seats for the finals when it was all in one arena was rough, but we couldn't leave him by himself. The E-rankers had it covered though—and we managed to snag enough entrance passes for all of our close friends. Benny, Jessie, Celine, Mel, Rime, Lament, Wren, Alden, Sydney, Megan, and Sloane were all coming with, hoping to cheer on my terrifying teacher and maybe get their faces on camera cheering. Some of the other teams we'd made friends with had their own invites too.

"You're sure you're healed up?" Callie asked with concern as Abel actually stretched before we headed to the arena. Warm-ups weren't his usual style.

He just waved it off. "I'm fine. I called and talked to Shane's cousin, who put me in touch with Valk. He won his match, and we both agreed that the best possible outcome is one of us winning, so we talked through a couple of combinations to maximize our combat potential." We all turned to stare at him questioningly, but he just winked. "No spoilers."

"I'm surprised," I volunteered. "I'd have pegged you for the lone warrior type. I wouldn't have figured you would team up with someone you didn't know."

Frowning, he nodded at Lament. "Yeah well, pigsticker over there showed me that I can't take this lightly. Chances are some of these bastards are tougher than she was, and while I'm confident I can take any G-ranker around, I'm not confident I can take *four* of any G-ranker around. If I'd been fighting four of her—even before she shamelessly cheated and lost anyway—I'd have been in trouble. Barely."

Lament twitched, and Wren tried his best not to snicker. The other members of their team had stayed behind, but Wren was a friend, and he was enjoying Abel tormenting his captain. Of course, like he'd said before, Abel didn't hold it against her, but he *did* love to mess with people, and regularly poked her about the loss. The pigsticker comment was particularly cutting, since he'd smashed her spear in the fight and she had no way to get a new one on-planet that was up to her standards, especially with the rank-up.

To her credit, Lament didn't argue the point. She wasn't sorry, and had admitted that, but she also had a good fight and the consequences were all on her. She considered the right to shit talk Abel's due for winning.

I decided interrupting would be the nicest thing I could do here. "Did we get confirmation on the finalists? I never checked."

Callie nodded. "The Walking War and Firn both made the finals. Helix didn't shockingly—got bounced out by some shapeshifter. Along with Abel and Valk that's the top five right there. The shapeshifter is from the Cult, as far as I can tell. Whereas I think Wilder, the Walking War, has ties to the Empire. Nobody is sure who the Final Frost Heaven is backed by, if anyone, but Firn is supposed to be damned scary."

Abel shook his head. "He's not a shapeshifter—he's got a racial trait. He's a Hyde. Valk sent me some videos of his matches. He's... not weak. Aside from being able to take on a massive supernaturally powerful form, he has some kind of black energy like what that asshat in Doomtown used." He pointed at my uncle. "Zeke says it's called the Rath and the Ruins, and it's a martial art from the Cult, though not directly created by Black Sorrow. Much less prestigious and powerful than the fist art that Alec uses. It recreates her power, Enshrining Darkness, though in a lesser form."

That was surprising to me, but when we looked at Zeke he just shrugged. "He paid for the info, so it wasn't helping too much to give it to him. Is Natalie coming with us or is she going on her own?"

"Her own. She and Perit and their other teammate got tickets easily. Speaking of tickets, we should go, shouldn't we? It's going to start soon."

During the conversation, most of us had trickled out to wait in the car. Jessie started it up and everyone packed in tightly, even with the expanded space. We got there pretty quickly from my view, since we didn't talk much on the drive. Everyone sort of mutually agreed to let Abel concentrate, and even my usually relaxed mentor himself was quieter than expected.

When we arrived, we all headed up to sit in the stands, not finding anyone we knew. We'd brought our own party, so to speak, so we didn't need to add to it. We were in assigned seating because otherwise there was no way we would have ended up together, the whole place being packed to the rafters. Or would have been, if open top arenas had rafters. It was pretty full, was the point.

Rather than the sand pit, this arena boasted a huge square ring surrounded by flat ground. The ring itself had an overlayed pentagonal shape indicating where each of the contestants would stand, equidistant from the center and from each other.

Before the match started, Midknight strode out onto the platform.

Callie tensed, and I put a hand on her arm. As much as I hated that asshole, and as much as I wanted her to get another chance to teach him a lesson, I knew this wasn't the time. Politically, this situation was a time bomb. We couldn't afford to throw gas on the fire when there was so much happening…

I looked around suspiciously. This would be the stupidest (and as such, in some ways the smartest) time to attack again. If the Cult thought they had a method to counter the defenses here it would provide a huge amount of reputation. But what was the point? By the time it ended the winner would be chosen.

Was I being paranoid? Or was this my Fate sense latching onto a stray thought?

Midknight cleared his throat. "Citizens!" he intoned, voice booming a bit more ominously than it had last time. He was hamming it up for the larger crowd. I wasn't sure what caused the shiver down my spine, but the effect was clearly felt throughout the arena. "We bring to you the final battle. The last moment. These warriors have bled and fought and cursed to reach this hallowed stage, and this is their reward. Glorious combat."

I got the incredibly strong urge to roll my eyes, and realized it was coming through the bond when Callie *did* roll her eyes. I smirked at her from behind my mask, but neither of us spoke as Midknight continued. "Power. Skill. Determination. All important qualities, important building blocks on the path to success. But in truth, these blocks are all made of a single material, one substance that makes up the blood and bone of every truly great warrior. Victory."

He gestured widely to the ring. "And as with all true Victory, only one may claim it. Only a single warrior may emerge at the peak. These five competitors will now show you how those building blocks are forged and reveal the way they're laid down, so you might follow that path yourselves one day."

"Wow," I murmured under my breath, making sure to pull on Callie's Stealth so I wasn't heard. "He *really* likes the sound of his own voice." I'd thought Callie had been being hyper critical when she mentioned that, but it seemed like she was just being literal.

My girlfriend used Stealth herself to stifle a giggle, and Midknight either didn't hear or didn't care as long as others couldn't, as he pressed on. "The competitors may use any means within the rules. They may team up, may even fall upon a single person as a group and beat them down. Anything is permitted. But at the end, when this finishes, only one will be crowned the victor. These five champions represent the strongest of their generation. Roland Wilder of the War God Regiment, Apollyon of the Starchaser Pavilion, Firn of the Final Frost Heaven, Valk of the Wish Curse Palace, and Jack Carrax of the Weeping Clown Tomb. Which of them will emerge victorious? Only time will tell."

He snapped his fingers and shadows leapt up, obscuring the five points of the ring and receding to reveal the contestants. "You may begin." He slammed his palms together and the armor exploded into a shadowy mist, obscuring the ring for a moment before it faded away, revealing the five combatants standing across from each other, waiting for the right time to attack.

Everyone watched with bated breath. Abel was standing to the left of Valk, close enough to reach quickly, of course, but the five of them all just… stood. This was combat at the highest possible level. These were all people like Abel, monsters in human form. The second one of them moved things would begin with a bang and they all knew it.

I took in the forms of the enemy. The Hyde, Jack Carrax, was a tall, pallid looking man with sunken eyes and a hungry expression. His matted, greasy blonde hair hung limply to his shoulders under a tall top hat, and he wore an apron covered in blood.

Firn was a small, delicate looking girl with purple hair and blue eyes the color of ice. She wore a pair of purple shorts and a black sleeveless shirt with a purple silk jacket. Her skin was chalk white, almost bloodless, and her expression was as cold as the ice she used in combat.

Finally, Roland was a short, dark-skinned man with a wide, amiable smile and close-cropped hair. His eyes were hazel and were the only part of him that didn't scream kind and approachable, his gaze analytical and danger-ous. He had on a functional set of leather armor, dyed red hide covering his entire body except for his face. I wasn't sure what the hide was, but it appeared to be F-ranked.

The lull before the fight lasted for almost an entire minute, the final five analyzing, waiting, deducing, until finally the tension snapped like a rubber band. Jack turned, shifting from a tall, thin man to a monster, easily ten feet tall and grotesquely bulging with muscle, arms so long they scraped the ground from a standing position. He hurled himself at Firn, who flicked a wrist to conjure a massive wall of pitch-black permafrost in front of herself.

My gaze was dragged away as Abel used his spatial lubrication to flash across the distance to Valk, one of each of their hands clapping together as the air blurred. Suddenly a massive manifestation of Abel's other hand appeared cupped in front of them, but this time it wasn't normally colored. Instead the hand was made of blue gel.

The gel was Valk's ability, and it was lucky it was because a wave of G-ranked swords came spearing down from above to pincushion our guys, stopped by the gel-formed hand before getting close. Roland surged forward to engage, and I turned to look at Callie with worry. Those attacks had all been terrifying.

I hoped Abel would be okay, but all I could do was trust in my mentor. However this went down, one thing was sure—this would be one for the history books.

Chapter Sixty-Seven

ROLAND WILDER, the man known as the Walking War, was every bit as terrifying as his moniker suggested. While Firn battled with the Hyde (who was managing to just barely degrade her permafrost with his dark energy, and then smashed holes in the weakened barrier with his massive fists), Valk and Abel were teaming up to combat the storm of conjured swords sweeping down on them from above.

While he didn't seem able to manually control the things one at a time, Roland *was* able to direct the torrent of conjured weapons, turning and shaping the attack pattern to try to avoid the hand. Abel stepped forward, making a circular motion with his palm, and created a rotating trail of lubricated space leading inward. The motion had the effect of making a sort of vortex in space that sucked in all the swords the other man was trying to get past Abel's manifestation.

It was an interesting and terrifying move, though I could see how Abel couldn't normally use it. Without the gel power, Abel's manifestations were part of him. It wasn't direct translation, but them being harmed affected him. Now though, his manifestation was catching the swords like flies in amber.

Which, as it turned out, was kind of the point. Roland had purposefully filled the hand with swords, something we didn't know until he used the next wave as a path, stepping on swords in the air and heading up after them.

This seemed like a supremely bad idea, but I realized as he got sucked in that the palm was packed so full of swords there was barely any gel left. With a wave of his hand Roland dismissed the swords, and suddenly there were big open holes in the construct, and Roland stepped off a summoned sword and dashed through it.

Abel, not one to shrink back, flickered forward to meet him. Roland grabbed a sword from his summoned masses and brought it to bear in a powerful swing that Abel diverted easily with his power. I expected Valk to jump in, but I realized I'd been so concerned with the big show I'd missed the red bearded man leaving. Looking around, I spotted him engaging the Hyde. I was confused as to why he wasn't in position until I saw the dark energy wrapped around the whips on his hands.

I wasn't the only one who had noticed—the distraction had been plenty of time for Firn, whose black ice dragon came howling down from above to swallow Jack whole. Seeing the opening, Valk turned and sprinted back to the fight between Roland and my mentor.

The swordsman had been trying unsuccessfully to get his blade on Abel, who had been using trails of lubricated space to divert every blow, never coming into contact. Roland wasn't a pushover though, and he noticed as Valk came in behind him. With a stomp, a barrage of swords erupted from the ground like spikes to perforate both fighters.

Abel avoided easily, and Valk used the dark energy whips to tear the blades apart. Before either could counterattack, there was a roar as Jack came hurtling out of the ice dragon, shattering the black frost as he threw himself bodily at Valk.

Abel flickered again, stepping into a trail of lubricated space that took him in an arc around the edge of where Valk was preparing to combat Jack. Valk didn't hesitate, lashing out at Roland with the whips as Abel intercepted the Hyde.

The towering form of the monstrous brawler brought his hands down, collecting dark energy, and Abel dipped to the side to avoid it. Reaching up to pluck off his mask and slip it into his pocket, Abel flickered sideways, circling the Hyde and leaving a trail of duplicates, overlapping them again as he completed a second circle and empowering himself with his Cicada Stacking Step.

I blinked at the realization that Jack was *stronger* than my mentor. Whatever being a Hyde did for you, it apparently prioritized Might and got some kind of natural strength modifier like the Wendigo had. Jack lashed out with another punch, but this one Abel met head on, using a coating of warped space to prevent his hands from being degraded by the dark energy of the Rath and the Ruins.

Jack snarled at him, baring yellowed, uneven teeth, and snapped something we couldn't hear through the barrier before redoubling his efforts, attacking twice as fast, raining down blows. Abel whipped his jacket off and hurled it up at the other man. Jack slapped it aside nearly instantly, but that nearly was all the opening Abel needed. He used his spatial lubrication to slip around behind the Hyde.

Wrapping his arms around the giant man's waist, Abel bent over backwards, lifting Jack off his feet and slamming his skull into the dark stone of the ring. His tophat, which had somehow stayed on this whole time, went flying as his head slammed brutally into the stone, cracking the F-ranked material with the force of impact.

Abel would have followed up, but before he could attack, he seemed to sense danger. He pulled Jack in front of him as a rain of razor-sharp black icicles came down on both of them, using the giant Hyde as a human shield to intercept the ice spikes.

Which turned out to be extremely wise—every place the permafrost slammed into Jack, ice spread over his body, darkening his flesh with frost-bite. Even though we couldn't hear him, the expression on his face made the pain clear. Firn had apparently taken the distraction as time to build up something really nasty, because once Abel tossed aside his shield she didn't do that again.

Jack just writhed on the ground in pain, ignored as Valk faced off with Roland and Abel matched Firn head-on. My cousin's guard was doing shockingly well, his dark whips easily matching the torrent of blades Roland was bringing to bear. That dark energy was dangerous, and even G-ranked blades couldn't stand up to it in combination with the force the whips were bringing to bear.

At this point, Valk was the one bringing the pain, and it was gratifying seeing the calm and cheerful Roland get serious, deflecting blows and being forced to abandon and resummon the swords he had in each hand as they became unusable under the assault.

Abel meanwhile had rushed Firn, who reacted by erecting some sort of spherical shield with nine large heads emerging from it, each a sucking tube of black ice with consecutive rotating rings of black frost teeth. Abel was bouncing from tube to tube, sliding down them on lubricated space trails to speed himself up and tying the damned things into knots.

I even saw one about to catch him, but as it chomped down he shed one of his Cicada shells, his strength dipping by a chunk but his body surviving the attack completely unscathed. He took advantage of the gap to push off, heading for the shield while manifesting a massive fist, condensing several blows together even on top of the enhancement from the Cicada Shedding Step.

His fist image hit the shield of dark ice and shattered it, smashing Firn *into* the stage, creating a crater deeper than I was tall. Abel turned on a heel, flickering in an arch along a trail of space I hadn't noticed him making, and came down with a smashing axe kick on a distracted Roland, who took the blow to the shoulder and was forced to the ground with a grunt. Judging by the expression on his face I was guessing his collar bone was either broken or cracked.

The two of them turned to Jack, who had dragged himself to his feet to glare at them. The Hyde took a step forward, and both of them prepared to fight, but Jack just toppled over face first. With him down, the two final competitors turned to each other. Valk spoke calmly, saying something I couldn't hear. I wished they'd left the shield noise permeable after Midknight vanished.

Abel flashed forward, and Valk whirled his whips in front of him in a defensive barrier. Sadly for him, Jack's black energy had been used up quite a bit fighting Roland. I'd seen the effect waning as the fight went on, but now it was barely present. Abel slipped out of another Cicada shell, leaving behind a duplicate as he flowed behind Valk. The red bearded warrior shredded the shell, but realized too later what had happened as Abel hammered a spinning back elbow to the base of his skull.

He fell to the ground heavily, and Abel looked around the area, eager for more despite the sweat and obvious exhaustion. The dome began to fall.

The armored form of Midknight stepped up onto the stage, choosing to avoid any more suspense. He approached Abel, grabbed his hand, and held it aloft triumphantly.

"Your champion!" he roared. "Winner of the ten spots for the Moonsong Glade, to be distributed however he sees fit. The rest of them fought bravely, but in the end only one warrior can—"

He was cut off as a blast of black energy detonated in the center of the stage, both Abel and Midknight being thrown clear.

I saw the armor dissolve from the blast, and Abel hit the sand rolling, having survived the explosion by virtue of being further away and having Midknight's armor between them. In the center of the ring stood three figures, each clad in a dark robe, the air around them crackling with familiar black energy.

The one at the front of the triangle formation (a flushed, boyish-faced E-ranker with curly red hair surrounding a round face set with bright green eyes) grinned widely. "Sorry to interrupt!" he boomed. "I'm afraid we disagree with the results. Actually, we disagree with the tournament entirely. We've decided the Black Sorrow Cult will take the slots, and since you did such a poor job distributing them, we'll be taking this planet for good measure."

I froze, staring down at them. Of course they would try something—they'd been way too quiet lately. But this... this was crazy. I turned to Zeke. "They can't do this right? They know you're here! It would be insane for them to attack a world with a B-ranked protector on it."

Zeke just shook his head. "This is faction business. This kind of thing happens. Callus would normally be too backwater to warrant a takeover attempt, but under the circumstances... I could see it. Still, the planet is my current home, and I have loved ones here besides you." He seemed confused. "There's no way they could be stupid enough to think I'd ignore that."

As if he'd heard Zeke's words, the redheaded cultist turned to grin up at us. "But please, don't think we're looking down on you bringing only a trio. We have many more agents placed around the planet, and even more than that, we made sure to bring some extra special helpers who will make sure that things are finished up fast."

The two figures behind him stopped holding back, and I felt the world slam down on my shoulders as the weight of their Impact affected the air. My eyes widened as I struggled to breathe under the suppression, and not because they were trying to hurt us. They weren't—they were just that powerful. A level of powerful I recognized, though I couldn't pinpoint exactly where they fell within their rank.

B-rankers. They were both B-rankers. This was insane. Why were they here? What was going on? People like this shouldn't be on Callus.

Zeke stared at them with a glimmer in his eyes I'd never seen. Real, genuine fury was radiating off my uncle as he stood. Their eyes locked on him, and the redhead smiled. They knew he was here, and they'd come anyway. I just hoped they'd bitten off more than they could chew. Otherwise, we were all dead.

Chapter Sixty-Eight

"YOU HAVE a lot of guts coming here like this." With Zeke's words came a tide of power, pushing back the aura of the two B-rankers through his own and with sheer force of personality. Zeke wasn't worried at all, and it showed in the way he spoke. "You might not worry about some small-time scuffle between the Unity and the Cult, but there are other interests here."

The redhead didn't seem worried (apparently he was as crazy as all the other cultists I'd met). "You won't get involved, but in case you did, we arranged some entertainment for you. Finding out there was an unknown B-ranker on the planet was an annoyance, but luckily, we managed to get the details from a reputable source. Isn't that right Miss Selka?" His smug grin turned to take in where I could see Natalie sitting.

The teal haired woman next to Nat, clearly her own guardian, rolled her eyes. "Stop trying to start trouble, Kix. I'm a neutral party. As long as my charge remains safe, I'm not obligated to take a side, and while Natalie might think an alliance with her cousin is best, I'm not nearly so convinced."

It occurred to me that while Nat might be aware that Zeke was B-rank, and even knew his name, she hadn't passed the latter bit of information on to her guardian. Apparently the lack of trust ran in both directions. She and her guardian clearly had a much different relationship than we did.

Zeke looked mildly annoyed at the woman, but not upset. "Selka. That sounds familiar." He was talking normally now, as were the others, but with the Perception of everyone here and the cameras, it didn't seem to be a problem for anyone. He snapped his fingers. "Ricardo's daughter. Your mother is that little Countess with the teleportation power. The hair should have tipped me off. Surprised someone from Malachai's branch contracted you as a guardian, given how much he and your grandmother hate each other."

She glared at him. "Inter-branch cooperation is important. Grandma knows that. And no *real* Wyndham would ever violate the sanctity of the Candidate selection. Not that some random's pet B-ranker would know that."

Wow… apparently Nat hadn't told her guardian *anything* about me. Maybe Zeke's little jab about branch politics wasn't that far off.

My cousin was pinching the bridge of her nose in exasperation. Neither of us were in danger, granted, but it hardly made her guardian being a shady asshole any less mortifying. Zeke just looked unperturbed. "It's always so cute when the little ones make plans. I assume you realized that the location and importance of this planet made it a prime target for annexation and decided to arrange this to both get rid of my ward and advance your own?"

"Pretty much," she said with a shrug. "It would be suicide to attack you, and bad form even if I survived, but this way my hands stay clean and I make a nice profit. I'm not defecting or anything, but unlike you I have no obligation to protect your Candidate."

Zeke just smiled wryly. "I'm guessing you don't know who he is? Or who I am? Because while a pair of mid to upper B-rankers would be sufficient for most, I assure you I can handle myself just fine. Tell you what. Since I don't dislike ambition, I'll give you a chance. Help me take care of the rabble while I deal with thug one and thug two and I'll let you slink off after this without doing anything drastic."

She just snorted. "Drastic? You think you can take on a pair of nearly peak Arch-Bishops and still be alive to hurt me? Everyone knows the cultists are hell to kill off, and in pairs they're more than a match for anyone their rank. Crazy bastards will self-destruct if they think they're losing. Outnumbered, you have no shot."

Sighing, Zeke shook his head. "Come on, don't be stupid here." He reached into his coat and pulled out an old, brittle-looking mask. "I don't have a teleportation volto mask anymore. My last one broke. Unless you were planning to spend the remainder of your life with your soul trapped in porcelain I'd take the offer." He held up the mask in the air beside him, then released it, leaving it hanging in the space he left it in. Under the mask, a form manifested, a black robe too dense to see a shape. "Besides," he said with a bloodthirsty smile, "who said I was outnumbered?"

Snapping his fingers, a bag appeared, a large black duffel. He unzipped it and started to remove masks, leaving them hanging in the air. Under each mask a robed figure manifested, each one floating up and away to take position around us in an aerial formation. Selka's eyes went wide with terror as she stared at Zeke, then down at her Candidate in an expression of fearful dismay.

"I... I didn't know," she stuttered. "I swear, I didn't know. I wouldn't have contacted them if I had." Zeke just looked at her calmly, and she swallowed, standing and bowing. "Not a single cultist will remain on this planet by the time you finish," she said formally, and then, suddenly, she was gone.

Amusingly, she did *not* inform her former allies who Zeke was, though she clearly figured it out herself. Clearly we were far enough from wherever Zeke usually did his thing that random B-rankers didn't know who he was, because the hooded figures didn't back down.

The redhead's ever-present grin slipped, replaced by an annoyed scowl. "Bitch," he snapped. "I'll let their excellencies deal with her after they finish with you. Your brat has been responsible for the deaths of several of our operatives, including a promising young talent here to attend the tournament. He needs to pay, and since we're here anyway, we can just send a few messages all at once."

Zeke smiled. "Really? I thought you guys found out his mother is the Star Queen and decided to enforce that shitty blood feud you nutcases have with those stuffed shirts at the church." At Kix's shocked expression Zeke put on a faux embarrassed face. "Oh no, did I say that out loud? Now everyone knows. Of course, once they see what I'm about to do to your little buddies I don't expect they'll find the risk worth it."

I'd been shocked when Zeke blurted that out, but looking at his face, I understood. He must have blocked the broadcast temporarily. The rage in my Uncle's eyes told me in no uncertain terms that none of these invaders were leaving here alive. As for the rest... most of them probably didn't even know what he was talking about and had no way to contact anyone outside Callus anyway.

Kix, meanwhile, was turning red, his face looking like he'd had an aneurysm. "H-heretic! How dare you protect a heretic? That bitch has killed more of our Saints than any ten A-rankers in the entire Church, and the Radiant Pope murdered our Saintess of the Drowning Shade, our Lady's own flesh and blood daughter!"

Zeke rolled his eyes. "Oh come on, that happened before he even broke through to S-rank. None of us were even alive. Besides, Drowning Shade was a psychopath, even by Ascendant standards. I've met serial killers lost in full recursion that weren't unstable enough to have spawned some of those stories."

The redhead was shaking like he was going to explode. "You *dare!*" he screamed, his voice cracking. "Defaming our lost Saintess, speaking ill of our Lady's bloodline. Crimes! Crimes against the Cult! Blasphemy! Heresy! Sacrilege! You'll die for this. You and your brat and every person you've ever met!"

"See," Zeke said, turning to me. "This is why no one likes dealing with cultists outside strict mercenary assassination contracts. One wrong word and they turn into gibbering lunatics." Looking back at the other man he clicked his tongue. "Also, heresy is the holding of an opinion counter to a religious precept, and usually carries the assumption of being a heretic, and heretics can't, by definition, blaspheme, which is defined as 'showing contempt for god or sacred things.' Can't hold contempt for something you don't believe exists."

Before the redhead could retort, Zeke held up a hand. "Don't mistake me —I know Black Sorrow is real. I'm just making the point that you're contradicting yourself here. Regardless, this whole fight is deeply inconvenient to me. I don't have the materials to make two more B-rank masks. I'll have to seal your souls until I can make a shopping trip to get the materials for a porcelain that can contain them." He shrugged. "Oh well, doesn't matter I suppose. Any artist would be glad to have a new canvas to work with."

The two Arch-Bishops, predictably, didn't take this threat well, but before they could do more than step forward, Zeke snapped his fingers. Two of the masks began to glow, the hooded manifestations under them vanishing and appearing around the ring. A third mask's specter gestured, and the remaining contestants were subsumed in suddenly liquid earth, then spat out beyond the now self-repaired stage. The two mask figures raised their arms and a cube of glasslike energy appeared, then shifted as the second figure warped the energy, creating a defensive perimeter.

Zeke took a step, vanishing and appearing inside the ring with the three cultists, while all the other robed figures, seven of them in total, drifted through the shield as if it wasn't there to join him. Smiling grimly, he reached into the bag again, withdrawing one last mask, then snapped his fingers to dismiss the duffle as he raised the porcelain to his face.

As the mask covered him, I felt a sort of… shift in the air. Zeke's body language changed, like someone throwing off an old cloak. Perception was important, and he was making no effort to hide the differences. His stance screamed aggressive and sadistic, and even the two hooded Arch-Bishops stepped back, clearly realizing that they had picked a fight with someone with whom wise men did not fuck.

The floating robed figures had spread out to surround the enemies, slipping the edges of the ring to create a second line of defense. Zeke cracked his neck. "Oh dear, this one is always so bloodthirsty. Perhaps I should have used one of the others." He shrugged. "Oh well." He flickered, appearing in the middle of the B-rankers, right behind Kix, and shoved an arm *through* the E-ranker's chest. "Too late now."

The two B-rankers whirled, one bringing to bear that black energy and the other releasing a massive cloud of red lightning that literally turned the shield into a seething black box riddled by red sparks. When the energy faded, Zeke was back in his original spot, safely behind a line of defense erected by his masks. There was no evidence at all of the attack, since Kix's body was obliterated by the other B-rankers.

Zeke just clicked his tongue. "Killing your own subordinate. How gauche. Especially since he would have been fine." Their fists clenched and he cocked his head. "What? Did you think I actually attacked him? Didn't you hear me earlier? I don't have a teleportation mask." He flicked a hand and a perfect copy of him appeared to one side, high-fiving him before vanishing. "But we've had enough fun for now. Let's get started." And with a snap of his fingers, both he and all his mask bearers disappeared.

Chapter Sixty-Nine

IT TOOK me almost no time to figure out what that mask did from context. Illusions, obviously. But despite knowing that I also knew I had no chance of piercing through them. No one here did. Trying to bypass B-rank perception would be pure delusion.

Zeke was far too much of a performer to let this end without a show, so I trusted the illusions wouldn't ruin our chance to watch them battle. Apparently, he was making enough of an impression here that the other two were genuinely worried. The taller of the hooded Arch-Bishops snarled. "You seek to unnerve us with your games, but you've shown your weakness. This shield exists to protect this planet and your charge. Should we take it down, any casual attack would reduce this world to dust."

He started to gather dark energy in his hands. It... hurt. Just looking at it hurt. The energy Pietro had used had looked wrong, but it was nothing compared to this. Like the difference between a dark room before bed and the soul crushing depths of the deepest cave in the world. It was just conceptually incomparable. Callie grabbed my hand, squeezing it as I struggled to tear my eyes away from the energy. The worst part was that I suspected the shield was already mitigating the effects somewhat like it had with the attacks.

Being able to box in a pair of B-rankers by himself was terrifying to me.

Zeke was stronger than any of us had given him credit for. He wasn't just B-rank, he was to B-rank what Abel was to G-rank. He was a monster.

His voice echoed cheerfully from the empty air. "I wouldn't do that. That shield is made from a combination of very powerful abilities. The direct defensive applications are impressive, but the secondary effects are what really make it shine. Aside from filtering out harmful conceptual elements before they can damage the lower rankers here, the defenses also—"

The Arch-Bishop cut him off by unleashing a *torrent* of the gathering power, a beam of energy packing into the size of a needle, so dense I almost threw up just seeing it. The beam struck the shield... then bounced off it in three different directions before spearing the other Arch-bishop, the red lightning guy, through the shoulder. The hooded figure howled in pain and literally *ripped* his arm off his body, hurling it onto the ground as it was consumed along with his cloak in a swirl of rotting darkness.

Zeke's voice continued his explanation as if there had been no interruption. "—deflect direct attacks along the inside of the defensive perimeter. It's made for aftershocks, but if you try to break it directly there's a back-lash. It took me *ages* to find that power interaction. Most B-rankers don't focus on defense."

The red lightning guy, who was revealed to be a large red-haired man with mutton chops and dark eyes, glared at both his companion and the air around them. "Damn it Absalom! You have to stop doing that. This is why we got reassigned to this frontier nonsense. You can't just overpower every-thing." He looked down at his smoking shoulder. "Can you remove this corruption? I can do it but it'll take time we don't have."

Shuffling uncomfortably, the still-robed figure took a step toward the other man and froze. There was a shift in the air and three masked figures appeared in a triangle formation. They raised their arms and a whirling vortex of brilliant white flame sprung up, swallowing Absalom. As the injured one saw his partner attacked, he tried to rush to his aid.

Zeke's four other hooded figures swirled into existence around him. Two of them threw their hands out and dark chains lashed from the ground, binding him in place at the neck, legs, and his remaining arm. One of the other masked figures made a drawing motion and a huge bow and arrow coalesced above. The last one pointed at the arrow and power spilled down the length of the weapon, infusing it with a yellow glow so sharp it almost hurt to look at.

There was a rush as the arrow released, but the vortex burst, and a flash of dark energy imposed itself between the red-haired man and the arrow. Absalom's robe had burned away, revealing what looked like a desiccated corpse with its mouth sewn shut. Dark gems were set where its eyes should have been, and it punched the arrow head-on, trying to destroy the energy. It channeled an absurd amount of power, even more than last time, and swung it in a close-quarters blow meant to destroy the attack.

Its blow hit... nothing. The image of the arrow vanished, and the corpse man choked, looking down at where he'd been bisected by the *actual* arrow, which had been fired from the ground, where it had been hidden under an illusion.

Zeke stepped out of thin air as he saw the corpse fall, snapping his fingers. The three masks responsible for the white firestorm manifested around the plummeting figure's top half, unleashing another attack. By the time the flames faded there *was* no top half left—just a pair of spasming desiccated legs hitting the ground.

Zeke clicked his tongue and turned to the remaining B-ranker, who was staring at his partner's legs in terror. "This is the problem with cultists. No sense of flare or imagination. You all pride yourself on being sneaky and dangerous, but give you an ounce of power and all you can do is slug away."

The other man pointed shakily at one of the masks. "That's... that's an Arch-Bishop of the Red Revenant Church. Those were flames of purification."

Zeke shrugged. "Partly. They were amplified by a few other powerful abilities, but purification was definitely in the mix. Theodore Stoddard. Dreadful man. Tried to have my nephew's mother assassinated so he could move up in the clergy. He did have a gift for purifying flame, though. Comes in useful when up against Black Sorrow's Enshrining Darkness."

Snapping his fingers, a small flask appeared in his hand. He opened the top and there was a swirl of crystalline energy as runes lit up along the flask. There were millions of runes on it, so dense I wouldn't have been able to see them if not for my Perception. In the sky where the fire had struck, a phantasmal dark-bluish-purple outline of the corpselike Arch-Bishop appeared, screaming so loudly the stitches in his mouth had torn open.

The image of the man clawed at the air as an invisible force dragged him toward the flask. Zeke gestured to one of the masks and the same dark chains holding the redhead grabbed Absalom and restrained him, allowing him to be sucked into the flask. Zeke screwed the top back on the flask, staring at it for a few seconds before flicking it with a sharp, "Stop that." Then he put it away.

"What did you just do?" the red-haired man asked in revulsion. "Was that his soul? Give it back! You can't take a soul that belongs to our Lady!"

Zeke snorted. "Imagine only being at Indigo as a B-ranker. I think Black Sorrow would thank me for cleaning up trash like that. Maybe not. I don't much care. I told you morons I'd be harvesting you for materials. Did you think I would go back on my word on a System-wide broadcast? A man's word is all he has. Would you like to struggle? I'm still not sure what your ability is, and if you want to show off I'd be happy to allow it."

The man looked sick. "You're a monster! Our souls belong to the Lady. How many of our brethren have you used to create these abominations? How many have you stolen from the Red Revenant? You can't do something like this in front of all these people and expect to get away with it. The Cult will——"

"Do nothing," Zeke said, cutting him off in amusement. "I've been active for quite some time, my friend. The Church and the Cult know about me. You think they care? If they hunted down people for things like this I'd hardly be first on the list. Morgan Lark can consume the very stats that make up a person, yet the Vampire remains free, assumed to be the next being to become a god. Do you know why that is?"

The cultist didn't respond, so Zeke continued. "Because power is all that matters. I'm strong, which makes me valuable. If you think *I'm* scary, you should see my best friend. When it comes down to it, you've played with forces best left alone. You weren't sent by the Cult itself—you and your little buddy decided to take this planet on your own. You wanted to prove yourselves, didn't you?"

"We... we just wanted to be recognized for our power," he said blankly. "We wanted the respect our positions were due. There are so many Arch-Bishops, and we had to work our way up the ranks the hard way. We didn't get any special privileges like some of the children of the Saints and Popes. We're members of the Cult, too—we just wanted them to acknowledge us."

Zeke just chuckled. "Of course you did. But you have no concept of what a *real* B-ranker looks like. There are real monsters out among the stars, my boy. You might be a cultist, but you aren't powerful enough to interfere in high-level faction business. People like Sasha, like my buddy Elijah—they're in a whole different world than you."

He turned his eyes on the crowd, and somehow, I could sense him looking past them all, to everyone watching the recordings. "This is your one warning. All of you. Elijah Wyndham's son is under the protection of Janus. If you are of a match with him, are willing to pit your heirs against him, be welcome. Hone his edge. Help me mold him. But if you think you can interfere with the Candidate selection, interfere with *my family,* this is all that awaits you."

He walked toward the still-chained redhead, and like he said, he let the other man use his powers. The cultist hurled red lightning at my uncle, and one of the masks appeared, erecting a small clear shield that I believed was similar to the one they were in. The red-haired man screamed, hurling bolts of crimson electricity, but none of them even came close to Zeke.

My uncle arrived in front of the man. With a snap, he slipped on a glove with pointed talon-like fingers that lit up with a multitude of runes, just like the flask. Then he shoved a hand *into* the other man. Not through him—there was no blood. His hand vanished into the chest of his enemy, and as he withdrew it, I could see the struggling purple soul as it was *ripped* from the cultist's body.

When he finally tore it loose, the body slumped over to the ground, limp and motionless, breathing but empty. Another finger snap brought out a second flask, and Zeke popped the cap with a thumb before stuffing the struggling spirit into it. Dismissing the glove, he recapped the flask and put it away. He waved a hand and the bodies vanished, as did the shield, and Zeke turned and walked out of the arena, past a staring Abel who had crawled over to lean against the wall and watch.

The rest of the crowd was... quiet. That had been brutal, even by Ascendant standards. Zeke had been sending a message, and it was one that I knew came from a place of real anger. Seeing him do that should have horrified me, and part of it did, but it also made me proud. My uncle was strong and loyal and had my back. Despite how brutal he could be, I was damned glad he was on my side.

Chapter Seventy

HEALING OR NOT, we had to carry Abel out of the arena. My mentor was in bad shape, though not as bad as the armor Midknight had worn, which had been mostly destroyed. Callie had been… quiet since we saw him get wrecked, and I wanted to pull her aside to check on her, but we had other problems.

Zeke rode home with us this time, as did Natalie and her guardian along with Perit and Valk. We were all pretty quiet until we got to the house, at which point I finally broke the silence. "Alright… what the actual fuck? Like, to all of that Zeke. Can you tell me what happened now that it's over?"

My uncle shrugged. "Stupid people doing stupid people things." He cut a look at Selka, who wilted slightly but didn't argue. "I made an example of them, so they shouldn't try it again, though you can bet they'll try other things. That's your problem, though."

I couldn't really complain about that. "What about the other factions? Abel won, but the Empire, the Faerieland—are they really just going to back off because you smacked around a couple B-rankers? Like, won't they send more people to come and fight you?"

Zeke just snorted. "No. First of all, there are a hundred of these. Losing two B-rankers, even trash like them, is a blow over something this insignificant. Sunk cost fallacy isn't something the upper echelons of the Black Sorrow Cult engage in, or any higher-ups from the factions. Going to war over a random border planet would be ridiculous. Second of all, they can't spare enough people to kill me off, especially knowing they'll lose most of them. I'm basically unkillable under A-rank and everyone knows it."

Selka nodded quickly. "It's true. Janus is infamous among B-rankers. He's predicted to reach A-rank in the next decade."

Seeming to sense my skepticism at the time frame, Zeke snickered. "I know it seems like a while to you, but in the upper ranks you need hundreds of thousands or even millions of stat points to rank up. Not to mention... other things. The next decade isn't bad. I think that was part of why Eli did what he did. I'm sure you of all people can imagine how frustrating it is to be giving out points that let people rank up fast when you lag behind."

I hadn't experienced that, but he wasn't wrong. It was easy to picture. "Well, that whole thing was certainly dramatic enough to diffuse things. I guess that means it's really over. We... we won." I felt myself melt into my seat gleefully like some magic switch had been flipped. I couldn't believe it. We'd been working so hard for such a long time for this, been through so much.

Callie looked shocked too, her eyes wide as she thought through exactly what it meant for us to have made it. Abel was grinning, despite his injuries. I couldn't see Mel's face under her mask but Jessie and Benny looked thrilled. We'd separated from the others after the mess at the tournament, planning to meet up again soon.

"So..." I said uncertainly, "how are we handling the Moonsong Glade? You can't get in, right Zeke? I was told it was F-ranker exclusive. How long will we be in there? Are you just going to wait outside? Can you suppress your power to come in with us?"

"Nah," my uncle said casually. "Your mask will let me keep an eye on you. If things go too badly I'll break in and help, but it would destroy the glade which would be... bad. Even for me. I probably will wait outside. Plenty of the older generation will be out there. I'll make sure they don't ambush you when you come out for whatever you get. Though I think we should get you all some proper spatial gear before you enter."

"Like a ring? A real one? How would we even get that? They don't really have them available on Callus, at least not that I've seen. I've got some solid cash reserves, but we don't have access to a supplier." It was a similar problem to the issue of my weapon. I really wanted something E-rank, but despite probably having enough for a relatively low-level E-rank weapon, there weren't any on world.

His grin was wolfish. "Well sure, which is why you'll be picking up what you need at the field market outside the glade. Someone always starts one. That large an influx of newcomers always spawns a bazaar. People need consumables and weapons before entering, not to mention that it ends up being a huge conglomeration of powerful elders from different forces waiting around for months on end."

"You think they'd have an E-rank weapon I could use?" I asked excitedly. "I definitely need a new stick to hit people with. Hopefully something that can take a beating."

Abel snickered. "You know, I understand the preference for blunt damage, but you could pick up a more traditional weapon and develop an actual Skill for it. Maybe a staff? Bit longer than your usual but it wouldn't hurt to give yourself some range. It could synergize with your combat style too. Pole vaulting would be a good complement to your movement skills and open up more lines of attack."

My mentor had been mostly quiet since the tournament. He seemed happy to have won, but I saw him giving Zeke awed looks that made it hard not to snicker. As I nodded my agreement to look into a staff weapon, a question popped into my head. "That reminds me—was that really a B-rank fight? Don't get me wrong it was crazy, but I was figuring it would be... larger scale."

My uncle just smiled. "It was—you just couldn't tell. That shield protected you. It was dampening the Impact to prevent not just physical but conceptual damage. Looking at B-ranked attacks directly without any protection can damage your soul. Impact is a qualitative difference in level. Sound is just vibration, sight is light bouncing off an object. The size of the attacks wasn't massive because they were in a confined space and that wasn't necessary, but make no mistake—those moves would have killed you just by observing them if I hadn't protected you."

Selka chimed in. "Not to mention, any one of those casual blows would have atomized the planet and everyone on it. B-rankers operate in the ten million range of stat points. Any blow you're capable of throwing they can beat by thousands of times, and that's not even counting the qualitative leap that is D-rank or the effects of higher-ranked Skills. If I were you, I'd commit that fight to memory. You'll be benefiting from it for decades, even if you can't see why yet."

I tried thinking back to the fight, to the movements, the abilities, and I could kind of see what she meant. There was... something there. Something just out of reach, like looking at a crack in the ground that's only a few inches wide but then realizing it goes down for miles. I was only seeing the crack.

The others almost all seemed nearly as distracted by the statement as I was. Mel, though—Mel was all business. "I'll keep that in mind, but I want to know that Abel's win is going to be safe. He worked his ass off for that. How do we know they won't try something before the ceremony. Speaking of, when *is* the ceremony?"

"Tomorrow," Zeke said bluntly. "The actual date for the Moonsong Glade is in a month to make sure everyone's teammates have the best chance to rank up, but no one was comfortable waiting on the ending ceremony. Tomorrow they announce the top placements and allow everyone in the tournament to rank up. You'll all be reaching F-rank." He glanced at Abel. "Provided you're willing."

My teacher nodded firmly. "No more waiting. I'm confident I've gotten the most out of G-rank, and I want to take the next step. I wanted a good fight to go out on, and I definitely got that. It's going to be brilliant ranking up and getting to fight it out with people so much stronger than I am on a relatively even playing field."

That was a good point. The idea that some people would be five times stronger than we were but still within our ability to harm was kind of crazy. Not that I was going to be fighting peak F-rankers, but the point remained. This would also be a huge opportunity for me to make sure I was able to reach the higher levels of F-rank in an area without E-rankers to take advantage of the gap.

"Wait," I said, remembering something. "We'll be in the glade for *months?*" I'd asked for a time frame earlier, and I guess I had one, but that was kind of crazy.

Zeke shrugged. "For you at least. Some people might stay longer, but I absolutely refuse to let you miss out on the soul trials. The Ruined Soul

Temple is one of those places I mentioned to you where you can train soul strength outside of a clan. Once in a while the temple holds trials for people training there, and they offer prizes that can increase the speed of soul refinement and even reward special Skills and unique gifts."

That sounded intriguing. "So this would be a way for me to increase the grade of my soul to two ahead before D-rank? Because I know you said that's important."

"All of you, if you're ready," he said, looking over the others. "The Ruined Soul Temple is technically neutral territory, but practically speaking, it's hard for anyone outside the higher ends of a faction to get in. There are so many people scrambling for entry, there's no possible way to accommodate them all. The cream of the crop have their own soul refinement methods and locations, but for something like the soul trial even clan heirs will be showing up."

My eyes widened. "That's why everyone is paying so much attention to the Glade!" I said sharply. "When everything else is equal, a boost in Impact might be the thing that puts them over the top in the trials."

"Exactly," said Zeke with a nod. "I didn't want to bring it up and increase the pressure, but now that the tournament is over it's best you know what's coming. The trial is a unique opportunity. You can get things there that even wishes would have trouble giving you, at least from any people low-ranked enough to bother with any of you. Some people have even managed to pick up a second ability."

My head snapped up. A second ability would be... big. Especially for me. The current Wishmaster had his position specifically because he had two abilities, something that gave him the skills and power to beat even my dad out for the position. Not to mention it would enable me to have a surefire Skill that would always rank up without detracting from my effort in other areas. If I got a weapon ability for instance, I would be a natural. It would prevent me from ending up a Master Candidate like Abel, but that wasn't ever really in the cards for me anyway.

Seeing his comment had its intended effect, Zeke grinned, leaning back and closing his eyes. He wasn't going to sleep—Zeke just liked to tune things out sometimes when he was bored. His relaxed expression changed when his ring vibrated and he looked down to see a text, his face paling as he swallowed hard. "Huh. Apparently Stella wants me to come down for a visit so we can talk."

He tried to sound nonchalant, but there was a quaver in his voice that made me laugh. Good to know my terrifying uncle could still feel fear.

Chapter Seventy-One

THE CEREMONY WAS HELD at the same arena as the finals. It was a huge luxurious building (without even the wear from the battle, which they had repaired)—forty thousand people weren't enough to fill it up, though it was hardly empty with every one of the ten thousand starter teams having shown up. There were a few E-rankers here too, possibly for security, and to my shock, I saw a fucking B-ranker standing next to Midknight.

I turned to look at Zeke, who noticed where my attention had gone and chuckled. "Attempted invasions are bad for morale. They sent an executive from the Cluster branch to oversee the rest of this. I don't recognize her, but I'm guessing she's a heavy even among people at her rank."

The B-ranker was... impressive. A tall, dark-haired woman in a pitch-black body suit covered with shining stars. Her black hair shared the spacelike impression, as did her mask, and in the depths of her dark eyes I could see galaxies forming if I looked too long.

Callie, not surprisingly, knew her. "That's Asteria. She's pretty much my dad's boss's, boss's, boss. She has a star based spatial ability, though I don't know of anyone with the details. People who make her use it usually don't survive the encounter."

After a second of thought, Callie knowing a high-end B-ranker made sense. The Systems and Clusters in the Conglomerate were feeders for the

Unity to gain renown for their top members. I knew that renown was weighted, so normal mortals probably didn't rate the effort, but I was betting people like Midknight knew *all* the big-name Unity capes, and he'd have drilled them into his daughter's head.

Mel whistled. "I want to be her when I grow up. You can feel the badass coming off her in waves."

We'd managed to find plenty of our friends in the crowd. Sydney, Megan, Sloane, Wren, Lament, Teague, Alec—there were tons of us all crowded together, though most of the teams were talking to whoever was nearby. Given how hectic things were, longer distance conversations seemed unlikely.

"You all ready?" Benny asked with interest. "I still don't know how this works. Is this just an excuse to draw more attention to the highest-placing fighters before rank-up? Or is there some sort of significance to ranking up all together like this?"

Zeke shrugged. "Opinion is divided on that actually, but ceremonies like this *usually* have better yields. Whether that's because they put the rank-up on display and draw attention or because of some weird resonance from all the Impact, I couldn't say. I do know that they're good for the planet. Not enough to take this one to a proper D-grade, but they'll push the process ahead for sure."

Benny looked annoyed. "Damn. Kind of wish I'd made it in time for this bit, but I'm still a hundred plus points short."

My best friend was probably building to a nice long whining session, but the poke in the ribs from the girl standing beside him shut him up. I gave Celine a grateful smile she couldn't see behind my mask, but before I could comment, everyone got really quiet.

"Welcome," came a surprisingly soft, melodic voice. Every eye in the place focused on Asteria. She was suppressing her aura, but she was letting something… else out. Some strange aspect of herself that made her seem like more than us, even without the pressure. I wondered if Zeke had that. If he did, he was much better at containing it than she was. "My name is Asteria, and I am the vice Guild Master of the Axiom Cluster."

She looked over us all slowly, the sympathetic look on her unnaturally perfect features seemingly at odds with her tall, muscular physique. She looked like a war goddess, but she had such a peaceful gaze. Her galactic eyes were hidden behind a small domino mask with that same starry sky distortion as her costume, but somehow, it just pulled focus to their depths, like she was sucking us all in.

I felt a sharp jolt and turned to see Zeke frowning at her, withdrawing his fingers after having pinched her (he must have crossed the distance and come back in an instant). "Sloppy," he muttered in annoyance.

Her eyes jerked up to settle on him, and my uncle raised a brow. Her porcelain cheeks colored a bit and things... shifted. It either hadn't been on purpose or she was embarrassed to be caught, but she seemed much less intimidating now.

Clearing her throat, she returned to addressing the now confused crowd, all of whom were still reeling a bit like I was. "You've been through a great deal recently," she said gently, bringing us all back to the topic at hand. "You all show great bravery coming here, though you need not worry now. I'm here to keep you safe. I'll be staying on-world for a while, working from Callus as a preventative measure, and I'll need to count on all of you that are local to support me."

Zeke snorted lightly, clearly not buying it, but this time she didn't react. Asteria continued on for a while, announcing the names of the final five, in order based on ability. She also announced the top ten, of which I was a part, and we were all called up to be shown off as the "stellar example of heroism and ability" that we were (her words, and I'm almost sure that there was a pun mixed in there secretly, which made me like her more).

Finally, she finished telling us all what we'd accomplished, passed out some monetary rewards for the top ten (I couldn't remember if those had been mentioned or if they were hush money, but I got another hundred G-rank coins so I wasn't complaining) and then officially let us all know that we were eligible to rank up now. There was even a big countdown as we all got ready to accept the rank.

The actual shift in the world around us when we accepted the rank-up simultaneously was *massive*. The feel of that much Impact shifting at the same time was insane. I knew that since it was qualitatively within the limits of the planet there was no danger of damage, but it still felt crazy, like a hurricane made of hammers bludgeoning us all, rather than the single wall of force I felt from a B-rank aura.

I felt plenty of changes, and had to look over my stats to figure out what they were, but once I did I found myself flabbergasted. I'd gotten a staggering amount of points over the course of this tournament. Thirty in Might, thirty in Perception, twenty in Fantasy, thirty in Vitality, twenty in Creation, and twenty in Focus. Which left me staring at my new stat screen after rank-up.

Wishmaster Candidate Status: F-rank.

Ability: Intermediate Wish—Six times a day, grant an Intermediate wish in return for proper compensation. Wish must be feasibly achievable by the Candidate's own efforts within a three-day period with current statistics.

Might: 250
Impact: 32
Fantasy: 200
Vitality: 220
Focus: 168
Perception: 180
Creation: 180
Progress to next rank: 1230/10000

Stored: 7 shadow attacks, 10 Stealth charges, 9 triple-strength tranq blows, 7 triple-strength density-shifted attacks, 9 spider leg attacks, 2 heal bursts, 4 gravity attacks, 7 shadow clones, 22 scan heals (I-rank)

Pet: Wolf named Jin

Skills: Lesser Cooking Mastery, Lesser Inventing Mastery, Minor Piano Mastery, Minor Guitar Mastery, Lesser Balam Mastery, Minor First Aid Mastery, Lesser Paired Dueling, Intermediate Path of the Doom Sovereign

Path of the Doom Sovereign:
Monk: Stone Limb, Moonlit Night, Consecration of Flame, Ripple Running, State of Grace, Steam Arrow, Afterburner, Pit of Despair, Mountain Stance

Rogue: Mercy Kill, Double Trouble, Touch of Tears, Flurry of Blows, Heavy hands, Marked for Death

Diviner: Overlay, Song of the Soil, Rhythm of the Wild, Eye of Revelation, Danger Sense

My results were staggering, leaving me almost a quarter of the way to two thousand points after just one tournament, but that was nothing compared to the changes Callie had seen. My girlfriend's rank up had brought not just new stats, but a new ability, taking into account her new Skill synergy from Shadow Manipulation (which she had apparently ranked up during all the down time as the tournament progressed) as well as her lean into Perception towards the end of her accumulation.

Calliope Reynolds: F-rank.

Ability: Intermediate Abyssal Infiltration—Enter the shadows and emerge where you will within range. Shape the darkness to your call, moving it as if it were part of your body, and even extend your senses through the shadows to spy on your enemies.

Might: 218
Impact: 32
Vitality: 142
Fantasy: 150
Focus: 58
Perception: 375
Creation: 185
Progress to next rank: 1160/10000

Pet: Wolf named Rellia

Skills: Minor Tracking, Beginner Stealth, Beginner Trap Mastery, Beginner Disguise, Lesser Balam Mastery, Intermediate Shadow Manipulation Mastery, Lesser Paired Dueling

Aside from the standard twenty points of Impact, she'd gotten fifty points of Creation, forty points of Perception, twenty of Might, and thirty of

Fantasy. She was up to eleven hundred and sixty total, meaning she'd gotten a hundred and forty points off this rank up, but that was nothing compared to her Abyssal Infiltration ability.

Despite her control of shadows, Callie had never been able to fully enter them. She could (with preparation and concentration) *hide* things in her shadows, like she had with her bike, but she needed to spend a lot of time and materials making that possible and it effectively made it useless in combat. This new ability more than made up for it. Not only could she meld into shadows, she could extend her Perception through shadows to spy on people, and it increased her versatility with the shadows she had.

After she finished telling me about it, she threw herself into my arms and kissed me senseless. I could sense the happiness and relief through the bond. Callie, in a lot of ways, had been standing still since we'd met. It was easy to forget that while the rest of us had ranked up quickly to catch up to her, she'd been G-rank for years. Finally breaking that wall, not to mention evolving her ability into something truly amazing, made her really believe she could keep up.

I pulled back, smiling at her, and decided not to address her insecurities about being left behind. They were crazy, of course, but being told your emotions are dumb doesn't make you feel them less, and I'd learned enough not to make *that* rookie mistake.

I turned to Abel and Mel, both of whom looked pleased with their results, though they didn't share. We knew bits and pieces of what they could do based on things they'd shared and what we'd seen, but we didn't have access to their stat pages and I wasn't going to ask. Callie could bring it up if she wanted, but I trusted them to tell us if there was something we needed to know.

Asteria cleared her throat, bringing all of us back to reality from our upgrade highs. "It seems you've all broken through to the next rank. Congratulations, both to my own citizens and to our visitors. As discussed, the departure will be in a month. Any of our guests should feel free to remain and visit—I assure you you'll be quite safe here." Translation: stay if you want to, I'll be watching you all.

With that she made her goodbyes and turned to stride out of the arena, Midknight trailing behind her silently. I didn't know if it was the real him or an armor double, but Callie looked worried as she watched him go. I knew she didn't forgive him, and shouldn't, but he was still her dad and she was a bit worried after seeing that armor demolished by those B-rankers. She didn't mention it though, and I didn't push. We had bigger worries anyway. We had a month left (or rather thirty-one days counting today) to prepare and get Jessie and Benny ranked up. Good thing I had an extra daily wish—I'd need it.

Chapter Seventy-Two

A MONTH. A month of wishes, a month of stat gains, slow and steady, constantly trying to build up my friends.

Benny and Jessie were both within reach of F-rank. With Jessie's regular income of Might from her bond with Randall, not to mention my boost, and how close Benny already was, the seven hundred and forty-four points I had to throw around for the month was more than enough to get them both where they needed to go.

Benny was first. One hundred fifty-seven points. Seven days and six wishes each (though only half on the final day) got him to F-rank without a problem. Well, it would have been one short at a hundred fifty-six (thirty nine wishes, four stats each) but Benny had been working on jobs pretty consistently, and had managed to snag a point of Creation despite only doing drudge work.

He was, of course, thrilled to reach F-rank like the rest of us, and began training with Abel nearly immediately afterward, trying to get the best out of his new abilities, especially since Abel had pushed his Ragam to Expert and was even *more* terrifying now.

Benicio Cortez: F-rank.

*Ability: Intermediate Mechanical Embodiment—Allows
the integration of existing inventions into the user's body
for the purposes of strengthening and enhancing them.*

Might: 405
Impact: 32
Fantasy: 16
Vitality: 31
Focus: 463
Perception: 42
Creation: 31
Progress to next rank: 1020/10000

Pet: Wolf named Rolf

Current integrated tech: 10/10.
Torso: extending rope.
Right fist: triple punch.
Left forearm: long range attack attraction.
Left fist: minor slow acting tranquilizer effect.
*Right foot: density shifting to create heavier kicks and
more powerful jumps.*
*Left foot: momentum neutralization to allow stopping
instantly.*
Head: slight cognitive boost to allow more thinking time.
Back: ability to grow a shell to tank damage.
*Chest: pair of golden G-rank spider legs that arch up from
the shoulders.*
Waist: belt of spiritual calming.

*Skills: Minor Cooking Mastery, Intermediate Inventing
Mastery, Minor Haggling Mastery, Minor Stealth Mastery*

And of course, Jessie's upgrade was much easier to manage. Her Bond to
Randall over the course of the month gave her fifty-five Might, bringing
the stat to an even one hundred fifty. The entire rest of her development,
all four hundred and thirty-four points of it, was Vitality. A whopping

seven hundred and sixty-two points of the stuff, making her an absolute monster with the stat and exponentially increasing the power of her ability.

Jessica Evans: F-rank.

Ability: Intermediate Lifeweaving—Infuse living things with life itself and direct their actions while the user's power flows through them. Control has limited effect on sapient entities. Prolonged exposure to life energy may cause lasting effects in controlled subjects.

Might: 150
Impact: 32
Fantasy: 28
Vitality: 762
Focus: 25
Perception: 15
Creation: 8
Progress to next rank: 1020/10000

Pet: Wolf named Lily and bear named Randall (Beginner Beast Bond)

Skills: Intermediate Horticulture, Intermediate First Aid, Beginner Herbalism, Minor Flower Arrangement, Minor Beast Taming Mastery, Beginner Beast Bonding

Just under twenty days and one hundred and nine wishes for Jessie. Amusingly, after paying for the wishes with coins (the upcoming bazaar was going to be expensive) I ended up with four hundred and thirty-four G-rank chits, the same amount of points Jessie had added to her Vitality. Out of all of us I think Jessie came the furthest. During all the downtime she'd been training non-stop apparently. Horticulture and First Aid both hit Intermediate, and Herbalism hit Beginner.

Her biggest change was one small subtle shift in her ability description. The loss of the word non-sapient when it came to her ability to permanently enhance her controlled subjects. Her actual life force control didn't work on sapient beings still, but the change represented her ability to control beings in other ways (like Beast Bonding) and permanently enhance them even if they developed sapience. It was a game-changer for her.

My last thirty-eight wishes I used for myself, a hundred and fifty-two points sourced from the Beast Lord Garden crew. A hundred went into Fantasy and fifty-two into Focus (which was lagging behind), bringing those stats to three hundred even and two hundred and twenty, respectively. Getting everyone up to snuff was difficult, time consuming, and frankly exhausting. Mixed in with my own consistent effort to get used to my new Impact and adjust my fighting style, the month flew by in a blur of exhaustion and pain.

But eventually, it ended. On the last night of the month, thirty-one days after the ceremony and the last night before we left, we all gathered for a meeting on who would be coming. Natalie, Perit, Valk, Abel, Mel, Benny, Celine, Jessie, Callie, and me. Natalie's last team member, whose name I couldn't remember for the life of me, was apparently not important enough to come with us, and Benny had lobbied shamelessly for us to bring Celine in their place.

The elf herself was here, looking a bit nervous, but Benny was holding her hand for support, and it said something about how close their trials had brought them that she didn't seem bothered by the public display. I was happy for my friend. Callie... less so.

"Why would we *possibly* bring her?" argued my girlfriend. She shot Celine an apologetic look. "Not that I'm still mad. You made peace with Benny and almost died—I'm happy to let bygones be bygones. But this slot is priceless. We could get paid through the nose to bring someone."

That... was actually fair. Everyone had come here just for this. If word got out we had a spare slot for the Glade, everyone would swarm us to try and get it.

Benny nodded. "That's true, so why not let that person be Celine? She chose me over her family in the end, but her sister is the only one who knows. Her family is desperate to get someone into the Glade. Nalia would look like a rock star if she pulled it off, and that kind of reputation would be worth downplaying or omitting a few... indiscretions."

I whistled appreciatively. "Damn." Everyone looked at me. "That's sneaky —not just leveraging the family into letting Celine come with us, but making use of that exact same leverage to patch things up with her family and get rid of any evidence that Celine ever screwed them. Two birds one stone. Did you come up with that?"

He grinned proudly. "Celine has been giving me lessons in political theory. Pretty good, right?"

"Excuse me," interrupted Callie, "but we still haven't agreed. It would depend on exactly what Nalia is willing to offer. I'm sorry Celine, but this needs to be about what's best for the team. If that's you then I welcome you with open arms, but we need to shop around."

I could sense through the bond that Callie wasn't completely over the back-stabbing, which was fair, but she was willing to put it to bed for benefits, not to mention helping out Benny. Not that he seemed to notice—my best friend was glaring hard at Callie, though she ignored it. She had to do what was best for the team.

Celine seemed to understand though, because she just nodded solemnly. "Can I at least have a bit to call and try to get you some kind of benefits before you let anyone else know about the slot?"

Callie glanced over at Benny with a sigh. "Alright, I can do that much. See what you can get." Celine slipped out of the room and my girlfriend shot my best friend an apologetic smile. "Sorry Ben, I can't let an opportunity like this slip away. We need every possible advantage going into a dungeon." Glancing at Nat, she said, "Speaking of which—do you know anything about this place? Now that we have the entry permissions, planning ahead would be a good idea."

Nat just sighed. "No. The Moonsong Glade isn't a dungeon people normally have access to. It's in an unstable area of space, similar to the unstable spaces Mad Madigan used to make that Labyrinth we lured the cultists into. The space sort of fluctuates, which means access is only possible at certain times or under certain conditions. Same reason only F-rankers can enter. There *are* people alive who have been inside, but they're ancient, and chances are things have changed a ton."

"Then what do we know?" Callie asked in frustration. "Even out-of-date information is better than no information. It would give us a starting point."

Nat shrugged. "Not much. We know there were people inside, locals who lived on the planet as it developed into a dungeon. Lots of beasts. The Moonglow Dew is stimulated by external access, so it doesn't spawn except when the place is open. No clue why—something about Impact resonance. Other than that, we've got nothing. It's been a *very* long time since anyone was in there."

Callie sighed in aggravation as Celine came back into the room, leaning down to whisper in her ear. Callie blinked in surprise. "Wait... really?" She looked up at us. "Nalia is willing to offer a Skill Crystal of our choice as compensation. That would be a pretty huge opportunity, especially for Jessie. Life and beast Skills are specialties of the elves. Celine's woodcraft is a good demonstration of that. She can get something Vitality based that will massively help her combat efficiency."

"Ask for Shape of the Wild," Celine said immediately. "The crystal we have is at Intermediate, so Jessie should be able to learn it. It's a supplementary Skill for Beast Bonding that lets a person transform into their bonded companion. Given how strong Randall is Jessie would benefit from it a ton."

Jessie's eyes went wide. "I can be a *bear?* That's amazing!" She looked at Callie pleadingly. "Oh please let me be a bear. That sounds so fun. I can slap fish out of rivers and hibernate in caves!" We all looked at her and she shrugged. "It sounds relaxing. Plus I might be able to actually speak with Randall. Minor communication through the bond is one thing, but being able to *speak bear?* That sounds so cool!" Her voice was starting to run together as she talked faster and breathed less. If she hadn't been an Ascendant I'd have been worried about her suffocating.

My girlfriend's gaze was not amused. "Traditionally, when negotiating, it's best not to inform the other side of the negotiations that you can't live without the thing being negotiated over." Her eyes narrowed. "Which you're more than smart enough to know. You're trying to help Benny."

Jessie grinned back at her cheekily. "Maybe I thought he needed a bit of help. Come on. We like Celine. I mean sure, I was pretty pissed about her stabbing us in the back, but she did it for her family, and she changed sides in the end to help us. We would have had a much tougher time with the Burning Heaven Abyss without her. They had a Master Candidate."

Callie sighed. "Fine. I'll agree to her coming. The Skill Crystal is a good idea, and I do appreciate the suggestion. Do you think you'll be able to work that into your next rank up? Because it kind of fits with your whole theme." She turned to Celine. "Am I wrong assuming that Vitality plays a role in this Skill?"

The elf nodded. "Higher Vitality means a longer transformation. The power of the transformation depends on the Bond itself and the relative power of the two subjects. In this case both are F-rank, so that'll help." It would also give Jessie a Might bump from what turning into a giant bear would do for her reputation.

Nat said nothing about it, so she clearly didn't care, and Benny was thrilled as we sat and talked over the details before finalizing things. Callie called Nalia personally, and once it was all finalized Nalia had the crystal sent over, promising it would be there by morning.

Then we all started getting ready. The next day would be our departure for the Moonsong Glade. It was finally time to leave Callus. We were going to enter the wider universe at last.

Chapter Seventy-Three

THE NEXT MORNING, we all got packed up, ready to leave and prepared to set off. Cass was sobbing uncontrollably, hugging each of us in turn and begging us not to go, and I wasn't the only one whose heart broke as the little girl started promising not to feed her vegetables to the wolves anymore if we would stay.

I... hadn't been thinking about Cass when we decided to leave, but now that I was it tore my heart out. We'd been like her new family since we rescued her, and she was desperate to keep us from leaving. I wasn't the only one who thought so either, because she was so heartbreaking Zeke finally spoke up.

"You know... I could use an assistant," he said casually. "We're going to be waiting around in space for literal months with nothing to do. I mean sure, there will be other people around, but doing all the menial labor on my own isn't my style. Maybe if Cark wants to stick around I can pay him in advice or something. Give him a few pointers. He's not part of your Pavilion so there's no conflict of interest there. As long as he commits to never joining."

Cark looked hesitant, but I could see the eagerness too. He was part of a faction here, but he spent more time around the house than anything, trying to be there for Cass. Burning Fist had taught him a bit, but the guy wasn't, like, a *mentor.* Not to mention he didn't need to quit the faction. In fact, training under Zeke at *all* would be a hell of an education for later. Leaving Sage would suck for him, but he spent more time around the house than he did with her.

Finally, he looked over at Cass, staring at him with big shimmering eyes, and nodded, moving to call Burning Fist and gather his stuff. As he ran off, I turned to Nat. "I never bothered to ask but... how are we getting off planet? I've never left before so I don't know how it works."

She shrugged. "Varies based on distance. There are ships that can transit between worlds, but they're mostly System locked. Anything bigger or more powerful needs to be made by a high-ranking Inventor, which obviously makes them extremely rare. Even ones who focus on control when they reach Intermediate have trouble staying focused on singular projects for long. For something across the Cluster, I expect they'll use a Waywalker."

At my confused expression she chuckled. "Waywalkers are long distance teleporters. One of the clans has kind of a monopoly on the industry. Shipping and transportation often depends on stability, so having an organization with a standardized power that allows transport across space is key. They do a lot of work with the Merchant's Guild."

That sounded awesome. "So they just... tear open space? To anywhere? That kind of spatial power must be insanely expensive stat-wise. How do they have so many high-ranking members?"

She shook her head. "Nah, they use anchors. Send them to various planets and then connect the space between their current location and the anchor to open a portal. For a System-level jump, a D-ranker can manage. Cluster-level would be someone in the C-ranks. Past that it can get dicey. Cross Galaxy transport is extremely hard to arrange. The higher-ups at the Waywalker Convergence aren't really interested in being people's ride."

Zeke snickered from where he was sitting on the couch watching Cass play with Jin (the wolves were coming along with us because the Moonsong Glade would be a perfect environment for them to grow). When he noticed us looking at him, he smirked. "They really don't. We took a Waywalker here when we first came over from the Empire. Your Grandfather's branch is in Empire territory. This absolute ass named Charleston was our transporter. He was an A-ranker, but given our affiliation we were of similar statuses. Huge prick."

Everyone just stared at him in terror, remembering the power they'd seen in the arena and then imagining mouthing off to someone *stronger* than that. He didn't seem to notice. Finally Cark came back out with a bag, wincing slightly. "I'm good to go."

It occurred to me that while him and Sage didn't seem super serious, telling your girlfriend you planned to take off for another star System out of the blue was probably not a fun conversation. I didn't envy him that, but I wasn't going to poke at it.

We all headed out to the car to drive to... wherever we were going. Callie knew, apparently, and told Jessie before sitting in the back with me. "You okay?" she asked quietly. "I know you've never been off world."

I smiled at her attempt to ignore her nerves by focusing on mine. I could feel her nervousness through the bond, and I knew what she needed, so I just smiled and said, "Yeah, it's going to be a big change. I'll miss a lot of people here." I put an arm around her shoulder. "But I'm taking all of my favorites with me, so I think I'll be okay."

Her shoulders relaxed a bit as my words sunk in, but I knew it would take more than that to make her feel better. She was leaving her mom, her uncle, and the only place she'd ever known, too. Looking back on my life, I'd been steered toward solitude, so leaving with the only people I cared that much about was nostalgic but not sad. Callie hadn't had the luxury of that kind of mindset.

I mean sure, I'd miss Maria, Stella, Ian, and plenty of other friends, but I wasn't leaving behind a piece of myself. Not like Callie was. She'd called Amelia last night to say goodbye, and I'd held her after they hung up as she cried her eyes out.

But she wanted to do this. Leaving home sucked, but it was important, especially to someone as independent as Callie. At least this time she was doing it with her mom's blessing. And she'd told me she called Alexander and demanded he stop by and check in regularly. She hadn't cried after saying goodbye to him, but she'd been sad about it.

We talked a bit over the drive, keeping each other distracted so we weren't thinking about the trip. The closer we got to the Waywalker departure point, the less sure of myself I felt. I knew that was just fear of the unknown, though, so I ignored it and focused on talking things out with

Callie. We weren't the only ones nervous, of course, and after a few minutes Benny came to sit with us, bringing Celine with him.

Since Jessie was driving, Celine passed the Skill Crystal to Callie as she sat down. My girlfriend stashed it away and then glanced at Benny. "You doing okay? This is probably pretty scary for you too, right?"

He sighed and leaned back. "Yeah. Leaving my family sucks. I mean, Jessie is leaving Maria too, but they weren't really official and it's not the same. Not just her either. My parents are here. I know intellectually I haven't seen them since we visited home, and traveling further is just more of the same. But it feels like a bigger deal."

I clapped him on the shoulder. "We'll be back, man. And we'll have stories to tell and souvenirs to give them. I can even give them abilities if they want." It would be too noticeable to start doing that to everyone as I was now, but when we came back I'd be stronger. It would be much less of a problem.

He smiled at that. "That would be nice." He still sounded sad about leaving, but Celine squeezed his hand and we lapsed into silence.

Before we could talk more the car slowed down. Callie took a deep breath. "Alright... we're here. Is everyone ready? Have everything you need?"

Benny snickered at that. "Yes *Mom*. Let's go." Celine pulled him up as she stood and the two of them headed outside. We all filed out after, and I was surprised to find us before an arena.

Zeke nodded. "Smart place to put it. These places all have decent protections on them."

We headed inside and made our way down to the ring, where Midknight, Asteria, and surprisingly Frostbite were waiting. Rime was there, and we nodded to our former bodyguard. It would have been nice to take her with us, but our contract didn't extend that far. Not everyone wanted to leave the planet after all.

Asteria smiled as we approached. "Ah. Our champion and his party. Welcome. I trust you're all prepared to depart?" At our nods she gestured to one side. "Please take your positions." She tried very hard not to look at Zeke, presumably out of fear, which seemed to suit him fine.

We all lined up where she pointed, and she stepped forward, laying down a small stone with intricate carvings all over it. Tapping the top of it, she created a spark which flooded the runes across its surface. There was a flash of light, and then, before our eyes, the air *cracked*.

There was a shudder in space, and my head swam a bit as I watched the world itself tear apart, prying reality open until there was a portal sitting in the air in front of us. As it had opened, I'd been able to see the fluctuations of unstable space in the cracks around the edges, but now that it was open it was just... a hole.

Like looking at a window with no frame, on one side was one place, and on the other, a second. It was weird looking at the portal because it was two-dimensional and flat but showed three-dimensional space on either side. Zeke looked bored, but everyone else seemed shaken by the ability. It was a pretty impressive sight, I had to admit.

Asteria pointed at the portal. "Your path to the Moonsong Glade lies through there. The Glade isn't *quite* revealed yet, though it's accessible enough for them to arrange accommodations. You'll be dropped off on the floating city established outside the Glade while you wait for the other tournament winners and their teams. You will not be provided with a return trip and will need to arrange that yourselves."

That kind of sucked, but it also made sense. This was an open tournament. There was a net benefit to the Unity from all the publicity, but once the winners left, it was hardly their problem. We were nominally members of the Unity, but only junior members. It wasn't worth paying for us to come back without some sort of benefit to them. Granted, I could probably have arranged a trip for some wishes if I wanted to pay, but we had a next destination after the Glade, so there was no point.

Frostbite looked mildly annoyed, but she was an E-ranker, and Asteria was the one who made decisions. I was guessing our ally had tried to lobby for better treatment and got shot down. Someone as strong as Asteria had probably met plenty of Candidates, and while we theoretically had amazing potential, not all of us lived up to it.

Staring through the window, I saw a sprawling, massive city with a night sky background somehow far too close to be believable. I reached down to grab Callie's hand and she squeezed back. I felt her nervousness and excitement in equal measure through the bond.

With one last look around at the planet I'd spent my whole life on, I gave the others a short nod, then Callie and I stepped through the window together, emerging for the first time in the wider universe. As the others stepped through behind us and the window closed, I couldn't help but grin as my heart pounded. The sadness had mostly faded, all I could feel now was the anticipation.

Now was when the adventure really began.

About the Author

Malcolm Tent is, in fact, smarter than a fifth grader. He enjoys reading, writing, and spending time with his dogs. He's lycanthrophobic and addicted to Cajun food.

Author website:

About Timeless Wind Publishing

Founded in late 2020 by Lorne Ryburn and Silas Sontag, Timeless Wind Publishing is an up-and-coming indie publishing house. We love sci-fi and fantasy—progression fantasy, power fantasy, LitRPG, time loops, cultivation, system apocalypse—genre fiction of all kinds! We're prolific readers within these genres and endeavor to bring awesome books into the limelight.

We look forward to helping authors (aspiring and published alike) develop and expand an audience of readers who believe in their vision.

Our logo is an exotic cat from a Palmyrene ruin. The word along its back roughly translates to, "Alas!" or "What a shame!" This word is present on all gravestones in Palmyra. It's a recognition that all things come to an end… even the best people and stories. Alas!

We hope our readers will have "alas" moments when they finish our books.

Connect with Timeless Wind Publishing
TimelessWind.com
Facebook.com/timelesswind
Twitter.com/timeless_wind
Instagram.com/timelesswindpub